THE
NIGHTMARE
MAN

Also available by J. H. Markert, as James Markert

A White Wind Blew
The Angels' Share
All Things Bright and Strange
What Blooms from Dust
Midnight at the Tuscany Hotel
The Strange Case of Isaac Crawley

THE NIGHTMARE MAN

A NOVEL

J. H. MARKERT

CROOKED
LANE

NEW YORK

Copyright © 2023 by James Markert

Published in the United States by Crooked Lane Books, an imprint of The Quick Brown Fox & Company LLC.

Crooked Lane Books and its logo are trademarks of The Quick Brown Fox & Company LLC.

Library of Congress Catalog-in-Publication data available upon request.

ISBN (hardcover): 978-1-63910-170-2
ISBN (ebook): 978-1-63910-171-9

Cover design by Heather VenHuizen

Printed in the United States.

www.crookedlanebooks.com

Crooked Lane Books
34 West 27th St., 10th Floor
New York, NY 10001

First Edition: January 2023

10 9 8 7 6 5 4 3 2 1

For

The Fist,
All five fingers,
It's been a fun ride, so let's keep it going.

To Tracy,
My wife
You might not want to read this one.

Charlie Shircliff,
You always said I should write something scary.
Well, I hope this gives you nightmares.

Here I am lying down to sleep;
No nightmare shall plague me until they have swum through all the
waters that flow upon the earth, and counted all stars that appear in
the skies.
Thus help me God, Father, Son, and Holy Ghost.
Amen
—*A prayer from Westphalia, Germany, used to ward off mares*

"I am the corn. I am the fall. I am the harvest, little girl.
And you are my Little Baby Jane."
—*From The Scarecrow*

"We collect books in the belief that we are preserving them
when in fact it is the books that preserve their collector."
—*Philosopher Walter Benjamin*

*Novels by
Benjamin Bookman*

(Detective Mulky Series)

*Summer Reign
Some Fall Down
Winter Bones
Spring Showers, Dead Flowers
The Pulse
The Scarecrow*

1

Detective Winchester Mills smelled the Petersons' barn before he saw it.

The mailman had warned him on the phone. *The stench is bad, Winny.* Bad enough for Ernie Palponie—who'd seen, smelled, and heard it all during his thirty-three years of delivering Crooked Tree's mail—to stop at the edge of the Petersons' cornfield and lose his lunch. *The mailbox is overflowing,* Ernie had told Mills on the phone. *It isn't like them to leave town and not stop their mail. And both their trucks are in the driveway.*

Detective Mills had asked Ernie to slow down and take a couple of deep ones. Then requested he go knock on their doors, and to stay on the line. After a few minutes of listening to Ernie's heavy breathing as he reconnoitered the Petersons' house, the mailman reported back that he'd knocked—*Good and hard too, Winny*—but to no avail.

Mills told Ernie to continue on his mail route, and not to mention this to anyone. He'd take care of it. But Ernie was still there when Mills arrived, sitting on a back porch rocking chair, smoking a cigar he usually saved for the end of the day, staring out at the cornfield with an undelivered bag of mail on the boards between his old, dusty boots.

When Mills approached the house, Ernie exhaled cigar smoke, nodded toward the cornstalks. "They should have harvested that field by now. Something's not right."

"Sit there as long as you need, Ernie." Mills glimpsed the barn's slated roof down the hillside. It was only noon but he needed a nap. His hips hurt, which meant rain was coming. Breeze ushered in the smell of ozone and fall leaves, the hint of something foul.

The stench of crime.

A nuance Mills once admitted to Father Frank in confession he not only recognized, but secretly coveted.

A conundrum of sorts, Father. You can't have the catch without the crime, right?

Is this why you won't retire, Winchester? Every riddle has an answer? Every loose thread needs to be pulled?

To that he'd shrugged. At sixty-six, the fire in his gut still smoldered.

"Do you smell it, Winny?"

It took a second for Ernie's voice to register from the porch. Mills adjusted his hearing aid, turned away from the postman, and faced the barn. "Yeah, Ernie. I smell it."

"Any word on that missing girl?"

Mills said, "No." Eight-year-old Blair Atchinson was ten days missing now; the mere mention of it was a thorn in his side. "But I'll find her," he said to himself, not wanting to invite further discussion.

A wind gust unfurled more stench. Mills yawned into a fist, reached inside his shirt pocket for his pills, and dry-swallowed a Ritalin and an Adderall simultaneously. He didn't know which one worked better, but the Ritalin kicked in sooner and the Adderall lasted longer—in his mind, the perfect marriage.

A black Jeep Cherokee stopped on the gravel driveway beside the Petersons' house.

Mills grumbled. Detective Blue stepped out of the vehicle. If he hadn't paused to talk with Ernie, he'd have been inside that barn already, without the rookie. Now that Blue had arrived, the trek down that hill would be something akin to the tortoise and the hare. He'd told her he'd handle this one alone. Either she'd ignored him again, or Chief Givens had sent her, with a nod and the unspoken suggestion to follow the old man. Make sure he doesn't nod off while he's walking.

Chief Givens could kiss his ass. *You were in diapers when I caught the Bad Cop. A grade schooler when I faced down the Lamplighter. Golfing when I brought in the Boogeyman.*

"Hold up, Mills."

Her voice was bee buzz. He readjusted his hearing aid and held up for her on the hillside.

Blue called out to the postman on the porch. "Hey, Ernie."

"Hey, Baby," he answered.

Mills grunted. He refused to call her by her nickname. Ever since she'd married Danny Blue, the town's number one defense attorney, seven years ago, the name had stuck. Baby Blue. Blue was good enough for him. She sidled with him down the sloped lawn. She wore black pants, a white blouse, and a brown jacket to conceal the piece strapped around her shoulder. All legs and youth and spunk, while he'd doubled down on the opposite of every one of them.

He wrinkled his nose. "Detectives don't wear perfume."

"Yeah? Well, they don't wear diapers either."

He pulled his .40 caliber Smith & Wesson from the pancake holster at his waistband, and took the lead toward the dilapidated barn. Except for the newly painted white doors, the rest of the faded red structure looked beaten up by decades of harsh weather and wood rot. The stench hit them like a wall, and while she covered her nose with her jacket, he inhaled it deep into his lungs. His way of diving headfirst into the pool. To get acclimated.

She removed her Sig Sauer pistol from inside her jacket.

Too eager. Her shirt was untucked, which meant she was carrying the tiny .380 in her flashbang bra holster. The bulge at her right ankle showed she was also carrying her 9mm down low. *It was too much*, he'd once told her. *You're inviting an accident, Blue.*

"Mills, look." She pointed toward the barn doors. Muddy paw prints stained them. Claw marks had grooved portions of the wood to splinters, with streaks of blood dried to rust. "Looks like a dog was desperate to get inside."

The Petersons had a golden retriever named Gus. Gus had a limp, but was still active. He had a habit of chasing cars down the road and had gotten hit more than once. Mills surveyed the cornfields but saw no sign of him. He gripped the wooden handle above the paw prints and pulled. The door initially resisted, sucked in place like ice holding a car door closed, so it took another pull to fully open it. Trapped air escaped.

Blue covered her nose again.

A moth fluttered from the barn, spun frantically in the sunlight, and then returned to the dark. Mills stepped inside and motioned for Blue to follow.

She raised her pistol at a shadowy figure in the middle of the barn.

Mills placed a calm hand on her arm, lowered it. "It's just a scarecrow."

She let out a deep breath. "Who puts a fucking scarecrow in the middle of a barn?"

Language, Blue. Language.

The scarecrow was the height of a man. Straw hat. Face stitched from burlap, with coat buttons for the eyes, nose, and mouth. Checkered red-and-black shirt half-tucked into blue jeans cinched by one of Mr. Peterson's old belts. From the road, Mills had seen it plenty of times before. To keep the crows honest, Mr. Peterson liked to move the scarecrow around the property.

Sunlight angled through wall slats. Dust motes hovered. Blow flies buzzed like live current through the rafters.

"Jesus Christ." Blue eyed the wooden beams overhead.

Through the haze of blow flies, five sack-like cocoons hung from the center rafter in a neat row, like something out of a sci-fi movie. *Like something about to hatch.* Blue turned away, gagged. *Cocoons made from corn husks. Dried. Hand-sewn. Carefully threaded and stitched. Layers of them; thick enough to hold a body.* The second cocoon, the largest—if not the largest, the heaviest—was covered by the most flies. The bottom was ripped; soaked blood had run the husks thin. A man's hand had fallen loose, dangling limp and bloody.

Mr. Peterson, no doubt.

Without looking at her across the room, he said, "You okay, Blue?"

"I'm fine," she said from the shadows. She spat, wiped her mouth.

He'd told her not to come. He'd had a feeling it would be bad. The entire Peterson family, it seemed, had been bundled inside stitched-together husks, suspended in midair. Breeze entered the barn through the open doors. The husks rotated slightly, ropes pulled taut by the weight of the bodies. *I've seen this before.*

"Mills."

It's harvest time, Blue.

"Mills."

Scarecrows scare. That's what they do.

Something popped. Fingers. Blue's fingers snapped again in front of his face. Her voice was more urgent now, her breath smelling of the mint she'd popped after throwing up. "Dad?"

He looked at her. She never called him that anymore. Not since, as a child, when she'd told him she wished he wasn't. He brought himself back to the moment with a heavy exhale.

"Where'd you go?" she asked.

Where I always go, Blue.

"You've seen what before?"

"Nothing."

"You said—"

"I'm fine," he hissed.

She clenched her jaw, looked away. She had a soft spot and he'd just hit it. Another moth fluttered low to the ground. She watched it with an intense gaze.

He rubbed a calloused hand over his face, wishing he had kept his anger in just now. Wishing was one thing and doing was another. He followed where her index finger pointed. The Petersons' golden retriever, dirty and probably starving, stood in the barn's open doors.

Blue knelt, beckoned it closer. Gus approached, tentative at first, and then limp-hustled toward her, licking her hand rapidly, as if searching for food remnants. One of her mints, maybe. The dog whimpered, eyes upward, transfixed just as they'd been moments ago by what hung from the ceiling. He barked so loud it echoed. Gus broke free from Blue's hold and hurried to a spot directly under the last cocoon in line, the one most touched by shade and shadows.

Mills followed it, seeing immediately what the dog must have seen seconds ago.

Blue verbalized his thought. "No flies, Mills."

No flies, indeed.

This sack rotated more than the others. Bulges moved like toes wriggling in a sock. Whimpering sounded from within.

Mills unlatched the handheld from his belt. "Christ on a cross, Blue. This one's still alive."

CHAPTER

2

B EN MADE SURE the bathroom was empty, and then locked himself inside.

He had five minutes to kill before the bookstore manager announced him, and he needed to kill those minutes alone. Away from his fans. Locking a public bathroom with three stalls and four urinals in a crowded store was, as Grandpa Robert would have said, uncouth.

But he'd been desperate.

Someone rattled the door. He jumped. Sweat popped across his brow. "Just a minute." He paced, stopped at the sink, flashed a hand under the faucet, and water sluiced down the drain. He watched it instead of himself in the mirror; he didn't look like the man on the back of his jacket cover. Stress had aged him these past twelve months.

It had been a week since release day, his hashtagged "book birthday," and *The Scarecrow* was already number one on the *New York Times* Best Seller list, with his fifth book, *The Pulse*, regaining life at number nine. *Publisher's Weekly* called it his best work yet, a "once in a decade type scare fest for the Nightmare Man!"

Ben checked his watch, a Rolex he'd purchased after *Summer Reign* was translated into its thirtieth language. Grandpa Robert had once owned a Rolex. Ben had gotten the same model, a Submariner, Oyster Collection, with the distinctive Blue Dial face. He still had three minutes. He splashed water on his face, took some slow deep breaths. He used to look forward to his signings, the tours. They all did—him, Amanda, and Bri out on the road.

A family.

Three weeks ago, the day before his early copy of *The Scarecrow* had arrived by UPS, Clayton Childress, Ben's editor for all six of his books, had called to warn him it was on the way. Amanda had taken the call. Ben had left his cell on the island while prepping lasagna. She'd grabbed it before he could wipe his hands clean and snatch it himself. He'd given her the look. *Don't answer it.* She'd gone one better and put it on speaker. Clayton had overnighted the early copy and had promised it there by noon.

"It's your best work, Ben. The Nightmare Man has struck again. We really cranked up the scare with this one. How's the sequel coming? The Screamer?"

"It's coming," Ben had said, but the truth was the sequel Clayton and his bosses at McBride & Company so craved had hit a wall not even halfway through. He was in the same situation he'd been in before delivering *The Scarecrow* a year ago.

Two weeks, Ben.

Amanda had left the kitchen without questioning Ben on that sequel, walking hard on her way out just to let him know she was pissed. Pissed at his procrastination. Pissed that his writer's block hadn't been a one-book thing. His current work in progress was going nowhere. But what else was new? They'd been this way with each other for the better part of a year now. Since he'd stumbled home that weekend from the old family home of Blackwood, disheveled and disoriented and smelling of vice.

Ben braved a glance at the bathroom mirror. He had bags under his eyes, sprouts of gray around his ears. He was too young for gray. He raked a hand through his hair and exhaled twelve months of tension. It was go time. He practiced a smile into the mirror, and his mind went to Joaquin Phoenix as Arthur Fleck in *The Joker*. He took a slug from his flask of bourbon and slid it back inside the lining of his coat. He popped two mints and turned off the water. In the sudden silence of the cold bathroom, Amanda's voice resurfaced, the panicked quiver in it from when he'd returned from that weekend. *Ben, what did you do?* The way she'd looked at him. Angry, yes, but just . . . scared. *What did you do, Ben?*

One minute.

And then he heard it. The manager was jumping the gun. "Ladies and gentlemen, this is the moment we've . . ."

He closed his eyes again, blocked out the manager's voice. *Focus, Ben.* He straightened the cuffs on his shirt and headed for the bathroom door. He opened it with his trademark smile, and was greeted immediately by the throng. Some jackass started clapping, like he'd just done something he should be proud of in the bathroom. He still tasted bourbon; he'd need to pop another mint when he got to the table. He politely burrowed through the crowd toward where they had him set up near the back of the store, ignoring the admiring whispers and stares, and took his seat behind the pyramid of books.

The dust jacket showed a scarecrow in the middle of a high school football field. Reddish-orange sundown illuminated a background of dark trees and shadowed cornfields. With stalks that should have held husked cobs, but instead enclosed hands trying to break through the silks that contained them. As was the case with his previous two novels, Ben's name was bigger than the title. He and Amanda had joked about it happening one day—it meant he'd made it, really made it—but now that the letters of his name dwarfed what was below, he missed the days when the title and story held more sway than the man who'd written it.

The line stretched out the front door toward the neighboring ice cream shop. The Banana Split was giving twenty percent discounts on single scoops for anyone waiting in line for Ben Bookman's latest. Dick Bennington, Amanda's fellow news anchor, was covering the event, interviewing a select few from the line. He was coiffed and tanned, a Ken doll with a voice like Walter Cronkite. At some point he'd come over with a question Ben would be obliged to answer.

He's a dick, Amanda.

And you're jealous.

Of what? I don't like how he smiles at you.

What? Like you used to?

The brief discussion in bed last night after she'd warned him Richard was covering the signing; the rest was said with their backs to each other, staring at their respective walls.

Why do we need it covered in the first place?

Because not much else positive is happening in Crooked Tree.

Then you cover it.

You're my husband, Ben. Not my story.

Maybe they'd been better off when he'd *been* her story.

He spotted Amanda across the store, dressed in a beige knee-length skirt and blue blouse that accentuated her baby bump. In two months he'd be a father again. A boy this time. They'd barely discussed a name. Amanda looked even better than the day they'd met. She worked the room like all was right with their world, skittering from fan to fan like a bee, smiling and conversing and directing like it was *her* signing instead of the bookstore's. By the way she was framing her shots for Instagram and Twitter and Facebook Live, no one would begin to suspect their problems.

He scanned the crowd for their daughter, Bri, but didn't see her.

A young woman in jeans and a baggy sweatshirt smiled shyly as she handed him a book. "I've already read it." She looked down as if ashamed. "Twice."

"You've already read it twice?"

"Sorry."

"Don't apologize. It's only about ten times less than I've read it."

She laughed. "Well, it was amazing." His hand lingered above the page, waiting. "To Leslie," she said, and spelled it for him. "Please. Thank you."

"To Leslie. Please and thank you. Best wishes . . ." He closed the book, handed it back. "I'd say enjoy it if you hadn't already read it. Twice. But I hope it gave you nightmares."

It was his trademark saying; it usually came with a wink he decided not to give now. This was when the customer typically peeled away, but Leslie didn't. "Are the rumors true? About the next book?" He shrugged playfully—there were so many false rumors out there about him he didn't have time to fish for the right one. "Is it finally going to be about the Screamer? About the history of children gone missing from Riverdale?"

He forced a smile. "You'll just have to wait and see."

She was sweet, but he was glad she moved on. The next three in line said very little. He spotted Amanda again across the store, taking pictures. She snapped one, caught Ben watching from afar, and waved. For the crowd. For show. She didn't want to be here either. Three weeks ago, she'd been outside mulching, anticipating the arrival of the UPS truck, the early copy of his book. He'd watched from the bay window. Her curly auburn hair was pulled up in a loose bun. Jeans ripped at the knees. No makeup. A complete three-sixty from the perfect persona she played every day for the news cameras. He liked this version better. Always had—the problem was, she didn't. She'd hurried up the driveway with the small package, carrying it like it was his first novel instead of his sixth. Carrying it like it was a physical secret, concrete evidence. When she handed it to him in the foyer—cedar still flecked her fingers—she'd bit her lower lip like she would when nervous, or in the mood. The smirk of what now? *It's finally time to talk, Ben.*

"I can't believe I'm seeing you in person." The next fan in line stole him from his reverie. "I drove all the way from Tennessee. You okay, Mr. Bookman?"

I'm not twisted.

Ben blinked hard, smiled at the bookish woman. He signed his name, said he hoped it gave her nightmares, and thanked her for coming.

I drove to Blackwood, Ben. I saw the shadow of more than just you in that room!

He shook Amanda's voice away, signed books for the next ten in line. Out of the corner of his eye he spotted Brianna, at nine, sitting crisscross applesauce in the middle of the Young Adult aisle, reading way above her level. He smiled at her. His anchor. His heart and soul. He'd ignored that early copy of his book weeks ago, leaving it unopened on the kitchen island for hours before Bri had knocked on his office door and forced the issue.

He'd invited her in, along with Amanda, who'd hovered not only behind their daughter but behind the plan to get him to open that package.

Bri had his blue eyes and dimples and Amanda's curly brown hair. She'd smiled, on point, held out the package. "This just came in the mail, Daddy. Open it. It's shaped like a book."

Ben had faked excitement, glanced at Amanda, who'd stood with her arms rigidly folded. He made a drumroll sound while he tore open the package, and then showed his wife and daughter the hardcover copy of **The Scarecrow**, at the top of which said in quotes from Stephen King: "Ben Bookman is the new master of horror. The true Nightmare Man."

Ben had handed the book to his daughter.

Bri's eyes had grown large; her fondness for books rivaled his own. She flipped to the large photo of Ben on the back. "What's it about?"

"It's about a scarecrow who kills people."

"Ben." Amanda warned him with her eyes, her tone.

Bri, oblivious, focused on the back cover, her daddy leaning against a column with his arms folded. Strong jawline. Piercing blue eyes. Wavy brown hair. A brown jacket over a black T-shirt that read *The Nightmare Man* in red, blood-dripping letters.

Bri pointed to the photograph. "Why aren't you smiling?"

"I'm smiling now."

"But in the picture."

"They won't let me."

"Why not?"

"Because I'm supposed to be a serious writer who writes serious stuff."

"Scary stuff."

"Exactly." Ben leaned forward, elbows on his knees. "Seriously scary stuff."

"I like scary stuff," said Bri.

It was Ben's turn to eye Amanda and alter *his* tone. "I know you do."

Amanda averted her eyes; it was partly her fault the nickname "The Nightmare Man" had stuck in the first place.

Bri held out the book. "Can I read it, Daddy?"

Ben tapped his chin thoughtfully. "Hmmm." A thing he liked to do, to string Brianna along. They both thought it funny, until ultimately he'd point at her and say "No."

She'd laugh and leave it at that. But just as Ben was about to add, you're way too young, Bri had surprised them both by bluntly saying, "You smell like bourbon."

It had been a few ticks past noon on a Tuesday.

Ben stole a sip from his water bottle. He'd just ripped through ten more books, signing and speaking on autopilot. And then a man, a dozen or so spots back in line, grabbed Ben's attention. An orange John Deere hat pulled low on his brow. A white button-down untucked from jeans that sagged. Rugged boots, scuffed, the right one untied. Ben drank more water, kept his eyes on the man in the John Deere hat. His tan, weathered face was covered in salt-and-pepper stubble. His hands were large, fingers thick, dirty beneath the nails. Unlike all the others, he wasn't holding a copy of *The Scarecrow*.

What do you mean you finished the book? Ben? Is this a joke? His agent had said when he'd called her frantically from Blackwood before returning home that weekend.

Kim, just read it, he'd hissed. *But consider it delivered.*

Ben? This is well over a hundred thousand words. You wrote this in one weekend?

Finished it. I didn't go up there with nothing.

The man in the John Deere hat was only five spots away now, fidgety, playing with his hat, biting his fingernails, looking more strung out the closer he got in line.

Ben looked toward the YA section again but didn't see Bri anymore. His hand palsied through a signature, botching what he'd written. He apologized, started over on another book.

The man in the John Deere hat moved closer.

Across the store, Amanda had noticed him too, and had already located a security guard; this wouldn't be the first crazed fan to be escorted away from a Ben Bookman event—his books often conjured freaks. The man looked around like he expected to be ambushed. His movements grew hurried. A security guard approached from the coffee shop, but before he could get close enough, the man in the John Deere hat jumped the line and headed right for Ben's table.

Ben stood with caution, not outwardly panicked but ready to defend himself.

The man leaned forward, thick hands splayed out on the wooden tabletop like giant starfish. "How'd you do it?"

Ben stood strong, eyed the approaching guard. "How did I do what?"

"You know what you did." He pointed at the stack of books, to the cover of *The Scarecrow*. "I haven't slept in a year, you son of a bitch."

"Security," Ben called out, mainly to startle the man, to give him pause, to give himself time to think of a nonviolent way out of this, but all he managed to do was alert the crazed man, who turned with a clenched fist the size of a small pumpkin and punched the approaching guard in the chest, knocking him to the floor and leaving him gasping for air.

The man in the John Deere hat again leveled his gaze on Ben. "You stole my nightmare, Ben Bookman." His angry, rigid face suddenly turned soft, melted into a quiver. He removed a revolver from the folds of his disheveled clothes. Customers screamed. Instead of pointing the gun at Ben, the man put the barrel under his own chin.

"This is on you, pal."

And he pulled the trigger.

Before

*T*HE BEDROOM DOOR *creaked open.*

Footfalls pressed on hardwood. Ben squeezed his eyes closed, pretended to sleep, anticipating the curled knuckle of his grandfather's finger on his shoulder blade.

"Wake up, Benjamin. I've something to show you."

His sister Emily slept across the room. His brother, Devon, in a room down the hall. He'd been warned not to wake them. He slid his legs from beneath the covers. Moonlight cast shadows on the floor; he imagined they were fingers instead of branches from the oak outside.

Grandpa Robert waited for him on the third-floor landing. Tendrils of vanilla pipe smoke enveloped him. The candle glow in his right hand accentuated the furrows in his cheeks, the white stubble and stark blue eyes. His free hand rested on the banister that curled down to a deeper dark. Upon reaching the second-floor landing, the candle flame rippled and then went out. The darkness thrilled Ben, but didn't last long. With the sleight of hand of an accomplished magician, Grandpa Robert ignited the candlewick with a Zippo lighter that Ben heard and smelled, but never saw leave his grandfather's robe.

Grandpa Robert smiled at Ben, continued stoop-shouldered downward toward the main floor, holding the brass candlestick as steadily as a man half his age. They tiptoed past the closed door where Ben's parents slept.

Wind pressed upon the house and Ben heard whispers. Floors creaked and he imagined footsteps. His hand oozed down the carved banister as they descended, the main stairwell spiraling lazily toward the foyer and low-hanging candelabra that illuminated the mosaic floor. Ben followed his grandfather down a dark hallway. The walls, like nearly every wall inside the house, were made up of floor-to-ceiling bookshelves, with ladders that slid along well-greased runners, giving instant access to the mansion's vast, eclectic book collection.

Ben saw moonlight in the room at the end of the hallway.

He heard the birds.

He pretended to be his grandfather's shadow as they closed in on that room.

The room with the tree with no leaves.

The books with no words.

3

DETECTIVE MILLS HAD fallen asleep in the conference room, leaning back and snoring with the papers and photos from the Peterson case scattered across the table like a tornado had spun through.

He popped alert when Chief Givens smacked the doorway's threshold. "Mills! Go home and get some sleep."

Blue had said the same thing to him before she'd left the station twenty minutes ago.

Chief Givens ducked his head back in. "And that's an order."

Blue's order had been that of a daughter to her father, a clever diversion from the question he'd asked her just before she'd left the conference room.

Can I see the grandkids sometime soon? The pause, the exhale, the look away. Neither a yes or a no or a maybe. Just . . . *Go home and get some sleep.*

Mills yawned twice on his way to the car. On the five-mile ride home, he drove slowly, blinking hard and opening his eyes wide, a ritual he'd started years ago to keep himself from nodding off behind the wheel. The Rolling Stones' "Sympathy for the Devil" blared on the radio, an appropriate title for the pictures he'd left behind in the conference room. It had been two weeks since they'd found the Peterson family in the barn, hacked to pieces inside those cocoons, with no leads. They'd been murdered inside the house. Bloody size-fifteen boot prints had been found in the kitchen, up and down the hallway, on the stairs, and in all of the second-floor bedrooms, but most prominently inside the dining room, from which the cocooned bodies must have been bundled and sewn on the table and then carried, one by one, to the barn. They'd found four dead moths on the kitchen table, and a half-dozen live ones fluttering inside the Petersons' closed bedroom.

He'd heard his fair share of myths about moths, what they represented and meant and so forth, and not many of the so-called *sayings* were good. So he'd kept his mouth shut when Chief Givens asked what he thought about all those moths, dead or otherwise. Mills had grunted that he didn't, and moved on, mentally ledgering, though, like he always did, tunneling for some deeper meaning.

Mills rolled down his window and allowed in the crisp fall air. He filled his lungs with it, caught the hint of burning leaves and grilled meat as the town rolled by. Mills once overheard a tourist compare Crooked Tree to the sleepy, fictional town of Mayberry. But as far as crime went, Crooked Tree was closer to Gotham. And Mills considered himself more of a Batman than Andy Griffith, with no Barney Fife in sight.

The roads were empty. Most the town was at the bookstore for Ben Bookman's newest release. That's why Sam—she allowed him to ease off calling her Detective Blue during off hours—had left the police station in such a hurry. For whatever reason, she was a Ben Bookman fan. She, of course, had made a point to needle him about retirement before she'd gone. Like she did every day of late. She didn't like the way he was limping around, zoning out.

You just don't look healthy, Mills.

Retirement was out of the question. He'd just as soon die on the job. No one else at the station had an eighty-nine percent closure rate. Crooked Tree needed him now like it had needed him back then, and all the decades in between. For a town of only six thousand, the crime rate often surpassed those numbers from the cities, and this year had been one of the worst. Break-ins. Domestic violence. Fits of rage. Five months ago—after nearly half a year of breaking into homes and jumping out of closets and out from under beds scaring children—Mills had finally caught the lunatic the newspaper had dubbed the Boogeyman, real name Bruce Bagwell. Other than fright—he'd taken to painting his face in brown and black vertical stripes, with stark red paint around his eyes and mouth—Bruce Bagwell, a plumber by trade, never harmed a soul. But when the judge asked what he planned on doing when released, and he'd said *Scare more children*, he was sent the same afternoon to Oswald Asylum for an extensive evaluation that proved he was, in Blue's own words, *a fucking nut job*.

The investigation that weighed most heavily on Mills' heart of late was the missing girl, Blair Atchinson, who'd disappeared from her backyard just over three weeks ago, an occurrence that had given many in town pangs of dread. There'd been a handful of children in Crooked Tree over the past decade or more who came up missing. There'd been almost four years between Blair and the previous abduction, a seven-year-old boy named Matt Jacobson. Like the others before him, Matt was never heard from again. Mills had hoped—and by now assumed—those abductions were over.

He was wrong.

And now this.

The horror he'd found inside the Petersons' house and barn was the most bizarre crime scene he'd ever witnessed. *Those hand-stitched cocoons.* Mills rolled his window back up, no longer craving that Crooked Tree air. By the time he neared his home, the combination of Ritalin and Adderall he'd downed before leaving the station had jolted him alert.

The gravel driveway snaked through tall oaks and pines. He coasted to a stop outside the ranch-style home he and Linda had shared for thirty-nine years of marriage. It would have been forty next month had she not dropped dead, face down on the kitchen table, eight months ago.

Right in the middle of a bout of laughter.

Right in the middle of our nightly game of Uno.

Mills shut off the car and made his way inside. He hung his jacket on the rack beside the door, and then locked the bolt and chain. Samantha was right; he needed rest. His decade-long struggle with narcolepsy—late onset and believed by his doctor to have been the result of decades of poor sleep habits—made him painfully tired during the day. But insomnia kept him awake most nights, and it had only gotten worse since Linda died.

The kitchen was a mess from sink to stovetop. Linda had called him a slob and he owned it. A moth flew along the ceiling and settled on the faucet handle. He grabbed a flyswatter from the hook on the wall and killed it with one stroke. Goddamn things were coming out in full daylight now, which was why the moths found inside the Petersons' house hadn't been terribly alarming. He knocked the dead moth to the floor. It landed a few inches away from one he'd killed and meant to sweep up last night. He found a dustpan and tossed both dead ones in the garbage. Call it what you want, an infestation or ambush, no matter how many bug companies they'd called, the moths kept coming back. He kept a swatter in every room of the house for that sole purpose.

He fixed himself a frozen pepperoni pizza and ate it in the living room with a can of cola and his feet propped on the coffee table. He needed to vacuum. There was a dead moth on the carpet in front of the television. He needed to dust, too, but after the days he'd had since the Peterson investigation started, he'd felt the need to laugh, not clean. So while the amphetamines coursed through his system, he'd taken to watching *Seinfeld* reruns at night.

Five minutes in, he nodded off. But only for a couple minutes before he startled awake, spilling what was left in the can of cola on his pants. Once he went under, it never took long to reach REM sleep, which was why he always made it a point, if he felt himself growing drowsy, to not lie down unless he was fully prepared for what could follow. The nightmares were not as common and nowhere near as severe as they'd be lying down, which, for the first time in days, he now felt like doing.

The deep sleep.

He placed his dishes on the pile beside the sink and promised to do them tomorrow. The kitchen table beckoned. Mills poured two fingers of Old Forester on ice and sat at the square, wooden table, where the pack of Uno cards rested unboxed since that night. Beside the cards was a bottle of sleeping pills. He opened the lid, shook out four into his palm.

Put one back. Closed the lid. Three would do.

He'd eased himself up from the two and a half he'd been periodically taking for months. He crunched them with his teeth to get them into his bloodstream faster, winced at the bitterness, and swallowed with a gulp of water from the sink.

The bourbon he placed on the table; it would go untouched until he poured it out in the morning. He shuffled the cards and dealt out two hands, one for him and one for Linda. He played both. Lost. He shuffled, dealt again. Twenty minutes and three hands of Uno later, his eyelids grew heavy. His job flashed to the forefront.

To the unsolved Peterson murders.

The horrific details, unbelievably enough, he'd been able to keep from the news, despite the numerous attempts by that pretty news anchor Amanda Bookman to dig deeper toward the truth. Didn't matter she was about to give birth. Both of Crooked Tree's news channels had covered the Peterson massacre for days, as had all the national talking heads, but that had since trailed off, especially after the realization had set in that the police were not under any circumstances giving out any details of what they'd really found inside that barn.

Behind closed doors—specifically because of the scarecrow found in the barn beneath the cocooned bodies—they referred to the case as *Scarecrow.* The public knew only that the Petersons had been murdered, found inside the barn, and that there had been only one survivor. The Petersons' ten-year-old daughter, Amy, had been found inside her cocoon without a scratch. She was still in the hospital recovering from shock, and two weeks later had yet to say a word. Detective Blue had visited the girl every morning since she'd been pulled from that hand-sewn husk like a frightened newborn eager for air. According to forensics and the state in which the other four cut-up bodies had been found, the girl had hung there for days, two to three minimum, four at the most. She'd been bundled up with an apple, two bananas, and a bottled water, which she'd rationed out, with no more than a sip or two left by the time they'd cut that cocoon down. Unlike the rest of her family, she was bundled inside a blanket, so she couldn't break free.

The murderer had wanted the girl to be found alive. To tell and to talk.

To spread fear.

The sleeping pills had already mixed with what remained of the amphetamines.

His cell phone buzzed, but he was too gone to answer it. His skull felt heavy. His brain floated on hurricane waves. He picked up the Uno cards and dealt another hand. Linda won again. "But you didn't say Uno," he said aloud, chuckling as his mind spun, stopping abruptly when he realized how pathetic he felt. On a notepad, he tallied another check in her column. She was up twelve on him now. A name bubbled suddenly on his lips.

"Jepson Heap."

Although he knew no Jepson Heap.

Scarecrows scare. That's what they do, Blue.

He stood from the table. "Goodnight, Linda." He knocked the chair over when he stepped away. Used the hallway walls to guide himself to his bedroom. He fumbled the doorknob open, kicked the door closed with his heel, and stumbled to the bed. Some of what hung from the ceiling brushed the top of his head as he climbed atop the disheveled covers. He rolled on his back, eyes on the ceiling, heavy lids getting heavier.

By last count he was up to ninety-four dream catchers. Most he'd hung from the ceiling, pinned there either by nails or thumbtacks. The dream catchers leaked like water drops from the ceiling, swaying like muted wind chimes. Some leather. Some plastic. Some made of wood. All with the webbing needed to catch what was coming. He'd nailed dream catchers to the walls, atop the windows. Some hung from the corners of framed pictures, from the lamp shades, and several from the dresser—one on each of the five horizontal drawers.

Three dream catchers atop the headboard, three more at his feet.

His eyelids fluttered.

A moth landed on the windowsill across the room.

One dream catcher under the bed.

Ten more in the bathroom.

Mom . . .

Yes, Winny?

Why do they call them dream catchers if they were made to catch nightmares?

It's just what they're called, dear.

And what if it doesn't work?

It'll work, Winny. Now close your eyes and get some rest.

Mills drifted off to another time and place, to when the young, flaxen-haired psychiatrist sat bedside in a hard-backed wooden chair and patted his hair.

Told him, *Close your eyes and relax.*

And he did.

Pleasant dreams, Winchester. Pleasant dreams.

4

B EN SAT SLUMP-SHOULDERED in his office chair, staring at the hardwood between his bare feet, hair still wet from the shower he'd taken minutes ago, the shower Amanda had been asking him to take since their return from the bookstore. He'd relented after Bri—who, thank God, had been deep into a stack of middle grade books when the gun went off—walked by and innocently asked what that was in his hair. After feeling his head, his unsteady fingers tracing over hair hardened by dried blood and coming back with a kernel-size bit of that man's skull pinched between his fingers, he'd showered, standing under the hot stream until his heart stopped hammering.

"Where's Bri? I want to see her before she goes."

Amanda leaned against his bookshelf. "She's already gone, Ben."

"You should have waited until I got out."

"Mom and Dad were in a hurry. They're freaked out, too. There's cameras outside."

"You know them all. Tell them to fuck off?"

"They're chasing the story, Ben. A man blew his head off in the middle of a bookstore."

Ben rested his elbows on his knees. While Amanda scrolled on her iPhone, he surveyed his office bookshelves. Translations in forty-plus languages. Hardcovers. Paperbacks. Audiobooks. Movie versions. *Summer Reign* had been a blockbuster three years ago. *The*

Pulse was in the can and set for release in the spring. Rumors were already circulating about the movie version of *The Scarecrow*. He'd wanted this. All of it. The moniker—the Nightmare Man, the fame—he'd wanted it. Craved it ever since Grandpa Robert held his hand as a young boy and walked him through all the rooms at Blackwood, the thousands of books in his collection. *All for your perusal, Benjamin.*

"Did you see her? At the bookstore?"

"See who?"

"Jennifer. She was there, briefly. Wearing a Yankees baseball cap. Like she didn't want to be noticed."

His heart lurched at the sound of their former intern-turned-nanny's name. But no, he hadn't seen her. Jennifer Jackson, now a college senior and English major, had suddenly and without explanation quit a week after Ben returned from his weekend at Blackwood. The weekend he could only vaguely remember. Amanda blamed him. Jennifer had been like a little sister to her and now she was gone, leaving so abruptly some of her books and clothes remained in the spare bedroom upstairs.

"She doesn't look good."

"I didn't see her."

"I know you call her."

He swallowed the words he wanted to say. *You're fucking twisted, Ben.* "Maybe I am," he mumbled.

"Maybe you're what?"

"Nothing."

Weeks ago, Amanda snatched the early copy of *The Scarecrow* from his hands after he'd sent Bri off to play. Other than traditionally reading his first chapter to make sure it had a hook, she never read his books, and hadn't in fact read one of them since his first, the day before they'd met, when she'd interviewed him on the station's morning show months before either of them had become well known.

"So what is your ultimate goal as a writer, Ben Bookman?" she'd asked.

"To scare the pants off people," he'd said, leaning forward toward the camera. "To give them nightmares." He'd smiled when he'd said it, meaning every word.

She'd chuckled, and he'd fallen instantly in love with that laugh.

"The Nightmare Man," she'd called him on camera. They'd begun dating two nights later, where she'd admitted, because of the gore and creepiness, she'd only gotten through half the novel and had only agreed to go to dinner with him because *she just had to know.*

"Know what?" he'd said, leaning over their table of expensive sushi, as intrigued by her as she was by him, hoping she'd giggle again because the first time had nearly stopped his heart.

"What makes you tick," she'd said, biting her lower lip, eyes emerald green.

But then, as he'd eyed the early copy of *The Scarecrow* in the crook of her arm, the spine resting on the gentle swell of what would soon become their second child, painfully recalling the innocence of that first date, he asked a simple question. "Why? Why read this one?"

No flirting to her words this time. "To see what makes you tick."

"It's a novel, Amanda. Not a memoir."

She'd read it in two days, setting it aside on an end table immediately after finishing, staring deadpan into the fireplace. He'd stood in the doorway, waiting. "Well?"

"It was good."

"That's it?"

"Damn good." But then, without looking up, she'd said, "You're fucking twisted, Ben." Those words still hurt. Blackwood had done it. All those summers there. He and his older sister Emily, and their little brother Devon.

Fucking twisted like Daddy, because the apple doesn't fall far from the tree.

"Amanda?" Ben waited for her to look at him. "Amanda."

She sent a text, looked up. "What?"

He wrangled. *Tell her you love her. That you are not fucking twisted.* "Sometimes it hurts to talk," he said.

"Sometimes? You brood, Ben. Professionally."

"I'm a writer. I'm in my head a lot."

"I'd like a glimpse of what's in there myself. Although I'm starting to get a good idea. Like Jack Torrance from *The Shining.*"

They stayed silent, both brooding now. She returned to her phone. Ben said, "Who are you texting?"

She looked up. "Nobody. Everybody. You do realize if I wasn't married to you I'd be outside with them right now? So excuse me if my phone is blowing up." She started out of his office, stopped at the door. "You sit in your office and stare at the screen, Ben. You don't *do* anything. But *something* is in there churning. Jennifer saw it. She was scared of you, Ben. When she quit. I don't know what happened—"

"Amanda. I told you—"

"We all are," Amanda said, raising her voice, then settling, "scared of you. Since Grandpa Robert died, you haven't been yourself." She started toward his office door again.

"What I write . . . It's just words on a page."

She let out a soft laugh. "You're sleepwalking again. It gets worse when you aren't writing."

"Did I . . . ?"

"No," she said quickly. "You didn't . . . touch me. You stand in the courtyard, stare at the woods. Calling out for Devon."

He raked his hair, let it fall loosely. "Amanda, I'm sorry."

"I can't un-see what I saw that weekend, Ben." The blood on his shirt. Cigarette smoke on his clothes. *Why was her car there?* He'd been unreachable for three days, too quick to avoid her questions. Amanda finished her thought. "And I can't un-see what I saw tonight. Who was that man, Ben?"

"I told you. I've never seen him before. Same as I told Detective Blue."

She looked at her iPhone, thumb-scrolled, sent a quick text, and then read from her phone: "They found his wallet and ID on the floorboard of his truck. His name was Jepson Heap. Sixty-five years old. Wheat farmer. Three sons. Six grandchildren. A wife, Trudy, of forty-two years. But what did he mean, Ben? You stole his nightmare?"

"He was a crazy fan, Amanda. You've read *Misery*? We watched it together. Kathy Bates. *I'm your number one fan?*"

"He wasn't a fan, Ben. Your book, to him, was more than just words on a page. My God. I hate that place."

"What place?"

"Blackwood," she said with an edge, like how could you even ask such a stupid question? "I'm with your sister. I say we burn the entire house down."

"Blackwood didn't blow that man's head off."

She arched her eyebrows as if to say *didn't it?* Her phone pinged with another text. And another. And then three almost piggybacking each other.

"Who's that?" Ben asked. "What's going on? Is it Bri?"

Amanda's cell sounded. She answered it. "Yes. What? When?"

Ben followed her down the hall and into the kitchen, where she paced like she didn't know where to go. "Amanda? Is it Bri? Has something happened?" He was close enough to hear Richard Bennington's voice on the other end.

Amanda distanced herself from Ben. Her jaw tightened. She picked up the remote for the small television on the wall behind the breakfast nook, and turned it on.

Dick Bennington was on the screen with breaking news and a warning—what he was about to describe was gruesome in nature. A replay of what must have been broadcast live moments ago. Amanda tossed the remote on the island and left him alone in the kitchen. For *his* eyes; it was clear she no longer wanted to be in the same room. The television showed a farm house with a wraparound porch. A cornfield in the background. Photographs of a young couple. Mid-thirties, Ben guessed. Billy and Allison Reynolds, both smiling in the picture. They'd been found dead inside their screened porch a couple of hours ago.

"No." He approached the television, wide-eyed, heart hammering. "No."

"Odd handmade cocoons stitched together from old corn husks," Dick Bennington said on the television. "Layered thick enough to hold the weight of two adults, the woman . . ."

"Six months pregnant," Ben said, echoing the replay. "No." Ben gagged, hurried to the sink in time to empty his stomach. He heaved again, running the water and garbage disposal simultaneously. On screen, just as Dick Bennington was about to reveal more of the gruesome details, the Crooked Tree police shut him down.

But Ben already knew.

Amanda entered the kitchen again, eyes reddened by tears. She kept her distance. The island between them. Her at the threshold to the living room. A quick getaway, if needed.

He stepped toward her. She held her hand out to keep him at bay. "What did he say? Amanda? What did they find inside that house?"

"I think you already know. Don't you?"

"How would—"

"Because the scene was straight out of your fucking book, Ben. Every detail. Which means the Petersons' murder weeks ago . . . Oh my God, Ben." Her face went white, as if she too was about to be sick. He knew the look. The first two months of this pregnancy had been spent in the bathroom. "The Petersons," she mumbled.

"That was why the police were so tight-lipped." She glared at him, through him. "Just words on a page, Ben?"

"Someone read my book, Amanda. Some cruel piece of shit acting out some morbid—"

"Ben."

"Amanda . . ." He was almost pleading. "What?"

"Your book came out last week. The Petersons were killed almost three weeks ago."

Before

H<small>E SHOULD HAVE</small> *changed his shirt.*
  Linda had told him, hissed in his ear as soon as he entered the kitchen.

"Change your shirt, Winchester. There's blood on the collar."

She only used his full name when she was serious. He'd gone into the bedroom fully intending to change it before returning to the dinner table, where in passing he'd seen eight-year-old Samantha anxiously awaiting her father's return from work, as she did every day. A day he'd just as soon forget. A day from which immediately detoxing was more important than changing his damn shirt.

He removed a bottle of Old Forester from the bedroom closet, from a shelf too high for Linda to reach, and began his nightly detox with two deep swallows. He wiped his mouth with his shirt sleeve—there was a spot of blood on the cuff too—and then lowered the suspenders from his shoulders, letting them dangle like a pair of dead snakes. He removed his shoulder holster and placed it on the bed. The handgun from his waistline he placed on the bedside dresser.

Before entering the kitchen, he made a pit stop in the hallway bathroom. He closed the door, splashed water on his face. He flushed the toilet to mask the sound of the mouthwash he swished and spat into the sink, any remnants of the bourbon down with it.

When he sat at the table, Linda's eyes bored into him. She placed his plate of meatloaf and mashed potatoes in front of him with an angry clank.

He'd forgotten to change his shirt.

Truth was, he hadn't felt like peeling it off yet. He'd change it when he showered, before he'd remove one of the airplane bottles of vodka he kept duct-taped to the underside of the lowest shelf of the towel closet in their master bathroom.

Linda ate quickly, without looking up, without saying a word.

She had one rule for his job, and it was to not bring it home.

She cleaned her plate at the sink, and then busied herself there while they ate. He heard her voice from too many yesterdays. She worries about you, Winny. She worries about you dying.

And then Sam said it. "There's stuff on your shirt, Daddy." He glanced at his cuff, made a brief attempt to see the spots on his collar, and then casually scooped a forkful of meatloaf and potatoes into his mouth. "Is it blood?"

"Yes, it's blood."

Linda wiped her hands on a towel and left the kitchen. Mills watched her go, and then said to his daughter, "But it's not my blood. Eat up before it gets cold." She watched him in between bites. "Stop staring, Sam."

They ate quietly for a minute before she asked, "Whose blood is it?"

"Doesn't matter. He's behind bars now."

"The human cage?"

"Yes, the human cage." He put his fork down and watched his daughter eat across the table. "Sam, have I ever told you about the three Fates?"

She shook her head.

"In Greek mythology, they're known as the three weaving goddesses."

"Like Mommy weaves?"

"Yes, except instead of a quilt, they weave mortality threads." He held up a hand to stop her from asking what that was. "And, Sam, their tasks are clearly defined. Clotho, she—"

"Clotho's a weird name."

"Maybe so, but she spins the thread."

"What thread?"

"The thread of life. Clotho spins the thread. Lachesis measures it. And then at the end, when our time on earth is up, Atropos cuts it. You see what I'm getting at?"

"I think."

"Well, I talked to Lachesis the other day, Sam."

"You did?

"I did."

"What did she look like?"

"She's beautiful. Like you and your mother." This made her smile; she had three front teeth missing. *"And you know what Lachesis said? She said, Winchester, your thread isn't even close to being cut. And you know how I know?"*

"How?"

"Because I haven't caught all the bad guys yet."

CHAPTER

5

MILLS SMELLED SOIL and damp grass.

A shovel crunched through fresh earth. Dirt rained down on him in tiny pebbles and clumps. He opened his eyes to a shrinking blue sky and a dark silhouette. Dirt on his thighs. His chest. He was being buried alive. He'd had this nightmare before. Dirt hit his face, in his mouth. He couldn't spit it out. Couldn't blink away the grains. Couldn't move at all. The weight of it made it hard to breathe. The impact muted by the thickness, the layers.

It'll soon be over.

"Mills."

I can't breathe.

The sky, a peephole of blue surrounded by black.

There's something on my chest.

"Mills. Wake up." Something moved within the dirt. Grabbed his arm and shook it. Total darkness now. "Wake up!"

No matter how many dream catchers festooned his bedroom, they still came. The imagined weight on his chest was the typical paralysis that hit him within minutes of falling asleep. The doctors called it sleep paralysis. An intrusion of the rapid eye movement stage. He was transient and conscious; he could open his eyes during the episode, but couldn't move his limbs, his head, or torso. Sometimes he couldn't blink. Those first several times as a child, he'd thought he was dying, that the shadow man pressing on his chest was real, and not remnants of the nightmare that had seized him. His body was asleep but his mind was awake. Or maybe it was the other way around.

The pressure on his chest eased. His breathing grew more normal. "Linda?"

"No. It's Samantha."

His head rolled toward his daughter. Brain fuzz gave way to Sam's familiar features. Soft sandy hair and pretty blue eyes. It was dark out. He hadn't even made it through the night. He saw the wall clock. He'd only been out three hours. It was barely evening. He peered down. *How'd I get on the living room floor?* "Where's my clothes?"

"How many prescriptions are you on?"

"What do you care?"

"Because I'm not financially prepared for a funeral right now."

He leaned on his elbows. Thick silver hair covered his droopy pectorals. A roll of fat rounded his waistline. "I'm fine. Sorry you had to . . . see this."

She looked away. "I've been trying to reach you for hours. Have you not seen the news?"

"Did I ever tell you how me and your mother met?"

"What? No, but . . ." She sighed. "Fine, how did you meet?"

"We were freshmen in high school. She got detention for falling asleep in class. I'd been sweet on her. This cute little redheaded girl. She was popular and I was weird, so I didn't know how to approach her. The next class I pretended to fall asleep so I'd get detention, too."

Samantha looked to be fighting a smile. "And?"

"And Mrs. Needers gave me a detention. We slipped each other notes. I found out why she was so tired. She'd been having nightmares. I told her I'd take it away for her if I could and she said wouldn't that be nice."

Samantha smiled. "And the rest as they say is history."

He nodded, surveyed the room. "When can I see the grandkids again?"

"I can't talk about this now."

It had been a month since he'd seen them. David and Joseph were five and four, respectively. A month since he'd gripped David's wrist to keep him from touching the stove's hot burner. He'd pressed too hard, and the boy ran off crying louder than he would have had he gotten burned. The next morning, the boy had a bruise around his wrist. When Mills called to check on him, to see if he could come over later in the week, Samantha had said maybe it wasn't a good idea. Maybe they needed more time.

"More time?" he'd said. "The boy was about to burn himself, Sam."

"You scared him. You scare both of them. Just like . . ."

Just like what? She'd hung up. *You scare both of them.* The way she'd said scare—not scared—on the phone that day . . .

Samantha snapped him back to the present.

"God damn it." He sat up. "Would you all stop snapping in my face?"

"There's been another murder. Two. And a half."

He knew what the half meant, and the reality of it sickened him. "How many months?"

"Does it matter?" She wrangled with it, looked away. "Six."

"Where and when? The murders, Sam?"

Detective Samantha Blue pulled Ben Bookman's latest novel from a bag and showed it to him. His eyes caught the scarecrow on the cover. She opened it to a certain page and tapped it with a blue-painted nail. *No detective paints their nails, Blue.* "There's something in it you need to read."

"I don't read shit."

"Well, you need to read *this* shit, Dad."

He squinted in the sunlight, looked at Blue; forgot completely what she'd asked him to do. "You know your mother used to hold my hand at night."

Blue clenched her jaw, looked away. "Here we go . . ."

"She'd hold my hand until I dozed off."

"I didn't know that, Dad." She tapped the book, the specific page. "Read this."

"Can I get some clothes on first?" Her eyes bored into him and it broke his heart; those were *his* damn angry eyes. Her face was pale. "Sam, what is it?"

"A man named Jepson Heap blew his head off inside the bookstore a couple of hours ago. Right in front of Ben Bookman."

"Jepson Heap?"

"Name ring a bell?"

"No." But it did, and he could tell she didn't believe him. *Jepson Heap.* He'd heard the name before. "Do you have a picture?"

"Before or after he blew his head off?"

You're more like me than you know, Blue.

"What's funny?" she asked.

"Nothing." He opened Ben Bookman's novel to the first chapter, read the first line: *Scarecrows scare. That's what they do.* "And this is from a best seller?"

Samantha stood from her crouch. "Read the first page of chapter three. We've got something to call him now. And he didn't leave one alive this time." She left the room.

"Where are you going?"

"To get you some clothes," she called out.

The dream catchers. "No. Samantha, don't go in my room! I'll get'm myself."

It was too late. Her voice rang from down the hall. "Oh my God. Oh . . . My . . . What in the living fuck, Dad?"

He sighed, rubbed his face. "Told you not to go in there."

6

B EN SLAMMED HIS office door and paced.

Think, Ben. Think.

He opened his flask, swallowed three gulps. The burn trailed down his throat and spread across his chest like a spill. He heard footsteps in the hallway. He locked the door before Amanda could come in.

The knob rattled. "Ben. Open the door." When he didn't, Amanda pounded on it, shaking the beveled glass. "Ben."

"Give me a minute."

She knocked again, tried the knob. "Ben, open the damn door!"

"Amanda, please. I need time to think."

"What did you do?" She was crying on the other side of the door. Her voice softened. "What did you do?" He wanted to hold her, but not until he got hold of things himself; his body was a live wire. He couldn't stop shaking.

I don't know. But it's out of control now.

The home phone sounded. Amanda's silhouette moved from the door, leaving him alone.

His cell phone buzzed.

It was Kim, his agent. He couldn't talk now. He placed the phone on his desk. It vibrated against the wood until it went to voice mail. He sat at his desk, buried his face in his hands, and sucked in deep breaths until his heart rate settled. His phone vibrated again. Clayton this time. His editor. He let it go to voice mail too, and then touched the mouse pad on his laptop. The screen came to life. The cursor blinked, awaiting his words. He stared, fingers poised above the keys. How could he even think of writing now? Continuing what he never should have even started back then. Started for what he thought were all the right reasons . . .

He placed his fingertips on the keys anyway. Typed: *The Screamer* . . . And then he stopped, deleted the two words. Wrangling, he typed again. *The Screamer had found his next little mouse.*

Ben paused, made as if to delete the sentence, but something stopped him. He'd thought out the next scene days ago, but couldn't bring himself to write it. And now, after what was happening . . . How could he even think of moving forward with this book, this story line?

For Devon. That was why it had to be done. He was getting too close to finding the truth about Devon to stop now.

Ben swallowed, throat dry. He sipped from his flask and typed.

The Screamer tried to smile, but it was hard through the stitches and thread. He watched the Mulky girl from the trees. Hushes and whispers, he thought. He could corner this little mouse with hushes and whispers, he knew, but nothing worked better than the silent screams. From his spot in the woods, as a test, he let out one, just a quick burst.

The little Mulky girl's head turned toward the lack of sound.

So easy, the silent scream, like a subtle kiss of breeze. How nicely she would fit next to Little Baby Jane, the girl Meeks had left alive. Poor, poor Miserable Meeks. Poor stupid ol' Miserable Meeks.

Dead now because of that girl.

Because of Little Baby Jane.

That girl.

Ben thought of the little Peterson girl in the hospital, here now, because of his book, and pushed himself away from the desk, panting. *Fuck!* What had happened at the bookstore had unnerved him, but the dread he now felt had started when his own daughter left the house without his telling her goodbye. On impulse, he dialed Amanda's parents and paced his office while it rang. He needed to hear her voice. And a drink. He took a quick slug from his flask, wiped his mouth with a sleeve.

Amanda's father, Jim, picked up on the third ring. "Amanda?"

"Jim, it's Ben." Silence. "I need to talk to Bri."

"Ben, I don't know if that's a good idea right—"

"Jim, please . . ."

"Is Amanda with you?"

"Yes. She's . . . in the other room. Please, put Bri on the phone. I need to hear—"

"Daddy."

"Bri." Tears pooled his eyes in an instant—a floodgate opened.

"Are you crying?"

"No, honey." He wiped his eyes, gave an anxious chuckle. "Just happy to hear your voice."

"What's going on? Mommy said you're sick."

He closed his eyes, nodded. "I'm sick, yes. But I hope to be better soon."

"How soon?"

"Real soon."

"Like tomorrow?"

"Yes, I'll see you tomorrow."

A pause, and then: "Then you must not be that sick. Are you sick like that one time when you opened the box?"

The girl never forgot a thing. "Yeah, kinda like that."

"They won't let me turn on the television. Why was there police cars at our house?"

"Just a misunderstanding."

"Is it because of what happened at the bookstore? With that man?"

What did she see? "Yes."

"I heard the gunshot, Daddy. It was loud."

"It *was* loud. But it's over now." *Is it, Ben? Is it really over?*

"I'm not scared," she said.

He choked up again. "That's right. Because you aren't scared of anything."

"Well, one thing."

He heard rustling. Bri softly said *Okay*, and then Jim must have taken the phone back from her. "Ben, we need to hang up now."

"What's happening? Is something happening there?"

"No, we're fine. We don't need Brianna getting worked up before bedtime. She's getting worked up, Ben."

"She doesn't sound like—"

"I'm hanging up," Jim said with urgency. "Please. You take care of my daughter. We'll talk tomorrow."

In the background, Bri said, "Goodnight, Daddy."

"Goodnight, Bri." The line disconnected. He tossed his phone on the desktop, watched it spin. When it stopped, his gaze moved to the bottom right drawer of his desk, the one locked with a key he kept hidden on the third shelf across the room, under a hardcover copy of his second novel, *Some Fall Down*.

He tugged on the drawer handle, just to make sure. It didn't budge.

Amanda was outside his office door again, her shadowed silhouette looming on the other side of that frosted glass.

You take care of my daughter.

"You take care of mine," he said softly. He moved around the desk to the door and opened it. Amanda needed no one to take care of her. Under the makeup and away from the cameras, she was the toughest girl he'd ever met. He stepped toward her in a consolatory way, but she stepped aside, looked down, anywhere but at him.

"Amanda? Who was on the phone?"

"Detective Mills," she said.

"What did he want?"

Same thing he wanted thirteen years ago, Ben. Answers . . .

She looked up at him. "They want to talk. Said they'd be here within the hour. And to not go anywhere."

Before

*B*RI KNOCKED ON *his office door.*
      Ben hid his irritation. He'd told her more than once that if she
heard him typing, whatever it was could wait.

"*But what if it's an emergency?*"

"*Only if it's an emergency,*" *he'd told her with a smile.*

The next day she'd knocked on his office door to tell him Jerry, her
hamster, was out of food. And that she feared Tom, her other hamster,
was stealing it.

"*Bri, this is not an emergency,*" *he'd told her. "Hamsters can store*
food in their cheeks for years, I think. For decades, probably."

She was unconvinced, so he'd grabbed his keys and driven—with
thoughts and plots and murders still raging through his head—to the
pet store for more food.

Now he waited until after he'd finished his thought, his sentence,
one where'd they'd just found the bones of another of the Screamer's
victims—but he needed a clue left behind. He removed his glasses and
placed them on the desk beside his laptop. "Come in, Bri."

She opened the door. In both hands she held a cardboard box the
size of which might fit a grown man's shoes. "A man left this for you on
the porch."

He waved her closer. "Bri, I don't bite."

"*But I'm not sure if this is an emergency.*"

"Boxes are always emergencies. Let's see what's in it." He minimized his screen so she couldn't see what he'd just written.

"What were you working on?"

"I was looking up the word cute on Google."

"And?"

"And up popped a picture of you."

She rolled her eyes, handed him the box. *"Open it."*

He drumrolled, sliced the box open with his letter opener, and realized it had no addresses, just his name in black Sharpie. On instinct, he shielded the inside of the box from her when he opened the cardboard flap.

What he saw inside sucked his soul right out of him.

"Daddy, what's in the box?"

He closed the lid, stared catatonically across his office to the open door. *"Bri, you said a man dropped this off?"*

"Yes."

"Did you see what he was driving?"

"No."

"What did he look like?"

She shrugged.

"Did you see his face?"

"No. Why?"

"No reason."

"What's in the box?"

He closed the lid, kissed the top of her head, and told her to go play.

She stopped at the door. *"Daddy, your skin looks funny. Funny weird, not funny ha ha."*

That's because I'm about to pass out, Bri. But he smiled. *"I'm fine, honey."*

After a beat, she disappeared down the hallway.

When he heard Amanda's voice coming from the kitchen, he locked the box inside the bottom right drawer of his desk, and threw up in the garbage can.

7

Detective Mills leaned at the porch railing overlooking the Reynolds' cornfield, sucking in fresh air like the country might soon run out of it. Next to him stood the county medical examiner, Dr. Braxton Little, a stout, even-tempered man who'd been in the business as long as Mills. In all their years together, he'd never seen Little go so pale at a crime scene. He'd hurried from the Reynolds' living room and vomited in their backyard.

Mills clapped the ME's back, which was arched like a turtle shell. That, with the bald dome, was why everyone called him the Turtle. A name he'd taken so thoroughly to heart a decade ago he'd begun wearing nothing but shades of green and brown on the job. "You okay?"

Little nodded. The Turtle had once been larger; on doctor's orders, he'd recently lost sixty pounds, leaving behind loose skin around his neck that not only hung like turkey wattle but added to his Turtle resemblance. "Sorry, Winny. I've never done that before." The Turtle pulled a flask from his coat pocket and downed a quick swallow.

For a beat, Mills envied him. The ease with which he took that drink, with no guilt in the world.

Cornstalks swayed in the distance, eerie and silent under starless black.

Mills drew a deep breath and returned inside. Uniformed officers and techs roamed from room to room, focused, going about their jobs like ants on an anthill. The Reynolds couple had been found in the same type of hand-stitched cocoons as the Petersons weeks ago. Instead of the barn—and just like in Ben Bookman's novel—the couple had been hung from hooks that had previously held their porch swing, which was now on the floor facing their hanging bodies. It appeared as if the killer, who they were all calling the Scarecrow because of Ben Bookman's novel, had sat for a while on the porch swing to admire what he'd done, long enough to open fifteen peanuts and stuff the shells inside a coffee cup that held the two severed tongues they'd been unable to find up until that point. The uneaten peanuts, just like the second murder scene in Bookman's novel, had been carefully placed on the porch's floorboards, in front of the swing and in what appeared to be in the shape of a face. A face with eyes and a nose but no mouth. He and Blue had taken notes, snapped pictures, and scoured the place from basement to attic, both of them eager to get to Ben Bookman's house to question him.

Earlier, Blue had had no luck questioning Jepson Heap's wife—now widow—Trudy Heap, who'd been in such shock after hearing what her husband had done inside that bookstore that all Blue had been able to conjure from her was a tear-garbled "I don't know" and some slight head nods when asked if they could come back to question her in the morning. After she'd taken the dose of meds prescribed to calm her down.

While Mills finished up inside the Reynolds' house, taking special note of the eight moths he'd found tapping the overhead light inside the Reynolds' closed bedroom—with two more dead on the windowsill—Blue had gone to question their neighbor, the only one within a half mile. Like the Petersons, the Reynolds' property was out in the middle of nowhere, surrounded by corn on three sides and a road on the other. The neighbor, an elderly widow named Beverly Carnish, was a hundred yards away and Blue had gone on foot.

Mills checked his watch, stared out the kitchen window, avoiding any glimpse of the living room's blood-stained walls, where the bodies had been cut to pieces. With the blood splatter, they suspected one or both of them had still been alive when the psycho had started cutting. Blue had been gone thirty minutes and should have been back by now. Mills knew if it had been any other uniformed cop or plainclothes detective, he wouldn't have been worried. She'd been trained like any other. She'd earned the badge on her own. In high school, the boys had kept their distance, prompting Samantha one night during her senior year to tell her mother, in tears, that she feared the boys were *afraid* to ask her out. Which was fine by Mills. Samantha could be gruff. But they'd all known she'd end up becoming a Blue; she and Detective Willard's son Danny had just been the last ones to figure it out.

"You ready? Mills?"

He turned, found his daughter standing in the kitchen. Relief washed over him in one broad stroke. "Sorry. Didn't hear you come in."

"Your hearing aid on?"

He checked it. "Yes." Even though it wasn't. He and the Turtle both wore them now. They'd turned them off when they'd been outside together, convinced, when the Turtle's had started squawking, that some weird interference was going on. Mills brushed past Blue on his way out the door. "What did the neighbor say?"

"Not much." She trailed behind him down the porch steps. He nodded to the Turtle as the pathologist made his way back inside, seemingly rejuvenated. "Turtle okay?" Blue asked.

"He's fine. What did the neighbor say?"

"It was an old woman."

"Define old."

"Older than you." She pointed back toward the house. "Older than him." The Turtle had just let the door slam—Mills flinched, adjusted his hearing aid as they neared her Jeep Cherokee. "Two days ago Billy and Allison Reynolds knocked on their neighbor's door, with an apple pie."

The two of them stopped next to their respective car doors, watching each other over the hood. "And?" he asked. "After they brought the pie . . ."

"They asked Ms. Carnish if she'd seen anyone around the cornfield. She said no. They'd seen someone standing in their backyard three nights ago. Legs together and arms stretched out like a scarecrow." She briefly imitated the pose. "Straw hat and all. At first they thought someone had put a scarecrow in their yard as a prank, but when Billy walked outside to get a look, it was gone. He claimed to see the cornstalks moving, like someone had just fled into them. Turns out he had."

"Who had?"

"The scarecrow," she said, annoyed. "Billy Reynolds goes back inside to find his wife trembling and panicked. She'd been watching from the window. Saw the thing, what they'd both assumed to be a prop, run into the cornfield."

Mills looked away, toward the corn in the distance. "Only in Crooked Tree."

"And I'm assuming the next two nights went as they did in Bookman's novel." He hadn't read as much as she had but she'd filled him in on the car ride over. "The next night the scarecrow shows up again," she said. "But in a different spot. Stands out there until they notice him out the window. The stalking phase, just like in the book."

"Interesting MO."

"Billy Reynolds goes out again, this time probably with the rifle we found propped up beside the back door there."

"But again the scarecrow flees," Mills grumbled, watched the cornstalks sway.

"Until the third night he doesn't. But they never call the police."

"Because everybody in Crooked Tree carries a gun now." He watched her mull on it. "You're thinking if we'd been more public with the Petersons' scene . . ."

"That the Reynolds couple would have at least called the police? Aren't you?"

"No. All we had from the Petersons was a bloodbath and an old, dusty scarecrow in a barn. What we had was a crime scene that would have stirred up a big bowl of panic."

"Like we're about to have now." She nodded out toward the road. Three news vans lingered behind the roadblock. "Bennington got too much before we shut him down."

"And maybe that's a good thing now. But don't second guess yourself, Blue. That's rule number one. There's not a damn thing we can ever go back and change no matter how badly . . ." His voice caught in his throat, so he tried again. "No matter how badly we'd like to."

"So in hindsight?" she asked.

"Hindsight's a motherfucker, Blue. Rule number two."

"More like rule twenty. Hindsight's a motherfucker. Got it."

"When we entered the Petersons' barn, we had no way of knowing what we know now. About this son of a bitch using that writer's book like a goddamn blueprint."

"And you get on me for my language?" Blue paused after opening her door. "Why don't you like him?"

"Who?"

"Ben Bookman? *That* writer?"

"The self-proclaimed Nightmare Man?" He shook his head. "He comes from a family of weirdos. And the apple with him didn't fall too far from one of those Blackwood trees."

"You ever been there? To Blackwood?"

"Long time ago," he said.

"In a galaxy far, far away . . ."

"Something like that." He opened his door. "You haven't been there, have you?"

"Since I'm a little old now to be grounded, yes, I've been there. Me and some friends. Senior year. Danny went with us. One summer night we drove out there, just to say we did."

"Just to say you did." He scratched his head. "That was stupid, Blue."

She shrugged. "We didn't stay long. It was creepy. And we'd never seen trees like that before. We heard some noises. Hightailed it out of there."

"Which was why your mother and I warned you never to go."

"Sometimes teens need to get burned before they realize for themselves that fire is hot."

"One of your mother's favorite quotes."

"A useful one," she said. "Why did you go to Blackwood, Mills?"

"Sam, can you cut it with the Mills shit?"

"Want to tell me about it?"

"No."

"What happened?"

"I was there to investigate the disappearance of the Bookman boy. Ben's younger brother, Devon."

"And?"

"And nothing. Conversation's over, *Blue*." A news van pulled away. His temper was the reason she'd frozen him out from seeing his grandchildren. Mills looked back at his daughter. "Was the pie good?"

"What?" She wiped her mouth, defensively.

"The pie," he said. "You visited the old neighbor. She offered you a piece of the apple pie the Reynolds had brought over three days ago. Because that's what old people do. They offer you pie. And because we raised you to have proper manners, you sat with her for a bite. No harm in that." He nodded toward her. "But you left crumbs on your blouse."

She looked down, brushed them off, and got in the car. He did likewise. She glanced at him as he buckled, and then she chuckled.

"What's funny?"

"Your fly's open."

He looked down, mumbled, "God damn it." He zipped up, nodded toward the road. "Just drive." A mile down the road, he said, "All I'm saying is you could have brought me a piece."

"Of what? The pie?"

"Yes."

"Then say that."

8

"THAT STORY YOU told back at the house," Blue said with a sideways glance toward her father as she drove. "About how you and Mom met. In detention."

"What about it?"

"It was cute." Cornfields and pines blurred past. Cute wasn't a word typically mentioned in the same sentence as Detective Winchester Mills. He grunted. She looked to be prodding for more, in a detoured way trying to get to the truth of all the dream catchers hanging from his bedroom ceiling. Or maybe she'd noticed he was on enough prescription meds to bring down a T-Rex. "You know . . . ," she said. "How you offered to take Mom's childhood nightmare away?"

"I remember the story, Sam." Downtown Crooked Tree zipped past. A town chock-full of working-class poor. Houses, once new, had fallen to disrepair. Too many storefronts boarded up. Too much crime. After an awkward minute of watching blacktop disappear like a running treadmill beneath the tires, Mills said, "What's your point?"

"Wouldn't that be neat?"

"Wouldn't what be neat?"

"If you could, you know, take somebody's nightmare from them."

"You've been reading too many Ben Bookman novels." Mills held Blue's copy of *The Scarecrow* on his lap. He pretended to read in the hopes she'd shut up. He'd already reviewed the paragraphs where the killer had pulled his inspiration, mirroring the two literary crime scenes, down to the peanuts on the Reynolds' porch.

He felt her glance as she drove, and then she said, "I tried to question Jepson Heap's wife earlier."

"You told me already."

"I didn't get anything out of her."

"Told me that too."

"In the living room," she said with caution, as if tiptoeing where she didn't belong. "They had dream catchers hanging all over the windows."

"What's your point?"

"I think you know what my point is. Your bedroom?"

"Just drive."

"But—"

"I don't want to talk about it, Sam."

They didn't talk about anything the rest of the way to the Bookmans' residence, on the wealthier side of Crooked Tree, a small percentage compared to the rest. There were so few in Crooked Tree who Had and so many who Had Not. And no one as wealthy as Ben and Amanda Bookman.

Blue parked at the curb outside the massive house, where a half dozen media vans and twice as many reporters had already set up camp outside the Bookmans' property. The front lawn was tiered, the landscaping manicured, the horseshoe driveway a landing pad for the Bookmans' two cars, one a Lexus sedan and the other a BMW SUV. With mature trees and acreage that stretched a quarter mile to the nearest neighbor, the Bookmans had managed a bit of isolation in the middle of suburbia. Good for them. The American Dream was alive and well. He'd give the author some leeway in regard to the Haves and Have Nots. If a man can make millions making stuff up, more power to him. Word was, the Bookmans gave a good amount of it to charities. But after seeing the wraparound porch and the thousands of stones and bricks it enclosed, as well as the four chimneys, all of which appeared to be billowing smoke for only three goddamn people, Mills couldn't help feeling a pang of annoyance as they approached the obnoxiously large front door.

Reporters hurled questions across the dark night. Mills and Blue ignored them.

Mills waved to Officer Chuck Black down the road; he'd been parked outside the Bookmans' home for security purposes ever since Jepson Heap blew his head to bits inside the bookstore. Officer Black rolled down his window and gave Mills the finger.

Mills chuckled, nodded back.

Blue knocked on the front door, saying to her father, "Call me when you grow up."

"I'll make sure to do that."

Amanda Bookman opened the door a few seconds later, done up like she was getting ready to go on air any minute. Mills knew Amanda Bookman only slightly better than he knew her husband; she'd been the lead "investigator" for Channel 11 News for the Peterson murders three weeks ago, and the disappearance of that little girl, Blair Atchinson, the week before that. He'd spoken on air with her three times recently, and often in the past. She'd been pushy at times, but always professional. So while Mills didn't trust reporters in general, he had respect for her.

And he could tell she'd been crying.

Amanda ushered them in and shut the door behind her. She watched the reporters out the nearby window, closed the curtain, and offered them drinks they both declined.

Ben Bookman paced in front of the fireplace and didn't acknowledge their entrance into the living room. While Amanda was put together, Ben was disheveled and apparently under the influence, making no attempt to hide the flask he nipped from even as Mills and Blue took their seats on the couch facing two ornate reading chairs on the opposite side of the coffee table.

Amanda sat in one of the chairs and watched her husband pace. "Ben."

He raked a hand through his hair and sat, not in the chair next to his wife, but in one at the coffee table's end zone.

Mills leaned forward, elbows on thighs. "Mr. Bookman, I'm Detective Mills and this—"

"I know who you are," Ben said, lowering his voice, looking away. "I remember you."

Blue eyed both her father and Ben. When neither of them elaborated, Blue got down to business. "And so you know why we're here?"

Ben's eyes were red-rimmed and glazed. He exhaled, as if resigned to dropping the tough-guy act, but then unabashedly took another drink from his flask. Amanda looked away—not only away but in the damn near opposite direction. "Of course I know why you're here."

Mills said, "I'm assuming by the smell that you're drinking whiskey."

Ben looked him in the eyes. "That a crime?"

"No. Just perhaps not the best idea under the circumstances."

"I didn't do anything."

"We never said you did." Blue and Amanda shared a glance, and then looked away from each other.

Amanda was still pissed about being shut out weeks ago by the police, Detective Blue specifically, about the Peterson murders. It dawned on Mills now that perhaps Amanda thought she could have helped the investigation, and thought this second set of murders was on their heads and not somehow her husband's.

Mills said, "Do you know what's going on here, Mr. Bookman?"

"No." He sighed, softened his tone. "And call me Ben."

"You don't recall ever meeting Jepson Heap?"

"The bookstore was the first I'd ever seen him. Look, haven't we gone over this?" He looked at Blue. "In the store. I answered every question."

"You were still in shock then," she said.

Ben said, "And I'm damn near drunk now."

Mills wasn't amused. "We didn't get much out of Jepson's wife, but by the looks of the meds on his coffee table, he'd been popping Ativan like candy."

"For his anxiety," said Blue. "Like he was trying to kill himself that way instead of snapping like he'd done."

"Would have been a lot cleaner," Ben said.

Blue looked at Mills, then studied Ben for a beat. "You think this is funny?"

"No. I don't." Ben watched the floor. His jaw trembled. When he looked back up his eyes had pooled with moisture. "I just spent thirty minutes cleaning Jepson Heap out of my hair, Detectives. It was my little girl who noticed parts of him still in there."

Blue said, "I'm sorry."

Mills was undeterred. "And what he'd said about you stealing his nightmare?"

"He was deranged. Delusional. A lunatic. Okay? You're better off asking his wife."

"We plan to more thoroughly," said Blue. "Once she calms down."

Mills said, "Once we *all* calm down."

Ben chuckled, and for the first time offered the flask over the coffee table. "Touché."

Mills hesitated, and then reached for it. He ignored Blue's look of disapproval. But instead of drinking, he merely smelled it. He handed it back to Ben, brushing his finger as he did so. Mills said, "I don't drink anymore." He leaned forward. "The book, Ben. Tell us about the book."

"What's there to tell?"

Amanda scoffed, fidgeted in her seat.

Mills studied them both, his eyes flicking from one to the other. "Perhaps it's none of my business, but it's clear you two are fighting."

"Ask him what happened last fall," said Amanda.

Mills folded his hands, searched deep for some patience. "What happened last fall?"

Ben raked unsteady fingers through his hair again. "That's when I wrote the book."

"This book? *The Scarecrow*? The same—"

"Yes. The same book that's now become a blueprint for some psychopath out there."

Mills nodded, didn't appreciate getting interrupted. Blue scribbled on her notepad. Mills waited for more from Ben, but it was like pulling teeth.

"He wrote it in three days," Amanda said, with caution.

"You wrote *The Scarecrow* in three days?"

Ben didn't answer, so Amanda did. "He had nothing before he went out there."

"I had a third of it done," Ben corrected.

"Went out where?" asked Mills.

"Ben . . ." Amanda raised her eyebrows, prodding him, Mills could tell, for some truth she'd been after for much longer than them.

"Blackwood."

"Your grandfather's place?" Blue asked. "A year ago?"

"Yes."

"When did your grandfather die?"

"Six months before that."

"So roughly a year and a half ago?"

"Thereabouts." Ben chewed a fingernail. "He didn't just die."

Blue looked up. "Says in the reports Dr. Robert Bookman died of a heart attack. At Oswald Asylum, if I remember correctly. *His* asylum."

"Reports are wrong."

"Oswald isn't his?"

"No. That he died of a heart attack."

"I was there," Mills said. "I saw him before the medics arrived. No hint of foul play." This surprised Blue, as he knew it would. Ben, too, clearly wanted more, but Mills wasn't about to give it. "He died of a heart attack."

"You know something I don't, Detective?" asked Ben.

"Ben . . . Don't," said Amanda. "He was ninety-two years old. Let it go."

Her interjection seemed to fuel him. "I don't doubt he died of a heart attack. While visiting Oswald Asylum. He visited Oswald every day. What I doubt is whether or not something other than old age caused it."

"Like?" asked Blue.

Ben looked away. "I don't know." He let it drop.

Blue scribbled on her notepad; probably sensing the unease in the room, and changed course. "You have a sister? Emily Sanders?"

"Yes."

"Formerly Emily Bookman . . . And where is she now?"

"Upstate New York. A psychiatrist with an accountant husband and three kids who seem to excel at whatever they do."

"And this bothers you?" asked Mills.

"No."

"Sounds like it does."

"They're fighting," Amanda said. "Ben and his sister. Robert left Blackwood to Emily."

"Why Emily?" asked Blue. "Why not to both of them?"

"She's older," Ben said quickly.

"Emily wants to sell Blackwood," Amanda said. "Ben wants to keep it. He wants to move us there. Right in the middle of the woods." Her sarcasm gained steam. "The *perfect* house to raise our children. When they're bored, they can run down the hill to Robert's lunatic asylum."

"It was just a suggestion," Ben said, monotone. His eyes drifted to Amanda's baby bump, as if it had gone unnoticed until now. Something about their attitude screamed *unplanned.*

Mills asked, "Why does your sister want to sell Blackwood?"

"Too much upkeep," said Ben, at the same time Amanda said, "Because it's creepy as hell." And then Amanda added, "I suppose both are true."

Mills asked, "What about your parents, Ben? They're both deceased? And this is why Blackwood went to a grandchild?"

Ben gazed at him—they both knew what happened to his parents—but it was Blue he spoke to. "What's it say in your notes? Even Wikipedia has that somewhat correct."

Blue flipped the page, found it. "Michael and Christine Bookman both passed away in a car accident when you were about to turn eighteen."

"Sounds about right." Ben slugged more bourbon.

Blue said, "And that was three months after your little brother, Devon, went missing?"

"Yes."

"And is still missing to this day?"

"Yes." He glanced at Mills. "Just another Crooked Tree cold case."

Mills took that as the shot it probably was, but didn't react.

Blue referred to her notes again. "Your parents were leaving Blackwood. The accident happened a mile from the house. The car was traveling nearly eighty miles per hour down that hill. Your father was behind the wheel. They went off the road into a ravine, killing them both instantly."

"Car was smashed like an accordion," Ben added.

Mills caught a twitch in Ben's eye. "Am I to assume you don't think this was an accident? Just like your grandfather's heart attack wasn't just old age?"

"I'm not saying it wasn't old age . . . Just some things that didn't add up in the way he was found."

"Like what?" asked Mills.

"His . . . Never mind," Ben said. "We're not here to talk about my grandfather."

Blue eyed Mills, then returned the questioning to Ben. "Your parents?"

Ben sighed, as if to regroup. "They were going too fast on those turns. My father had been drinking."

"You suggesting it was suicide?"

"Or they were in a hurry to flee that house," Amanda added.

"Why would they be in a hurry to flee the house?" asked Blue.

Ben looked away. Mills watched him, saw more signs of a man hiding something.

"Who wouldn't be in a hurry to leave that house?" Amanda added, breaking the silence. "I always was. Still am. Grandpa

Robert's death hit us hard. I might not have loved the house but we all loved the man. It hit Ben particularly hard." Amanda watched her husband, as if waiting for his permission to tell more, which he gave with a punctuated nod. "Robert was more of a father to Ben than a grandfather. Ben never really got along with his own father."

Ben laughed, a quick ironic burst of emotion. "That's an understatement."

Amanda shifted in her seat, and as if by reflex, touched her baby bump. Mills noticed Blue staring at it. "After Robert died," Amanda said, "Ben had a slip. He started drinking. Couldn't sleep. If there's such a thing as writer's block, Ben had it. With the looming deadline, he drove out to Blackwood for inspiration. He was desperate."

"To finish the book?" asked Blue.

"He'd hardly started."

"I was well into it," Ben mumbled, but didn't elaborate.

"An idea. A premise, at best," Amanda said. "I'd hoped he'd go out there and clear his head. Come home with a few solid chapters."

"And he caught lightning in a bottle," Mills said to Ben, sharing Amanda's skepticism.

"That's a saying for a reason," Ben said. "I was inspired. It always happens there."

"In that fucking room," said Amanda.

Apparently, she'd forgotten her company. Or maybe she was at the end of her rope and no longer cared. Either way, her harsh words gave Mills pause. He went cold and clammy. He felt Blue's whisper of *are you okay* against his ear, and nodded—but he wasn't.

"What room?" Blue asked.

"The room Robert called the atrium," Amanda said. "It was attached to the house, but not exactly part of it. We weren't allowed in there, even as adults, without him escorting us."

"Sounds bizarre."

"It was," Amanda said.

"What was in the room?"

"Books," Ben said, eyes distant.

"I've read of the book collection at Blackwood," said Blue. "One that rivaled libraries."

"That was in the main house," Ben corrected her. "The books in the atrium were not allowed to be read."

"Not allowed . . . I don't understand."

They had no titles. They were marked only by numbers on the spines.

The room had gone quiet. Mills looked up, found three sets of eyes on him.

"How do you know that?" asked Ben.

Mills took in their questioning gazes. "Know what?"

Blue said, "You just said the books had no titles. They were marked by numbers?"

Ben eyed Mills skeptically. "How'd you know that? He never let anyone in that room."

"I once knew your grandfather. Before your brother disappeared. Now back to *The Scarecrow*. You wrote it in three days inside that room?"

"Yes. Can we hurry up here? We know about the couple found today. It matches one of the murders in the book. To a T."

"The second one," offered Blue.

Ben was about to add something, but then went quiet.

"What?" Mills asked.

"Nothing. Have you read the book?"

"We haven't had time. We have someone on it. Tell us what we need to know."

"Tell me about how the Peterson family was found."

Blue hesitated, probably because Amanda's reporter antennas had just gone up. "Exactly how the first set of murders went down in your book. Our killer found a family that matched the number of victims. Even the ages were close. All within a year or two. Amy, the one left alive, was the same age as the little girl left alive in your book."

"Jane. In the book," Ben said. "Her name was Jane. They called her Little Baby Jane."

Mills leaned forward. "How do they catch him?"

"The girl, Jane. Eventually she talks."

"And?"

"And what?"

Mills clenched his jaw. "I'm sure it's against any writer's code of ethics to give away an ending, but who is it? In the book? The Scarecrow?"

"A man named Meeks. Michael Meeks. He went by Miserable. Miserable Meeks. He . . . he escaped from an asylum."

"Original," Mills mumbled, with sarcasm he didn't attempt to hide.

"Maybe so, but it sells," Ben shot back.

Blue said, "I've read your other books. The Riverdale Asylum is at least mentioned in all of them. This is where your fictional Meeks escapes from?"

"Yes."

"If I remember correctly, the asylum in the book is very reminiscent of Oswald here in Crooked Tree."

"Real life influences art. It's just the way it is."

"Did your grandfather ever take you there as a kid?"

"To Oswald? Yes. A few times."

"Seems an odd place to take a kid," Mills chimed in.

"My parents were unreliable. My grandfather was stuck with us, often."

"This Meeks," Mills said. "The book. Just give us the quick plot. Detailed as you can."

Ben said, "Meeks, as a boy, bounced from foster home to foster home. He was a loner. Antisocial. The other foster kids picked on him. Every home, abuse followed him. Physical. Mental. Sexual . . . At his final stop, Meeks was thirteen, the age when most boys start showing signs of becoming a man. But not him. He was still a sliver." A weird glow swept over Ben's face. Mills and Blue both saw it. "A little leaf. There were two boys at the foster home who took an immediate disliking to Meeks, a set of fourteen-year-old twins named Murphy and Thomas Pope. Murph and Tommy. You'll learn all of this near the end. They'd twist his skin until it bled. They held ice cubes on his skin. Made him strip naked, put his testicles in a bowl of ice water and made him stand there until he passed out."

Mills and Blue exchanged glances as Ben spoke: the fact that he was getting so worked up over a character in a novel, and telling it in such graphic detail.

"You see," Ben said, "Miserable Meeks was a nervous boy who believed everything. They burned cigarettes on his back. His legs. Parts of his body no one could see with clothes on. These twins. *They* made him into a monster." Here, Mills noticed, Ben looked down at the floor and appeared to get emotional. When he looked up again, his eyes were wet, like before. "Because *something* has to make a boy bad, right? There has to be a *reason*." He shook his head, wiped his eyes. "It started with small things. Mice. Chipmunks. He caught them. Took out his rage on them. Eventually he took pleasure in seeing them die. He craved it. But then he started killing crows. There was an old coal chute behind the house. That's where he hid the things he'd kill. One day the twins followed him. Shined a flashlight into the chute, and there he was, organizing feathers and bones. That night, the twins woke Meeks up. In Murphy's hand was a dead crow, one they'd taken from his collection inside the coal chute. They laughed, told him to eat it. Thought it was funny, making him eat crow. They said to eat or they'd tell, and he'd go to a place much worse than where he was. A place with bars and cold food and guards who liked thirteen-year-old boys who were just slivers and little leaves."

Mills shared another glance with Blue.

"He wouldn't eat the crow," Ben said. "They tried to force it in, but that only made him sick. He got sick right on the floor. They rubbed his face in it, and made him clean it up, which he did. With a smile of triumph. He stood by the window until morning, watching the neighboring cornfield, saying nothing. Just smiling." Ben tapped his temple with a bent index finger. "Thinking."

"You speak of Meeks like he's real," Mills said.

"Isn't that a writer's job? To make the characters seem real? To come alive?"

But this started inside your *brain*, Mills wanted to say.

"Just words on a page, Detective." Ben stood, paced behind the chair. "But in the book? It's about revenge, plain and simple. Revenge on all those who wronged him on his road to perdition. In his twelve years inside the Riverdale Asylum, Miserable Meeks made a list. He makes it through only half the list before he's caught. It's the little girl, Jane. Little Baby Jane. Eventually, she awakes from her coma and talks. Detective Mulky, the protagonist in all of my books, he already had an idea who the killer was, because Meeks had escaped from the asylum, and he'd told another inmate there what he'd planned on doing. Becoming the Scarecrow. Stitched cocoons and all. The stalking. The burlap mask he ultimately ends up stitching into his own skin. But they didn't know how to find him. Except for the innocent little girl who asked him why."

Ben smiled. "That sweet voice swept Miserable Meeks off his feet. Pulled him back to his *own* innocence. She asked him why he did what he did. It was his moment of weakness. His pause. That brief hiccup of time where he found what was left of his soul. And it was that moment that ends up killing him in the end. He said when they were at a foster home when he was nine, *her* father didn't do anything to stop the bullies. He just watched. Pretended to not see. He was bigger and stronger and he didn't *do* anything." Ben took a swig from his flask, and pointed with it. "Little Baby Jane was brave, despite what she'd just witnessed him doing to her family. She asked him if he was the devil and he said no. He told her he was the scarecrow. And do you know what scarecrows do?"

Ben seemed to have slipped into what could have been Meeks' fictional voice. "She shook her head. Scarecrows scare, he said. That's what they do." Which was the first line of the book, Mills recalled, watching as Ben finally sat back down. "Before tying her up, he asked Little Baby Jane if she knew how moths are born. While he was pulling her cocoon across the yard and into the barn, he explained it all to her. From the eggs come the larvae. The caterpillar. And then the caterpillar makes a cocoon. Some even dig holes in the ground, where they live until they're ready to emerge as fully grown adult moths." Ben smiled again. "You see, the Riverdale Asylum was Miserable Meeks' cocoon, and it wasn't until he escaped that he became fully grown."

After a moment to process it all, Mills said, "Mr. Bookman, I've read enough crime novels in my lifetime. And there are far too few that are unique. Psycho acts out the crimes straight from the novelist's pages. I'm sure it's been done before. But what I don't get is that the Petersons were murdered weeks *before* the reading public got their hands on the book."

Ben shook his head. "Thousands of people read *The Scarecrow* before it was released. Literally, thousands. The publisher releases early copies, long before publication. Book bloggers. Early reviewers. Newspapers. Magazines. Free grabs off NetGalley."

"Anyone local?"

"Local, not local. Here, there. Anywhere. But at this point it wouldn't matter if it was someone from California or my back yard. If they read it and wanted to act on it, then that's what they did. Planes, trains, and automobiles?"

Blue said, "Who local would have read it?"

"Trevor Hendricks at the *Gazette* did an early review. Debbie Glasscock at the *Crooked Tree Journal*. Shit, little old Bettie Hottington at the library read it two months ago. Said it scared her pants off. Maybe she has a needle and thread and some old corn husks hiding in her basement." Ben sighed, rubbed his temples. "Look, I'm sorry. But that's all I know. If you want more, leave me your cards and I'll text you the names and numbers of my agent and editor and publicist. They'll have a more thorough list of early readers. Start there."

Mills stood with a grunt, suddenly anxious to leave the house. "We'll be back in touch. Don't skip town."

"Right. I know how this works." Ben pocketed the card Detective Blue slid across the coffee table. A moth fluttered into the room, bounced off the ceiling before nose-diving for the floor lamp. It settled inside the canvas, wings pulsing. Ben flicked the lampshade. The moth scrambled out of the room and into the kitchen. He turned, locked eyes with Mills. "What?"

"Moths."

"Damn things are everywhere. That's where I got the idea." He watched them both. "For Meeks and his manifestation."

Mills eyed the lampshade where the moth had just been, as if it had left a visible residue. "That's the only part of the crime scenes so far that don't match the scenes in your book."

Blue touched Mills' arm. "Let's go, Mills. Not the time or place."

"Moths," said Mills, undeterred. "We found them at both crime scenes. *Dozens* of them inside both houses."

Blue lights flashed outside on the street. Ben moved away from the lamp and looked through a split in the curtain. "Shit."

More news vans had pulled up behind Officer Black's squad car. He'd flashed his light bar as a warning, and kept it cycling. Officer Black was now out of his car and physically holding the press at a distance no closer than the curb. Dick Bennington stood out there with a dozen others, in the very spot Amanda would have been had her husband not been the center of it all. Parked behind the real news crews was an obnoxiously bright yellow van with red letters on the side panel marking it as from *The Story*.

"And there goes the neighborhood," Mills grumbled, watching the regional tabloid that claimed to *Tell the Story and Nothing but the Story*.

"Christ." Ben closed the curtain, turned away from it.

The moth had returned to the lampshade, casting shadows on the ceiling. Watching the moth, Blue said, "We'll get to the bottom of this."

Mills said, "But not everyone works as fast as you, Ben."

Ben looked ready to retaliate, but held back. He walked them to the door. They stepped out to the well-lit veranda, where another moth fluttered against a recessed bulb.

Mills followed the moth's flight. "When you get a chance, let us know your whereabouts for the dates in question."

"You mean you need my alibi?"

"We wouldn't be doing our job otherwise."

"Strictly protocol," said Blue.

"I understand," he said to her.

"The sooner the better, so you can move on with your life," Blue said. "In the meantime, we'll have a car outside your home twenty-four/seven, for your family's protection."

They shook hands, promised to keep each other apprised of any pertinent information. Mills started down the porch steps, but stopped at Ben's voice.

"Detectives . . ." Ben leaned in the open doorway with his arms folded. The reporters were having a field day snapping pictures of him. He seemed to enjoy it. "Do you plan on reading the book?"

"Of course," said Mills. "But if there's something we need to know until then . . ."

"In the book. The scarecrow takes his next victim two days later. It's a single old man who gets it next. A recent widower."

Mills clenched his jaw. "That some sort of a threat, Mr. Bookman?"

"No. Just a friendly warning."

Before

BENJAMIN WAS TEN *and Emily twelve when Grandpa Robert told them about the Baku.*

During their childhood summers at Blackwood, Benjamin and Emily—who was prone to nightmares—had always shared a room. A recurring nightmare tortured Emily for five consecutive nights. It wasn't until that fifth night, after Ben had jumped from his bed and hurried across the room to comfort her, that she'd told him about it.

"It's those trees," she said.

Ben loved the Blackwood trees, the way those dark branches twisted and turned like live oaks, so he listened intently to his sister as she explained. "As soon as I fall asleep they come alive. This is not funny, Ben."

"I'm not laughing."

"You're about to. You're smiling."

"Because we're not scared of the same things, Em."

"You're not scared of anything."

"Go on. The trees?"

She leaned on an elbow. "Those crooked branches become arms and they pull me in and suffocate me. I can't breathe. And that liquid that sometimes seeps from them, it's not future syrup as Grandpa claims. It's . . ."

"It's what?"

"It's rot. And blood. A whole mixture of things I can still smell even after I wake up."

"It's not real, Em. It's all in your head."

She huffed, turned toward the ceiling, and pulled her blanket to her neck. "The moths drink it. The stuff that comes from the trees."

On that sixth night Grandpa Robert entered their room with only a candle to illuminate his handsome face. He pulled a tri-legged wooden stool between the two beds and told them a story. Ben sat up against the headboard, anxiously anticipating, while Emily hid all but her nose and eyes beneath the covers. She was mad Ben had told Grandpa Robert of her nightmare.

Grandpa Robert's feathered hair had long ago transitioned from yellow to white. In the candle glow his blue eyes sparkled. His velvety voice conveyed truth and trust, and for that, the two of them remained rapt, eager, and listening to every word.

"The Baku," he told them, "is a mythological spirit from Chinese and Japanese folklore that is said to devour nightmares. It takes on the form of a chimera." Grandpa Robert liked to tell stories. He'd stressed that last word, which coaxed Emily into asking what that was. "The chimera is another mythological beast," he said. "This one is composed of various parts from other animals. The Baku is typically made up of a bear's body."

"I hate bears," Emily said.

"But with the nose of an elephant. The feet from a tiger."

"Cool," said Ben.

"Cool if you're a creep," said Emily.

Grandpa Robert grinned; his face reminded Ben of every story he'd ever told them. In Ben's mind, Grandpa Robert's face was the imagined hero in any story ever told or written. "The Baku has the eyes from a rhino. The tail from an ox." Emily shook her head like she didn't want to believe it. Grandpa Robert assured her with a theatrical nod that it was true. "After God created all the animals, the Baku was made up of the leftover parts."

"How is this supposed to help my nightmare?"

Grandpa Robert grinned. He'd left the bedroom door cracked open. Ben could see, from a certain shadow, that little four-year-old Devon was out there listening too.

"In ancient Chinese legend, the Baku was hunted for its pelt. The pelts were used as a talisman to protect people from evil spirits. Eventually the Baku's mere image over the bed would suffice. But when someone would awaken suddenly from a bad dream, they could call out to the Baku." He placed the candle on the floorboards, leaned forward with his elbows on his knees, and lowered his voice. "Baku-san, come eat my dream. Baku-san, come eat my dream. Baku-san, come eat my dream."

His voice floated to silence. Wind gripped the windows.

"And then what would happen?" asked Ben.

"The Baku would come into the child's room and eat the nightmare, Benjamin. And the child would peacefully return to sleep." He held up a long index finger. "My dear Emily, the Baku can also be called to protect before falling asleep."

She shook her head. "I don't want the Baku in my room. I'd rather be smothered by the trees. I'd rather hear of the Sandman again. Or Mr. Dreams. Don't they do the same thing as this Baku, but they're not as freaky?"

Grandpa Robert chuckled. "Yes, my dear Emily, they can all rid us of our nightmares."

"I call them mare killers," said Ben. "But Mr. Dreams is the best of them all."

The story of Mr. Dreams and the Nightmare Man had always been Ben's favorite. Devon's too, but it had become old hat as many times now as Grandpa Robert had told it. The Sandman was the legend he'd told, for the first time, the previous summer, in much the same way as he now told about the Baku, after Emily had had a bad nightmare about the stone tower on the northeast corner of the house. In some European folklore, the Sandman was a character who brought good dreams to children by sprinkling magical sand onto their eyes at night.

Of the three stories—Ben hoped there'd be more—Emily liked the Sandman the best, but Ben now was enthralled to hear of this Baku.

Grandpa Robert faced Ben. "But caution must be used when calling the Baku. If the nightmare is not scary enough. If the mare has climbed atop us and dribbled only a pittance of scare, if the Baku is not satisfied, if the Baku is still hungry . . ."

"Then what?" Emily asked, voice shaky, clearly wanting to get this over with.

"Then the Baku will devour your hopes and dreams as well." He eyed them both. "Leaving you to live an empty life from that point onward."

Emily's eyes darted from her grandfather to her little brother. Devon's shadow was gone in the hallway. Grandpa Robert, as if *waiting for just that, stood from the stool, ruffled their hair, wished them pleasant dreams, and left the room as quietly as he'd entered moments ago.*

With the room now black, Emily buried her head beneath the covers.

Twenty minutes later, after Benjamin heard his sister snoring, he whispered to the night, "Baku-san, come eat my sister's dream . . ."

THE DETECTIVES PULLED away.

Ben closed the front door, rested his forehead against the wood, and thought about damage control. Only after closing his eyes and opening them again to a floor that spun beneath his feet did he realize how drunk he was, how drunk he'd been when answering their questions. Questions too reminiscent of the ones Detective Mills had asked him as a teenager, when Devon disappeared. The old man surely suspected him, if not of the murders, of something else.

Just as he had back then.

Ben had convinced himself that tough and guarded was the way to go—to keep up with his public persona—but, in hindsight, he now realized he'd been on the edge of uncooperative. A privileged prick. And now, after they'd gone, the tension had only been ramped up, not deadened by his behavior. "You're the unreliable narrator now, Ben." The words whispered to himself brought about a smile. The best characters were the ones who changed the most throughout the story. Wasn't that what Grandpa Robert had once told him? But when had his story begun? A year ago at Blackwood? When he'd published his first novel? When Devon disappeared? He pounded the front door with his fist. "When does my story start?"

The answer flashed back to him.

He'd been twelve years old. Grandpa had sneaked him downstairs to the atrium. The first of three secret trips into that room.

The third and final night was still vividly etched in his mind. The soaring bookshelves. The dark leafless tree in the middle of the room, its crooked limbs hugging the curved glass of the ceiling, branching out in twisted arches like the bones of an open umbrella, the ribbed vault of a European cathedral. Moths had clung to the dark tree bark. Above his head, birds had fluttered, perched on gnarled branches—blackbirds, cardinals, a blue jay, and one buttery yellow warbler. The atrium floor was made of brick, uneven and clunky from where tree roots had tunneled like mole trails.

His grandfather had handed him a book, and then strictly went over the rules, of which there were three.

Open the book when prompted.

Close it precisely when told.

And there will be no wavering, Benjamin.

And to that Benjamin had nodded, only to open book number 456 and find it utterly free of words, every page blank. He'd looked up, confused and disappointed. After all these years of wondering. *Was this some kind of joke? And what was rule number three?* His grandfather then coaxed him with that blue-eyed glare to give it time, to look at those blank pages, to be patient and wait.

"Ben?" Amanda's voice yanked him from the past.

He pounded the front door with his fist. *He tested you and you failed.* That's when your story started. That's when your course changed paths, your relationship with your grandfather forever altered. Ben's lips were inches from the door, his breath hot against the wood. "Three rules." He closed his eyes to beat down the rising nausea, the reality of the reporters out there. Bits of Jepson Heap's brain clogging his shower drain. "Benjamin, close the goddamn book!"

"Ben?"

"Three rules."

"Ben!"

"I'm sorry, Devon. I thought I knew what I was doing."

"Ben, you're scaring me!" Amanda shouted.

He turned to find his wife standing at the kitchen's threshold with a suitcase in hand. "Amanda, what are you doing?"

"You were just talking to yourself."

"Why do you have a suitcase?"

"What three rules?"

"Nothing."

"And the detectives, Ben? The way you were talking in there? If they don't already suspect you for the murders, they suspect you for something."

"You don't think I did this, do you? Amanda?"

She looked down, shook her head. "No. But I know you've done *something*. You did something. You're *doing* something, Ben. And until you tell me what . . ."

"Where are you going?"

"Mom and Dad's."

Seeing the suitcase was too much reality hitting home. "What will you tell them?"

"That I don't feel safe here." She was crying. When he approached to console her she held her hand outstretched. "Don't, Ben. Don't touch me."

"I'm not who they think I am. You know that. I'm not the villain, Amanda."

"So you're the hero?"

"I never said that."

"Heroes don't lie to their wives. They don't lie to the police. You're hiding something. You've been hiding something for a long time, Ben."

Yeah, well, so is Detective Mills, Ben thought. "Something wasn't right when Grandpa Robert was found dead inside Oswald Asylum, Amanda."

"What? Not this again . . ."

"His watch was on the wrong arm," he said, thinking out loud. "Left instead of the right. And his shirt had been misbuttoned. Amanda, you know he was anal about how he dressed."

"You're doing it again."

"What?"

"Avoiding the now." She walked toward him. He wanted to wrap her up in his arms and cry on her shoulder, but he stepped aside to let her go. So much for Crooked Tree's young celebrity couple. With a nine-year-old daughter and an unplanned baby boy on the way. How could they bring another child into the mix now? A child conceived from passion, yes, but of the harmful kind, one stemming from an argument that had nearly come to blows.

"I'm losing it, Amanda. The man talking to those detectives was not me."

"No, it wasn't." She touched the swell of her stomach, then looked away

The gesture hit him like a punch. For months now he'd been trying to forget the evening their unborn baby was conceived, and at the same time cling to the thrill of it. She'd taken him, yes, she'd been the aggressor, she'd been so enraged—*is this how she did it to you, Ben?*—on the first flat surface she could find, the kitchen table, with the Minnie Mouse salt shaker digging into his spine. They'd finished quickly, all arguments forgotten, panting, shamed, turning their heads simultaneously to find Brianna standing dazed next to the refrigerator with a stuffed unicorn in her arms, sleepwalking, as she was prone to do. *Like father, like daughter.* As far as they knew, Bri had remembered none of it, although she'd said very little the next morning at breakfast. But the raw, uninhibited passion of that moment still clung to him even now—Amanda finishing like a deadweight atop his chest, panting, their heartbeats sprinting in unison, staring into each other's eyes with an emotion closer to confusion and regret than love.

He saw the same look now as she brushed past him toward the front door and reached for the doorknob.

"Dick's out there," he said. "Every news channel. Even the tabloids, Amanda. Do you really want to leave now and give the impression that something is wrong? That we're unraveling?" She laughed at that. "You walk out that door, every reporter will think I've done something. That I'm guilty somehow." She focused on her phone, sent off a quick text. "What are you doing?" A texted reply came back within seconds. She slid the phone into her purse, changed direction toward the kitchen. "Who did you just text? Was that Dick?"

"*Richard* is meeting me around back. Away from the noise. He's taking me to my parents'. Your reputation will be safe for another night."

They neared the back door, where he assumed she'd sneak across the courtyard toward the hedgerow and meet up with Bennington and his car parked somewhere along the crowded street. He hated the desperation in his own voice. "What will you tell Bri?"

"That she and I are having a sleepover. That Daddy's still sick and we don't want to catch it."

A bitter pill, but better than the truth. "And when she has her nightmare?"

"I'll hug her."

"And tell her what?"

"That Mommy and Daddy love each other." She opened the door, surveyed the moonlit backyard. No cameras or reporters in the bushes. She turned back to him with tears in her eyes. "Did you fuck her, Ben?"

"What? Who?"

"Jennifer. Can you at least tell me that?"

She'd been tiptoeing around the issue of an affair for twelve months now, but she'd never mentioned their former babysitter's name. Amanda knew Jennifer had gone out to Blackwood that weekend; not *with* him, but she'd met him there at some point. After Amanda's numerous failed attempts at reaching Ben, she'd driven out there. Jennifer's red Camry had been parked beside Ben's SUV. She'd gotten back in her car, sat for an hour, and then returned to Crooked Tree, where she'd waited another day and a half for Ben to finally return. He'd been adamant that Jennifer had only driven some research out to him. That was all.

"No, Amanda. I didn't." He couldn't bring himself to repeat Amanda's exact words. I didn't *fuck her. My God.* Jennifer, although he couldn't deny she was smart and funny and carefree—*Jesus, Ben, admit she was growing on you; that you'd begun flirting.* Since Amanda hadn't budged from the back porch, he said it again. "No. I can't believe you'd—"

"Don't tell me what I can and can't believe, Ben. That girl was an emotional wreck when she told us she was quitting. *Something* happened."

He couldn't deny it, and for the first time, didn't try to. He couldn't account for everything that happened that weekend inside Blackwood's atrium and they both knew it.

Amanda stepped down into the shadows of the courtyard, and stopped next to the stone fountain, where water trickled into a shallow pool from the mouths of devilish winged chimera. "You know how you once told me that you don't have nightmares? That you don't fear?"

Where was she going with this? Because he did have a nightmare. One he'd never told her about. Never told anyone about, because that had been rule number three.

Tell no one.

"Who is Julia?" asked Amanda.

Ben couldn't look at her. "I don't know. Why?"

"Because you say her name at night when you sleep."

10

S TILL PARKED OUTSIDE the Bookmans' house, Blue leafed through the pages of *The Scarecrow* and found the next murder in the book before even starting the car.

"Here it is." She jabbed her fingernail into the page like a dagger. "Read it."

Mills glanced toward her hand, toward the page she'd indented with the pressure of her nail, but then focused on the media swarm down the street. "Detectives don't wear fingernail polish, Sam."

"The next crime scene is a solo shot. The victim is a sixty-seven-year-old retired electrician."

"I'm sixty-five. And I can barely change a light bulb."

"He's a recent widower."

"Start the car," he said.

She started it, but didn't pull away. She was stubborn enough to sit here all night, so he threw her a bone. "I get it. I'll sleep with my gun tonight." He saw a lanky reporter from *The Story* approaching the car. "Now drive."

She put the car in gear with so much force he thought she'd broken the shaft, and then squealed the tires to make haste. "As soon as I get back to the station I'll start compiling a list."

"Of what?"

"Of old men. Widowers. *Jesus*, Dad. A list of people we can warn. Are you awake?"

Mills closed his eyes as she drove, and was nearly asleep when Blue somehow channeled his thoughts. "Back there," she said. "You sounded like you know more about Dr. Bookman's death."

Here we go.

"The heart attack? I didn't know you were there when it happened."

"I wasn't."

"You said—"

"I was there visiting another patient when Dr. Bookman was *found*. There's a big difference." He opened his eyes, watched her drive.

She glanced at him. "Why are you smiling? It's weird."

"Just remembering the first time I took you out driving. How tightly you held the wheel, and now you're driving with two fingers."

"Tell me about what you saw at Oswald Asylum."

"Which time? I've only visited that place about once a week since it opened."

"You know what I'm talking about. Robert Bookman's death?"

Mills started to speak but stopped. "What do *you* know? Your notes seemed extensive."

"Just doing my job. Quit stalling. Oswald? Robert Bookman?"

"What else did you have in your notes?"

"I asked you first."

"I'm your father."

"A father who fell asleep in the conference room today."

"And who is also your superior."

She sighed, gripped the wheel now with both hands. "Is this better?"

"Yes, that's better."

They drove for a few miles of meandering country road in silence. "Just the basics," she said. "That Robert Bookman was a child psychiatrist. He specialized in sleep studies. Specifically children with anxiety and nightmares. PTSD. Those sorts of things." Her grip on the wheel eased as she regurgitated notes from memory. "Dr. Robert Bookman had Oswald Asylum built in 1976. Opened officially in March of seventy-seven. Lucius Oswald was the first patient there. Some believed it was the Oswald family who funded the asylum, but it was mostly Dr. Bookman's doing. Mostly old Bookman money. Rumor is he named it after Lucius Oswald *because* he was the first patient. That he had the asylum built specifically *for* Lucius Oswald, and others like him."

"Other lunatics."

"Mentally ill," she corrected. "And most at Oswald tended to have violent pasts."

"Very good," he said. "I'm impressed."

"But the town wanted no part of his asylum," she said. "The mayor at the time, a Mr. Sam Haversmith, says in a quote from the *Crooked Tree Journal* . . ."

"Now defunct."

"Now defunct," she concurred. "That '*We have enough lunatics here in Crooked Tree as it is. We don't need more. And certainly not on our taxpayers' money.*' So that's when Dr. Bookman carved out a wedge of his own property at Blackwood. On the outskirts of the woods overlooking Blackwood Hollow. Right at the bottom of the hill. In the winter, it's visible from the main house atop the hill. Most noticeably from the tower."

"And Lucius Oswald?"

"He died inside the asylum in 1991."

"From what?"

"From AIDS. But it doesn't say how he contracted it."

Mills sat more erect in his seat, more engaged now. "Most likely scenario was a love affair with a male attendant named Curtis Lumpkin. Lumpkin was fired from Oswald Asylum in the spring of eighty-eight. He was caught fondling a sleeping male patient. When Lucius Oswald began deteriorating, and was found to have the virus, they went hunting for Curtis Lumpkin but could never track him down." Mills watched his daughter navigate the twists and turns of the country roads, and then slow toward the long gravel driveway that led to his home. "But why was Oswald there in the first place?"

"He was mentally ill," she said. "He was afraid of his own shadow. He was delusional. Schizophrenic."

"Yes, he was all those things. And more. But why was he important to me?"

"He was your first arrest."

"Ding, ding, ding, ding. We have a winner." Cornfields pinched the road, and through the trees ahead, glimpses of his house were visible. "I'll put in a good word for you at the station. For a promotion."

"I'll earn it on my own, thank you. But what I don't get is why? Why did Robert Bookman find it so necessary to build the asylum for Lucius Oswald?"

"Because he was nuts, Blue. Truly nuts."

"Mentally ill," she corrected again, slowing the car along a dark curve. "But, according to my notes, he wasn't always. Mentally ill. A bit odd, perhaps. A loner. But . . . What?"

She'd caught him grinning. "You never cease to amaze me with how deeply you dive."

"He never harmed anyone," she continued.

"Until he did."

"An accident."

"Manslaughter."

"No intent, except perhaps to scare. Which was why he chased people in the first place. He seemed to get his rocks off making people run away from him." Blue coasted to a stop on the dust-gravel outside her childhood home, and left the car idling. "Dad?"

"What?"

"I asked you a question." She waited, realized he didn't remember what that question was. "I know it was at this point that Dr. Robert Bookman swept in and starting fighting on Lucius Oswald's behalf. He was the reason he got asylum time instead of jail time."

"Not much of a difference in my mind, save for the drugs administered."

"Construction on what would become Oswald Asylum started soon thereafter," she said, glued to her point. "My question is, why was he so intrigued by Lucius Oswald, an adult, when all of his work previously was with children?"

"Find me a man or woman who wasn't once a child, Blue . . ." He winked. "And I'll tell you where I hide all the money."

Before

*D*ETECTIVE *WILLARD BLUE looked haggard and worn down as he sat on the sawed tree stump outside Blackwood, dangling an unlit cigarette between his pale lips.*

Unlike Detective Mills, who, on the surface, was initially able to compartmentalize work from home life, Willard couldn't help but put all of his hats in a blender and turn it on high. Willard's son Danny was seventeen. Mills' daughter Samantha was three months younger. The two were inseparable. And although now their two children looked like young adults, both with their minds already set on careers, it hadn't been long ago that they'd been prepubescent and innocent and carefree like little Devon Bookman.

Mills didn't have to ask; he knew this was where his friend's mind had ventured as he sat stoic on the tree stump, staring off into the woods, imagining if it had been his *boy gone missing.*

Ten-year-old Devon Bookman—if his parents' scattered recollections could be trusted; they both appeared under the influence of drugs, alcohol, or both—had been missing now for at least twelve hours. Possibly as few as ten. Mills and Blue had scoured the woods to no avail, and still had teams of exhausted men and women out there combing the dips and hollows.

The father, Michael Bookman—who had a long-ago repaired cleft upper lip Mills couldn't help but notice, plus missing little fingers from a birth defect—told them Devon had been wearing black and blue Batman pajamas. This, the older sister Emily confirmed. She was the only one of the Bookmans, other than the patriarch Robert, whose mind seemed trustworthy. Batman pajamas, she'd said, and Nike basketball shoes. You're sure about the shoes? Yes. I had a habit of checking on my brothers at night. Especially when we stay here.

Why here?

Devon . . . he liked to wander about.

And he was in bed when you checked on him. At roughly ten o'clock last night.

Yes. He'd fallen asleep with his shoes on. Atop the covers. I was afraid I'd wake him up so I left him that way.

From Robert Bookman, who arrived home from an out-of-town consultation around the time Devon had been missing for the thirteenth hour, they'd learned that his Rolex watch was missing from the locked desk drawer of the atrium.

From Benjamin Bookman, the older brother and middle child, they'd learned that Devon was crafty and clever, and liked to sneak into that room whenever Grandpa was away. More importantly, his little brother knew how to get into the room's desk and locked drawer and prance around in a ten thousand dollar watch big enough to slide over his elbow and wear around his nonexistent bicep like a sweatband.

So as they searched the woods, they had those points on their minds—Batman pajamas, Nike shoes, and a Rolex watch that could have easily slid off the boy's arm.

"You okay?" Mills asked his partner.

Detective Willard Blue nodded but didn't look up from his seat on the tree stump. His cigarette dangled, soggy where his lips touched it. Detectives were nothing if not peculiar. Blue never lit his cigarettes for the same reason Mills poured his alcohol just to stare at it. They wore their peculiarities like badges of honor. Men who'd done enough wrong in their lives to at least understand the concept of doing better.

Mills touched his partner's shoulder. "There's something upstairs you need to see."

Willard tossed his cigarette to the ground and produced another from the inside lining of his sport coat. "Do I get a hint?"

Mills looked over his shoulder as he neared the front door and gargoyle knocker the size of a clenched fist. "The older brother."

Blue exhaled behind him; nervous energy, Mills knew, and not cigarette smoke. That exhale, for years, had held a slightly different sound. One with a quiver. "Is this about that weird-ass story about the 'mare'?"

"Yeah. Sort of." They were both still rattled from what Christine Bookman had told them twenty minutes ago about her oldest son, Benjamin Bookman. The one who had dreams of becoming a horror writer. About him truly believing he was a mare, some mythical being that sat on the chest of sleepers and gave them nightmares.

Inside Ben's third-floor bedroom, Mills led Willard to the desk he'd gone through ten minutes ago. He slid out the middle drawer, gathered the pile of sketches, and handed them to his partner. "Leaf through those. If you can stomach it."

Willard went through them, one by one. When he handed them back, his hands were shaking. For the first time in six years he reached for his lighter.

The drag on that cigarette was a long one.

11

THE LAST THING Ben said to Amanda before she'd disappeared into the shadows beyond the courtyard had been to text him when she made it to her parents' house.

Thirty minutes after she'd left, she did so with a quick *Made it.*

He'd responded: *Good. Thank you. Hug Bri for me.* But he couldn't help wondering if Dick Bennington was still with her. Had he just dropped her off, or stopped in for a visit? Dick was who Amanda's parents had always hoped she'd marry. The two of them had attended twelve years of Catholic school together, and despite Amanda swearing otherwise, Ben was sure they'd at some point tried dating.

The reporters were still out there, talking, occasionally laughing. Like any part of this was funny. He didn't fully trust the police, but he trusted the reporters less.

He sat on the hallway floor next to the closet where they kept the board games. From there, he couldn't glimpse a window, and if he couldn't see a window, the reporters couldn't see him. He checked his phone. Wishing Amanda would respond with a *Bri says hello* or *Bri sends hugs back*, but it'd been five minutes and she'd sent nothing. But he'd gotten another call from his editor: his fourth message—two of them texts—since the news broke the scarecrow story nationwide a couple hours ago. His agent had sent three texts and left two phone messages. He texted them both back, *I'm safe*, and almost typed, *I'm fine*, but couldn't bring himself to lie even through the phone.

He had a month to deliver his next book, and he was only halfway through. Just slightly more than he'd completed a year ago before finishing *The Scarecrow* in that one weekend. It wasn't unheard of to write that much in three days, just unlikely. He admitted it. Very unlikely. But here he was with *The Screamer* and a deadline looming large. Another panicked situation like a year ago.

But this was different. *The Scarecrow* had been the book he'd always wanted to write, ever since he was a boy, but couldn't bring himself to do it. The writer's block he'd experienced with it a year ago had not been due to any lack of idea or premise, as Amanda had suggested to the detectives earlier, but more to do with the unknowns of it all. The mystery inside him that had been building since the days his grandfather had secreted him down into that room and allowed all of what had happened to happen. Bottom line is he'd been just as scared to write it as he'd been thrilled, called even. Scared of the unknown, that his books may have been building up to some great crescendo and *The Scarecrow* was the tipping point?

It was nonsense.

Just words on a page.

Without fully realizing he'd done so, he found himself in his office, sitting at his desk, opening his laptop. Now that the unknown had begun to reveal itself as real-life horror, how could he even think about finishing things? Because when he sat down now to write *The Screamer*, it not only rained, it poured. It flowed out like no thoughts ever should. Maybe it was guilt that had conjured his first book, and then the second, and on and on, but it was sure as hell guilt now that had him slamming on his literary brakes.

The cursor blinked at him, waiting. He flexed his fingers over the keyboard.

Why didn't you tell them? You didn't tell the detectives everything they needed to know. He grinned; it felt uncontrollable. They'd read it soon enough.

Ben leaned back in his chair, finished what was left in his flask. He stared at his laptop screen, the blinking cursor, wondered exactly who Julia was. He remembered only that she smelled good. Like roses and lavender and scented candles.

With all the mental strength he could muster, he pushed himself away from the desk. He paced like a caged animal. He didn't smoke, but he suddenly needed a cigarette. But Jennifer had been smoking that weekend, even though she was definitely *not* a smoker, and was, in fact, a fitness freak who had run with Amanda every morning and practically lived in yoga pants. *My God, what was she doing there? You asked her to bring your iPad. You'd been in a hurry to get to Blackwood. You grabbed your laptop but forgot the iPad.* He wrote on the one and researched on the other. *You and Amanda had already started fighting. You're not easy to live with when you're not writing, Ben. That's why you called Jennifer instead of your wife. You'd been flirting with the goddamn babysitter for weeks and Amanda was aware. That's why she'd begun to turn cold toward Jennifer even before that weekend. You forgot the iPad on purpose.*

He sat back down, fingers hovering over the keys, cursor beckoning like some doorway through which his wicked words would soon come crawling, one after the other, until things really started to happen.

Should I or shouldn't I? People are dying, Ben.

He looked to the locked drawer to his right, the one holding the box. *Back to the screen, Ben. The blinking cursor. Detective Mulky's girl, the next victim.*

After six novels, *The Screamer* had finally taken center stage in the fictional town of Riverdale. He typed two sentences—the beginning of the Mulky girl's abduction—and then immediately deleted them. He leaned back in his chair again, exhaled into his hands as if cold, and just as he started typing again his phone buzzed. It was his sister. He hadn't spoken with Emily in more than a month; their last call had ended with him yelling, clicking off while she'd been in mid-sentence, something about her contacting realtors and selling Blackwood, books and all. If he didn't pick up, she was stubborn enough to drive down from New York.

"Hello."

"Ben? What in the heck is going on?" Emily had always been the good girl. He could never even get her to cuss. "Do I need to come down there? Ben?"

"Emily, I'm fine." He laughed. *I'm fine.* He'd said the same thing to her one summer at Blackwood when he was ten, when she'd sneaked up behind him in the woods to find the dead sparrow in his hands, the recently plucked wings resting on dead pine needles below.

"Ben, what in the world are you doing?" she'd asked that day.

"I'm . . . seeing what it sounds like . . . when the wings come off. For my story. I . . . I found it already dead."

"Ben, stop," she'd said. "What is wrong with you?"

"Nothing. I'm fine."

Now he squeezed his eyes closed. "Really, Emily. I'm fine."

"Ben, are you drunk? Have you been drinking?"

"Yes. And yes."

She sighed into the phone. He could see her now, rubbing her temples, wanting to shout but holding back because, unlike Bri—who was often up late—her kids were kissed, tucked in, and ready to be read to by eight thirty every evening. Like clockwork.

"The police were at your house? Do they actually think you did this?"

"No." He rubbed his own temples. "I don't think so."

"You don't think so?"

"Have you read the book?"

"No, Ben. I haven't." She'd read enough of his stories growing up and swore to never read another. "But from what I'm hearing, the murders are identical. Ben . . . ?"

"Yes."

"You're not well."

"I've never been well, Em. Isn't that what you always said? That's why Grandpa left Blackwood to you? Right?"

"Oh, Ben . . ." She paused, as if fighting some truth still unknown to him. He missed her, despite all. "I don't want to get into it now. That's not why I called. I'm worried about you."

"I'm—"

"I know, you're fine. You're sitting there alone and you're fine. Amanda took Bri to her parents' because you're fine. I know you're having trouble. Talk to me."

Words snagged in his throat. How much does Emily know? She and Amanda talked more than he and Emily did.

"Did . . ." Emily paused as if to regroup. "Did you cheat on her?"

"Would you believe me if I said I don't know?"

"You don't . . . Ben? Really?"

"It's complicated, Em."

"You either did or you didn't. What's complicated about—"

"I don't . . . remember everything."

"Do I need to come down? Benjamin? I feel like I should come down."

"No. Don't. It's not safe. Not with me. That's why Amanda left. That's why . . ." He wiped his face, his wet cheeks. "I don't know what I did."

"When? With Jennifer? Or at Blackwood?"

"Both," he said. "Something happened, Emily. My memory is spotty. But something bad happened. That book . . . It's been festering for years, but I wrote it in a blink I barely remember." She didn't respond. For a moment he thought he'd lost her. Panic came upon him in a flash. "Emily?"

"I'm right here."

"Then fucking say something, sis."

A pause. And then, "Something." He smiled; he could feel her smile through the phone. She said, "I'm coming down."

"No. Please. Trust me. It's not safe to be around me. That's why Amanda took—"

"You said that, Ben. Amanda says you still call her. You still call Jennifer?"

To say I'm sorry. "We don't talk. We haven't spoken since she quit. She ignores my calls."

"Why do you keep calling her? Whatever happened or didn't happen, you've got to let it go."

"I'd never knowingly cheat on Amanda."

"And the dog ate your homework." It came out quickly, a reflex from a trained psychiatrist. "The excuses, Ben. Nothing's ever been your fault."

"Amanda says I'm sleepwalking again."

"And you think you might have done something . . . while you were asleep?"

"I don't know. But it's possible, right? I mean . . ."

"Amanda told me."

"Told you what?"

She exhaled. "That there's been a couple instances with you during the night, with . . ."

"That's fucking great. So big sister knows everything about me now."

"Ben . . ."

"You're a doctor, Emily. Say it. Yes, I've apparently had sex with my wife a couple of times while I was asleep. What did she say? What did she tell you about it?"

"That you were more forceful."

"What? Like I raped her or something?"

"No, Ben. My Lord, no. Just that you were more aggressive. More assertive."

"I'm gonna throw up."

"But she let you do it. She . . ."

"She what, Em? Christ, this is not where I thought this call was going."

"I can honestly say, me either."

"Then what? Amanda? Sleep-screwing?"

"Amanda said she wanted you to do it. It . . . okay, this is weird."

"Just say it."

"It turned her on. She was afraid to wake you up. So she played along. And you've done it more than just a couple of times."

"How many? Emily?"

"Twelve."

"So she keeps track. She charts it? Like I'm a fucking werewolf?"

They both sat silent for a moment. Ben said, "Emily, the same detective who investigated Devon's disappearance is handling these murders."

"Which one?"

"The shorter one. With the blue eyes we said couldn't be real. He's an old man now with a limp. The partner is dead. Some of his questions, they reminded me of back then. Dad, he . . . ?"

"He what? Dad what?"

"Dad, he called me. Before they left the house and died in the car wreck. He called me from Blackwood. Mom was crying. Dad was panicked. I mean really out of his skin, you know?"

"What did he say?"

"Something about knowing the truth. He kept saying he knew the truth about us. And that he was out there."

"Who was out there?"

"I don't know. Devon, maybe?" Ben waited for a response from his level-headed sister, but when none came he verbalized a thought that had been hounding him since the detectives left a couple of hours ago. "Em . . . Do you think Devon is still alive?" *Please say yes. Tell me I'm not crazy.* Nothing. "They never found him. You know?"

"Ben. Devon is dead. It's been thirteen years. You've got to let go . . ."

"I can't. I'm close, I think."

"Close? To what? Ben, what are you talking about?"

"I've been looking for him. All these years. I think I know a way to find him now."

"Ben, no. You're talking crazy. Devon. Is. Dead."

"But we don't—"

"We do," she said definitively; after hearing it, he realized that's what he'd really wanted all along—confirmation from big sister. Emily said, "Whatever you're doing, stop. He's gone." Her words drifted to silence. And then she asked, "What happened next? With Dad, the day of the wreck?"

"He hung up. I called back. I left messages but he wouldn't answer. I called Grandpa, but he wasn't at Blackwood. He was at his office in town seeing patients. But when I did finally get hold of him and told him Mom and Dad were acting strange, he told me to stay put."

"And you didn't?"

"No. I drove to Blackwood. Fresh off my new license."

"That was stupid, Benjamin. Why did you never tell me this?"

"I don't know. It was like . . . I couldn't believe what I'd seen and didn't want to."

She sniffled; her relationship with their parents had been better than Ben's, but still strained. "What did you see, Ben?"

"Grandpa Robert was there at the accident. I saw his truck in the distance, so I stopped a good ways back. I didn't want him to know I'd come. I got the binoculars from the glove compartment. I went into the woods and watched. Mom and Dad were dead in the ravine off the side of the road. Both went through the windshield. But Grandpa, he wasn't even looking at them, not like you might think he should have been. His son and daughter-in-law."

"What was he looking at?"

"The woods. He even walked into them. He was looking for someone. I know he was."

"Or something," she added. "He told us it was a deer that startled them off the road."

"Driving that fast, though?"

"There were deer all over those woods, Ben."

"I saw someone, Emily."

She dry-swallowed deep through the phone. "What do you mean you saw someone?"

"It was a man. Completely bald. Tall. Thin and tall. Black pants and shirt. Like he was trying to blend in with those trees. I think that's who took Devon, Emily."

"And you're just talking about this now?"

"No. I told Grandpa. Back then. I confronted him that afternoon. Admitted I was there. What I'd seen . . ."

"And?"

"And he told me he'd look into it."

"That's it? He'd look into it?"

"Couple of days later, he told me the police had scoured those woods for days looking for someone. And that they were continuing to look. And that settled me, because, you know, Grandpa had that look he'd give. You know the look when the case in his mind was closed. End of story. Don't ask any more questions. You know?"

"I know the look, Ben."

"Well, that's what he did. He gave me the look. And then he hammered it home that it was a deer that caused the wreck. That they'd actually clipped it. Front left side. Said the left headlight was smashed, and had blood on it. But of course it was fucking smashed . . ."

"Ben, stop yelling. Don't speak like that."

He closed his eyes, loosened his grip on the phone. Remembered back to that day. "Of course it was smashed. They were going so fast. And the next day, he made it a point to come find me. Told me he'd found the deer they'd hit. It was dead. Said he buried it. I asked where. He hesitated, but said about thirty yards into the woods from where they hit the ravine."

"Well, there you go, Ben. You can turn your mind off now."

"But I went and found where he'd buried that deer, Emily. I dug it up."

"You what?"

"Yeah, I dug it up. There was a deer there, like he said, but it wasn't one that had been smashed to death. Didn't look like it had died from broken bones and fucking busted innards."

"Ben . . ."

"The deer's throat was cut. There was a bullet hole up near the left hind leg. Another in the head, like somebody had seen it struggling and had to put it down."

"And you think Grandpa did this?"

"Yeah, maybe. To hide something else."

"Grandpa wouldn't hurt a fly, Ben. He'd literally trap them in the house, in a cup, and set them free outside. He never allowed hunting in his woods. He didn't even own a gun."

He agreed with all of this, but he'd seen what he'd seen. "A few years later I got to thinking. That afternoon, he was just telling me what I already knew. I knew the police had scoured those woods looking for Devon. I'd gone through them too, walking them for days. That's what he was reinforcing. That they'd searched the woods for Devon. Not for the man I saw on the day of their accident."

"The man you *think* you saw?"

"You don't believe me?"

"I don't know what to believe, Benjamin. I've *never* known what to believe. All I know is that I lost a little brother and both of my parents in a span of three months. You used to see everything in those woods. Wasn't a day gone by that you didn't tell me you saw a goblin, or a troll, or a mare. You saw mares lurking behind every twist and turn of those woods, Ben."

"But that was all make-believe, Emily. A brother trying to scare the pants off a sister who was easy fodder. But this . . . I saw him. I know I saw him."

"And you've been looking for him ever since?"

She'd said this tongue-in-cheek, but the verbalizing of it was a gut-punch validation. "Off and on," he admitted. "Yes. I've been looking. I've never stopped looking."

"Ben," she said. "Devon is dead. Let it go." She sniffled. He wanted to reach out and hug her through the phone. Admit he used to scare her because seeing her vulnerable was proof she wasn't perfect. Scaring her kept her close. He could protect her from all those things that weren't really there. *Why did you used to cut yourself, Em?* He remembered the track of white scars she used to hide under long sleeves, even in the summer. The way she'd never go swimming, never put on a bathing suit like all her friends. "Ben, you still there? What's going through your head?"

"Nothing." *Why did you used to cut yourself, Em?* Even now it made him want to cry.

"Look," she said. "I gotta go."

"Emily, wait . . ."

"Ben, we'll talk soon. Be safe. And please tell me if you need me to come down."

"Emily . . . did Grandpa ever let you into that room?"

She hesitated, and then hung up on him, which was answer enough.

And rule number three, Benjamin.

Tell no one.

12

Mills' cell phone vibrated on his lap, woke him up. He'd dozed for only twenty minutes on the living room couch, not enough to catch remnants from his brush-up with Benjamin Bookman earlier in the day, but enough to get his mind active. When they were questioning the Bookmans, Mills had taken that whiskey flask from the author solely so he could inconspicuously touch him in the passing of it—what he, for as long as he could remember, had called a *brush-up*. Sometimes it happened with a handshake, the brushing of a shoulder on a crowded sidewalk, the fleeting touch of a finger during the handoff of a whiskey flask. The brush-ups didn't always take root, and truth be told he didn't always want them to, but ever since he was a boy he'd been tortured by his uncanny ability to take on the burden of other people's nightmares.

This one he'd done on purpose, with the hopes of getting a glimpse into Ben Bookman's mind. To see what made his mind tick.

He sat straight on the couch, rubbed his face.

Lock your doors. You see anything resembling a scarecrow, you call.

The last words Sam had shouted to him before she'd driven away an hour ago. And now she was calling. He hit the green ACCEPT button on his iPhone and put it on speaker.

"Clever," she said, without any preamble.

"What's clever?"

"What you did in the car. I asked you a question and you expertly evaded answering."

"What are you talking about, Sam?"

"Dr. Bookman. You were at Oswald Asylum when he died? Actually, no, you corrected me. You were there when they *discovered* that he'd died. We were in the midst of a quid pro quo that was never returned."

"Remind me. I'm old." He realized then that he'd never locked the front door either, so he stood with a grunt and headed that way.

She must have heard the bolt click. "Did you just now lock the front door?"

"What do you want, Sam?"

"What did you find inside that room when Robert Bookman died?"

"Nothing. He was in his nineties. The man died of a heart attack."

"Bullshit."

"Fine." He returned to the living room and plopped back down on the sofa. "Out of respect for Dr. Robert Bookman and what he meant to the town, there were some details left out of the newspapers."

"Even kept from the family?"

"You a reporter now?"

"Strictly off the record."

"Yes. What I found would have only tarnished a good man's image. So I did a bit of innocent concealing on Robert Bookman's behalf."

"Or what you found could have shown he wasn't as good a man as people thought?"

"I don't think so, Sam. But we all have our dalliances. Apparently Robert Bookman had one of a more frisky nature."

"Barf," she said. "I'm waiting."

"Not a word."

"Not a word. But this is pertinent."

"Which is why I'm telling." He propped the phone on his knee and rubbed his tired eyes. "It was the morning nurse who found him. She took two steps into the room. A room she had to unlock with a key, mind you, because the overnight nurse had locked him in. But I'll get to that in a minute. The morning nurse screamed. I was downstairs interrogating another patient I'd arrested two weeks prior."

"Who?"

"What's it matter who?"

"Details."

"Sally Pratchett."

"The Tooth Fairy?"

"Yeah. The Tooth Fairy. Judge Lowe deemed her crazy enough for Oswald. Rather than sending her to prison. Dr. Bookman had fought for her to be released to him at Oswald and Judge Lowe agreed. She arrived the day before. I wanted to see her in prison for what she'd done. I was pissed. Needed some more answers from her."

"And then the nurse screamed?"

"Yes, and I hurried upstairs before anyone else could. Found Nurse Miller distraught on the landing. She pointed toward the room. Said she thought Dr. Bookman was dead, which he was. I told her to call an ambulance and then I went in. When I saw his wrists tied to the posts of the headboard I closed the door. I'd known Dr. Bookman for decades and didn't like seeing him like that, naked and exposed. I shouldn't have done it, but I cut the ropes and disposed of them. I found his clothes on the floor, and managed to get him mostly dressed before the ambulance arrived. He died of a heart attack. No one needed to know what he'd been doing beforehand."

"Or during."

"Or during," he said. "I had a quick talk with Nurse Miller, and she agreed. It was hard for her to see Dr. Bookman like that. We chalked it up to old age. Maybe some Alzheimer's creeping in. But she, like so many, loved him like a grandfather. She'd once been a patient of his. One of many who'd eventually work for him."

"And she still works there?"

"Yes."

After a few seconds of what sounded like Samantha writing something, she said, "Who was it? Who was he with when he died?"

"The overnight. Nurse Allen. Attractive young woman. Brunette. Late twenties. She'd been working there for only four months. She panicked. Locked him in and hurried out. Told her coworkers she was sick and had to leave." Mills waited. "Sam? You there?"

"Yes. Ugh. Barf."

"You asked."

"He was sixty years older."

"Like I said. Dalliances."

"It's not a dalliance. It's sick. You questioned her?"

"Of course. She admitted to being in the room with him when he died."

"During?"

"I assume they'd been in the middle of it. She couldn't talk much through the tears. She was still in shock. She quit the next day."

"Where is she now?"

"I don't know. I didn't put a tracker on her. But Dr. Robert Bookman, pillar of our community, died of a heart attack. Found on the floor of an upstairs bedroom inside of his own asylum. Died working. End of story."

"Do you ever regret it? Covering that up? Seems a noble thing for you to do for someone you didn't know that well."

"No," he said. "Rule number three, Blue. No regrets."

"Right. Got it. Let me write that down."

He yawned. "We done here?"

"No," she said. "Unless you knew Dr. Robert Bookman better than I thought?"

"Quit fishing, Sam. I'll repeat. Are we done?"

"No. Check your email. You can do it right there on your phone."

"I know how to check my damn email."

"Good. I just sent you a list. Including you, Crooked Tree has twenty-two widowed men over the age of fifty."

"I probably know most of them."

"I've got Maxwell calling them now, but if you want to reach out personally go ahead. Just to be safe, I also included six younger male widowers who don't fit the age demographic. It would be careless for us to not warn them too. Although there's probably not a soul in town not looking out their windows."

Eager to get to the list, but truthfully unsure of how to check his iPhone for email while he was still engaged on the phone call, he hurried her on. "Is that it?"

"How old was Devon Bookman when he went missing?"

He straightened on the sofa. This was information she could easily find in their records. She was digging for firsthand dirt he'd never been willing to offer. "He was ten. Last they'd seen him he was asleep in his room at Blackwood. Right in the middle of their yearly summer stay. They woke in the morning and he was gone. Bedcovers casually tossed aside like he'd gotten up to pee. Or maybe wander the woods like he was prone to do."

"Was he a sleepwalker?"

"Possibly. At least Emily, the older sister, alluded to the fact that he was prone to wandering. Fell asleep in his Batman pajamas, but with his shoes still on. Why?"

"Most boys that age wouldn't wander into the woods at night. Alone."

"Apparently the boy wasn't scared of much. Now Ben, on the other hand . . . He was a sleepwalker. According to the mother and sister. Might still be, I don't know."

"You were the lead?"

"Yes. Willard was the sidecar. We flipped a coin when the call came in."

"Why? Seems like a case both of you would want."

Mills ran a hand over his face and exhaled heavily, recalling the sketches they'd found inside Ben Bookman's center desk drawer that day. "The people in that house were one of two things, Sam. You either embraced Blackwood's history, or you were scared to death of it. Devon was more like his older brother Ben. If not for the age gap, the two brothers looked like twins. Devon was a big boy for his age. Both boys embraced the house. Their older sister Emily hated it. She was so angry when we questioned her, she could hardly speak."

"Angry at who?"

"Her father. Her mother. Ben. The grandfather. All of them, really."

"What about Ben's parents? Which side did they fall on? With Blackwood?"

"The father, Michael, was terrified of it."

"Even though he grew up in it?"

"Yes. The mother, Christine, fell more along the lines of her two boys. She'd married into the family, some said, *because* of that house. *Because* of those woods. She was a free spirit, to say the least. It was her idea to stay there every summer."

"And her husband went along with it, even though he hated it there?"

"He was enamored of her. He'd do anything she said. She was an attractive woman. Way out of Michael Bookman's league. Ben Bookman gets his looks from his mother, no doubt. As does the sister Emily. Devon did too. They're all what one might consider model types. Whereas Michael Bookman was average, at best. Born with a cleft upper lip. Lucky enough to come from a family that had the money to fix it up. Six fingers on one hand, four on the other, until he chopped two of them off with a butcher knife." He flicked a speck of lint from his pant leg. "So the story goes."

"So Devon would be about twenty-two, twenty-three now?"

"Thereabouts."

"You think he's our scarecrow?"

"No, I don't."

"You think he's dead?"

"Most likely."

"You think his disappearance is connected to some of the other missing kids over the past decade?"

"I don't know. Possibly. Willard thought so. But Devon's disappearance started it all."

"But you suspected the family somehow?"

"Yes," he said. "I had a hunch. They grieved, but not like I'd seen other families grieve in a situation like that. The mother was despondent. She was on something, no doubt. Heavy stuff too. Not just pot. We questioned Ben's father *outside* because he refused to go back in. Said the walls were listening. He was a basket case. Wouldn't take his eyes off the woods."

"You never found anything on him?"

"No. And I know what you're thinking. Michael Bookman didn't drive off that road because of any pressure from us. We'd backed off by then. Never found anything to stick. Once the cases went cold, we didn't have the manpower to keep searching."

"You used to brag about your closure rate. On cases."

"Once as high as ninety-five percent."

"And the five percent?"

"The missing children."

"Danny blames those missing children for his dad's death. Not the children, but the unsolved cases. He said they chewed his dad up."

"Willard was a good detective. And an even better father."

"That's not where I'm going with this."

"Then where are you going?"

"I don't know. Danny still feels burned by it all, losing his dad as a teen." She paused. "It's hard to be a teen without a father."

She may not have meant it as a jab, but he took it as one. He'd been married to the job. Of that there was no question. "Willard worked as hard as he did so that Danny would never be the next one to come up missing. He devoted every waking hour to those cases to keep them from growing cold."

"Yet they still did."

"Yes, they did," he said, "And the last one was four years ago."

"Until Blair Atchinson."

"Yes, until Blair."

He'd hoped she was finished, but she wasn't. "Tell me about Ben Bookman's sleepwalking. What did you learn from the mother?"

It was moments like these that Mills knew Sam was made for the job; she had the ability to sift through the soil and find the roots, in this case the one thing in his mind connecting the events from both past and present. Ben Bookman's sleepwalking.

"In folklore, do you know what a mare is?" he asked.

"No."

"The root of the word nightmare is the Old English word *mære*. With an a-e. According to lore, and every country and culture seems to have their own name for it, a mare was a nocturnal visitor known to sneak into people's bedrooms at night. A spirit or demon that would climb atop whoever was sleeping and sit there."

"Morbid."

"Or they'd lie down on top of the sleeper. They'd apply pressure on the person's chest and suffocate them with bad dreams. Nightmares. When I have my episodes of sleep paralysis, I can still feel them on me. Like I'm half in and half out."

She asked, "What does this have to do with Ben Bookman's sleepwalking?"

"When Devon went missing, the mother, Christine, said very little. Except when I asked her about Benjamin. Without being prompted, she called him a good boy, beneath it all."

"Beneath it all? Beneath what?"

"He was dark. That's one of the few things we were able to get from the sister. She said there's a darkness in my brother. Christine, the mother, out of the blue, said he's a sleepwalker, you know? Said when Ben was six years old, she was sleeping alone, and had a nightmare. Woke up screaming and unable to breathe. Opened her eyes to find Ben lying down on top of her."

"Okay . . . I used to run into your bedroom as a child. Mom . . . she'd wake up to find me asleep beside—"

"His eyes were open, Sam. His hands were pressing down on her chest. Like *he* was the goddamn mare."

"Jesus."

"She played it off like it was no big deal, but I could tell she wished she'd not told me about it." He swallowed hard, the memory coming back to him fully detailed and sprawled wide like a reopened wound. "She said he'd been sleepwalking. Like he was known to do. Said he'd sleepwalked into the woods a couple of times without knowing what he was doing. One time when he was ten, he went outside and started a damn fire. He was about to roast a marshmallow on a stick he'd chiseled to a point with a steak knife he'd swiped from the kitchen, when she shook him awake. He swung at her, with the knife, before dropping it, realizing what he'd nearly done to his own mother. That's when she realized she shouldn't ever shake him awake when he was sleepwalking. After that, she'd always walk him back to bed if he didn't make it back there on his own, which he sometimes did."

"And he'd just go back to sleep?"

"I suppose."

"How would a six-year-old boy even know what a mare is, without being told?"

"The lore of the mare is displayed right on that mosaic floor when you enter the house, so it shouldn't have been too much of a surprise. She did tell us that's what Ben wanted to be when he grew up. A nightmare. She said if he couldn't *become* a mare, he'd become somebody who could give others nightmares."

"Like a horror writer," she said. "Do you think Ben might have done something similar to his little brother, Devon. Pressing down on his chest like he did his mother's? Like a mare of folklore would? And he accidently killed him. Buried him somewhere on the property?"

"That was always my theory."

"And Willard?"

"He didn't believe it as I did, but he never dismissed it entirely."

"But you could never prove anything either way?"

"No, but the family is good at hiding the truth. I never knew what to believe. But you see why I don't completely trust him now?"

"Because if he's still sleepwalking . . ."

"It's possible. I don't know the extent of the disorder, but if it's severe enough, I guess it's possible. That's why I want a search warrant."

"We can't get a warrant because of some moths."

"I know, but something's not right here. And it hasn't been right for some time."

"So Chuck isn't parked outside the Bookmans' house just for their protection?"

"No. He's to let me know if and when Mr. Bookman goes anywhere. Especially in the middle of the night." She didn't speak for several seconds. "You okay, Sam?"

"Yes." But her voice had a noticeable quiver to it. "Check over the list I sent. Lock all your doors. We'll talk to Jepson Heap's wife first thing in the morning."

"Goodnight, Blue."

"Goodnight, Mills. Get some sleep." He was about to sign off when her voice caught him again. "Wait." Something about the way she said that word, wait, made him feel like a badly needed anchor. A father again. "The story you told me earlier."

"What story?"

"About you and Mom. When you two were little. In school. Detention. Did she ever tell you what her nightmare was? When you said you'd take it away from her if you could?"

"Why are we back to this?"

"I just want to know."

"Being buried alive." He could still smell the overturned soil from his most recent version of it. "She used to have nightmares of being buried alive."

"Used to? So her nightmare *did* go away?"

"Yeah. As those things tend to do over time. It went away."

He ended the call, stood at the window, and watched rain begin to fall.

Before

WINCHESTER MILLS WAS *eight years old and living in Roanoke, Virginia, when he first saw sixteen-year-old Norman Lattimore walked on a leash by his father.*

Norman, despite his age, would act up every night, screaming in terror from the house next door. Winchester's mother, attempting to explain the screams, said Norman's mind was more like that of a little boy. The poor thing heard voices. Winchester's father didn't call Norman a poor thing; he called him retarded, and grumbled nightly he wished the Lattimores would move back to Charlotte, where, according to the rumors, poor Norman Lattimore had lost his marbles.

Mr. and Mrs. Lattimore referred to the sudden changing of their son's behavior as the time when it all started. Implied to the Mills family one evening that Norman had at one time been normal. At that moment, just as Mrs. Lattimore—the poor tired thing—handed over an apple pie she'd baked to apologize for the nightly disturbances next door, young Winchester decided he'd start referring to his odd neighbor as Abnormal Norman.

A swath of grass twenty feet wide separated their house from the Lattimores', and Winchester's second-floor bedroom window mirrored Norman's across the gap. So Winchester took the brunt of the noise at night. He'd learned to sleep with a pillow over his head to mute the screams.

Abnormal Norman, to a born observer like young Winchester, became more of an intrigue than anything else. Norman never left the house. Some whispered it would do the boy good to get out, but the one time Norman was allowed out, he'd jetted off into the nearby woods, and it had taken them hours to find him, barely breathing on the outskirts of a pond where the locals liked to fish. With coils of vine he'd fastened together in perfect Boy Scout knots, he'd attempted to hang himself from a tree. Luckily, the branch had snapped under his weight.

It was only weeks ago that the Lattimores, who agreed it would do the boy good to get out of the house, tried it again. But this time on a leash, the same one, Winchester noticed, they used to walk their little brown mutt they called Choco. They'd attach the leash to one of the loops on Norman's jeans. It wouldn't take much force for Norman to run from that leash his father held so tightly wrapped around his wrist, but Abnormal Norman seemed content enough to simply be outside. The walk soon became a daily thing, typically around lunch. Winchester's parents agreed the walks seemed to do the boy good, but they didn't want their boy outside when it happened.

It just looks bizarre, his father said, walking a grown boy on a leash.

One day the Lattimores walked Norman earlier than normal. Mother was out back hanging laundry on the line. Father was at work at the car factory. Winchester was playing out front, tossing up acorns and hitting them with a wooden baseball bat, periodically glancing toward the Lattimores' house, either anticipating the front door opening or catching a glimpse of Norman's silhouette in his upstairs window.

That day, Norman and his father walked out the front door before lunchtime.

They paused, noticing Winchester playing out front. For a moment it appeared Mr. Lattimore would steer Norman in the opposite direction, but Norman wasn't having it. He would make his daily walk in the same daily direction. Norman was tall and gangly, his dark hair disheveled and in bad need of a cut and comb. Winchester froze as they passed. Norman didn't look up.

But he did mumble something under his breath.

Winchester stepped closer for a better listen, thought he heard Norman grumble something about not being strong enough.

"That's enough now, Norman." His father jerked the leash in a tired, exhausted way, and then flashed Winchester a tired, fake smile.

It took a moment for it to register that Norman may have been talking to him. By the time Winchester had realized it, the Lattimores had already reached the next driveway.

Two days later, Norman Lattimore waved to Winchester from his upstairs window. Winchester waved back, but didn't look away. Norman then opened his window, and without any sign of agitation or warning, jumped out.

13

B EN FELT LIKE a moth trapped in a lampshade.
The hours waiting for Amanda to call had made him restless. So when the real moth made another appearance, tapping
sporadically off the hallway light, Ben went after it. He needed
something to do. Something to take his mind off Devon. He'd been
thinking about his little brother since he'd hung up with Emily.
Ben followed the moth from room to room before cornering it in
his office. It bumped off the ceiling fan's globe light and settled on
the corner of his desk next to the stapler.

Although similar to the butterfly, the moth was nocturnal.
They'd seemingly infested Crooked Tree decades ago and never
left. Until now, he'd never taken the time to closely analyze one.
To really study the details. The body was stout and looked to be
molded from cigarette ash. It lacked the clubbed antennae of the
butterfly, and certainly the color, although some of the ones he'd
seen on the atrium's tree over the years had been as colorful as
some birds. The moth's saw-edged wings folded flat as it rested.
It twitched and Ben did likewise. Without taking his eyes off the
insect, he slowly unshelved a paperback copy of *Summer Reign* and
brought it down hard, catching the moth flush, reducing it to dark,
sifted gunk and crinkled wing. He was in the process of swiping it
into the garbage when his ring tone sounded.

Without looking to see who it was, he said, "Amanda?"

A man answered. "Mr. Bookman?"

"Yes? Who is this?"

"Trevor Golappus. I'm a reporter from *The Story*."

"*The Story*? How did you get my number?"

"That's not important. I won't take much—"

"It sure as hell *is* important. How did you get my cell phone number?"

"Mr. Bookman, please. Let's not get . . ."

Ben lowered the phone, opened his office door, and stormed down the hallway toward the living room. He watched through a sliver of closed curtain. The mustard yellow van was still parked at the curb, but behind the more reputable news vans where the tabloids belonged. He gripped the phone hard enough to crush it. "You've got thirty seconds."

"Is it true you're having an affair with your ex-nanny, Jennifer Jackson?"

Ben hung up, opened the front door, and hurried down the porch steps, unconcerned with the approaching reporters and cameras. Mr. Bookman this. Mr. Bookman that. He said nothing, and made a beeline toward *The Story*'s van, where the reporter Trevor Golappus had already gotten out of the driver's seat and extended his hand to help calm the waters.

Richard Bennington—who'd already made it back from Amanda's parents'—noticed Ben's clenched right fist and jumped in between them. Ben raised his hands, as if in surrender, like he'd calmed, but as soon as Bennington let his guard down, Ben sidestepped him and grabbed Golappus by the collar. He jabbed, a quick snakebite punch, hard knuckles against the man's right cheekbone. Bennington yanked Ben away. Cameras flashed. The street crowd swarmed. Golappus slithered back inside his van, threatening a lawsuit but keeping his door open and his phone camera running.

Bennington had three inches on Ben and, by the feel of the hands and arms holding him back, about thirty pounds of muscle. "Keep cool, Ben."

Ben kept his cool. "I'll break the fucking camera, Richard. Get him out of here."

"It's a public street, Ben. Ignore him. He's gutter."

"He's dead, is what he is." Ben pointed toward the yellow van, raised his voice. "You're dead!" And then, before he could stop the words. "You're fucking next, you son of a bitch."

Cameras and van lights turned the night bright. Ben shielded his eyes. Bennington turned him away, urged him back toward

the house, even acted as a shield himself as his fellow reporters—
Amanda's coworkers—shouted questions about the scarecrow and
the book.

"Let's get you back inside."

"How'd he get my number?"

"Just lock yourself back in, Ben."

"How'd he know about . . . ?" He let it trail away.

"How'd he know about what?"

"Nothing." Ben wrestled his arm free, and returned inside as
rapidly as he'd exited, realizing after he relocked the front door how
much worse his temper had just made things. He calmed himself
with some deep breaths, and then refilled his flask in the kitchen.
How'd he get my cell number? Who would want to help ruin me? And
then it donned on him. *Bennington. Fucking Bennington.* The same
asshole who'd just helped him back inside. It made sense. He had a
feeling Richard was in love with Amanda. *But would he go that far?*
His gut said yes. Instinct told him to walk back out there and throw
down in the front yard, but then again, instinct had just gotten him
on camera threatening the life of *The Story* reporter. It would be
viral within the hour.

You're next? Where had that come from?

He drank from the flask, wiped his mouth.

His phone went off again. This time he checked the number.
"Amanda?"

"Ben, what in the hell are you doing?"

"He called you that fast?"

"Who?"

"Who do you think?"

"Ben, shut up. Just . . . stop. Listen to yourself. If you turn the
news on now, you'll see yourself threatening the life of a reporter. A
gutter, but—" Ben cut her off with a laugh. "What?"

"Nothing. Just that your boy called him the exact same thing.
Gutter."

"Fuck you."

"You must be outside. You never cuss in your parents' house."
For some reason they both found humor in it. "Is it true news
anchors cuss like sailors as soon as the cameras go off?"

"Yes. What else would we do?"

"And they sometimes don't wear pants under the desk?"

"And we have porn running silently in the background to keep
us focused."

"Really? I didn't know that one."

"No, Ben. Well, actually a few times, yes." She laughed, but then, as if the brief burst of civility between them had been wrong, she stoked the fire again. "What did he want?"

"Who?"

"The reporter from *The Story*?"

"Nothing."

"He wanted nothing? You marched out in front of all the reporters, the same ones you've spent all day avoiding, because he wanted nothing?"

"He was just being an asshole. Look, I know Bennington gave him my cell."

"You don't know that."

"No?" He paced next to the kitchen island, took another drink. "So you were about to call before this happened?" She didn't answer, because it may or may not have been phrased as a question, so he said, "How's Bri? Can I talk to her?"

"She's already in bed."

"Okay. Probably for the better." Talking to him in this condition would have only gotten her worked up and asking questions. "Kiss her for me."

"I already did."

"You told her it was from me?"

"Yes, Ben."

"And you hung the little picture above the headboard?"

"Yes. I hung the stupid picture."

"And she said the thing?"

Amanda sighed. Loud. Point taken. "She said the thing, Ben. As stupid as it is."

"She's just messing with you, Amanda."

"Yeah, I get that." She sounded defeated. She didn't like him much right now. She didn't like when Bri said the *thing*. And she didn't like the picture above Bri's headboard at night. To her, the small framed painting of the Baku was creepy. But Bri didn't mind it. One day she'd even told Amanda it was cute. That it helped her go to sleep knowing it was there, although she'd whispered to Ben after Amanda left the room that she didn't really need the dream-eater because nothing scared her, and like him, she favored Mr. Dreams over the Baku and the Sandman.

"Amanda . . ."

"Yes, Ben."

"It was Grandpa Robert's idea for me to write. I'd read damn near every book in that house. If it was something scary, I'd read it multiple times. I had an imagination. He said, 'Ben, why don't you put those thoughts down. On paper. Write it out.'"

"Write it out? Write what out?"

"The bad stuff," Ben said. "Write out the bad stuff. He thought maybe that would help. You know? Get the thoughts out of my head and onto the paper."

"What thoughts? My God . . ."

"A boy can't help what pops into his head, Amanda."

"And it did?"

"Yeah. It did. I found an old typewriter in the basement and started on that. Emily, she noticed a difference right away. Mom and Dad too."

"Ben, why are you telling me this?"

He chewed his lip. "I'm not twisted."

Ben and Amanda listened to each other say nothing for a few seconds, and then she told him goodnight. Before she hung up, he said, "I poured out all the alcohol. In the house." He was lying, unsure why he'd even said it. It had sounded desperate. He just thought that's what she'd want to hear. What she'd wanted him to do for months now. But she said nothing.

Ben thought of Devon again after they hung up. Of their father Michael and his demons, his lopping off two of the six fingers on one hand just to make them even with the other. Of their mother, Christine, and her addictions. Her snorting white powder as often as Emily popped gum. Christine and Michael Bookman, one gorgeous and knowing how to flaunt it, the other deformed and bounced around life like a lump. The perfectly imperfect pair, Grandpa Robert called them.

Ben took his flask back to the bedroom and worked his way through it. The alcohol slowly pushed Devon and their parents back where they belonged.

He drank until his eyes grew heavy.

Drank until he drifted off.

14

DETECTIVE MILLS WAS off the phone with Blue for no more than five minutes before gathering his coffee buddies in person to warn them about Blue's completed list.

He'd fumbled his way through a group text he had going with eight of them, and requested they meet at Hardee's pronto. Even with it being such late notice, not to mention dark and bordering on old-man bedtimes, five of the eight showed up for his spur-of-the-moment meeting. As if they'd somehow inferred the reason, the three other men who'd been widowed were all in attendance.

Mills made the fourth and most recent widower of the bunch.

Gus Cantorie, an ex-Marine, in regard to the scarecrow, said to bring the motherfucker on. He'd sit on his porch with a bottle of Beam and a shotgun all night and wait. Ever since his wife Darlene had died from ovarian cancer two years ago, Gus had been on the verge of shooting someone anyway. He was downing straight black coffee like it was water and digging into his Thickburger like it might be his last.

Bill Santino, on the other hand, simply nodded. His coffee mug shook in his hand. Mills invited him to stay at his house. Bill declined, said he'd put his fate in the hands of the Lord. Bill was a retired Catholic deacon who owned no guns. Mills told Bill he'd stake out in front of his house himself. Bill was grateful, but declined that as well.

Mills asked if any of them had read Ben Bookman's latest novel. Two of them had purchased it, but none had cracked it. Most of them liked e-readers for the enlarged print.

"Little Peterson girl in the hospital still isn't talking?" Gus licked mayo off his fingers.

"No," said Mills. "But we know from the Reynolds couple that the scarecrow stalked them two nights prior. Just like in the book. Like it had latched on. We're assuming it came back the next night and then ran off again."

"It?" asked Sammy Valsant, the newest in the coffee crew, not a widower yet but unfortunately close; his wife Lou Anne had a failing liver.

"We don't know for sure if it's a man or a woman. Not with the mask on, but I'm assuming a man."

Gus said, "Did it have tits?"

Mills had no time for Gus' shit. "If he's mimicking the novel, it'll be a man. The killer in the book ends up being a man named Miserable Meeks."

"Weird-ass name," said Gus.

"Weird-ass story," said Mills. "But this story is now our reality. The character Meeks was orphaned as a boy. Spent some time in the fictional Riverdale Asylum." He leaned in and the men did likewise. "Breaks out and gets to killing. I know it's not much, and when the Peterson girl starts talking, hopefully she can shed some more light on what to watch for, but in the days leading up to the murders, the victims notice a scarecrow in their yard. At night. Arms outstretched like he's stuck to a post. Maybe they'll be walking past the window or something and boom!" He slapped the table and the five men jumped. "In the book it's called the Stalking Phase. Victims assume it's a prank. They'd go out to look and the scarecrow would be gone. Fled into the corn or woods or what have you until he comes back the next day." Mills sipped coffee, making sure he had their attention. "By then he's gotten into their heads. Messed with their minds. That's one of his missions, to create fear. The children see the anxiety in the parents and the anxiety spreads. The children have nightmares. Then fear spreads like warm butter on hot toast."

"When does the scarecrow decide to kill them?" Bill asked. "In the book."

"It varies. But eventually the owners will come out to give chase and the scarecrow doesn't flee."

"And that's when they get the axe?"

"That's when they get it," Mills warned. "So my point is, we shouldn't just be looking out for tomorrow night. I'd expect it to start stalking tonight. In the book, the murders are all about revenge. But that's not what we're dealing with here. It's likeness. Any sign of him, you call me right away. Or call nine-one-one. You understand me?" Head nods all around, even from Gus, mid-chew. "That goes for you gentlemen still lucky enough to have wives, too, just in case this son of a bitch makes a detour from the book."

Assured now that his friends would do as told and take the threat seriously, Mills left them to their sandwiches and drinks.

He'd been too wired to eat anyway. His cell phone buzzed in the parking lot.

Glancing at the number, he realized he'd missed a text from Blue while he'd been inside with his pals.

Tried Jepson Heap's wife again. Still too frazzled to talk. I get the feeling she won't until we catch whoever this is. We'll try again in the morning. Get some sleep.

The incoming call was from the station. When he answered, Chief Givens said, "You sitting down, Mills?"

He opened his car door. "About to."

"Where are you?"

"Hardee's." He lowered himself behind the steering wheel with a grunt. "Had a craving for a Thickburger. What can I do you for, Givens?" He'd never called him Chief. The boy was twenty years younger than Mills, a fancy suit more concerned with climbing the ladder than catching bad guys, and Mills would forever resent him for it.

"Anderson, the new kid, he's the fastest reader we got. He's plowing through the book like a savant."

"Get to the point."

"That Peterson crime scene wasn't the first."

"What are you talking about?"

"In the book, the murders that the Petersons' mirrored might have started off the story. To the reader that was the first, but you find out two-thirds of the way through that there was another murder, a set of twins the scarecrow kills two weeks prior, and they aren't found until *after* the old man widower gets it. I assumed Blue sent you the list, since you're on it?"

"I got the list."

"And then you went to Hardee's."

"And then I went to Hardee's. What I do on my own time is sacred." Mills wracked his brain for the details Ben Bookman had given them hours ago about the fictional Meeks. The twins in the orphanage who'd tormented him. The ones who'd tried to make him eat the dead crow. What were their names? *Murphy* . . . "Murph and Tommy Pope."

Chief Givens said, "Yes. Those were the twins killed in the book. Found late. So Bookman told you about the twins, but not that they were the true first victims?"

Mills didn't like Givens's accusatory tone. "No, he did not."

"Christ. I've a notion to bring him in now."

"We still don't have enough," Mills said, and they both knew it.

"Obstruction? Lying? Intentionally evading an ongoing—"

"The man was two hours removed from seeing a fan blow his head off in front of him."

"Oh, Jepson Heap was no fan, Mills."

"Bookman was still rattled when we talked to him. And . . ."

"And what?"

"Drunk. He was drunk."

"Uh huh. Something you'd know about, I guess."

"Fuck off. Are we done here?"

"Find out why Bookman held back that bit of information."

"Already planning to."

"And Blue, she's compiling another list. This one of twins in the area."

"*Missing* twins," Mills said.

"Yes," said Givens. "Missing twins. By the time the Pope twins are found in the book they're already Fright Night." He used their morbid term for decomposed. "But don't you think we would have been alerted by now if we had a missing set of twins on our hands?"

Mills got behind the wheel and closed his car door. "For once, it seems we agree."

Before

BRIANNA'S VOICE LURED *Ben from his bed.*
 He moved quietly down the hallway toward her bedroom, to eavesdrop but not startle. She was a sleepwalker, like him, had been ever since she'd graduated from the crib. It wasn't uncommon for her to talk in her sleep. Ben found her sitting on the side of her bed, in profile. From his vantage point in the hallway, only half the bedroom was visible, and Bri sat as if in conversation with someone on the other side of it.

 "You're silly," Bri said. "I don't believe you."

 Ben inched closer. "Bri?"

 She snapped awake, groggy, but alert to his presence now. "Daddy?"

 "You were talking in your sleep, honey." At the doorway, he noticed the bedroom window was open. A moth beat against the frame, and then flew out.

 "I was hot," she said. "Before I went to sleep."

 Ben lowered and locked the window. "You know you're not supposed to open your windows at bedtime." He'd once gone out his window as a kid, sleepwalking.

 "I'm sorry."

 "Let's get you back to bed." She lay down willingly. He pulled the covers to her chest and handed her one of a dozen stuffed animals she kept atop the puffy comforter. "Bri, do you remember talking just now?"

 She shook her head on the pillow. "What did I say?"

"You said . . . you're silly. Who's silly? Do you remember?"

She seemed so unbothered. "He said you and Mommy don't love each other. That you're going to get a divorce."

Ben bit his lip, looked away. "That is silly. You know that, don't you, Bri?"

"I know that, Daddy."

"Good." He kissed her forehead. Kids were smart. Too smart. He and Amanda would have to work at this, to disguise better, to do better. "Now go to bed. Love you."

"Love you, too, Daddy."

He stopped at the doorway. "You said he *a minute ago? Who told you this?"*

Eyes closed, she rolled on her side, hugged a pillow. "The Nightmare Man."

"You know the Nightmare Man isn't real, don't you? It's just a story."

"I know, Daddy," said Bri, although her tone didn't convince him.

"And the media," he said. "It's just a silly thing they call me. Because of my books."

"I know," she said sleepily.

Ben waited in the threshold until Bri fell asleep. He returned to his room, feeling like his soul had been scooped out. As a kid, Grandpa Robert had told them all the stories about mares. How they crawled up on the sleeper's chest and brought about nightmares. The Nightmare Man was the leader of them all. He sneaked into children's rooms at night and planted nightmares in their heads. His words whispered into their ears became seeds. This was after he and Emily, as kids, had asked where nightmares came from. Ben, in turn, had told Bri the same story months ago, when she'd asked the same question of him.

Amanda had then told their daughter that nightmares happened when you ate food too close to bedtime. Especially Oreo cookies, which was what Bri had sneaked, with milk, when she'd thought they weren't looking. Bri had obviously chosen to adhere to his version, no doubt seeing the connection to what the newspapers and magazines called him, the Nightmare Man, prompting them both to remind her that his nickname was just for fun.

For his public persona.

Like Grandpa Robert's stories, all make-believe.

Ben watched his daughter until she snored lightly. He kissed her on the forehead and returned to bed himself.

* * *

An hour later, Bri screamed in all-out terror.

Ben was down the hallway in seconds, Amanda right behind. They held their daughter on the bed, one stroking her hair while the other rubbed her back, whispering, "Everything is all right" and "Everything is fine."

After Bri calmed down, Amanda lifted her daughter's chin and looked into her eyes. "Did you have a bad dream, honey?"

"It was a nightmare." Bri wiped her eyes, looked from parent to parent. "I had a nightmare that you two hated each other. You were screaming at each other so loud my ears started bleeding. And then, Mommy, you ran out of the house. But you had no arms. And Daddy, you were next. You left too, and you didn't have any arms either. Neither one of you could hold me anymore because you didn't have any arms and then you left me all alone."

Amanda hugged Bri tight, watching Ben over their daughter's shoulder. His fault, he knew. He shouldn't have told her the story of the Nightmare Man. "We love each other, honey," said Amanda. "We always will." As if to give proof, Amanda leaned over and kissed Ben on the lips. She looked back at Bri and said, "You see? All better now."

They tucked her back in and she slept all night. That became their nightly ritual, because the nightmare came often.

It was the only time Ben and Amanda ever kissed anymore.

15

Ben startled himself awake, hit the back of his head against a wall, not the bed's headboard as he would have expected. He'd fallen asleep on their bed, but he was no longer there. By the smell of the surroundings, no longer inside the house. Amanda's reassuring voice to Bri—*You see? All better now*—was miles away. As was the memory.

His eyes adjusted to the dark. He was inside their barn. He scrambled upright, tripped over an old rake.

A bat fluttered in the shadows. Moonlight shone in slivers through the barn's wood slats. A spider crawled on his right hand. He flung it off, watched it scurry into a thicket of old leaves and hay beneath the rusted tractor with the stuffing-plucked seat. He was shirtless. His feet were bare and he wore only boxers. He'd been fully clothed when he'd fallen asleep—*How long ago?*—thinking of that night Bri first had her reoccurring nightmare.

Get hold of yourself. He shivered, breathed into his cupped hands like one might into paper bag when hyperventilating. *You're at it again, Ben.*

It was cold enough in the barn to see his breath.

He scanned the barn's floor for his clothes, but couldn't find them. He must have undressed inside. He opened the barn door to cool, crisp air and unexpected footsteps.

A uniformed cop walked the grounds ten feet away. They saw each other simultaneously. Officer Black turned, aimed a pistol at Ben. "Jesus H . . ."

Ben ducked, clutched his chest to keep his heart from jumping from it.

Officer Black lowered his gun. "What are you doing out here, Mr. Bookman?"

Ben didn't answer; he didn't know what he was doing out here half-clothed.

They stared at each other for a few deep ones, feeling each other out. Both men flinched when a voice chirped across Officer Black's walkie-talkie: *Is everything okay, Officer Black?*

"All good here," he said into it, curious eyes still on Ben. "Just a raccoon," he lied, hooking the walkie-talkie back on his waistline along with his weapon, and then spoke to Ben. "Everything okay here?"

Ben hugged himself, shivered again. "I'm fine."

"Do I need to check out something in that barn for you?"

"No." Ben started for the house, hoping Officer Black would follow. He doubted the officer would find anything incriminating in that barn, but he didn't know for sure. He didn't have time to check it out himself. Once he heard Officer Black trailing up the dewy lawn behind him, Ben said, "I sleepwalk sometimes."

"You look awake to me, Mr. Bookman."

"What about you?"

"What about me?"

"Out for a stroll?"

"Just reconnoitering the rim, Mr. Bookman. Making sure all is as it should be."

"And is it?"

"It was until you nearly made me drop a load in my pants."

"Well," Ben said. "Same here."

"What pants?" After a few more steps, they both sniggered at that, enough, at least, to loosen whatever tension had been built up from their meeting outside the barn. Officer Black said, "Detective Mills sent me to knock on your door. Said he's been trying to reach you."

"Yeah, well, my cell. I left it inside."

"I figured." Officer Black gave him another head-to-toe glance and wished him an awkward goodnight. Ben did the same, and they went their separate ways, Officer Black back around to his squad car parked at the curb and Ben back inside. He realized, once back in the kitchen, that he'd left the back door open a crack, which was one of his sleepwalking MOs. Any time he ended up outside, he'd leave a door ajar, as if his subconscious thought he'd be unable to get back in if he didn't.

Ben locked the back door and headed straight for the bedroom. His jeans rested in the middle of the floor like a puddle. His shirt clung to the bed's footboard. Knowing he wouldn't be going back to sleep, and probably shouldn't now, he slid both back on, removed the empty flask from the back pocket of his jeans, refilled it with Old Sam from the kitchen, and returned to the bedroom. He checked his watch. Eleven o'clock. It had only been five hours since Jepson Heap ended his life, and Ben's book signing, but it felt like days. His nap and short bout of sleepwalking had only been a blip, but long enough to leave him groggy, disoriented, and still buzzing. Probably still drunk. He dropped to the floor and grunted through two dozen pushups to clear his head, get his heart going and his body ready for another night ride. Unlike previous nights, with Amanda and Bri out of the house, he wouldn't have to wait until the middle of the night to sneak out.

He checked his phone.

Both detectives had called. Mills, three times. His daughter twice. He assumed they'd dived deeper into the book. Found out what he'd held back earlier. That the Peterson crime scene would not officially be the first. He didn't want to talk to either one of them, but knew if he didn't, they'd soon come knocking.

He dialed Detective Blue.

"There you are. We've been trying to—"

He cut her off. "I fell asleep." *Too forceful.* He softened his tone. "I'm sorry. I fell asleep. I just saw the messages."

"I know."

"You know? How do you know?"

"Officer Black said he found you coming out of your barn. Half clothed. Said you'd been sleepwalking."

"Word travels fast."

"And you threatened the life of that reporter from *The Story*? Got in a good lick too. He's pressing charges."

"Figured he would." Dizzy, Ben sat down on the side of the bed and massaged his temples. "What's so urgent that you and your dad felt the need to call me five times?"

"You're withholding information, Mr. Bookman. You didn't warn us there was possibly another murder committed, before all of this. One that mirrors the two twins in the book. Mr. Bookman, you there?"

"I forgot."

"Bullshit."

"Do you understand the stress I'm under, Detective? A man pulled a gun—"

"I know what Jepson Heap did, Mr. Bookman. In your story, the twins were living together in a trailer with a woman, sharing her as a wife. Meeks kills them first. Cuts them up. Stitches his cocoons and hangs them from a basement ceiling pipe while he leaves the woman strapped to a chair to watch. She's dead too by the time Detective Mulky, in the book, finds them. It's unclear whether *your* scarecrow—"

"*My* scarecrow?"

"This all came from your mind. It's unclear if this *shared wife* was left alive on purpose, but she's dead from starvation when Mulky finds them."

"He hated them that much." Ben shifted in his seat. "He hated those twins so much he took it out on the woman. He knew she'd eventually starve to death." He waited. "Detective Blue? You there?"

"Yes." She sounded defeated.

"Never mind," Ben said. "I gotta go. I'm sorry. I need sleep. I'm dead on my feet." *You're losing your mind, is what you're doing, Benjamin. You've got work to do. There's no time for sleep.* He hung up, waited two minutes before standing from the bed, sure she'd call back, but she didn't. *You should have warned her about the end of the book.* If they had someone speed-reading through *The Scarecrow*, they'd find out soon enough. Probably within the next hour or two. All they had to do was read the reviews. The cliff-hanger all his fans were talking about. He'd known all along it would begin and end with the Screamer.

Somehow, he'd always known.

But now that he'd opened Pandora's Box—and with some of the pieces beginning to fall into place like they were—he doubted he'd be able to get them back in.

Like trying to put toothpaste back in the tube.

He left through the kitchen door, made sure no one was watching the back side of his house, and then hurried back to the barn. In the shadows, he found his mountain bike where he'd left it the previous night, propped against the wall behind the lawnmower.

He walked the bike out the barn's rear door, mounted it, and pedaled into the woods.

16

MILLS STOOD AT the toilet and waited.

The urge to pee had been strong, but he'd been standing now for two minutes and had yet to muster a trickle. Maybe he should have kept the follow-up appointments after his run-in with prostatitis in the summer. Bladder was healthy as a Cadillac, but the enlarged prostate looked, in Dr. Goodwin's words, *like it had been in a fight with a ball-peen hammer.* But he wasn't about to let the doc stick a finger up his ass again, so he'd take his chances.

You can be such a big baby, Winny.

Linda's voice brought about a smile that didn't last long. Back sore and tired of standing, he turned around and sat on the toilet instead. On the back of the commode, right next to a book of matches and a candle he hadn't lit since Linda died—because what was the point?—rested Ben Bookman's novel. He'd left it there an hour ago, when he'd been unsuccessful in peeing then as well, and had given it ten minutes of reading before giving up and retreating to the kitchen for a bowl of clam chowder warmed up from a can. He was skimming, now well over halfway through *The Scarecrow*, and had just gotten to the part where the Pope twins were found. Bodies decomposed to Fright Night, like Givens had said. Bookman's earlier warning rang true, not only as a heads-up to Mills, as a widower, but as a reminder that Crooked Tree's version of the killer could be accelerating his pace just like Miserable Meeks in the book.

The air vent next to the commode kicked on and heat brushed his bare knees. He'd sit there until it turned off. After every page or so of reading he'd look up from the book to watch out the bathroom window toward the sloping hillside and woods below. The trees swayed, moonlit and dark. Sam had already compiled a list of twins in town, twelve sets in all, and had begun contacting them.

Unable to focus, he put the book down on the back of the toilet. He'd watched the news earlier while eating clam chowder in the kitchen. They'd been mostly successful keeping the gruesome details of the Petersons' crime scene undisclosed. The Reynolds' crime scene had been shut down quickly as well, but not before rumors of the macabre had leaked to the press, with whispers of the Reynolds couple being bundled and hung inside cocoon-like corn husks. After the press had learned of Ben Bookman being questioned, two and two had been tallied to four so quickly the police, no matter how many "no comments" were uttered, could do nothing to stop it. And now they were teetering on that fine line of not spreading fear as he assumed the Scarecrow wanted, or fueling the fire and doing their duty of warning the public that a madman was on the prowl. Mills knew how the town would react. Not with caution but panic. They'd watch over their shoulders, check twice before getting into vehicles. Fear would spread like morning fog. They'd sleep in shifts with shotguns on their porches. Some wouldn't sleep at all, because fear of the Scarecrow had already spread like a virus.

Within hours of it being broadcast on the local news, the national channels pounced, and then an hour later the first "scarecrow" sighting had taken place in the suburbs of Atlanta, Georgia. Another in Dallas, Texas. Thirty minutes later, a man was interviewed by his local news channel in Boise, Idaho, having just fired his rifle at a prankster dressed as a scarecrow and "stalking" out by their pond before fleeing the bullets, laughing. Like the clown craze from years ago, when sickos everywhere dressed as clowns with the sole purpose of terrifying people. Like a plague, Mills had thought then, and was realizing the similarities now. The pranks would make it more difficult to tell the fakes from the real, which in the end could cost more lives.

Mills closed the book and looked out the window toward the woods.

He jerked back and nearly slipped off the toilet seat.

Well, I'll be a son of a bitch. The urine came now. *There you are.*

He blinked hard, making sure what he now saw out the window was real. At the bottom of the hillside, on the outskirts of the trees, stood a figure dressed as a scarecrow posed as if stuck to a cross. Feet together, arms splayed out to the sides, head tilted to the left shoulder. From the distance all he could make out was the straw hat and rolled trouser cuffs, but he knew what it was.

So I'm next? Now that the initial shock had passed, he realized this was what he'd wanted all along. Come after me so he wouldn't harm anyone else.

He finished peeing, stood slowly from the toilet, pulled up his pants, and buckled without taking his eyes off the figure out there. "Stay right where you are." He moved down the hall and grabbed his pistol from the counter. As he passed through the kitchen, CNN was telling the story of a teenage boy in Phoenix, Arizona, who'd been gunned down and killed twenty minutes ago after "scarecrow" pranking his best friend, shot by the father who'd been on edge and had no clue it was the same boy who'd spent the night in his basement the weekend before.

Mills had walked out of range of the television. He grabbed his shotgun, and then stepped out to the back porch and high decking overlooking the hillside. Just as he'd figured, the scarecrow was gone. His brain told him to plow down that hill and enter the woods and not come back out until he had the bastard's head on a platter, but his body knew better. He hadn't gone down that steep hillside since the hip had started singing. He wasn't about to leave himself immobile at the foot of the hill like baited meat.

Shadows moved between the tree trunks. He should call Blue, or Chief Givens. He'd gotten as far as hitting the green button before turning it off and sliding the phone back into his pocket. No, he told himself. If that was the real deal, he'll be back tomorrow night for a showdown. If it was a prankster, he probably wouldn't have the balls to return. He pulled his phone from his pocket again, searched until he found Officer Black's cell number, and called it.

Chuck picked up on the second ring. "Officer Black."

"Chuck, it's Winny. I need you to go knock on the Bookmans' door right now."

"Something happening?"

"I don't know." Mills already heard Chuck breathing heavily, which meant he'd wasted no time getting out of the squad car to approach the house. Mills watched the woods as he waited, saw movement. Against his better instincts, he started down the deck's steps and carefully navigated the dewy decline toward the trees.

A minute later Chuck said, "I'm knocking, Winny, but no one is answering. And I just saw him a little while ago, so I know he's home."

"Where'd you see him?"

"Reconnoitering the rim. Found him coming out of the barn. I thought I told you this."

"No. You didn't."

"I called, anyway. You didn't pick up. Must have been Blue I told."

"Must have. But what was he doing in the barn?"

"Came out naked as a jaybird, save for his boxers. Claims he was sleepwalking."

Sleepwalking, my ass. "Try the doorbell." He heard it chime through the phone. "Knock harder."

"What's going on here, Winny?"

"I don't know yet. Maybe nothing."

"No one is answering."

"His car still there?"

"Yes. And his wife's car is here too. But we have reason to believe she snuck out a couple of hours ago with a coworker. Want me to bust the door down?"

"No," said Mills. "There's no call for that. We'd have lawyers so far up our ass we'd need a colonoscopy to get'm out. He's probably asleep." *If not walking again.* "Thanks for checking, Chuck. You're not as much of an asshole as I thought."

"It would take one to know one, wouldn't it?"

"Let me know if you see anything funny, because that sure wasn't. But maybe go take another look around back too."

"Will do, Winny."

They signed off. The phone dropped like a rock into his pocket. Mills had made it to the tree line, but saw no movement. No sign of anything, other than his own breath coming out in steamy plumes from his nose and mouth. *Where'd you go, you son of a bitch?* He scanned the woods with his rifle raised, finger on the trigger.

Thirty yards deep in the shadows, something big moved.

Too big for a deer.

Moonlight found a way through the canopy of trees, briefly glinted off what Mills realized was an axe blade, and then the dark swallowed it all up again. Something rustled. Heavy footsteps on deadfall. He didn't think a prankster would have taken it as far as bringing a damn axe. His heartbeat sped, uncomfortable; that combined with the freezing temperatures now clamping down on his chest, slowed any progress he'd begun to make toward whoever was out there.

Footprints marked the ground, some full, some half-pressed into the mud and wet leafy gunk of the woods, but clear enough to eyeball the indentations as well over a foot. Fourteen to fifteen inches, in Mills' best estimate. He heard movement again, deeper and to the right, toward where the trees funneled to the road. He followed it with the shotgun barrel, and fired high into the trees just to startle. Bats fluttered. An owl hooted. But whoever was out there was gone. Whoever it was, was younger and faster and stronger, and Mills was in no condition to chase. He surveyed for five more minutes and then slowly worked his way back up the wet hillside.

Back inside and out of breath, Mills locked his doors and made sure all the windows were secured. He poured himself two fingers of Old Forester and took his seat at the kitchen table. On the counter next to the refrigerator, a moth had landed on the trap he'd made days ago, a combination of flypaper and fish oil, and now the little black-winged bastard was stuck there, wings getting slower by the minute, like pulses from a dying heart. He dealt out two hands of Uno while the moth fought the stickiness. His cell phone rang before he had a chance to play the first card.

He answered. "What is it, Sam?"

"Oh good, you're awake."

"I'm always awake."

"Except when you're not."

"What is it, Sam? I'm busy."

"I heard from Judge Maxwell. He won't issue a search warrant on Bookman's house."

"It was worth a try." Mills stared at his bourbon. "Did he say why?"

"Not enough evidence. Not *any* evidence. If we find something substantial then he'd reconsider, but he's not going to jump the gun on what he called an abnormality and a hunch."

"Abnormality? Who's the abnormality? Me?"

"I don't know. Look, is everything okay? You sound rattled."

"Everything's fine, Blue." *Except the scarecrow latched on to me twenty minutes ago, and so tag I'm it.* But all he said was, "It's late." He eyed the bottle of sleeping pills on the table. The dying moth across the kitchen. "Hug those kids of yours and get some sleep. Tell them Grandpa Winny loves them. You might have to remind them who I am first."

"Funny." Blue sniffed on the other end, and then hung up.

Throat thick with memory, he recalled the exact night Sam had turned on him.

The night he'd sworn he'd stop drinking, and eventually did. He'd been deep into a bottle of Beam with work files spread out on the kitchen table like Linda asked him *not* to do when Samantha was awake. He'd been trying to figure out how to pin down that crafty son of a bitch the newspapers had by that point dubbed the Yellow Light Bandit, but whose real name, once they'd finally caught him a year later, turned out to be Henry Bannister. Mills and Willard Blue had been looking for Yellow Light for months with no success, and the lack of progress had made both men overly stressed. Bannister attacked only at night, with his handheld yellow light to startle, and his switchblade to maim—his trademark X carved in the middle of the forehead—while he, in his Richard Nixon mask, stole anything he could grab of value before vanishing into the dark. Thirty-nine victims in all; no deaths, but so many had been rattled that a few admitted they wished they had been killed. The night of the accident with his daughter, Mills had thought Samantha was asleep. But when he'd gone to the bathroom to unload some of the alcohol he'd consumed while going over the files, he found his nine-year-old daughter looking at the pictures he'd left face up on the table. More mad at himself than her, and knowing he would hear it in both ears from Linda, he stormed toward Sam and grabbed his little girl without thinking. She dropped down at the same time he pulled up and her little arm broke at the elbow, the pop so loud he instantly became nauseous and ended up hurling in the sink while she cried on the floor and Linda came running out in her nightgown.

The rest of the night was a blur—the hospital, the tears and shouting.

Samantha had been nine then. She was thirty-two now.

Long time to stay mad, Blue.

He played the first Uno card and then looked at Linda's hand for her best possible play. Sometimes he'd intentionally make a bad play for her, as she seemed somehow to win on most nights. He didn't want her lead to get too unsurmountable. But tonight, he'd let her go ahead and win. The earlier brush-up with Ben Bookman had left an unsettled feeling in his gut, and for whatever reason he'd been thinking of Linda all evening. But what did it have to do with Ben Bookman? Or did it have anything at all to do with him? Brush-ups weren't always foolproof.

The nightmares, of late, had been coming with vivid realness not felt since he was a child, when Dr. Robert Bookman had told his parents that he was a unique case, indeed. *Rare, even. Impossibly so.* With a mind, it seemed, made purposely *for* the planting. *Fertile,* the psychiatrist had told them. Blue might think him crazy with all the dream catchers, but while they never kept the nightmares from coming, they at least helped dampen things.

Tonight he was hoping to channel Ben Bookman.

Even though he'd swallowed the two and a half pills earlier, that sleep hadn't lasted long before Sam had found him on his living room floor and ushered him off to the Reynolds' crime scene. Now he craved the deep sleep. The pills he'd taken hours ago—even though they probably still coursed through his bloodstream—felt long gone now. Mills opened the sleeping pills and palmed three into his mouth. He crunched them down to pasty dust, closed his eyes, and chased the remnants with water from the sink. He poured out his untouched bourbon and returned to the table. He placed another card down on the pile and said to the empty chair across the table, "Sorry, honey. Draw two. And I'm switching the color to blue. No, make that red."

The room had already begun to spin.

Thoughts of the scarecrow grew distant. His eyelids grew heavy, his focus slow.

He drew a card for Linda. As he perused the splayed cards in his hand for the next play, he glanced at the moth stuck to the flypaper on the counter.

It was finally dead.

Before

*W*INCHESTER WASN'T SURE *exactly when he and Linda had begun doing it, such a small trivial thing as munching on pretzel rods during their games of Uno and pretending they were cigars.*

But they'd both latched on, and now it had become enough of a thing for Linda to stock the cabinet with multiple bags of them.

He wondered if Linda even knew she'd begun to flick imaginary ashes onto the table in between her plays. Unlike him, she'd never been a smoker, although her mannerisms were spot on. He made a play. Draw two. She smiled, placed her card down and told him with a nod to draw four, you son of a bitch. Inside, Mills smiled. Not all that much actual talking went down when they played anymore—not the verbal kind, at least—as they'd long past mastered the art of communicating without it. Sometimes, their facial expressions said more than words could.

He sneeze-farted and started laughing, which had felt good at the time—not necessarily the passing of gas, but the laugh—because he'd caught a really mean son-of-a-bitch home burglar that afternoon and the arrest had left him gloomy and feeling old. She'd laughed because he'd laughed, and there wasn't much in the world he liked more than hearing that.

Their bodies may have gone to pasture over the years, but that cute little chortle hadn't changed one iota since they were kids.

"Oh, Winny," she'd said, wrinkling her nose as if his gas had come with a stench, which he didn't believe it had. He didn't smell anything.

She looked up at him with a grin—not just a grin, but the *grin— one he hadn't seen in months. Hell, years, if he was being honest. Sex to them now was holding hands, just as it was as early teens, like things had gone full circle. The fault lay all on him. Erectile dysfunction is just gonna have to be my function, Linda. Her grin unnerved him more than anything, so out of the blue. And then she said, "Winny?"*

"Yes?"

"Let's go have a replay of our honeymoon."

"What? When?"

She pretended to exhale from her pretzel cigar. "Now."

Had he been in mid-chew he would have choked on his pretzel; if ET had walked into the kitchen at that moment and asked him to phone his fucking home, he wouldn't have been more startled than he was now, gazing across the table at his wife and hoping he hadn't just witnessed the first sign of Alzheimer's.

She laughed her distinct laugh again; he laughed right along with her because he didn't know what else to do. Didn't know if she was being serious or not, because in her old age she'd finally learned how to kid around, and he adored that too.

She guffawed. He did likewise, laughing so hard tears dripped.

Her bosom shook the tabletop.

He slammed the table playfully with a fist.

Her face reddened like it was set to burst, and then her laughter ended in a snap, like a speeding car had gone from ninety to zero in a break with no skid, no warning, no time for him to reach out and grab her. Her eyes grew large, like she'd just been goosed, and then her head dropped like a deadweight on her folded forearms.

She'd stopped moving.

At first he thought she was joking, but when he called her name she didn't answer.

"Linda?"

No response.

He hurried around the table, and found no pulse.

17

Ben's legs were on fire, but he refused to slow down, as he navigated the worn path up the wooded hill from Route Road to the back of his property, familiar now after a dozen nocturnal ventures made in the past months while Amanda and Bri slept.

His morning bike rides were common. It was a way for him to exercise without getting hounded by local fans. Early on in his career he'd been a walker, but the slow pace made it easy for others to sidle up for questions and autographs, which he didn't mind signing, except when his family was around. He didn't like strangers approaching his wife and kid. Running worked for a while, but even that eventually drew unwanted running mates. Amanda had bought him a bike for Christmas six years ago and he took to it like a fish would water. He made it a point to ride at least ten miles a day, and he'd been doing it nearly every morning for years, so on the evenings he sneaked out, he had a ready-made excuse if caught.

He couldn't sleep. He hadn't gotten his ride in during the day. He needed the fresh air, to clear his mind and think. Writers needed to think. And, even in the dark, he knew the trails like the back of his hand, especially those hugging the hills of Blackwood and Oswald Asylum and the hollow in between.

The uphill slope to his house was not steep, but a gradual, meandering climb through four acres of trees and trampled grass that made it necessary to stand as he pedaled. He was sweating profusely by the time he stopped, resting on his bike at the crest of the hill, where fifty yards of tall grass leveled out to his home in the distance. The twenty-minute bike ride from Blackwood was connected by hiking trails made long ago, and bike paths more recently, interweaving streets and backroads, woods and cornfields, like one large spiderweb of transit circling and cross-hatching the town.

The plan was to return his mountain bike to the barn and sneak back in through the kitchen to avoid the police and reporters, especially with what he now had inside his backpack. He didn't expect to find all the lights on inside his house. The back of his house now crawled with police and forensic crime units. The barn seemed to be the focal point of all the sudden chaos, the boards now painted by cycles of red and blue light from the cop cars.

He walked his bike backward ten yards to hide in the shadows of the trees.

Detective Blue had just exited the back door of the house with a cell phone to her ear. Techs and uniforms moved through his kitchen, his living room. Officer Black stood outside the open barn doors, chatting with another uniformed cop and pointing to something inside. Ben's initial thoughts went to his wife and daughter. *Please tell me they didn't come home.* He removed his phone from his jeans' pocket and fumbled it to the ground. He dropped his bike, rooted through the tall grass, finding his phone wet with dew. During his ride back, he'd missed three calls from Amanda. Another two from a number he realized was Detective Blue, who was calling now, again, as if she somehow knew he was nearby and spying. He waited as his cell phone vibrated and hummed, and then went quiet. He let it go to voice mail, and saw that he had several messages. Two from Amanda. Two from Detective Blue, with another on the way. Instead of listening, he called Amanda back.

She picked up on the first ring. "Ben? Where are you? Where have you been?"

"I was out. Out riding."

"At this time of night?"

"I needed to clear my head. I was trapped inside that house." Only now did he realize that the alcohol he'd consumed throughout the day had worn off; either that or the adrenaline from the past hour had soaked it up like a sponge. "There's police inside our barn. They're in our house, Amanda. Why are they in our house?"

"I . . . I told them to go in. They busted the door. Ben, you weren't answering. They called. They knocked on every window and door. They had a warrant."

"For my arrest?"

"No, a search warrant." By the sound of the breeze waffling through the line, she'd gone outside, probably to her parents' courtyard. "Detective Blue showed me the search warrant."

"In person?"

"No. Through the phone. She sent a pic. I'm not sure if I had to, I don't know all the rules, Ben. But I was worried. About you."

"I'm fine."

"You're not fine. And you've . . ."

"I've what?"

"You've done it before. You tried to kill yourself before."

He closed his eyes, hunkered down in the shadows under the trees and rubbed his temples. "That was years ago. After what happened to Devon. That was *before* we met. It hardly broke the skin, Amanda. You know this."

"But I couldn't get hold of you, Ben. Why didn't you answer your phone?"

"I was riding." *That's not all you were doing* . . . He pinched his inner voice away. "And now the cops are in our house." Silhouettes and shadows moved inside his office. Given time, they'd bust open his desk drawer and find that box mysteriously delivered to his house weeks ago.

"What are they going to find, Ben? Why should this worry you? I let them go in because I assumed we'd have nothing to hide. What are they going to find?"

"Nothing." Ben watched the barn. Two crime scene techs entered, along with Detective Blue and a female African American cop he knew named Maxwell. "Amanda?"

She sniffled. "Yes."

"How did they get a warrant so quickly?"

"You don't know?"

"No. I told you. I've been out—"

"They found another body," she said abruptly. "Inside our barn."

He suddenly felt weak-kneed. He widened his stance for balance. "Our barn?"

"Yes."

"Who is it? An older man? Widower? It's too early. In the book it's not until—"

"I don't know, Ben. But from the tone of Detective Blue's voice, it was bad."

"He's gone off the book." Ben watched techs mark off the barn's perimeter with crime-scene tape. "He's changed course. Amanda, I didn't do this. I need you to believe me."

"At least tell me where you are?"

"You know where I am. You've been tracking my phone since that weekend. We both know it." He almost said *in the woods watching our house*, but balked, with the stupid notion his phone could be bugged. *Watching the cops.* Although he'd lost track of Detective Blue.

"Go to them, Ben. Tell them everything they need to know and put it to rest."

"I can't. Not yet."

She sighed, defeated. "Then run, Ben. Run and look guilty."

"But . . . Amanda . . ."

"What?"

"I found the watch. I think I found Devon."

He waited, heard her crying. And then she hung up. Ben turned his phone off, heard footsteps on deadfall, the snapping of a branch.

Detective Blue stepped from the shadows, her gun drawn.

18

MILLS SQUIRMED IN bed, eyes flicking beneath closed lids.
He was in that room with the glass ceiling, surrounded
by the books with no words. The room with the tree. Hundreds
of moths clung to the bark, wings pulsing, crawling over one
another, up and down the trunk. He'd been there before. As a
kid. Once.

The psychiatrist, Dr. Robert Bookman, had screamed. *Get him
out. Now!*

But he wasn't a boy anymore, and this was not his nightmare.

Seductive laughter drew his attention across the room, to a
college-age brunette kneeling on the sofa in a sky-blue men's shirt,
unbuttoned to mid-chest.

He'd seen her before, several times around town, but didn't
know her.

But Ben Bookman did.

She'd just spoken her name aloud. Ben seemed confused. *That's
not your name,* Ben told the young woman. Her laugh lingered like
an echo.

Ben Bookman sat at a desk, red-eyed and typing, blood coming
from his right nostril.

The young brunette beckoned him with an index finger.

Come closer.

Fingernails painted cherry red, still wet. She teasingly lifted the
bottom of her shirt, revealing soft skin, trimmed pubic hair. She

laughed flirtatiously, let the shirt slide back down around the curve of her rear end.

Is this how you want me, Ben?

She grinned. Bits of red lipstick stained her teeth. She moved seductively from the sofa toward him, one foot in front of the next, as if navigating a balance beam.

Don't fear me.

That's not your voice, he said.

She oozed a fingernail down his arm, leaned in, breathed against his ear, and nibbled the lobe as her fingers unbuttoned his shirt.

I can't, he said.

You can, she answered, on tiptoes, her mouth moving toward his.

Water suddenly gushed from her open mouth, in torrents.

Mills opened his eyes, jerked up against the headboard, heart pounding and hair soaked. He surveyed the bedroom in a panic. The Turtle stood bedside with an empty jug Linda used for lemonade and tea.

"What the fuck?" Mills heaved for breath. His drenched shirt stuck to his chest. Dream catchers swayed from the ceiling. The nightmare had ended like they all do—abruptly. Without warning. To him it had always been more of a rip with time.

A book slammed closed.

A jug of water tossed unexpectedly.

"You were having one big bastard of a nightmare, Winny. I tried nudging you, but you weren't having it."

Mills blinked water from his eyes. "What are you doing here? What time is it?"

"Midnight. We've got some weird shit going on."

Mills smelled semen, felt something cold and sticky on his right upper thigh. Even though the Turtle wouldn't be able to decipher the remnants of a wet dream on his pants from the drenching of water he'd just thrown, Mills felt his face flush warm, and he hoped his old friend's sense of smell was as bad as his hearing.

"You smell something?" asked the Turtle.

"Just your typical reptilian stench." Mills covered himself with a blanket, playing it off like he was drying his wet clothes.

The Turtle raised his right arm and sniffed his shirtsleeve. "Blue's been trying to get hold of you for two hours. Said you might as well retire if you can't learn to answer your phone."

Mills grunted.

The Turtle looked up toward the ceiling and all the dream catchers. "What nonsense do you got going on in here?"

Mills heard words from the Turtle's mouth, but his mind was too preoccupied by the nightmare he'd just had. The voice coming from that young woman. *Roses and lavender.*

Her scent still lingered like a seductive perfume.

Mills stood from the bed with a sheet wrapped around his waistline. "I don't know," Mills said, still discombobulated.

"Maybe you do need to retire."

"Maybe you need to kiss my ass."

"I'd rather not." He checked his watch again.

"You late for a date or something?"

"Yeah," the Turtle said. "Something like that. Get dressed. I'll get some coffee going."

Lured from the nightmare the way he was, the sleeping pills still coursed through his system, and would linger for some time. Mills stumbled from the bed, grabbed the bedpost to right himself.

The Turtle clutched his arm. "Maybe waking you up was a bad idea."

Mills waved it away. "Where we going?"

"To the station. Blue's got Ben Bookman in the Box. She's letting him fester for a few before she starts grilling him. She needs you there."

"She doesn't need me there."

"Okay, wants."

"It's the middle of the night. What did Bookman do?"

"We don't know exactly, but we found a body in his barn. And actually the night's just starting."

Mills stood rigid. "Another cocoon?"

"No. Even more bizarre. I'll explain in the car. Go get ready."

Mills brushed past him, eyed the empty water jug in the Turtle's hand, and mumbled, "Asshole."

"Just hurry up. Oh, and get this. We finished the book. That little girl Miserable Meeks kept alive. Little Baby Jane? She's the reason he ends up getting caught."

"We already knew that."

"But then she gets kidnapped. *After* Detective Mulky guns down the Scarecrow."

"Nice plot twist."

"At the very end of the book. The last line, actually. A cliffhanger. Girl gets taken from the hospital."

Mills immediately thought of the young Peterson girl in the hospital now, the one kept alive to mirror Little Baby Jane. "We need some officers guarding—"

"Way ahead of you, Winny. We have one outside, one at the elevator, and another outside her room. But we're getting spread thin. Givens is talking about help from the feds."

"We don't need the feds," Mills said, remembering the visit earlier in the evening from the Scarecrow. *The stalking.* "I got this contained."

The Turtle nodded down the hallway, toward the bathroom.

Mills took a quick shower, just long enough to rinse off the residue from the nightmare and pry his eyes open. He changed into fresh clothes, but still felt groggy; eyeballs heavy as boulders and lids just as thick. Brewed coffee wafted from the kitchen, and that helped. He grabbed his cell phone from his pants on the floor. He'd missed five messages from Blue, one from Chief Givens, and the one from Officer Black he must have missed earlier. Instead of listening to them, he shot a quick text to Father Frank, and pocketed his phone. He snapped his suspenders on his way into the kitchen—an old habit Linda had found annoying—and the Turtle handed him a cup of coffee.

"Black as a hole and hot enough to do damage."

Mills nodded thanks, and blew into the steam before sipping. The coffee burned a trail down his throat and he welcomed it. He checked his pocket for his amphetamines. He'd need a good dose of those when the coffee wore off.

"You ready?"

"Born that way." He followed the Turtle out the door, into the midnight chill. "You're gonna have to drive, though."

The Turtle's head swiveled. "Figured."

"And run me by the church. I need a quick confession with Father Frank."

"It's midnight, Winny. And Blue's waiting."

"It'll take five minutes. He knows I'm coming."

Before

BEN STOPPED IN *mid-sentence when he heard his wife's voice from the bedroom.*

She was talking to someone, but Bri had gone to sleep an hour ago, and there was no one else in the house. Maybe Bri had had her nightmare and he'd been so engrossed in his book he hadn't noticed. But he didn't think so. He stood from his desk, stepped into the hallway.

"Amanda?"

"Is this how you want me?" she said from the bedroom.

Was she on the phone? His first thought was Dick Bennington, but when he stopped at the threshold to the open bedroom, he found Amanda at her vanity desk. Not on the phone, but scantily clad in black lingerie and hooked stockings, an outfit she'd bought for him as a birthday present years ago but hadn't worn in a while.

"Amanda," he called from the doorway.

She laughed, glanced at him through the mirror, and puckered her lips, luridly moist from the deep red she'd just coated on. But it wasn't Amanda. It was Jennifer, their former nanny. "Amanda's not here anymore, Ben. It's just me and you again." She stood from the chair. "But Amanda says hello. She says you're wrecking her just like you wrecked me, Ben. Her perfect life. And what's left of mine. But that's okay, isn't it?"

She approached on tall, thin-heeled shoes. She giggled.

"Jennifer?"

"Jennifer's gone for now, Ben."

"Julia," he whispered.

She froze. Jennifer's seductive grin melted into a look of confusion, and then panic.

"Ben?" It was Amanda's face again. She looked down at herself, to the lingerie, the painted nails and high heels, and then back to him. "What's going on?" She wobbled. "What did you do inside that room?" The color rushed from her face. "Did you fuck her, Ben?"

That seductive laughter.

Voice lodged in his throat, Ben couldn't answer.

She turned to glass and then shattered into a million pieces, bits of her scattering across the floor like tossed dice.

Ben woke up in bed, panting.

Amanda slept beside him.

CHAPTER

19

B EN HAD OVERHEARD Detective Blue refer to the room as the Box, and it fit.

Cold, sterile walls painted white on three sides, the fourth wall much the same except for the metal door in the middle of it. Probably had hidden windows in here somewhere. Walls disguised as windows. At least that's how he had described Detective Mulky's room in his third book, *Winter Bones,* where Mulky held a man he thought was the killer for an intense interrogation, during which time the real killer struck again and Mulky looked the fool.

This he found convenient to tell Detective Blue in between questions on his alibis. But he could tell she was stalling. "You waiting for your old man?" he asked.

She ignored him, pretended to flip through pages on her notepad.

Truth was, he was stalling too. She'd established he was in town for both sets of murders, and now needed time to think. Homicide techs were still inside his barn, inside his house, going through every room. His stuff. Upon finding him in the woods, they'd confiscated his backpack. How long before she asked him about what he had in there? What he'd found down in the Hollow. They'd allowed him to drive himself to the station for questioning, to avoid speculation from the media swarm. He was a suspect now for something, but they wouldn't say what.

He'd yet to be arrested.

"I want to talk to my wife," Ben said.

"You can, in time," said Detective Blue, without looking up from her notes.

"Where is she? I tried calling her from the car."

"Do you really want to know, Mr. Bookman?"

He nodded, fidgeting with the Styrofoam cup of water they'd given him.

"She's in the room next door. Box number two."

He started to get up, abruptly, but she stood with him, one hand out and one on the gun at her waistline. He sat back down. "What do you want from her?"

"Same as you. Answers." Detective Blue sat back down. "The Petersons, according to the tests, were killed eighteen to nineteen days ago, which puts it late October. Twenty-fifth or twenty-sixth." She referred to her pad of notes. "On October fifteenth you flew to Mobile, Alabama, as the keynote speaker at the annual Fright Night Conference."

"Yes. We've gone over this. Twice."

"And the next week, on the twenty-first, you flew to LA to meet with movie execs about writing the screenplay for *The Scarecrow*."

"And I flew back on the twenty-third. So, yes, I was in town during the times in question. I was in town yesterday when the Reynolds couple was murdered."

"Back to yesterday. Actually, the night *before*, when we believe the Reynolds couple was killed. What were you doing?"

"Writing. Working around the house. Staying out of the spotlight." *Drinking myself into blackouts.* "I told you this. I was playing Monopoly with my daughter. You can ask my—"

"I already did, Mr. Bookman. It checks out. According to your wife, your daughter won."

She always wins. He exhaled, hoped his relief wasn't too obvious. "Where's my daughter? If my wife's in the other room, where's my daughter?"

"Still at your in-laws'."

"Is there protection there?"

"Does there need to be? Is she in any specific danger?"

Ben's eyes bored holes into her.

"Of course we have someone there watching the house, Mr. Bookman. But we're running thin. Both on time and manpower." She scribbled something, looked up. "Monopoly, huh?"

He watched, untrusting. "We like to play, yes."

"You were home the entire night?"

What did Amanda say? She's testing me. "Yes. I was home the entire night."

"Okay," said Detective Blue, reflectively. Amanda must have lied for him.

"What?"

"Nothing. Just that those bike trails through your woods look pretty well trod and trampled. Where'd you go tonight on the bike?"

"Out for a ride."

"This late?"

"Needed to clear my head. Get out of the house." He leaned with both elbows on the table. "What was found in my barn? Or should I say who?"

"Why would you ask that?"

"Why else would homicide be there?"

"So you played Monopoly with your daughter."

"Her name's Bri."

"Your daughter Bri. She won. And you were home the rest of the night?"

He hesitated, just long enough for her to notice. She somehow knew he'd gone out that night. That's why she kept asking. "Okay, fine. I went out for a drive."

"Bike?"

"No. Car. You wouldn't drive a bike."

Half grinning, she said, "What time did you go out for a *ride* that night?" She watched him. He watched her.

He missed his wife, and decided to cooperate so maybe he could see her. "Ten. Ten-thirty. Thereabouts."

"Where?"

"Gas station."

"Ferns?"

"Yes."

She wrote, looked up. "At least that checks out. You're a celebrity, Mr. Bookman. Three people saw you at the gas station that night. Around that time. Any reason why you and your wife both said you were home all night when you weren't? Did you discuss this beforehand?"

"We had a fight. An argument. After Bri went to sleep, I went out to cool my jets." He held up his cup. "Can I have more of this warm water? It's delicious."

Detective Blue looked over her shoulder and made a hand gesture toward the window-wall. A few seconds later, Officer Maxwell, the African American uniform Ben had seen earlier around his taped-off barn, walked in with a bottled water this time.

Detective Blue smiled at Ben. "No upcharge for the sealed bottle."

Ben thanked Officer Maxwell and waited for her to exit before talking again, although she was no doubt now on the other side of that wall listening. "How detailed do you want it?"

"As detailed as you can give it, especially with your reputation on the line."

"I stopped at Ferns for a six-pack of Yuengling, three of which I admit downing while cruising backroads." He held up his hands in a mock defensive gesture. "I returned home as soon as the alcohol started kicking in. I promise."

"And the other three lagers?"

It wasn't the next question he'd anticipated, and it caught him off guard. "I finished the last three beers on the outskirts of our property. Pulled off the road and parked for an hour in the woods. I could see the back of my house from where I was."

"Why? Why didn't you just go home?"

"I felt like sitting there, Detective. On my property. I told you, we'd had a fight."

She wrote something, flipped backward several pages, wrote again.

Ben had parked in that exact spot in the woods one night after a dinner party with Amanda's news crew. Amanda had been tipsy from wine; he'd been the designated driver and had limited himself to one gin and tonic. He'd coaxed Amanda onto his lap, with the car still running and Pink Floyd singing about tearing down a wall. *At least turn the car lights off, Ben. Mom and Dad can probably see us from the house.* He'd reached around her. *Those aren't the lights, Ben.* They'd made love in the driver's seat, uncomfortable but passionate. When they'd finished, she'd fallen asleep on his lap, her arms still clutching him, her face on his shoulder. He'd replayed all of this as he downed those final three beers.

"I finished the beers and returned home," he said. "We continued our argument as if I'd never left."

"And that's why your wife failed to mention that you'd left the house? Because the argument continued, unfettered."

He shrugged. "Look, I wasn't gone that long. There's no way I had time to turn the Reynolds' house into a chop shop. And do what was done to that young couple."

Detective Blue looked up; she had her father's eyes, and a smile that must have come from her mother, because he'd never seen her daddy show one. "Can I ask what you were arguing about? You seemed to have been arguing when we visited earlier today."

He checked his watch. "Yesterday. Technically."

"Mr. Bookman, I know what time it is. And I'm losing my patience."

"So am I."

"You're not the only one missing their family. Chief Givens was two seconds away from getting a warrant for your arrest. Right now I'm the only reason why you haven't been."

"What did you find in my barn?"

"Why were you and your wife arguing?"

"Her reporter friend, Richard Bennington. Sometimes I find him a little too . . . clingy. To my wife. Childhood friends and all. I have suspicions they'd grown a little too close of late."

"Like you and your former babysitter? Jennifer Jackson?"

Ben stood abruptly. "Am I allowed to leave?"

"Yes." She didn't bother standing, and didn't seem bothered by him hovering over her. "But I don't think you want to do that. Not yet. Sit down, Ben."

Whether it was her tone, or using his first name, or the fact that he really had no place to go without being hounded, he sat back down. "What do you know about Jennifer Jackson?"

"Only that we can't find her anywhere. You?" He shook his head. "But not for lack of trying?" She waited, placed her cell phone on the table between them, turned it on, and flipped it around so he could see the headline of *The Story*'s latest tabloid. "This was published online three hours ago." Ben glanced at the headline. *The Nightmare Man's Love Affair with His College Nanny*. "Lame title, I know, but is it true?"

"Look, you know as well as I do that *The Story* is a tabloid that doesn't know fuck-all about anything it prints. If it's ninety-nine percent false—"

"It's a hundred percent true," she finished for him. "I know the saying."

"I might as well have Martians flying out of my ass."

"Do you?"

"What? No." He glanced again at her phone, and the picture beneath the headline. His arm around his former nanny, both drinking cocktails inside the Four-Leaf Clover, a popular Irish bar just outside Crooked Tree. It was taken over a year and a half ago, on the night of Jennifer's twenty-first birthday. The picture—*where had the reporter gotten it?*—had been cropped in a way that showed only the two of them laughing, with no glimpse of Amanda on the other side of him. The waiter had taken it with Jennifer's phone. "It's bullshit and you know it."

"Why would I know it? I don't really know you."

"Everyone thinks they do. Because they read my books. Most of my protagonists turn out to be shitheads, so I'm one too. Is that it? I'm the unreliable narrator?"

"Well, are you?"

He chugged from his water bottle, and then remembered the flask in his jacket pocket. He pulled it out next. The flask felt better in his hand than the flimsy plastic bottle. "You mind?"

"Knock yourself out." She probably hoped it would loosen his tongue. Maybe it would. He'd take his chances. She said, "Article says you two have been lovers since you spent that weekend at Blackwood a year ago."

"It's wrong. I haven't even seen her in months. I don't know . . ."

"You don't know what?"

He sipped Old Sam from the flask. "I don't know what happened that weekend."

"The same weekend you wrote *The Scarecrow?*"

"Much of it's a blur." He rubbed his forehead, looked up, tired-eyed, and nodded toward her phone. The screen was growing black. She tapped it to refresh the article. "Was it him who wrote it? That son of a bitch outside my house?"

"That son of a bitch you threatened to kill while the cameras were running?"

He smiled. "Is that what this is about?"

"His name was Trevor Golappus."

"He must have written it inside his damn car."

"He probably did. I counted three typos. He left. And then *you* left." She sat back in her seat, smiling proudly, arms folded. "You want to ask me again who we found inside your barn?"

His voice quivered. "Who?"

"Trevor Golappus. Twenty-four years old. Dead. Hours after you threatened to kill him."

He leaned back so quickly the chair almost buckled. "This is bullshit. Someone's out to get me. Someone was listening out on the street. Somebody—"

"*Everyone* was listening, Mr. Bookman. That video was at two million views by midnight. Of course someone heard it. But there was only one person who threatened to do it."

"I've never harmed anyone." He leaned back toward the table, pounded it with a clenched fist. "I'm a lot of things, Detective Blue, but I'm not a killer."

She leaned in too, close enough for the two of them to arm wrestle should she get the urge. "Are you ready to start helping us then?"

"Tell me what you want to know. I can tell you don't give two shits about some rumored affair."

"Why did you not tell us about the twins being the first murders in the book?"

"I wasn't thinking clearly. I should have, but I didn't. I was pissed. And for that I'm sorry. Have you found all the twins in town?"

"All accounted for," she said. "Over the phone, at least. We have someone now knocking on doors to double check."

"Because you can't always assume parents are telling the truth?"

"I've been doing this long enough to know too many parents are shitheads."

"How was that reporter found in my barn? Was it like the others?"

"No."

"No cocoon?"

"No cocoon."

"Then how was he found?" he asked. She sat stoic. A vault. "You aren't going to tell me? You ask for my help, and—"

"No. At this point in the investigation, Mr. Bookman, I am not going to tell you."

"But you don't think it was me? Otherwise you'd have me in cuffs, right?"

She shrugged, checked her phone, and flipped to another page. "We got into your computer. Can you tell me about your current book? *The Screamer*?"

"Why do you keep checking your phone? Why isn't your dad here?"

"Your current work in progress, Mr. Bookman? What's funny?"

"Nothing. Just that most nonwriters don't use that term. Work in progress."

She raised her eyebrows, which was her way of asking him again.

"We off the record, here?"

"I'm not a reporter," she said.

"What do you want to know?"

"I know Little Baby Jane was kidnapped from the hospital at the end of *The Scarecrow*. And because of that, we have security at our hospital here guarding Amy Peterson. Am I to assume, in the book, it was the Screamer who took Little Baby Jane? And the book you're working on finally brings the decade of missing Riverdale children to fruition?"

"Yes. That's the crux of it."

"Mr. Bookman, I'm going to be honest. You're still a suspect. In all of this. We know your brother Devon went missing thirteen years ago. And we know Crooked Tree has another dozen children gone missing over the past decade. Is there something else we should know about?"

"I . . . I don't know. I don't really know myself what all's going on."

"Where did you go tonight on your bike?"

"I told you. Just out for a ride."

"We found a bone in your backpack. Forensics has it now, but upon first glance it looks to be human. Possibly part of a leg. Where did you find it? And are there more?"

"I found it in the woods."

"Where?"

"I don't know. Miles from here."

"Could you find it again?"

"Maybe. In daylight." She studied him. He studied her. "What?"

"Do you remember the last line you wrote today? On your current novel?"

He swallowed hard, looked away, back again. The line he'd written and deleted a handful of times. He must have neglected to delete it the final time, or maybe he'd thought it better to leave it in. He took another drink from his flask, hated himself for not only wanting but needing it. "Refresh my memory. It's been a long day."

"Detective Mulky's little girl gets kidnapped. Ring a bell?"

"Yes. It's a plot twist. No one will see it coming."

"Is Detective Mulky, by chance, patterned after my father? And as *his* little girl, should I be worried about my life?"

"In your line of work, there wouldn't be a day goes by I wouldn't be worried. That's why you carry a gun." He mimicked typing on a keyboard. "I use my fingers. I'm not brave like you."

"Are you trying to flatter me?"

"No."

Her cell phone buzzed on the table with an incoming call. She looked annoyed; he couldn't tell if it was at him or the call, or maybe both, because it apparently wasn't the call she was expecting. She answered it with a look toward Ben that said, *give me a minute.* And then her eyes went large. "How old are the twins?"

Ben sat rigid in the chair, heard a woman's voice on the other end of the line say, "Teenagers. Fifteen, I think. Jeremy and Joshua Blakely."

Detective Blue stood from the table, half turned her back to Ben so that he couldn't so easily hear. She hung up a minute later, faced Ben. "We're going to have to continue this later."

"Who was that? What's going on?" Ben stood. "They found a set of twins?"

Before she could answer, the door opened and Chief Givens ducked under the threshold with Officer Maxwell in tow. Maxwell unlatched handcuffs from her waistline, whispered something into Detective Blue's ear that gave her face a sudden jolt, and then the detective nodded toward Ben.

Ben stepped away from the table with his hands up. "Wait . . . What's going on?"

Officer Maxwell said, "You have the right to remain silent, Mr. Bookman . . ."

"What is this?

You know what it is, Ben. They got into the box. They found the key on the bookshelf, opened the desk drawer, and got into the box.

20

A s THEY WALKED down the center aisle of St. Helen's Catholic Church, Father Frank reminded Detective Mills it was no longer necessary to use the old confessional.

"Nobody uses that old stuffy box anymore, Winny." Father shuffled along, used the end of each pew as a crutch. "Nowadays most prefer face-to-face. A conversation rather than a confession."

Mills had known Father too long and refused to see his face when sins were confessed. It mattered little to Father Frank—although the old white-haired priest hadn't fully given up hope—that Mills didn't attend church, and hadn't in quite some time. Not since the days, as a boy in parochial school, when Sister Rita would pull his ears and thump his knuckles with that ruler. It also mattered little, to Mills at least, that he didn't even believe in God, as the Turtle reminded him a few minutes ago in the parking lot.

But Mills did believe in the power of the confessional. The old wooden box was murder on the lower back, but he believed the hard-angled, Spartan-like bareness of it was part of his penance. An ornately carved partition with a square grated window separated himself from the priest. Mills leaned toward it. "I won't take much of your time, Father."

"Take as much as you need, Winny. You already woke me up. What's troubling you?"

"I cheated on my wife."

"Linda?"

"I didn't have another one."

"She's dead."

"Really, Father? I hadn't noticed."

Father sighed, probably right now rubbing his temples behind that partition because too many of these confessions had become mundane and old hat. "Who was the other woman? Or is it none of my business?"

"That's the thing. Now that I think on it, I don't think it counts."

"Counts as what?"

"Cheating."

"Tell me what happened?"

"I think I lusted after another woman. In my dreams. Just about an hour ago."

"Go on."

"I don't think you're taking this seriously, Father."

"I'm not."

"I wouldn't be here in the middle of the night if this wasn't building to some crescendo. I hadn't been able to get it up for years. But last night, in my dreams, I must have. You know what I'm saying?"

"I think so. But I don't see this as a sin. Or even anything remotely close to some of the things you've confessed in the past, Winny."

Mills intertwined his thick fingers. He'd figured as much, but it was good to hear. "I still play Uno every night. With Linda. I've got her place set up at the kitchen table and I deal out two hands. I keep a tally of who wins. She wins more than you'd think. We'd pretend those pretzel rods were cigars. I can't bring myself to go that far, though, you know?"

"Because pretzel rods are sacred?"

"Maybe I should go."

"Sit, Winny." On the other side of the partition, Father Frank's wooden bench creaked, which meant he was uncomfortable and shifting. "How are you doing? Are you sleeping?"

"No. Not in a way that would be considered normal."

"Because you can't or don't want to?"

"Little bit of both. I need pills to stay awake and pills to put me to sleep, and I'm not so sure they make the best dancing partners."

"I recall telling you that's probably not the best idea."

"Sometimes I think I flirt with death."

"Do you want to die, Winny?"

"Maybe not die, but perhaps have my role in this life be over."

"And how is your relationship with Samantha?"

"Tenuous."

"And your grandchildren?"

"At the moment, she won't let me see them."

"Why not?"

"We were good for a while. Then I hurt one of them. By accident."

"Were you drinking?"

"No. Still sober. But the boy was about ready to get burned on the stove. I gripped him too hard and put a bruise on his arm. Sent him off crying."

"I see. Our past is a sticky shadow sometimes."

"That it is. I guess I don't always know my own strength."

"And your temper?"

"I'm trying. But it's hard with the lack of sleep? Stress of the job . . ."

"And the nightmares." He hadn't phrased it as a question. Like it was a given Mills was still plagued by them. "You're still having them every night?"

"Every time I sleep. Which isn't every night. Sometimes I go several without sleeping."

"Because you're scared, Winny?"

"Yes."

"But also brave."

"I suppose."

"The bravest person I've ever known. Most in your condition would be in an asylum."

Mills swallowed. His throat was dry and his eyes felt heavy. The confessional box was stuffy, but the tight confines of it relaxed him like a womb would.

"And the severity of the nightmares? Winny?"

The priest's Peter O'Toole voice brought him back. "Yes."

"The severity? Still getting worse?"

"Yes. Like when I was a boy. When I moved here to see Dr. Bookman." The deceased psychiatrist's name gave them both pause. "I remember something. I must have blocked it out for years. But I was in that room. As a boy, Dr. Bookman took me into that room."

"What room are we talking about? His office downtown?"

"No, Father. To Blackwood. We went to his office a handful of times. But he told my mother he'd never seen anyone with nightmares so strong. So life-changing. He asked if he could take me to

Blackwood. For an experiment. We were desperate. He took me in that room."

"What room?"

Mills leaned close to the partition's window, lowered his voice in case anyone on the outside could hear. "I can't say."

"Can't or won't?"

"Won't." Mills rubbed his temples, tried to organize his thoughts. "Have you been following these murders? The Scarecrow? I think it all has something to do with that room."

"The room you won't talk about."

"There's more. The main reason I'm here. We've talked before about folklore. About mares. My sleep paralysis. Spirits riding on people's chests and giving them nightmares . . ."

"Yes, Winny, we've gone over this. It's your mind playing—"

"Do you believe in possession?"

After a pause, the priest asked, "Why?"

"Do you?"

Another pause. "Yes."

"Have you ever, you know, done one? An exorcism?" He knocked on the partition. "Father, you still in there?"

"Yes."

"Have you—"

"Yes, Winny," Father Frank hissed, like he was the one now confessing. Sometimes their confessions went from jovial to serious in a blink.

"Can you tell me about it?"

"No. I cannot."

"Is it like an attorney and client thing?"

"No. It's . . ."

"It's important, Father."

"Why?"

"I don't know." He rubbed his face, closed his eyes hard. "I don't even know what I'm talking about. It's all confusing. But . . ." He thought back to the snippet of Ben Bookman's nightmare, the seductive young woman on the couch, and went for it. "You ever heard of someone called Julia? Father?"

"Why?"

"Have you?"

"Yes. But I ask again, why?"

"I don't know all the way. Just trying to connect some dots. Her name came up recently."

"How?"

"Like I said, I don't really know exactly why she's important. Only that she might be." On the way to the church, the Turtle had showed Mills the article about Ben and the Bookmans' nanny that had just been published hours ago in the digital tabloid newspaper *The Story*. Mills immediately tagged the nanny as the young brunette he'd just seen in Ben Bookman's nightmare. The one who called herself Julia. "What about Jennifer Jackson?" Mills immediately regretted the question; it was silly to think the old priest would know her, but since Julia had lured a reaction from him, he thought maybe Jennifer would too. "Father?" Mills waited for the shifting on the other side of the partition to settle. "Father? You okay?"

"Yes, Winny. Are we finished here?"

"Did that name ring a bell? It did, didn't it? Father?"

"I cannot talk about certain things."

"But you know something?"

"Winny, as usual, I'll continue to pray for you."

"But Father, I think this all ties into the Scarecrow. This is—"

The partition shook as if it had taken a blow from a fist. "I will continue to pray for you."

Mills let the dust settle. "You've been praying for me for a long time, Father. Since I was a boy."

"As I don't know, at this point in our lives, Winny, what else to do."

"So this is my burden alone?"

"Not alone. You know that. Come to me, all of you who are weary and burdened, and I will give you rest."

Mills nodded; he'd heard it before.

Maybe one day he'd believe it.

The Turtle waited for Mills in the church parking lot, car idling under a rimless basketball goal, thumbing the steering wheel like he was still annoyed they'd made this stop at all.

Mills got inside, slammed the door.

"Feel better?"

"No. Drive."

"This is why I'm agnostic." The Turtle pulled out of the lot, heading for the station.

Mills felt his cell phone vibrate in his pocket. It was Blue. "Yes."

"Finally. Jesus. Where have you been?"

"I was sleeping. I'm on my way."

"You're taking a detour. I just had Ben Bookman arrested. He's not going anywhere."

"On what grounds?"

"From what we found inside his office, take your pick, but right now we got a tip from a neighbor on a possible twin situation. One one two five East Rochester."

The Turtle must have had his hearing aid turned up, because he changed direction abruptly and headed south toward Rochester without being told.

"Be there in five. What do we have?"

"Set of sixteen-year-old twins. Jeremy and Joshua Blakely." Blue sounded as if she'd just gotten in her car. "Elderly neighbor read the book and started playing detective. Long story short, she hadn't seen her neighbor's boys in several weeks, when typically they spent their evenings throwing football or baseball in the street."

"Did we not already contact the parents?"

"We did. On the phone. Royal Blakely, the father, said his twins were fine. Local electrician with a side business cleaning gutters. He sounded hurried, though. Awkward. So we sent officers out. Got no word when we knocked on the Blakelys' door, but this was when the neighbor saw out her living room window that we'd been there. And that's what got her to thinking. She eventually told us she hadn't seen the twins' mother in a while either."

"I don't like the sound of this." Mills eyed the dark streets as the Turtle flicked on the car's light bar and increased his speed on the straightaway.

"Well, I just woke up the boys' principal at Crooked Tree High, and Jeremy and Joshua hadn't been to school in five weeks."

"Five weeks? Why the fuck wasn't this reported."

"Because Royal, their father, when the principal called, had an easy explanation. He and his wife had a fight. Brandy Blakely filed for divorce, and up and took the boys with her back to Iowa. Said Royal even broke down crying on the phone."

"Any luck tracking down the wife?"

"None. Brandy Blakely grew up Brandy Stipes. She was in the system. Bounced around from foster home to foster home. But never once lived in Iowa."

Before

"MRS. BOOKMAN, CAN I ask you a few more questions about your son?"

"Devon's dead, isn't he, Detective?"

Before Mills could gather the nerve to concur, that yes, he assumed by now that Devon was dead, she answered her own question.

"I can see it in your eyes. You think he's dead." Christine Bookman puffed on a cigarette and exhaled out the side of her mouth. Red lipstick stained the butt. Who took the time to put on lipstick when their baby boy was two days missing? "And you're still coming around asking questions because that's just what detectives do. And call me Christine. Mrs. Bookman just sounds too blah, and formal. Don't you think?"

"Okay, ma'am."

"You have spectacular eyes, Detective Blue."

"Thank you, but I'm Mills. Detective Mills, ma'am. Detective Willard Blue is my partner."

She seemed to ignore this as she homed in on his eyes. "They're so blue, and lurid. Like paint yet to dry." She shifted in the doorway, studying him like he was actually something to look at. She wore a yellow cotton bathrobe that ended at the knees, and no shoes. Upon first glance, she wore nothing underneath. The cotton belt at the waistline wasn't secured as tightly as it should be, revealing curves and flesh no *stranger should see. She inhaled on the cigarette, exhaled a plume of smoke—politely away from Mills—and opened the front door wide enough for him to step through. But not so wide that he couldn't smell her perfume, or whatever bath scents she must have just drowned herself in before coming to the door. "Please. Come in."*

He stepped inside the foyer, atop the ten-foot-square mosaic floor Willard couldn't stop talking about back at the station: "Who orders a floor done like that, Winny?"

Christine caught him staring down at it. "It was Bernard's favorite painting. An oil on canvas called The Nightmare. *Painted in seventeen eighty-one by an artist named Henry Fuseli." She squatted to the floor, rested a bare knee on the tiles. The bathrobe slipped, showed clear thigh up to the hip.*

"Bernard?" he asked, eyeing the thousands of tiles needed to complete the image.

She ran the hand not holding the cigarette over the mosaic floor. "Bernard Bookman. It was he who built this house. Late eighteen hundreds. Like Robert, he worked with children. And their nightmares. First of the line, I guess you can say."

The mosaic showed a woman deep in sleep, her arms draped over her head. A demonic incubus sat crouched atop her chest, and in the background, a horse head watched from the shadows. The perfect blend of horror and sensuality. She pointed. "Mare-rides. Hints of intercourse with the devil. It's brilliantly done, don't you think?"

He studied it, nodded in agreement.

"The paleness of her skin and nightgown contrast so powerfully with the darker reds and ochres of the background." Christine paused, and then to his astonishment, lay down directly atop the sleeping woman portrayed on the floor, mimicking her exact position. She closed her eyes, play-acting, pretending to sleep, and then just as suddenly rolled upright again. The sudden movement exposed more of what was beneath her loosening robe. He recalled what Willard had said back at the station.

"She's bizarre. Probably on ten kinds of drugs, Winny. I'd bet my life on it." Which was why he'd urged Mills to go it alone on this hunch about those terrible sketches.

Christine placed a loose strand of her strawberry blonde hair behind her ear and pointed again at the floor. "You see the strong contrast between light and shadow. It's called the chiaroscuro effect. Bernard had this floor commissioned for his wife Lena, after she died from consumption. I've seen pictures of Lena. I can show you. It's amazing how strongly she resembles the woman in this mosaic."

"That's okay, Mrs. Bookman. I need to get going soon, so if we can—"

"On a business trip to Italy, one where Bernard went to help two desperate children plagued by nightmares, female twins in a small coastal village outside Grosseto." She paused, tied the waistband of her robe as if suddenly modest. "On his way through Tuscany, he interviewed five reputable mosaic artisans for the job at Blackwood. He picked a nervous little craftsman from Florence named Niccolo Tribiolto."

Mills wanted to get down to business, but she continued reciting details, as if doing a presentation on the history of the mosaic. "The artist arrived by ship the following month. He worked tirelessly, and at first progressed quickly, but as the months moved on, his pace became lethargic. His work was brilliant, but taking too long. The housekeepers would often find Niccolo sitting atop the unfinished mosaic floor, staring, as if in a trance, down the hallway toward the atrium, listening to the birds and moths. Do you know of the room, detective?"

"I've seen the room, yes."

"Near the end of the project, in the middle of the night, Bernard found the young artist standing outside the atrium, staring through the glass. Bernard walked him back to the mosaic, begged him to finish, and before going to bed, warned the Florentine to never go inside that room. The next morning, Bernard found the floor finished. But young Niccolo had fallen asleep upon completing it, right atop the tiles. Bernard nudged the young artist, realizing the man was dead."

Mills looked up from the mosaic. "Cause?"

Christine Bookman shrugged, folded her arms. "Officially undetermined. You know the doctors back then. Guessing was sometimes the norm. But Bernard wrote in his journal that he may have died of fright. Could you imagine?"

Michael Bookman, Christine's husband and the missing boy's father, appeared in the hallway, exiting the kitchen, holding in both hands a bowl of cereal. He ate as he shuffled, never acknowledging Mills' presence at the door, before disappearing into another room.

"My husband is mentally ill." She stood on her tiptoes and whispered into his ear. "He's a grown man and still has nightmares." Her lips lingered next to his ear, long enough he feared she might kiss him.

She backed down. "I never loved him. That lip might have been fixed as a boy, and those fingers, but he still looks like a creature."

"Mrs. Bookman, please, I'd like to ask some questions and then I'll be on my way. About your oldest son, Ben."

This startled her. "Benjamin? What about him?"

"I found some sketches in his drawer the other day that have me troubled."

21

ASIDE FROM THEM taking his cell phone, that last physical connection to the world outside the vertical bars of his cold new jail cell, courtesy of Detective Blue and the police station's finest basement jailhouse, Ben, for the moment, welcomed the isolation those three adjacent cells provided.

The other two cells stood empty. The quiet allowed him time to think.

They'd no doubt found what he'd kept hidden inside that wooden box locked in his desk drawer, and they'd come to the wrong conclusions. But at least the arrest had been done in the secrecy of the police station. As far as the press knew, he was still here for questioning.

He'd gone in around midnight, and it was three in the morning now.

Before long they'd begin to wonder why he was still inside.

For the first thirty minutes, he'd tried to make small talk with the guard, but the officer wasn't having it. Ben paced the tight confines of his cell. He sat on his cot, reached for his pockets, for a phone and a flask that were no longer there. Boredom and nerves sent him pacing again. After twenty minutes, he sat on the cot, stretched out on the hard springs. The pillow was flat and smelled of mildew, but when he closed his eyes, sleep actually seemed possible.

Before he could drift off, a door clapped open. He sat up in a hurry. Someone was coming down. A woman, by the sound of the footfalls on the stairs. He moved to the bars, hoped for it to be Amanda. She'd forgiven him for everything and was here to make things right. But it wasn't. The woman who emerged from the shadows and nodded to the guarding officer after he'd told her *ten minutes* wasn't seven months pregnant. But she did have three kids of her own in New York, and was starting to resemble their dead mother.

"Emily?"

His sister emerged from the shadows, stopped on the opposite side of the bars. It was the middle of the night and Emily was done up in a beige business suit, dressed as if she were about to meet her next psychiatric patient. Her face was long, pretty, and so much like their mother's that he did a double take.

"Ben, what did you do?"

"Em . . . I don't know." Instantly, he feared for her; unlike Bri and Amanda, the history of Blackwood directly involved her. "Go back home. You shouldn't have come." As soon as her hand touched his own between the bars, he knew he hadn't meant it. As much as he'd tormented her with pranks and scared her with stories growing up, she'd always been the safety valve when shit got real—when Grandma Jane died from cancer, when Grandpa Robert passed at Oswald Asylum, and to talk sense into him in the days after their parents ran off the road and died in the car crash. "I told you I was fine."

She wiped tears from his cheeks. "That's why I came. Fine for you, Ben, has always been a call for help. A red flag when there's no shame in waving the white." In a slow-motion collapse, Ben slid lower toward the floor and she followed him, mirroring him on the other side of the bars. "You don't always have to be tough, Ben."

He felt her hand on his hair, on the side of his face, and for the first time since Devon went missing thirteen years ago, Ben sobbed.

Emily shushed him, held him, told him now, as she did repeatedly back then, "Ben, it wasn't your fault."

CHAPTER

22

ADRENALINE HAD JOLTED any remnants of the sleeping pills from his system.

Before Mills stepped from the Turtle's sedan, forty yards down from Royal Blakely's property, he'd already seen a picture of the man they were about to confront. It was from a DUI three years prior, the only mark they could find on Royal's record. He was built like an offensive lineman, six foot four, three hundred pounds of country boy fat and gristle. Mills had immediately recognized the man as the electrician who'd come to his house eight months ago to replace the ceiling fan above the kitchen table. He'd been polite, calling Linda *ma'am* more than once. If Royal was their guy, it made sense now that Mills may have seen glimpses of his nightmarish mind and those cocoons before stepping into the Petersons' barn weeks ago. They'd been close together inside the kitchen. Come to think of it, Mills may have even shaken Royal's hand after he'd handed him the check. Either way, a brush-up had most likely occurred. According to Blue, who'd already spoken to Royal Blakely's boss at Gus Mitchell Electric, they'd let him go two months earlier. Royal had been one of their more loyal electricians until he'd suddenly gone off the deep end a year ago. Started off with small things. Forgetting a tool here and there. Then it progressed to botching jobs and eventually just not showing up. Royal wasn't much of a talker, but admitted to his boss that his wife had moved out a couple months ago and took the twin boys with her to Iowa.

Another lie. Or the same lie to more than one person.

Alongside Detective Blue and Officer Maxwell, Mills closed in on Blakely's house. Their footfalls penetrated an otherwise quiet night. Maxwell veered off behind a cluster of trees toward the rear of the house. Royal's truck was parked in the driveway. Two of the four rims were missing. The truck bed was full of trash, not in bags, but thrown in loose. Looked to be living off McDonald's and Wendy's. Blue winced as she passed. Mills breathed it in like it was a dose of potpourri, but cringed when he caught a whiff of human excrement. Soiled diapers were visible inside the heap. Adult diapers by the size of them.

"You coming?"

Mills hadn't realized he'd stopped moving. He followed Sam to the front door. She shooed a moth from the knob, opened the screen, and knocked on the wooden door. She gave it a few seconds, knocked again, harder this time.

Officer Maxwell's voice sounded through a radio Blue had somewhere on her body. "I see movement. Living room," Maxwell said, through static. "Good Lord, he's a hulk."

"Is he coming to the front door?" Blue asked.

Maxwell said, "He was, but then he stopped. He's pacing. Animated. Talking to himself, it looks like. Unless there's someone else in the room I can't see. There's sheets over the windows, though, not curtains. Seems to be multiple ropes strung across the room. Like clotheslines. He's moving again. Toward the front door."

Mills stepped in front of Sam as a bolt unlatched and the knob turned.

Royal opened it wide enough for his face to show. Big brown eyes gazed down beneath bushy eyebrows. His long hair was uncombed, a series of dark crow's nests and a wild beard in need of trimming. Charles Manson came to mind, and somewhere behind all the crazy was the same man who'd repaired their ceiling fan and called them sir and ma'am.

"Royal Blakely," said Mills. "I know it's late, but we need to ask you a few questions."

Royal closed his eyes, contorted his neck like he was trying to pop the kinks out, and then spoke in a deep voice. "I gotta go." He sniffled, nervous. "Dinner's on the stove."

He started to close the door, but Mills wedged his foot in there. "Can we talk to your twin boys, please? Jeremy and Joshua?"

He shook his head slowly. "They moved."

"Where?"

"Nebraska."

"We heard Iowa."

"Same difference."

"No, not really."

"Mother took'm." Royal sniffled again. "Dinner's on the stove."

"Can we come inside for a minute?" Blue tried to see around his massive frame. Rancid stench emanated from the house behind him, something decayed and foul.

Royal made as if to close the door, but Mills' foot still blocked it. Unable to look Mills in the eyes, Royal said, "I'm sorry."

"You're sorry?" asked Mills. "For what?"

"I kept her fed. I tried to keep her fed. Dinner's on the stove." He shook his head like he was trying to uncross some tangled wires. "But you took too long."

Blue stepped closer. "Mr. Blakely, you tried to keep who fed?"

"I gotta go. It's almost harvest time."

That did it. Mills glanced toward the floor, toward Royal's mud-stained boots, every bit of fourteen to fifteen inches. He'd been working, about to go out, or had just returned from somewhere. *Son of a bitch.* "It's him."

Maxwell's voice crackled over the radio. "Jesus Christ, he's got an axe. Behind his back, Mills, he's holding an axe."

Royal pushed Mills back far enough to get the door closed.

"I'm going in," Maxwell screamed. A window shattered.

Mills plowed his shoulder into the door, jarring it, realizing then that Royal hadn't locked it. Blue turned the knob, pushed the door open. Royal had disappeared. Rope festooned the front hallway in crisscrossing patterns from wall to wall, like Maxwell had described of what she'd seen in the living room.

But it wasn't clothes on those lines.

Mills touched what hung from them, rubbed it gently between thumb and index finger. "Corn husks."

Blue had already ducked under the dried, hanging husks. Garth Brooks sang in the background, from behind a closed door off the hallway.

I tried to keep her fed. But you took too long.

"Don't move," Officer Maxwell shouted from an adjacent room to their left, a room Blue had just entered too hastily. "Drop the axe and put your hands in the air."

Blue joined in. "Drop it. Now. No . . . no. Drop it. You take one more step and I'll put one through your heart."

"Temper, Blue," Mills whispered, ducking under the last strand of husks hanging across the hallway. Something heavy clunked against hardwood. The axe, Mills assumed, had just dropped to the floor.

Officer Maxwell said, "Now put your hands in the air. Both of them."

Mills stepped into the living room as the two women approached Royal Blakely, who stood with both hands in the air, head tilted down, chin to chest. Mills couldn't see his lips through all the untrimmed beard hair, but Blakely was mumbling, "Scarecrows scare. That's what they do. Scarecrows scare . . ."

The windows had been blacked out by bed sheets. The sofa and recliner had been stacked in the far corner, out of the way, so that he could work throughout the room. At least a dozen ropes had been hung like the entrance hall, from wall to wall, from fireplace to kitchen, where another had been tied from the kitchen faucet to the oven's door handle. Dried corn husks hung everywhere, like old, stiff clothes, all in various stages of evolution from sewn, stitched, and dried. The smell of urine and feces was thick in the air. Garbage littered the floor. He'd been living like an animal.

Blue and Maxwell got Blakely to his knees, and were cuffing his hands behind his back when Mills approached. Blakely looked up, as if truly seeing Mills for the first time, and then crab-walked back toward the wall. Terrified. Maxwell and Blue fumbled with his arms, but managed to contain and cuff him—but only, Mills noticed, because Royal had allowed it. They stood back, panting, both appearing surprised it hadn't been harder. Like he'd finally given up and wanted to be caught.

His eyes avoided Mills. "The ears were robust," he said. "The silks, dark brown and slick to the touch . . ."

"What's he saying?" Maxwell asked.

Blue said, "He's reciting lines from Bookman's novel."

Mills' attention drifted to the desk across the room. The old school typewriter on it, the white page tucked in and curled. He blew dust from the keys, cobwebs from the carriage. He turned the knob on the old, black machine, eased the page out, and read what had been typed, the same words, the same name over and over and not stopping until three-quarters down on the page: *Jepson Heap. Jepson Heap. Jepson Heap . . .*

"You stole my nightmare, Ben Bookman," Mills whispered to himself, recalling Jepson Heap's last words inside the bookstore.

A leather journal rested on a pile of crinkled corn husks, stacked there like fabric swatches. Unlike the dusty typewriter, the journal looked recently used. Mills flipped through, stopped on yesterday's date.

The words *Detective Winchester Mills* had been written diagonally across the page. His heart backfired like the old Model T it was, and sweat broke out across his forehead. He flipped backward, through pages of insanity—pictures of cocoons, bloody body parts, axes, sharp tools. The more Mills turned the pages, the more violently his hands shook. Dates that coincided with the previous murders showed stick figure drawings of the entire Peterson family. Above the smallest girl he'd written, *Amy Peterson*, and below, *Little Baby Jane*, connecting Bookman's novel to the real-life counterpart. And in parentheses, *Keep Alive!* The stick renditions of Mom and Dad Peterson were marked by exaggerated circles as breasts and a phallus way too large for the man's body. Underneath he'd written: *Ha.*

Had Blakely done more to their bodies than cut them up? More than what was in the book?

Mills fought the urge to turn around and fill Royal Blakely with holes. He turned back another page in the journal, found sketches of the Petersons' barn, outside and in, down to the details of the ceiling beams from which those bodies had ultimately been hung. He turned forward several pages, found the stick figures of the Reynolds couple holding stick hands. The wife, pregnant with an exaggerated unborn fetus in her womb. Beside it, Royal had written: *Oops!* Mills grew short of breath. His left arm felt numb, tingly. The urge to vomit came without warning, and he let loose on the floor next to the desk, the splatter landing a few feet away from the mask Royal must have been using as the Scarecrow. Not a mask that fully cloaked his head, but rather one—from the thread and stitching on the outlining of it—that he'd been literally sewing onto his own face. He dropped to a knee. He glanced across the room at Royal and noticed the red scars and cuts and scabs, both fresh and new, around the outside of his face, in and out of the hairline.

"Dad?" Blue was beside him now. He clutched her pant leg.

Stench wafted in from the entrance hallway, the closed basement door. Light glowed around the door frame. Garth Brooks had switched to anther song, "If Tomorrow Never Comes." One of Linda's favorites. Now it was tainted. "Dad?"

Mills wiped his mouth on his shirtsleeve and stood, weak-kneed. "Help me up."

"You're pale as a ghost. Your heart?"

He shook his head no, even though he knew it was. He sucked in a breath, reiterated he was okay. He handed her the closed journal, but their gazes remained on the basement door.

"I didn't want to do it," said Royal, from his knees across the room.

Maxwell aimed her pistol at Royal's head. Her eyes ping-ponged back and forth from Mills to their prisoner, waiting for an order for what next.

Blue opened the journal. Mills watched over her shoulder.

The first page, like the page in the typewriter, was full of Jepson Heap's name, scrawled every which way and even backward, on the lines and in the margins.

Like a little kid, doodling.

The next few pages showed the origin and designs of what would become his scarecrow costume. Sketches of cornstalks and renditions of how they could be sewn together. Pages upon pages of cocoons, trials and errors and scratch-outs, like an architect before finding the perfect one. Another page showed Jepson Heap's address, a sketch of his farmhouse—both circled in dark ink—and a crude stick drawing of Jepson and his plump wife, Trudy. *Just put a fright into him, Royal.*

Blue fanned forward a few dozen pages, stopped on one marked two months ago. More stick figures. A man, a woman, and two boys. He'd written *ME* above the man, and below, *Miserable Meeks*. Above the woman he'd written *Brandy*, and below, *Keep Alive*. Above the two sons had been written, *Jeremy and Joshua*, and the names of the fictional twins, *Murphy and Thomas Pope*, from Bookman's novel.

"Christ on a cross," muttered Mills, turning his head to watch Royal whimper something undecipherable. "He killed his family. The son of a bitch killed his wife and kids."

Blue had already begun to make her way toward the hallway.

I tried to keep her alive . . .

Maxwell watched them both. "What's going on? Mills? Blue? What's in that journal?"

Blue radioed for the Turtle.

Mills told Maxwell, "If he so much as sneezes, shoot him."

And then he closed in on the basement door.

Before

"D*ADDY?*"

    "Yes, Bri?"

"If moths don't like light, why do they always fly toward light bulbs?"

"Well . . . before we had electricity, moths would use the moon to navigate. And they still do. The artificial light confuses them. They go round and round in circles."

"Like maniacs?"

"Yeah, like little winged maniacs."

"And that's why they don't come out during the day? Because they don't like the light?"

"Correct. They hate the light."

"Makes sense then."

"What does?"

"Nothing."

23

B<small>Y THE TIME</small> Ben composed himself, the ten minutes with his sister was almost up.

Emily reached in between the bars, lifted Ben's chin so their eyes met. "What can I do? And don't tell me to go home."

"Trust everything I tell you. No matter how crazy it sounds."

"Ben, I'm here. Okay? No matter what."

He put his mouth next to the bars to get closer to her ear. "There's a box I kept locked inside my desk at home. I know they've arrested me because of what's in it."

"What's in the box, Ben?"

"Devon's other shoe."

"Other shoe? What are you talking about?" It must have dawned on her then; her eyes grew large and she covered her mouth with a hand.

He nodded. "When Devon went missing."

"They only found one of his shoes in the woods. The left one."

"A few weeks ago a package arrived at my door," Ben said. "With no mailing address. No return address. Inside was Devon's missing right shoe." He gave her a moment to process; she'd closed her eyes as if she might get sick. "You remember the investigation, Em. The detectives thought I had something to do with it. Detective Mills still does. But someone has had it all this time, Emily. His shoe. For years I searched for clues. For him. I stopped for a time. I'd given up. But since I got that other shoe, I . . . I've been sneaking out at night. I found bones, Emily. Bones from more than one body. In the woods. At the Hollow. Bones I believe are from all the missing kids."

"Ben, what are you saying?"

"There's someone out there . . ."

"I know, pretending to be a character in your book, and now—"

"It's the Screamer." Silence. She stared at the floor. "Em? Look at me."

When she looked up her eyes were red, tear-filled. "Ben, don't. Don't go there."

"That's what Dad called him. I told you when Mom and Dad died. I saw a man with a shaved head in the woods. That's who took Devon. That's who I think's been taking the kids. Devon was his first. He's out there." He gave her time to respond, but she looked lost for words.

The guard called from the stairwell. "Three minutes."

"I found his watch with all the bones." Ben lowered his voice. "Grandpa Robert's Rolex, the one Devon would wear around his arm. We assumed he'd had it on when he disappeared. They took my backpack tonight, Emily. The watch was in there, along with one of the bones. That's why they arrested me, I'm sure. Because it's all suspicious. It's fucking out there, and it doesn't make sense."

"The box. The missing shoe, is it some kind of warning?"

Ben nodded, raked a hand through his hair. "Maybe. I don't know. It wasn't the only thing in there. There were some other things that don't make much sense to me. A dead moth. A tooth. An old coin . . ."

She wasn't listening. "And you're still writing it? Your next book? My Lord, Ben."

"It's gotten me closer to the truth, Emily. I never thought I'd find Devon alive. I know that. But at least . . . I found his watch. I have the shoe. At least now we can bury *something*. It can end now. We can have closure."

"I've already *had* my closure."

The guard's voice sounded from across the room. "Time's up, ma'am."

Emily looked over her shoulder. "You said three minutes."

"I'm sorry, we've got someone coming down. We have to clear out. Now."

Emily stood.

Ben gripped her arm, accidently pulled up her sleeve to reveal an old white scar. One of many he'd seen up and down the underside of her arm. She yanked her arm back, straightened her sleeve. "Why? You've never told me why?"

"Why what?"

"Why did you used to cut yourself?"

She turned away.

"Emily, did Grandpa take you into that room when you were a girl?"

She faced him, couldn't lie. Unlike her brothers, Emily could never lie. "Yes."

"Did you follow all the rules?"

"Yes, Ben. I did."

"Because I didn't."

"Ma'am, let's go." The guard appeared nervous now, beckoning with both hands to come on.

"You asked what you can do for me? Go to Blackwood. Take Amanda and Bri and go to Blackwood, as soon as you leave here."

"Ben . . . Why? That place is wrong. Everything about it is . . . wrong."

"Just go. Trust me. Wait for me there."

"Ma'am," the guard raised his voice. "Now."

Emily turned away, hurried up the stairs, followed by the guard.

Ben waited by the bars, eyed the two empty cells beside him. A minute later, the door above unlatched with a loud pop. Multiple pairs of footsteps descended, different weights and totally out of sync. Detective Blue showed herself first, and then her father, Detective Mills, who looked like he'd died and come back to life, but only barely.

Next came two uniformed officers.

Heavy footfalls pressed down the staircase now, one creaky step at a time. Chains and handcuffs. Feet shuffled. A large, bearded man was guided toward the third cell. Six and a half feet tall, with a stench of rotten garbage.

A guard opened the cell, and the bearded man walked in on his own. He faced Ben two cells down, staring until Ben's eyes repelled. With urgency, Ben pleaded to the detectives, "What's going on?"

Mills stepped forward, dead on his feet. "Ben Bookman, meet the Scarecrow, Royal Blakely." And then both detectives headed for the stairs, exhausted.

Ben watched them go, thinking they'd for sure come back and release him, but they didn't. And when they didn't he started to panic. "Wait . . . You're leaving me down here with him?"

Detective Blue's voice rang out across the room. "We could move him to the middle cell if you want."

"I'm ready to talk," Ben shouted, gripping the bars like his life depended on it.

"When the sun comes up," said Detective Mills.

They disappeared one by one up the stairs. All of them. The guards, the officers, Detectives Mills and Blue. The door latched closed like a hammer blow on metal.

Ben turned to find Royal Blakely watching him, one small cell separating them. The writer and his character.

Ben started for his cot, but then heard Royal say, "Thank you."

Ben stopped cold, turned back toward the bearded man. "What did you say?"

"Said thank you."

"For what?"

"For everything."

24

MILLS LEANED HIS elbows on the conference room table and let out a healthy yawn.

Something about the pleasant birdsong out the window rang false. The sun was up, and the horrors from last night had somehow produced a beautiful sunny morning, but Mills knew better than to think they'd crossed the finish line. Royal Blakely may have been behind bars, but there were still too many questions left unanswered, namely Blakely's motive—specifically what in the hell had happened to the man to cause such a change in personality over the past year, what any or all of it had to do with Ben Bookman and that room at Blackwood, and last, and possibly most telling, what kind of sense to make of the human bone and Rolex watch found inside the backpack Bookman had been wearing when Blue had brought him in.

Across the room, on a beat-up sofa Mills had fallen asleep on more than once over the years, the Turtle peeled back the wrapper of a Snickers bar and bit into it, fingering through a level of Candy Crush while he chewed, all part of his morning ritual.

Mills had told him, "Go home. Get some sleep. We'll call when somebody dies." And that he was a medical examiner, not a detective. At which point the Turtle had told him to mind his own business, and that last night had been the biggest thrill he'd had since he and his deceased wife Ann had gone skydiving back in the last century. And that Turtles didn't need much rest anyway.

Mills had asked if that was true, and Chief Givens, who'd been trying to get caught up on everything, had mumbled, "Who gives a fuck?"

Sitting catty-corner from Mills and reviewing notes she'd taken during her interrogation of Ben Bookman hours ago, Blue rubbed her eyes, wiped away remnants of the brief power nap she'd taken in the break room to bridge her to the morning. She sipped hot coffee and willed herself onward.

Chief Givens was the only one fully alert—he lived off coffee, and hadn't been through the tension of catching Royal Blakely last night, so he was eager while they were all digging deep for what little they had left in the tank. Blue waited until Chief Givens left the room for a refill to ask Mills, "You okay?"

He nodded. He'd taken three sleeping pills less than five hours ago, and shouldn't have been lucid enough to do what he'd done inside that house. Adrenaline had a way of taking over when the body and mind were dragging, but then came the low, and no matter how many times he yawned and stretched, he was feeling it now. The conference room was cold, eternally cold, yet he was sweating as if it was summer and the A/C was out.

Blue shared a glance with the Turtle. Mills saw it, and knew immediately they were in cahoots about something.

As if that was the Turtle's cue, he placed his Candy Crush game face down on the cushion beside him, made sure Chief Givens wasn't yet back on his way in, and said, "Winny?"

"What?"

"I've never seen you get sick like that. Last night at Blakely's. Anything you need to tell us?"

Mills watched them both. "No."

"Like, any chest pains or whatnot?"

"The only pain I'm having is in my ass, from a combination of you two and this chair."

"You need to go to the hospital. Listen to me now. I'm a doctor."

"For the dead."

Blue said, "By the looks of you, you're not far from it."

"I'm not done yet, Sam. You know that. My thread has yet to be—"

The door opened and Chief Givens returned with a fresh cup of coffee. He sat at the head of the table, where he'd left his notepad open. He wore an expression that told them he knew he'd just interrupted something, but didn't care. "So, both twin boys?"

"Cut up and cocooned," said the Turtle. "Decomposed. I'd say two months dead, but we'll narrow it."

"And Royal's wife?"

"All of eighty pounds when she died."

"Which we think was?"

"Within the past twenty-four to forty-eight hours. Again, we'll get it narrowed."

Blue said, "Like in the book, he tried to keep her alive. He kept saying we were too late. That he tried to keep her fed."

"Noble."

"Toward the end he was using an IV and feeding tube," said the Turtle. "Crudely put together and administered. Infection to all get out."

Chief Givens scribbled some notes, dropped his pen. Mills resented the fact that he was fresh and they were all dead on their feet. "So we have him? This is over?"

"It's him," Mills said, eyes closing. "It's the same dude I saw in my woods."

Blue said, "Excuse me?"

He opened his eyes. "Oh, he stalked me. Sometime before midnight. Apparently I was gonna be next."

Blue tossed her pen on the table and stood abruptly. "And you were gonna tell us this when?"

"I was going to take care of him when he showed up again. I figured if he'd latched onto me, then everyone else was safe."

"Why do I feel we're running this investigation on two separate roads?"

"And I'm taking the one less traveled?"

"One way to put it. Mom said you spent your entire career on that road." Blue sat back down, retrieved her pen. "So you're the great martyr, Detective Winchester Mills. Taking one for the team."

Mills grunted, closed his eyes again. Their give-and-takes had become commonplace. Truth be told he liked them. "Yet another reason to never retire," he said aloud.

"What is?" asked Blue.

The Turtle chuckled, took another bite of his Snickers.

"Those on your diet?" Mills asked the Turtle.

"No."

Chief Givens ignored them, probably used to their banter by now, and turned another page on his notepad. "What about

Bookman's barn? You think he killed the reporter? Sounds too cut and dried to me."

"No," Blue said. "I don't think he did."

"Then why did we arrest him?"

"For his own good." Blue rubbed her face. "Plus he won't stop lying."

"Christ." Givens dropped his pen now. "You can't arrest someone for lying."

The Turtle said, "Liar, liar, pants on fire."

Mills smiled, started to nod off.

"A celebrity to boot," added Givens. "Who could sue our asses—"

"We found some weird shit in his house, okay?"

Mills sat alert. "Like what?"

"Like his little brother's missing shoe from thirteen years ago. In a box he'd locked inside a drawer. It's all been bagged and tagged."

"Son of a bitch," said Mills. "And you were gonna tell *me* this when?"

"I'm telling you now," said Blue.

"And you talk about the road less traveled?"

The Turtle said, "That was actually you who said that, Winny."

"Shut up."

Blue said, "We were a little preoccupied last night, okay?"

Mills scoffed, shook his head. "I suppose we were. But son of a bitch."

"What?"

"I don't know. Just that I always thought Ben Bookman had more to do with that disappearance than Willard did."

"You think he killed his little brother?" asked Givens, who, Mills knew, had been a rookie when Devon Bookman went missing.

"I don't know. Not sure I know anything anymore." He looked at Blue. "What else was in the box you forgot to tell me about?"

Blue sighed, took a deep breath and exhaled. "About ten different things. The shoe being the winner-winner-chicken-dinner. But there was a spool of thread and a needle. And a tooth."

"A tooth?"

"I told you, it was weird."

"We can't arrest someone for being weird, Blue," said Givens. "He's a horror writer. Maybe he kept all those for inspiration."

"A claw," she said. "Looked like it came from an eagle. Or a large bird, for sure. There was also a coin that may be from ancient Rome."

Mills laughed. "Ancient Rome, huh?"

"We're trying to authenticate," she said. "And then there's what we found on his computer. His new book."

"Catch me up," said Givens.

"Well, to answer what you mentioned earlier—no, I don't think this is over. Not with how we found that reporter's body in Bookman's barn. You saw the pictures?"

"Yes, I saw the pictures."

"It's morbid," said Blue. "But it's nothing like the Scarecrow. No cocoons. Body was left mostly intact. Just . . . I don't know. But back to what I found on his computer. His work in progress. As a fan of his previous books, I know there's a thread of missing children through all of them. All of them take place in the fictional town of Riverdale. Fans have been wanting answers for years, and it looks like his next novel, titled *The Screamer*, finally brings that plot point home. The first one to come up missing is a little boy mentioned as backstory in *Summer Reign*, his first novel. Ben is a world builder. The novels all share characters, town secrets, and the histories of each story as if they'd happened in real time."

"You've read them all?" asked Chief Givens.

"Twice," said Mills.

Blue said, "His second novel was *Some Fall Down*. Followed by *Winter Bones*. Then *Spring Showers, Dead Flowers*."

"Covers all four seasons," said Givens.

No shit, Mills almost said, starting to nod off again.

Blue said, "In his fifth novel, *The Pulse*, a young boy tells a story to a friend during a sleepover of a creature he'd seen in the woods. A monster with no hair. It has eyes and a nose but no mouth."

Mills snapped alert. "Like what we found on the porch. With the peanuts."

"Placed there by Royal Blakely as the Scarecrow, which is why I think he knows something we don't. And Bookman might too. In *The Pulse*, the boy refers to this monster as the Screamer. The other boy asks why he's called the Screamer if he doesn't have a mouth. And the one boy says he's not sure, but he lures children into the woods and eats them. The boy asked how he eats them if he doesn't have a mouth, and that goes unanswered too. But he's pretty sure that's where all of Riverdale's missing children are going. Rumors have been swirling for months that Ben Bookman's next novel after *The Scarecrow* would finally be about the Screamer. And it looks like that's true."

Mills could tell there was more. "And?"

"He's halfway finished with it. But the last line he wrote shows Detective Mulky's little girl being kidnapped."

"By the Screamer?" asked Givens, writing again.

"Yes."

"And?" Mills asked. "Spill it, Sam."

"Haven't you figured it out by now? Ben Bookman has been patterning his main character, Detective Mulky, on you. For years."

"Why?"

"I don't know. Maybe because you were the first detective he ever met."

"He met Willard the same time."

"Mulky reminds me more of you."

"How so?"

"His moods, for one. He's hard. He's tough. He's oftentimes a fuck-up."

Mills leaned back, grinned, hurt and proud in equal measure. "Language, Blue."

She avoided his gaze, paused, as if what she had to say next wouldn't come easily. "But he's also a hero."

Before

JEPSON HEAP LIKED to play in the fall leaves, dried brittle by the sun and crisp air.

He and his two older brothers, Jack and Jethro, would rake tall piles and jump into them from the back porch. They'd rake leaves into mazes and chase each other until the sun went down and mother would call out bath times from the porch. They were running through a maze on the day their daddy made the scarecrow. Jack and Jethro, who could be nice to Jepson on occasion, were in the middle of accusing him of stepping over one of the leaf walls, when their daddy fired his rifle from the back porch and yelled, "Goddamn crows," at the top of his voice.

Dozens of crows scattered from the cornfield, only to reform a minute later, as if daring their daddy to fire again. He did, but to no avail.

Daddy spent that entire night in the barn, building by lamplight a scarecrow out of burlap, stuffed with the same dried leaves they'd pulverized earlier in the day. He used old clothes and a belt and boots and a straw hat, and the next morning that scarecrow stood in the middle of the back yard, facing the house instead of the cornfield. Daddy took his morning coffee on the back porch, daring the crows to show themselves. They did, but not in such large numbers as before, and gradually the crows dwindled.

From day one, Jepson had been squeamish around the scarecrow, unsure of those coat-button eyes, just uneven enough to give him pause *every time he passed it. The first nightmare didn't occur until a week later, when Jack and Jethro had run into his room and told him the scarecrow moved overnight. Daddy had told the two older boys that he'd done it to keep the crows honest, but the brothers neglected to tell that detail to little brother Jepson. They thought it more fun to put on an act, to tell Jepson the scarecrow had come alive during the night and moved on its own. Not far, just thirty yards south toward the tractors and shed, but far enough to scare Jepson into a sleepless night.*

The two older brothers ramped up their deceit. Jepson was only nine and not all that bright, and wouldn't learn the truth until it was too late. Not a night went by that Jepson didn't have nightmares about that scarecrow. When Daddy found out the older brothers had been moving it, a couple of times having Jepson wake up to find it standing in the corner of his bedroom, he'd taken a belt to both of their backsides. By then, Jepson's nightmare had become the family's nightmare. Not that they shared the same fright—that was Jepson's alone— but none of them could escape the aftermath. With Jepson waking up screaming every night, none of them could catch a good night's sleep, which affected the overall mood of the household for nearly a year.

Jepson was ten when he stopped seeing the scarecrow in his dreams, and by then the scarecrow had become a walking, talking, foul-mouthed monster with a horrible mind of his own.

At least that's how Jepson described it to Dr. Robert Bookman.

25

"Am I free to go?"

"No, Ben." Detective Blue sipped from a coffee mug and took a seat on the other side of the table inside the Box. "You're not free to go yet."

"Am I still under arrest?"

"No. And technically you never were."

"You read me my Miranda rights."

"Fingers were crossed." She smiled. "Did Royal Blakely say anything to you overnight?"

"I could sue, right? Is this something I could take the department to court over?"

"Perhaps." The bags under her eyes were heavy, her blue eyes had lost a bit of their luster, but she somehow still shone. He'd gotten thirty minutes sleep, tops, and that had come right before she'd woken him up and removed him from the cell soon after the sun had come up. "You can call and ask my husband if you want. He'd probably love to take that case. Did Mr. Blakely say anything to you last night?"

"Wasn't much of a talker."

"Mr. Bookman . . ."

"I was Ben a minute ago. Can we go back to that?"

"So he didn't say anything to you all night?"

"He said thank you."

"Thank you?"

"Yeah, that's what he said. Thank you for everything. And no, I don't know what he was talking about." He leaned forward. "He's our guy, though, right?"

"That's pretty definitive, yes."

"Then why am I still in here?"

"There's still the matter of the dead reporter inside your barn. Trevor Golappus."

"I didn't do it. And if you thought I did, I'd still be down there with the caveman."

"I'm trying to protect you, Ben."

"From who?"

"Yourself. You're not making things easy. And we're not letting you go until you start making sense of some things."

"Like?"

"Like why did you write what you did? That last line of your current manuscript?"

"I was pissed. You all were grilling me. I was drunk. So I did what writers can do."

"What? Some kind of fictional payback? Can you see that this is no joke anymore? That there may still be someone out there wanting to act out your fictional world?"

"I thought I deleted it. That line."

"You didn't. Do I need to be worried? As my father's daughter? Because regardless of what you say, I know you thought of him when you conjured up your famous Detective Mulky."

"You're not in any danger. At least not from anything having to do with me."

"Why is your missing brother's shoe in the drawer of your desk? Ben? Help us."

"Is this some kind of a *help me help you* thing? Would you be giving me this extra rope if I wasn't who I am?"

"I'm not going to deny that I'm a fan. I always have been."

"You know I don't like the fame. Never have."

"You could have fooled me," she said. "But you know the saying about meeting your heroes?"

"Avoid it?"

"Something like that. Because the real deal might let you down."

"I apologize, since I've obviously done that."

"Not totally. I like a good redemption story, Ben. But I keep peeling away the layers, hoping to discover you aren't rotten at the core. We're running out of layers. Why do you have Devon's missing shoe? Some detectives, like my dad, might think you'd know better than to keep such evidence around. They might think it's a trophy of some sort. And that you took Devon all along. And if they keep digging through your house, which we are, we just might find items from all those other kids gone missing since Devon disappeared. They might just think *you're* the Screamer."

"That's ridiculous."

"No more ridiculous than what that crazy son of a bitch in the cell below did. He killed his family and kids, Ben, because of something *you* wrote. He evidently thanks you for it."

"A few weeks ago I received a package. Left on my porch. Don't know where it came from or who delivered it. But the shoe was in there. Along with all the other things you found inside that box. I don't know what any of them mean, except for the shoe. There's somebody out there trying to mess with me, Detective. And I think that somebody took my brother. I think . . ."

"You think what, Ben?"

"There's a man out there who thinks he's the Screamer."

"So first the Scarecrow and now this? Are the villains from all your other books out there somewhere too?"

She'd said it with a boatload of sarcasm, but it gave him pause. And the pause brought about a sense of unease between them. "Or he's pretending to be," Ben continued. "The Screamer. And he's been pretending for a long time."

"How long?"

"Before I'd even written my first novel. Before Devon even went missing."

"How do you know?"

"Because my dad was . . . My dad was afraid of him, okay? He had nightmares of him. The Screamer. That's what he called it. When my mom and dad died in that car wreck. I think it was this man my dad saw. That's what sent him off the road."

"Why do you think this?"

"Because I saw him. I saw him there in the woods. Bald as a pool ball."

"Why didn't you tell anyone?"

"I did. I told my grandpa. Even said I thought it was who maybe took Devon. And that Dad had seen him in the woods even before Devon disappeared."

"And he said what?"

"That he'd look into it. That the police had already scoured those woods around Blackwood and they didn't find any man. He said he thought I'd imagined him. That I was still reeling from what happened, and I believed him. He said he'd tell the detectives. Said he'd tell your father."

"Ben, I've looked at those reports countless times, and again right before I pulled you out of that cell. There's nothing mentioned about some man in the woods."

"Maybe your dad forgot to add it in."

"Or maybe your grandfather never told us."

Truth was a difficult pill to swallow. Unlike most who'd known Robert Bookman, Ben knew his grandfather wasn't perfect. He had flaws. He had demons. But why would he not push harder to find his grandson's killer?

"You've been going out searching for Devon since you got that box, haven't you? You think what you're doing might bring you closer to the truth of what happened to him. Why do you think they sent that box?"

"I don't know."

"To scare you?"

"I don't know."

"To make sure you write the next book?"

"I don't . . . know. Okay?"

"The bone we found in your backpack. Where did it come from?"

"The same place I found the watch. It was the watch Devon had on his arm when he disappeared. It was my grandfather's watch Devon used to wear around his skinny arm."

"So you think you found him?"

"His remains, yes. Along with the others. At Blackwood Hollow. Inside the caves."

"They searched the caves. My dad. My father-in-law. They searched every part of those woods. How did *you* find them?"

"There was a note in the box when I first opened it."

"What note? You said nothing about a note."

"I'm telling you now."

"Did you save it? The handwriting could have been useful to us."

"I threw it in the fireplace."

"Why?"

"I don't know. I panicked."

"Fine. What did it say?"

"*Where do all nightmares grow?*"

"And?"

"In the hollow. Deep down in the hollow. That's what Grandpa Robert always said. We'd ask where nightmares came from. The Nightmare Man plants them deep down in the hollow."

"The Nightmare Man?"

"Just another story Grandpa Robert liked to tell us. That there was someone since the first sleep that planted seeds in the heads of children at night. And that kids have something inside their brains called the hollow. That's where the nightmares are planted. That's where the seeds start growing. Deep down in the hollow."

"Blackwood Hollow," she said aloud. "The ravine behind Oswald Asylum."

"Yes. I've been looking there for months. Last night I dug deeper."

"Whoever sent that box obviously knows you."

"Or they were told the same story. My guess is a former patient of my grandfather's."

Someone knocked on the door and they both jumped in their seats. Without looking away from Ben, Detective Blue said, "Come in."

Officer Maxwell stuck her head in. "Somebody's here to see you, Blue. It's urgent."

"Who is it?"

"Jepson Heap's wife. She said now that he's been caught, she's ready to talk."

"How did she know the Scarecrow had been caught?"

"It's all over the news."

"How?"

Maxwell nodded toward Ben. "Ask him. It's his wife reporting it. All seven months pregnant of her."

26

MILLS AWOKE ON the couch to sunlight in his eyes. Discombobulation kept him still for a minute, and when he sat up, his body ached like he'd been in a car wreck. He hadn't done anything physically strenuous with Royal Blakely last night, but at his age, tension was enough to do physical damage. And there was the possible heart attack—albeit minor—but he was sure that's what it had been. He rubbed his face, vaguely remembered coming home, Blue driving, hounding him on his sleep habits and diet and general lack of exercise; Blue walking him to the door, to the couch, covering him with a blanket.

On the coffee table next to a brown box was a handwritten note from Blue.

Turtle says to rest and take it easy. Givens might have my ass for taking it from the evidence room, but here's the box of toys we found in Ben Bookman's desk drawer. See if you can make sense of them. And don't bother trying to go anywhere. I took your car keys, along with the extra set in the cookie jar. There were still a couple of peanut butter cookies left in there from when Mom was alive. I took them too. They were stale. Talk soon, Sam.

There was a postscript at the bottom of Blue's note.

PS, Turtle says to have your new healthy living exercise picked out by nightfall, and thinks you should take counseling for your stress, and start eating more fruits and legumes.

He crumpled the note, tossed it aside. *"He's* the fat ass." He googled the word *legume,* and when pictures of peas and dried beans popped up he tossed his phone down.

It was on one percent charge anyway.

Sunlight warmed his face as he leaned forward toward the box. He found a dozen or so items all individually bagged and tagged—the biggest one being Devon Bookman's shoe, the missing one that would match the one tagged inside the vault back at the station. The Scarecrow case had been about as gruesome as any he could remember, but nothing turned his stomach more than the disappearances.

Until Blair Atchinson disappeared a month ago, Mills hadn't thought of Devon Bookman for a long time—it had been almost four years since the previous child, Billy Boyle, had come up missing in the winter of '18. But Blair was an outlier. Despite the dots being out there, any lines drawn to connect all the others to Blair had always ended up crooked and contrived. While the other missing children disappeared during the night, Blair had disappeared from her fenced back yard in broad daylight, snatched in the five minutes it took her mother to run in and check on the green bean casserole. The only similarities the missing children had was that they were all under twelve, and all lived by either wooded areas or cornfields, which was the majority of Crooked Tree's terrain anyway. Mills had been convinced it was over until Blair disappeared.

Like bookends, he'd once said to Blue. Devon Bookman was the first, Blair the most recent, and they happened to be the only cases with a clue left behind—Devon's shoe, and one earring found on a tree stump behind the Atchinsons' house. Blair's mother had broken down crying when she saw the single Mickey Mouse earring cupped in Mills' right palm. She'd gone hysterical.

Mills rooted through the box, pulled out a bag containing a dead moth and another with what looked to be the tooth Blue had mentioned last night—this morning rather. But not until they'd all met in the conference room. He checked his watch. Shit, that hadn't even been two hours ago. Next, he pulled out a bag holding what looked like that Roman coin. And another with a sharp bird talon. Another baggie held what looked like a blade from a box cutter. He was about to reach in for more when his phone rang in the kitchen. Pain surged through his hips as he stood, box in hand, to go answer it. He lifted the phone from the wall next to the fridge. "Hello?"

"Why aren't you answering your cell?"

"It's dead."

"I just got a visit from Trudy Heap. Jepson Heap's wife."

Mills, still tethered to the wall by the cord and holding the box in the crook of his elbow, stretched himself to the kitchen table and plopped down on his most familiar seat. He'd had enough weird coincidences in his life now to know the dream he'd just woken from, of Jepson Heap's childhood scarecrow, wasn't just a dream.

He didn't believe in coincidences. "What did we learn?"

"I told you about the dream catchers on all of their windows. Apparently, they got desperate near the end. But unlike your nightmares, his was always the same. About the Scarecrow."

"And it evolved," Mills said aloud.

"What evolved?"

"Nothing. Just saying Jepson's nightmare, over time, must have evolved. Got worse." Silence. "Sam?"

"How do you know that?"

"Because that's what nightmares do. Now go on. What else did she say?"

"Talked a bit about the dream catchers. Wood. Plastic. Bent willow branches and sinews, feathers and beads. They collected them."

"The Ojibwa Chippewa tribe's word for dream catcher meant spider," said Mills. "They saw them as symbols of protection."

"She kept calling them Sacred Hoops."

"The Ojibwas used them as talismans. Natives believed the night air was filled with dreams. Good and bad. The dream catchers attract and catch them in their webs. The good ones ooze down the feathers and beads to the sleeper."

"The bad ones?"

"They get tangled up in the web. Burned up in the daylight. Now back to Jepson."

"As a boy, he had a fear of their family's scarecrow. His two older brothers made it worse." Mills knew all of this, but didn't stop her. "They would move the scarecrow around the property, even into Jepson's bedroom to make him think it came alive at night. His nightmares lasted for a good year or more. Until—get this—they took him to Dr. Robert Bookman. One visit, and the nightmare was gone. He didn't have the nightmare again until a year ago. Went four decades without dreaming of the Scarecrow, and then boom. It's back."

"Coinciding with that weekend Bookman spent at Blackwood."

"Yes, the weekend he wrote the book," she said. "Around that time, Jepson found something in the corner of his barn. A patch of cornstalks laid out on the ground for sleeping."

"Royal Blakely."

"Yes. Has to be."

"Is he talking yet?"

"No. Won't say a word. But Jepson thought it was maybe a hobo living in their barn. Next night he was set to go out there and check. He looked out the window first, and Mrs. Heap said Jepson went pale. There was a large man dressed as a scarecrow standing outside their window, looking in, arms outstretched like Christ on the cross. And then it was gone. That night, the nightmare returned for the first time since he was a boy."

"Did he return? Assuming it was Royal, did he return on any other night?"

"No. Mrs. Heap said they never saw him again."

Mills recalled Royal Blakely's journal, and what he'd jotted down in regard to Jepson Heap: *Just put a scare into him . . .*

"Because he'd accomplished what he'd set out to do."

"That's what I'm thinking."

"Where's the book come into play?"

"So for a year this goes on. Jepson had practically become a shut-in, until he heard about the book. He went to the store and bought one the day it came out. He read that book cover to cover in one day. The more he read, the madder he got. He highlighted passages. Underlined others. Circled words, made notes."

"Do you still have Jepson's copy? The one he made his markings on?"

"After his wife learned what he'd done inside the bookstore, she tossed it into the fireplace."

"Did she say which parts he claimed Ben stole? From his nightmare?"

"The Scarecrow himself. I'm sure Jepson wasn't the only child to ever have a bad dream about a scarecrow. But this was Jepson's exact version of one."

"Did Jepson's nightmares as a child ever involve these husks used as cocoons?"

"No. She said those were new. Like in those forty some odd years his nightmare was dormant, it was still evolving, like you said."

Mills considered telling her that one night back in May, he'd been given a glimpse of Jepson's nightmare. Just a snippet, but enough for him to catch a punch of déjà vu upon entering the Petersons' barn two weeks ago and finding the cocoons hanging from the ceiling. He'd seen it before. To his knowledge, he'd never had a brush-up with Jepson Heap. But Crooked Tree was a small town, and if they had been in the same vicinity at some point, that could have been enough to trigger it.

Had I known, I would have taken this grave burden off of his shoulders.

"Dad?"

I would have shaken his hand. Hugged him. Had enough of a brush-up to take that nightmare from Jepson for good.

"Dad?" she shouted. He snapped to, not realizing he'd taken another evidence baggie from the box until he saw it in his hand—the tooth again. "You see why we took your keys?"

"The Turtle can shove those legumes up his fat ass. Tell him that. And I want my car keys back, Sam. This isn't a time to be fucking with me."

"You sitting down?"

"Of course I'm sitting down. And I'm taking it easy. Why?"

"Because you're gonna need to be when you hear this."

"Goddammit, Sam, spill it."

"We found the remains at Blackwood Hollow." He didn't need to ask who they belonged to, something in her tone screamed it plain enough. "Forensics are there now. Inside one of the old caves. Dad, there's enough there to more than account for every one of those missing children. And more."

"Pick me up, Sam."

"We have it contained."

"Samantha!"

"It's under control, Dad."

While talking, he'd unknowingly slid Devon Bookman's shoe from the evidence bag. He fought the urge to throw it across the room.

"Ben found that Rolex watch there, too. He's convinced now. Devon is dead."

"You still have Bookman there?"

"No, we let him go a few minutes ago. You said yourself we couldn't keep him."

"How is he explaining this box?"

"It was delivered to him by an unknown subject. That's been confirmed by both his wife and daughter. His daughter was the one to get it off the porch and bring it to him. Even described the shock on his face when he opened it."

Mills closed his eyes and took a long, slow breath. He ran his fingers over the old, ragged laces of Devon Bookman's Nike, the weathered cotton tongue, damn well knowing he shouldn't be contaminating evidence with his own touches and prints and oils, but Sam had left him that box for a reason. His fingers slid inside the shoe and out again, and then he dropped it to the floor. Disgusted, he kicked it. It spun against the bottom of the refrigerator. Something protruded from it, clinging to one of the tattered laces.

"Dad?" He made his way over to the shoe, the phone still loosely cradled in his hand. "Amanda Bookman is on TV now, breaking the news on Royal Blakely . . ." His daughter's voice was static noise now that he'd homed in on what had come dislodged from the inside of that shoe. "It's only a matter of time before they learn of what we found at the Hollow."

"Sam, I gotta go. Keep me posted."

He hung up on her, then reached down and picked up Blair Atchinson's Minnie Mouse earring from the kitchen floor.

Before

IT BEGAN AS *a humming in Ben's heart, and then bloomed as warmth across his chest.*

The euphoria of something big, something impossible. The book became heat in his hands, as if the pages were about to come alive.

"Close the book, Benjamin."

And he did, without hesitation. Grandpa Robert watched him from the neighboring chair, smiling proudly, white hair feathered like dove wings.

The next night had been the same, except he'd climbed the ladder to find book number 1934.

The same feeling had emerged, the same push of adrenaline.

"Close the book, Benjamin."

And, again, he did. Without any explanation, Grandpa ushered him back to bed. Both nights he had trouble returning to sleep. He'd thought it impossible for his love and need of books to grow stronger, but inside that room, holding those books, he'd never felt more creative, more eager to not only read and smell the pages but to pick up a pen and write.

To Benjamin's surprise, on the third night, Grandpa Robert insisted he pick the book.

After careful perusal, Ben selected book number 1311 from the wall-shelf closest to the door. Grandpa Robert gestured for him to sit.

Ben opened the book when told, and within seconds the adrenaline returned. The pages moved. Just the breeze. What breeze? He would tell him to close the book any second now.

But what if I didn't? What if I waited a few seconds longer?

Birds circled above. Moth wings pulsed on the tree.

"Close the book, Benjamin."

Euphoria expanded across his chest like he imagined a drug would.

"Benjamin." More stern now. "Close the book."

He stared at the first page, this book with no words, waiting—for what? And then he saw it. Black ink. A spot at first, as if dotted from an ancient, freshly inked quill, and then a letter . . .

S

Grandpa Robert stood quickly from his chair. "Benjamin . . ."

Letter by letter, a word revealed itself.

Scarecrows . . .

"Benjamin! Close the book!"

Benjamin couldn't move. The words held him frozen.

Scarecrows scare . . .

Birds flew frantically below the glass ceiling. Moths pulsed their wings against the tree.

Scarecrows scare. That's what they do . . .

"Benjamin, close the goddamn book!"

Robert Bookman's words cleaved through whatever had enveloped him.

Benjamin shoved the book from his lap, where it rested a few feet away on the uneven bricks. His grandfather could have taken the book from him and closed it himself.

He'd wanted Benjamin to see.

Benjamin looked toward his grandfather, but Grandpa Robert refused to look at him.

"Benjamin, go to bed. And mention nothing of this to anyone. Ever."

27

THE BEAT-UP, BLACK 2010 Honda Accord brought back memories of Ben's first car at seventeen.

The car—the decoy Detective Blue had provided leaving the police station—had created a sense of normalcy he'd not known he'd needed until he'd gripped the sun-faded steering wheel and waited through two turns of the key for it to rev and rumble. It had been parked behind the police station, exactly where Detective Blue had told him, in between the dumpster and the hedgerow, with the key under the driver's side floor mat.

Flee town, Ben, and we'll be on you faster than a knife fight in a phone booth.

He'd laughed at that. Detective Blue said it was something her mother used to say. And then she reiterated that he could just as easily be down in a cell next to Blakely as out on the streets now assisting their delving into the unknown. He'd taken the baseball cap she'd given him, pulled it low over his brow, and promised her he'd keep her in the loop.

"Don't make me regret this, Ben," she'd told him.

She now had composite sketches of the tall, bald man Ben had seen in the woods thirteen years ago circulating.

"You've got two little ones, right?" he'd asked her. "Call your husband now."

"Way ahead of you. Danny's not letting them out of his sight. And your daughter?"

"She's with my sister at Blackwood, until Amanda can meet them there."

"You really think Blackwood is the safest place for your family right now?"

"Yeah, I do," he'd said, with no hesitation.

"Care to explain why?"

"Not yet. But aren't detectives told to follow their hunches."

"You're not a detective, Ben."

"I know," he'd told her with a smirk. "I'm a writer. I get to be everything wrapped into one."

He'd closed the car door and hurried off.

As far as he could tell, no one had followed him. While driving, he'd called Amanda; she'd finally picked up in the middle of his message, after he'd said he had a tip on another breaking story. Someone now possibly imitating his fictional character, the Screamer. "Make sure there's not a parent in town not keeping their child within reach. Better yet, Amanda, screw tiptoeing the line. Spread fear. Fear could save lives."

"Ben, are you sure about this?"

"Yes. Until he's caught, keep them in their house with the doors locked."

"Why didn't you tell me about that box, and what was in it?"

"I didn't want to frighten you."

"What about frightening Bri?"

"Does she appear frightened?"

"No."

"She watched me open the damn thing. She's the one who got it off the porch. I didn't know what was in it."

"Did she see anything?"

"No. Just my expression when I opened it."

"And you told her not to tell me?"

"Yes. I told her it was a surprise for Mommy. And to not tell you."

"Great. You're teaching our daughter to lie."

"Her knowing is the reason I'm out of jail right now, Amanda. And she was savvy enough to lay it all out there for Detective Blue when she was questioned. Now go. Send your crew to Blackwood Hollow. The police are there now. You won't be able to get within fifty yards of the remains. The bones I found are in the caves, but get as close as you can."

"Thank you."

"You're welcome."

"If only they'd let us in earlier . . . Ben, who is this person? You've seen him?"

"I think so. Thirteen years ago. I saw him in the woods at Mom and Dad's wreck. I told Grandpa Robert. He was supposed to tell the police then, but he never did."

"Why not?"

"I don't know. But I think he was hiding something too."

"And why do you think this man is still alive?"

"I don't know, Amanda. It's flimsy, but kids are still disappearing."

Or maybe I imagined him, like Grandpa Robert had told me when I'd finally gotten the nerve to ask him about the words I'd seen reveal themselves across the blank page of that book. You imagined seeing the Screamer in the woods that day, just like you imagined those words on the page.

But I hadn't imagined anything.

Scarecrows scare. That's what they do . . .

"Ben?"

Her voice yanked him back to reality. "The bones I found," he said. "Even if Blair is dead, her remains wouldn't have been as far gone as what I found in the caves. Maybe there's still hope for her."

"And you think this all started with Devon?"

"Yes. It . . . Yes." *With Devon and because of Devon.* Ben navigated the roads toward home, found himself picking up speed as he took the familiar turns nearing it. "But the man I saw . . . I know this was who took Devon."

"How do you know that, Ben? It could have been just a man hunting in the woods."

"I . . . Just report the story and meet me at —"

"God damn it, Ben, no more secrets."

He slowed on the turn leading up the hillside to his street. "Because I know who my father's nightmare was. I know exactly what he looked like, Amanda. And things are finally starting to make sense now."

Just as he'd feared, two news vans were parked outside his house.

He pulled his hat down, coasted by without looking their way, and parked two houses down, deep into his neighbor's driveway so the Accord was not visible from the road. The Creighton family didn't look to be home. They were both probably working, eager to get away from all the flashing lights bombarding everyone on the street for the past twenty-four hours. Even so, Ben would hurry, in case they arrived and drew attention to the unknown car parked under their son's basketball net.

Just a quick shower and a shave was what he'd told himself—he'd never felt more soiled than he did now, after spending the night in such close proximity to the filth wafting off Royal Blakely's body and clothes. But the truth was, he was hurrying back to get the sketches. Unless the police had completely ripped apart his office, the sketches would still be there, taped in an envelope on the underside of his desk. And they were. The same sketches Detective Mills and Detective Willard, years ago, had not only seen but tried to use as morbid evidence that he'd been the one to kidnap and possibly kill his own brother. He'd kept them out of spite. He'd kept them as a physical reminder of his little brother, a tethered thread he never should have begun pulling.

Six books and another on the way. *What were you thinking?*

He was thinking that writing those books might bring about answers. And they had. But too many horses had been let out of the barn now and he had no way to corral them back inside. He was done with the fictional town of Riverdale. Ben held the series of gruesome sketches in his hand, found a lighter inside the middle desk drawer, and did what he should have done years ago—lit them on fire. They burned, coiled and black; he held them until heat singed his fingers. He tossed the flaming pages into the wastebasket. Smoke sifted. Flames licked the sides of the can, and a few minutes later, the fire consumed itself and died.

He showered and dressed in less than ten minutes.

In the kitchen, he began to do what he'd told Amanda yesterday he'd already done. Bottle by bottle, he poured alcohol down the drain, and placed the empties on the island, lining them up by the dozens. Twenty-seven bottles later, half of which he'd hidden in various spots around the house, he began to empty the last one, a bottle of fifteen-year aged Old Sam he'd been saving for a special occasion.

He stopped after half of the dark, amber whiskey had glugged from the opening, fizzing like something alive into the sink. He grabbed a rock glass from the cabinet, poured a shot to help calm his nerves. "One more," he said aloud.

A young woman's voice behind him said, "Make that two."

He turned to find Jennifer, their former nanny, standing on the far side of the island.

28

MILLS SAT ON the sofa with the contents of the box spread out across the coffee table like some jigsaw puzzle ready to be tackled.

Beside him on the next cushion seat rested another box he'd just pulled from the dozens inside his home office. The top flap, in faded black Sharpie written over a decade ago, read: *Devon Bookman*. Typically, all investigative files were stored at the station, the older ones inside the cold, sterile room they called the Vault, but Mills, over the decades, had either photocopied or flat out taken whatever he deemed necessary. They'd been his cases, so he'd considered them his files. What Linda had always called a mess inside his office, he referred to as his life's work, and it had never failed to dawn on him—never more than now, especially—that he'd been blessed with some weird ones.

From his first case with Lucius Oswald, who they'd dubbed Chasing Jimmy, to his tenth case in Lou Ann Logjam—who they'd named the Witch for adding tiny doses of mouse poison to the cookies she handed out every day at lunch to her first grade class—to the Scarecrow and Screamer, there seemed to be an overly high number of cases that not only registered as bizarre, but macabre enough to name. Cases that when looked upon singularly might not register as overly odd, but added together— after finding Blair Atchinson's missing Minnie Mouse earring in Devon Bookman's missing shoe—it was hard to not notice the overall scope of things. It all started with Robert Bookman and Blackwood and his decades of working with children's nightmares.

Work that Mills knew well, as one of Robert Bookman's former patients.

Mills was looking for the sketches Detective Willard Blue had found in Ben's desk drawer that summer at Blackwood. Not the sketches themselves, as Ben had refused to hand them over and they'd had no real reason other than curiosity to take them. But while the boy had been out of the room, Willard had snapped pictures of each one before putting them back where he'd found them in the desk. Mills found the photocopied sketches in a manila folder near the bottom of Devon Bookman's evidence box. They shook him now as they'd shaken him then. Not so much the sinister pictures themselves, but the fact that they'd been drawn by a teenage boy. Murder and torture. Severed limbs. Devils and gore. Krampus biting off the heads of children at Christmas. Werewolves and vampires and blood. Baba Yaga hanging human bones as wind chimes outside her forested hut. Monsters from folklore. Creatures from nightmares. Mares riding the chests of troubled sleepers. Serial killer facts jotted down beneath crude sketches of their faces—Dahmer, Bundy, John Wayne Gacy, and more.

Mills scanned the photographs, and then froze on two in particular.

"Well, I'll be damned."

One was a clear sketch of the inside of a barn. A cocoon made of stitched corn husks suspended from a ceiling beam. Blood dripped from the bottom of the clumpy husk to the floor. In the shadows a scarecrow stood staring at his project. What the sketch meant, Mills didn't know, but the shock of it got him up from his chair and pacing. Ben Bookman hadn't just come up with the scarecrow book idea at Blackwood a year ago. He didn't know when these sketches had been drawn, but it had been at least thirteen years ago and *before* Devon Bookman disappeared. The seed for that story had been planted long ago.

The next picture showed a long, rangy bald man walking through dark woods, framed in such a profile that resembled how one might picture a glimpse of the mythical Bigfoot, caught unaware, its head swiveling toward a secret camera. It had a long face, dark eyes, and a nose, but no mouth. Mills wiped his face, exhaled into his open palms. "Jesus wept." He thought of the Reynolds' crime scene, the peanuts arranged in the shape of a face with no mouth on the floor of the porch, and knew this was Ben Bookman's Screamer. But even more, it resembled the sketch Samantha had just sent him of the man Bookman had seen in the woods thirteen years ago.

Leafing through the other sketches, Mills wondered now if some of the gruesome images were characters or scenes from Bookman's other novels. A moth fluttered across the room, clung to the far wall, wings pulsing. Mills quietly stood from the couch and approached it, but it flew away before he could strike it with the swatter he'd lifted from the end table.

He stared at the spot where it had clung to the wall, like it had left some kind of imprint or residue. He stepped back, widening the scope of his vision, until he could view the beige-colored living room wall in full. An idea struck him. It was a large, grand idea, and for it he'd need a large canvas. He started by moving each of the six framed pictures from the wall, resting them along the back side of the sofa, and then retrieved a black Sharpie pen from the kitchen. Linda was no longer around to test his sanity, so he went into it full throttle. He'd need as much room as he could get, not only to write but to pin the necessary files and pictures and notes as he stitched his thoughts together.

He started with one word, which he wrote in letters as large as his splayed hand.

Blackwood. And beneath it: *Dr. Robert Bookman.*

Near the top of the wall, angled thirty degrees in an upward tangent toward the ceiling, he wrote, *The Scarecrow,* and below it, *Jepson Heap* and *Royal Blakely.* Lower down on the wall, connected to the central circle by a line resembling the next spoke in a wheel, he wrote *The Screamer,* and beside it a question mark.

With the Minnie Mouse earring still confounding him, and unable to fight his better judgment, he found the number for Blair Atchinson's parents in his notes, and dialed. He didn't know exactly what he would say, but knew he had to follow his instincts. Blair's mother, Barbara, picked up after the third ring, and sounded as hollow now as she had in the immediate days after. But then her voice filled with hope, and he kicked himself for giving it.

"I'm sorry, Mrs. Atchinson, no, I haven't found your daughter."

"They called me earlier."

"Who?"

"Detective Blue," she said. "She wanted to warn me about what was just on the news. That they'd found remains at the Hollow. They don't think Blair was among them. Is that what this is about, Detective? Did you find somethingelse?"

He couldn't stop himself. "We have her missing earring." It wasn't why he'd called. He hadn't intended to give her that information.

"Oh, my Lord, where?"

"It was sent in a box to the police station, Mrs. Atchinson." It was a white lie that, in the grand scheme of things, meant little. "We don't know yet what it all means, but it's a sign that whoever took your girl may be reaching out to us."

"Like some kind of ransom?"

"We don't know yet, and this can't be repeated to anyone."

She lowered her voice. "Not even my husband?"

"No," said Mills, remembering how the poor, distraught father had been such a loose cannon. Too unpredictable, which, he knew, was normal under the circumstances. "Not yet. Please. Let us try and learn more. But I needed to follow up on a few things."

"Okay," she said softly. His heart ached for her. "But I don't know what else I can say other than what we've already gone over, Detective."

"I hate to bring this all back up for you again, but I want you to know I'm still trying." He cut to the chase no matter how odd it sounded. "But did Blair ever have nightmares?"

After a thoughtful pause, she said, "Yes. But don't most kids?"

"Yes, I assume. What about the time she disappeared? Was she having them then?"

"You mean more frequently?"

"Yes, ma'am."

"I suppose. Now that I think on it. She did wake up scared more often around that time."

"Well, it gets me thinking back to what Blair told you that day. The two of you were out playing in the yard. You said she was just staring off into the trees. Do you remember what you told me Blair said?"

"Yes. That it was quieter in the woods. The trees buffer the sound."

"And we didn't know what she meant. Quieter than what? We both asked." And most kids that age don't know the word *buffer* unless someone put it into their head.

"Yes. I remember. But what is this about?"

"I don't know for sure. But when she'd have her nightmares, did she tell you what they were about? Or what she'd see in them?"

"No. She'd never say. She'd claim not to remember." The charge he'd felt thrumming for the past minutes waned somewhat with those words.

And then Barbara Atchinson said, "But she was always holding her ears. When we'd hurry into the room, there she'd be, holding her ears."

The woods buffer the sound, not sounds . . .

"Like she'd just experienced something painfully loud?"

"Yes, I suppose."

"Like someone screaming?"

"Could have been."

"And it was quieter in the woods . . . ," he said, thinking aloud. *Only in a nightmare could something with no mouth make a screaming noise. Blair walked into the woods on her own.*

"Detective, is there something I should know?"

"No, Mrs. Atchison. Not right now. Just know that I'll spend every waking minute of my life trying to find your girl. I'm sorry if I troubled you again. I'll be sure and let you know if I learn anything more." He hung up, gripped the Sharpie tight enough to keep his hands from trembling, and then wrote *Blair Atchinson* on the wall, connected to the Screamer by a thin dark line. He thought of the earring falling out of the missing shoe, and beneath her name he wrote *Devon Bookman*.

Before

"STEP AWAY FROM *the car."*

Mills walked slowly down Route Road's emergency lane, weapon poised.

His target: a stocky, dark-haired man in a stolen police officer's uniform. The man made a move for the gun on his belt, but stopped inches from the handle.

"You so much as hiccup and I'll put a hole in your gut."

Mills knew the woman behind the wheel of the olive green Ford Taurus was Brenda Foxworthy. She'd been brave enough to call in the tip. Her door was open, and the man impersonating an officer had been in the process of pulling her out when Mills came skidding to a stop twenty yards away, siren blaring.

"Game's over." Mills inched closer. "Step away from the car. Both hands up. Now."

Brenda was crying inside the car. Afraid to move. The Bad Cop's hand was on her left shoulder, his thick fingers grasping a good hunk of her yellow blouse, pinching the pink flesh beneath it.

The man had dubbed himself the Bad Cop months ago. He was wanted now for the abduction and attempted *rape of eight Crooked Tree women, all red-haired and in the range of twenty-five to thirty-five years old. Brenda was set to be number nine. The Bad Cop would choose his victims carefully, stalk them for days, and then pull them over on low-trafficked roads when they were alone in the car. Before approaching the driver's side window, he'd bend down at the car's rear bumper and pretend he'd dropped something, at which point he'd stick a KA-BAR knife into one of the back tires. Regardless of the reasons why he pulled his victims over—usually he'd tell them for speeding— he always let them off with a warning, which buttered them up to his smile and what was to come next. After pointing out their flat tire and reminding them they were out in the middle of nowhere, it was difficult to decline his offer of a quick lift home, at which point he'd take them into the woods and attempt rape. Attempt being the key word, because afterward, when the suspects began to gather the courage to talk—they'd all escaped—their stories all matched up perfectly. The Bad Cop was not only impotent but also sensitive about the fact, and they'd scramble away as he sat there with his pants down, crying.*

Mills stepped closer; there was a clear bulge in the man's trousers now. Apparently the Bad Cop wasn't having impotency problems with victim number nine. Mills screamed, "Step away from the car. Hands up. Now!"

The Bad Cop's head swiveled toward Mills. "But I finally found her."

The man made as if to unbuckle his belt and attempt assault right there on the street, when Mills fired a warning shot over his head.

The Bad Cop ducked, and then went for his gun.

Mills put him down.

Then made no attempt to stymie the flow.

The Bad Cop bled out before the ambulance arrived.

29

H ER APPEARANCE HAD changed drastically, but Ben recognized
Jennifer immediately.

Gone were the running shoes, yoga pants, and ponytail. The
fun-loving smile and easy temperament. What he saw now on
the far side of the island was something harder, more guarded,
haunted. She'd dyed her hair raven black. A baggy sweatshirt
swallowed her. A black Yankees baseball cap, pushed low over
her brow, masked her eyes. For four years she'd been part of the
family.

"Jennifer, what are you doing here? I've been trying to get hold
of you for months. You didn't return my calls. Emails. Texts."

She drank from her glass of bourbon, but wouldn't look at him.
Even after she'd turned twenty-one, she'd always stayed away from
hard liquor. Now she swallowed it like a pro.

"I'm sorry." He didn't know what else to say.

She chewed on an unpainted nail she'd bitten to the quick.
"Sorry for what, Ben?"

"I don't know. For what happened."

Her eyes bored into him. "What *did* happen?"

"Whatever we did, it was bad enough to conceal and evade and
lie about." On instinct, he started around the island toward her.

"Don't," she said. He froze, retreated. She removed her cell
phone from her jeans, thumb-tapped a message, and placed it face
down on the island.

"Jennifer, it's been haunting me. We both know I sleepwalk. But I don't just sleepwalk. There's been other times. In the past . . ."

"That you fucked Amanda and didn't remember doing it?"

Her tone rendered him speechless. The year had changed her. He'd never heard her speak like that. He felt responsible. He downed his drink in one swallow and placed the glass in the sink. Gone was the bubbly high school senior who'd interviewed to be his intern, the college girl they'd asked to be their nanny, the sophisticated and upbeat young woman Amanda had begun to treat like a sister until a wall had gone up so suddenly. She produced a cigarette from her jeans, lit it and exhaled like a veteran. She'd never been a smoker.

"You were drinking heavily, Ben," she said, breaking the silence. "That weekend. You were drunk when I arrived. Shit, you were drunk when you called me." She swallowed the rest of her bourbon, inhaled deeply on the cigarette, and exhaled through her nose. "You were typing . . . like a madman. Like during one of your manic phases. Amanda worried. She'd watch from your office door sometimes and you wouldn't even know she was there." Another heavy pull on the cigarette. "Is it you writing the books, Ben? Or are the books writing you? She asked me that one time. Amanda did. Your characters. Some of their traits hit close to home. Sometimes the line is thin."

"What line?"

"What line?"

"Did I cross a line that weekend? Jennifer, did *we* cross a line?"

"I'm not a virgin anymore, if that's what you're asking."

He went rigid with panic. His temples throbbed like an aneurysm was coming.

"But it wasn't you, Ben. Rest easy." She exhaled. "But I didn't know at first. When I left Blackwood that weekend, I didn't know, and I wanted to know."

"Know?"

"If I was still . . . intact."

"*Christ.*"

"There was so much neither of us remembered. You because you were in one of your zones. Me . . ." She poured more bourbon. "It was some prick football player who took my virginity three weeks later. Trust me. But, Ben, I woke up naked. On the couch in that room. Someone had covered me with a blanket."

"I put the blanket on you. You refused to . . . to get dressed. To put your clothes on."

"Why would I do that? What were they doing off in the first place?"

"How much do you remember, Jennifer?"

"Very little. I remember blacking in and out. I still black in and out. Lose time."

Lose time?

She turned away, paced, came back again. "I dated a few boys in college. As you and Amanda knew, nothing serious." She met his eyes. "But I guess maybe I wanted a man. Is that what lured me out there? I wanted that reporter dead when I read that article. From *The Story.*"

"I did too."

"What would you say if I said it was me? That I killed him inside your barn?"

"Jennifer?"

She laughed, stubbed out her cigarette on the island top, and lit another. "No, Ben, I didn't kill the reporter. But I never had an agenda. It wasn't like he said in that article. I would never do that to you. Not to Amanda. Not to Bri." She teared up. "I miss Bri."

"She misses you, too. We all do, Jennifer."

"But it can't be like that again. Can it? I mean, not now. It wasn't like that article said."

"I know. I believe you."

"I can't deny having a crush. Stupid schoolgirl crush. Cloud nine, you know? Every day. Me, a nanny for my favorite author. And, like, in the weeks before . . . how we'd begun to flirt."

"I shouldn't have."

"We were just having fun, Ben. It was harmless. I would have never . . ." She moved her rock glass atop the hard granite island top. "So Amanda's pregnant?"

"Yes. Seven months."

"Didn't waste any time." She wiped her eyes. "I'm happy for you. Both of you." She checked her phone, scrolled, placed it face down on the island again.

"You've stopped going to class," Ben said. "When you wouldn't talk to me, I hunted down a couple of your friends. Anna and Beth. They're worried about you, kid."

"Don't . . . Don't call me that anymore. Because I'm not."

"You're months away from graduating. You've got your whole life—"

"That scarecrow the news is talking about . . . The one murdering people."

"They've caught him. It was a man named Royal Blakely."

"Something was in that room with us. Briefly. You saw that ceiling shatter."

"It was the wind. The ceiling is over a hundred years old. It cracked. It was the storm."

"Glass rained down from the ceiling," she said. "At first I thought someone was breaking in? We both know something broke *out*. You don't remember writing it, do you?"

"Not all of it." He moved closer. They were on the same side of the island now, their backs to the beveled edge, five feet apart but both staring out the window over the sink. Beyond the courtyard, the hill dropped off sharply toward the ravine below.

She held out the cigarette toward him. He took a drag, gave it back. She said, "We did cocaine. Do you remember?"

They'd pulled the bag from Grandpa Robert's desk drawer. The well-known child psychiatrist had his vices, too. Ben and Devon had spied on him one night through the glass wall when they were supposed to be sleeping. "He needed it to cope. With his work." Vaguely, Ben recalled snorting a line, and then another. His tongue and throat instantly numb. Jennifer had already snorted hers. But it wasn't Jennifer. She'd laughed while he snorted, but it hadn't been her. *It'll help keep you up through the night. It'll keep you juiced*, that voice had said. *So juiced you won't hardly remember a thing*. His nose had bled after the second round of coke. Drops plopping on his laptop keys. "You typed some of the novel for me. My nose wouldn't stop bleeding."

"I type faster than you do. You use two fingers." She eyed her phone, still face down on the island. "Fill in the gaps, Ben. Why did I wake up naked on that couch? What did I do?"

"Jennifer . . ."

"I want the truth."

"The truth as I remember it?"

"Yes, Ben, because I sure as hell don't."

He remembered. However cocaine-induced, sleep-deprived, and frightened they'd been, he remembered every bit of perverse pleasure he'd gotten from seeing her undress.

"What did I do?"

"It wasn't you. Your voice changed. *You* . . . changed, Jennifer. You said most of the time you'd blacked out. Well, when you were out, you weren't sleeping. You tried to seduce me," he said, but was quick to add, "But it wasn't you. It was her. Julia. Amanda says l dream about her. They're nightmares. I know it sounds crazy, but . . ."

"Ben, I know. I know all about the bitch."

"What?"

A hint of a smile, and then gone. "How did I try and seduce you?" she asked.

"You don't need to know. It wasn't you."

"Tell me, Ben."

"Why?"

"Because I was the one violated." She pushed him, punched his chest with both fists. "I was the one violated. Maybe not by you. By her. By something . . ." She clamped both hands to her ears, like she was hearing some loud noise only audible to her. She turned, walked away, stopped and came back again. He'd never seen her this restless. "Do you know what it feels like to have someone else inside you?" Jennifer placed a splayed hand on his chest, patted his shirt, fingers prodding the buttons. For a second he feared she was about to open one, but she removed her hand. She leaned back against the sink, folded her arms, and faced him knowingly. That smile again, there and gone before it could register any sense of relevance for him. The same smile he'd seen from her that weekend. From Julia, whoever she was. Whatever she was. "What did she make me do inside that room, Ben? Tell me."

"I told you not to open the book, but you did."

"Because you'd already opened one yourself."

He nodded. It was the same book he'd kept open too long as a boy. The same one he'd been wanting to reopen ever since, knowing damn well he shouldn't, knowing that he'd probably let too much of it out as a boy. "You kissed me. I knew it wasn't you. The way you laughed when you pulled away. You wanted more."

"You let me kiss you again," she said.

"Yes."

"And then you pushed me away."

He nodded.

"Say it out loud, Ben."

Why? "Yes. I pushed you away."

"Why?"

"Because you're not my wife," he shouted, and then softer. "Because you're not my wife. I love my wife."

She let that linger for a moment. "And what then? Ben? I want to know why I woke up sore the next morning."

"You kept at it. No, *she* kept at it. You were trying to undress me. Ripping my shirt."

She shook her head. "I don't remember."

"But then . . . you finally retreated. Across the room, sulking. You sat in a chair. For the longest time you watched the moths on the tree. You spent an hour painting your nails. Watching me, grinning as you touched polish to each finger."

"And then?"

"We don't need to do this."

"And then?" she asked, louder.

"You came over. You'd already ripped my shirt. You massaged my shoulders. To get me to relax. When I refused your advances, you scratched me. On the cheek. The right cheek. At first I thought it had been an accident. But then you laughed and scratched me again. On the arm. Amanda saw the scratches when I got home."

"And she assumed the worst."

"How couldn't she?"

"And then?"

"And then you went mad," he said. "*She* went mad. You tore into me, scratching, clawing. You bit my neck. It bled. I tried, but I couldn't explain it away. To Amanda." Ben rubbed his face, his stubbly jawline. "You retreated back across the room, to the sofa, laughing. You said . . . 'You're a stubborn one, Ben Bookman. I admire that,' you said."

"And then what?"

"I worked on my book. I tried to tune you out. For the longest time I tuned you out."

"Why did you need to tune me out? What was I doing?"

"Why does it matter?"

"What was I doing, Ben?"

"You were undressing. On the sofa."

Jennifer's eyes teared up. She was trying to be tough, but her jaw quivered.

"You were on your knees," he said. "On the seat cushions. Naked. I tried to not look. But you wouldn't stop calling my name. Pleading that I look. That I watch."

"How long did this go on?"

"Hours. Minutes. All fucking night. The entire weekend was a time warp. A . . ."

"A what?"

"A nightmare. The entire weekend was a nightmare."

"Thank you." Jennifer lowered her head, giggled toward her chest, and in the tone and timbre of that laugh, Ben knew something in her had changed.

Thank you? Like Royal Blakely had thanked him . . .

She looked up, slowly licked her lips, her eyes alive now. "Did I sound like this?"

"Jennifer?"

"Jennifer went away, Ben, but don't worry. She didn't go far." She approached, placed her hand on Ben's chest. He spun away, rounded the island, to keep a distance from her, and then as quickly and without warning as seconds ago, she was back.

"Jennifer?"

She watched him, confused. "She was just here again, wasn't she? She leaves crumbs."

Ben nodded, didn't need to say Julia's name.

"What was I doing?"

"You were trying to seduce me again."

"Because that's what she does, Ben. She's every happily married man's nightmare." She touched her temples, winced through pain of some sort. *Do you know what it feels like to have something inside of you?* She dropped her hands, refocused on him. "Not now. Then. On the couch. That weekend. What was I doing?"

He shook his head. *What do you think you were doing?*

"Ben? What. Was. I. Doing?"

"You were masturbating. Okay?"

"Why?"

"Because . . . I wouldn't . . ."

"Julia doesn't like to be turned away," Jennifer said, smiling, that brief flash of mischievousness in her eyes. She bit her lower lip. "What did I use?"

"What?"

"My hand?"

It dawned on him what she was talking about. "Yes, your hand. Jesus. Can we stop now?"

"And eventually I finished?"

"Yes."

"And I fell asleep?"

"Yes."

"And you covered me up?"

"You looked peaceful. I knew then she'd gone. It was not you, Jennifer."

"And the next morning I awoke. We spoke nothing of the previous night. There were papers scattered all over the room. I helped you finish the book. I helped you type because your nose wouldn't stop bleeding. There were bloodstains on the floor."

He stared out the window toward the woods. "She was gone."

"She was never gone," Jennifer yelled. "Don't you get it?"

He stepped toward her. She stepped away. "Let us help you."

"You can't! Nobody can. I've tried. Counseling. Therapist. A fucking priest. A secret exorcism, Ben! All because I opened that book! Nothing works, okay?" She looked away, back again. But it wasn't her. Maybe remnants, but not all. "I haven't been caught like Royal Blakely and some of the others, because what I do isn't a crime. Just wrong. Immoral. Unethical. But nothing to be arrested over, you see?"

"Others? What do you mean, what you do?"

"Do you know how many marriages I've wrecked in the past year, Ben? How many affairs since I've left that room? Thirteen men. Thirteen marriages I've wrecked, Ben, all in the past year. Because that's what I fucking do now. And I can't stop."

"Jennifer . . ." He trailed off, sounded pathetic.

"But I couldn't completely wreck yours," she said. "Your perfect little marriage." She laughed. "That old priest would never admit it," she said with a sly smile. "But he wants to fuck me too. Just like you do."

"I don't."

"But you did."

"I didn't," he said. "It was never like that."

"She doesn't like the strong ones. She doesn't like being turned down." Jennifer grabbed her empty bourbon glass and smashed it down on the marble island, cracking it into shards. "But I say fuck what she wants." She picked up one of the pieces and brought it toward her arm.

Ben yelled, "Stop. Don't!"

She did, biting her lip, not in a seductive way now but to dampen the pain of it all. A small cut on the top of her forearm, not very deep, just enough to draw blood, but right next to a line of scars showing she'd done this before. Not too different from what Ben had seen on his sister's arms. Jennifer grabbed a paper towel from the counter, dabbed at the blood, and faced Ben with her own eyes returned, like she was all better now. "The cuts keep her at bay. She doesn't like to be cut."

Ben swallowed hard, throat dry and body thrumming.

"What then?" she asked. "That weekend. I drove home."

"Yes. And I came home hours later."

"And you couldn't explain it away to Amanda."

"I couldn't explain it away," he said aloud, realizing someone was crying.

Ben looked over his shoulder. It wasn't coming from Jennifer. She was leaning against the island, arms folded, teary-eyed and completely frazzled, but making no sound. Her cell phone rested face up on the island now. She'd turned it over, as if for his eyes only. The crying was coming from whoever was on the other end, magnified somehow by the hard stone top of the island. Ben stepped closer, read the name on the bright screen.

Amanda Bookman.

The on-screen call minutes ticking toward 6:00. Still running. Still listening. Jennifer had called her. Left the phone running so that she could hear the entire conversation.

Ben lifted the phone. "Amanda . . . Say something." She hung up. "Amanda?"

Call ended. *Six minutes and nine seconds.* He gently placed the phone on the island as the room briefly spun in slow motion.

Jennifer dabbed at her arm with the paper towel, showed the bloodstain to him, like what she'd done was his fault. And maybe it was. Maybe it all was.

He wiped tears from his eyes, couldn't look at her arm—it reminded him too much of Emily.

As if Jennifer had just read his mind, she said, "I got the idea from your sister."

"Emily?"

"I've been seeing her too. It would break her heart to know that I'm a cutter, so don't tell her. She can't help either. Nobody can. But during one of our sessions, I asked where she got the scars on her arm. She was honest, as honest as she wanted me to be with her. She wanted me to trust her. In a sense we counseled each other."

"Jennifer, what are you talking about?"

"She said she used to cut herself when she was younger in order to rechannel the pain."

"What pain?"

"You'll have to ask her, Ben. I asked if it worked, the cutting. She said she thought it did then, but not now. She sees that now." Jennifer showed Ben her arm again, which had clotted. She dropped the stained paper towel on the island. "Your grandfather wasn't all you thought him to be." She pocketed her cell phone, turned her back to him on her way to the door. "No more secrets, Ben."

30

Two hours and a pot of coffee later, Mills had pulled from his office nearly two dozen boxes of old files from cases long buried and solved.

The living room wall had been transformed into something the FBI would have been proud of had they been looking simultaneously for their thirty most wanted, with a network of lines and arrows connecting it all like a spiderweb. While he'd solved hundreds of cases in his career, he'd never until now taken the time to analyze the collective puzzle each piece added up to creating. Or if he had, at one time, analyzed each piece, he'd never given thought that they could all end up as the same puzzle.

Adding to the dozens of names and files he'd written and tacked to the wall in the past two hours, he wrote *The Bad Cop: Kenneth Fontaine*, pinned the accompanying file below it, and then stood back to analyze and reflect on the bizarre memories from four years ago, during Fontaine's three-month crime spree.

Angie Deavers, victim number five, had been the first one to come forward that fall, and once she did, the rest followed, all claiming that Kenneth Fontaine—a forty-two-year-old elementary school math teacher—once he got them into his stolen police cruiser and locked the doors, would immediately tell them they'd been arrested by the Bad Cop.

The final victim, Brenda Foxworthy, like most women in Crooked Tree—and specifically those with red hair—had been on alert that fatal day. Brenda refused, like many other redheads had begun doing by then, to dye her hair, and knew she could possibly be a target: at thirty she fit right in the middle of the age range. Brenda had first noticed Fontaine in Bella's Diner, Mills learned later under questioning, watching her from behind his upside-down menu. Not only watching her, she'd told Detective Mills, but acting bizarre enough, especially for a man in uniform, to warrant a call to the hotline the news had been showing for weeks.

"He was sweating like he was stranded out in the desert, and used his untouched waffle to mop up his brow." That was when Brenda Foxworthy, despite being told to stay put when she'd called the hotline, had left the diner in a panic, but also willing to use herself as bait. Two miles down the road she'd spotted a police car in her rearview. The flashing bar lights and siren soon followed. The Bad Cop said she'd been speeding, which was true. Once he read her driver's license and saw her name, Brenda told Detective Mills, "It was like he was about to cry."

Kenneth Fontaine's wife, Dana, also a teacher at the same school, couldn't have been more shocked, not only by her husband's abrupt death on Route Road, but to learn *he* was the infamous Bad Cop they'd both been following every night on the news. In hindsight, she supposed he'd begun acting strange around the time the abductions had started. He'd fallen behind in his work. He'd begun staying out later after school, and coming home at odd hours. She broke down in hysterics when Mills told her, days after the incident on Route Road, that her husband had stolen the KA-BAR knife from a drunk Marine he'd killed and buried out near the empty grain silo Kenneth had been using as a hideout, living for days off what appeared to be a steady diet of Yoo-hoos and Butterfinger candy bars stolen from a gas station a mile down the road.

Everyone at Crooked Tree Elementary had been stunned, as Kenneth Fontaine had once been one of their most cherished and lovable teachers, prompting another faculty member in front of the flashing news cameras to say, "I guess you really think you know someone, but you don't." And prompting Dana Fontaine to swear, all the way up until she moved out of state two years later, that the man who abducted those young ladies was not her Kenneth. And even though the doctors—during the autopsy she'd insisted they perform—never found the brain tumor she insisted had to be there for his behavior to change so drastically and suddenly, she swore, even as she drove out of town, that something sinister had occurred. And that Kenneth was a victim too, not the perverted villain he was made out to be.

Brenda Foxworthy, Mills recalled, had been reluctant to say if she'd seen Kenneth Fontaine before, and ultimately decided, other than the composite sketches put together by the other victims that flashed nightly across the TV screen for weeks, that she hadn't. But two things specifically from that day stuck out to Mills now as he stared at the mess he'd made of the living room wall. One was Fontaine's blood pumping out onto the roadside gravel, and how Mills had stood there watching, with the briefest of notions that perhaps he should try and put that blood back in somehow. And number two was how Brenda Foxworthy, later at the police station, had described her frightening encounter, using the words, *It was as if he'd come from a nightmare.*

Mills pulled Brenda Foxworthy's cell phone number from the files and dialed. She remembered him well enough, and even though she at first seemed a little dubious talking about that afternoon four years ago, she proceeded to answer all of his questions.

"But back then, did you mean to say that he'd come straight from *your* nightmare?"

"I don't know what I meant to say, Detective. It was a long time ago."

"Did you used to have nightmares, Mrs. Foxworthy?"

She paused, and then, "Yes."

"About that man. That exact man? The Bad Cop?"

Another pause, this one longer. "Yes."

"May I ask for how long?"

"Years."

"How many?"

"I don't know. Five. Six, maybe," she said. "I was a girl. Ten years old. I saw a true crime show I shouldn't have been watching. About a rapist. I turned it off after ten minutes. It scared me. And then that night, I was watching the news with my parents. There was a police officer who'd done something bad. Roughed up a speeder. I asked my parents if there really were bad cops and my dad said, sure, there's probably a few out there, but the overwhelming majority are good men and women, sworn to protect us. I went to bed that night thinking about both that rapist and the bad cop. My mind must have put those fears together. I had a nightmare of it all."

"About this Bad Cop?"

"Yes. At first I couldn't remember a face, but the more I had the nightmare the more real he became. I'd scream out at night."

"And this lasted for five to six years?"

"Not every night, but yes. It was a reoccurring one for sure."

"A couple more questions, Mrs. Foxworthy. And again, I'm sorry if this has upset you again in any way, but it could help me with a case I'm currently working . . ."

"The missing kids?"

"Yes, ma'am. Among others."

"Go on then. Ask your questions."

"When did your nightmare of the Bad Cop go away?"

"I was sixteen."

"And when did it return?"

"Four years ago," she said. "Before the first . . . victim."

"Do you understand now that he was looking for you specifically?"

She started crying, and it made his heart ache for her. "Yes, I know that now."

"Because he was *your* nightmare."

"Yes. Somehow, yes."

"One last question. Were you ever a patient of Dr. Robert Bookman?"

Another pause, he sensed not so much to search her memory but whether or not to disclose it. "Yes. I went to him four times. On the final time it worked."

"Can I ask what exactly worked?"

"My doctor referred us to him," she said. "It was a long time ago, Detective, but I remember him turning the lights down low and putting on some nature sounds. He talked me to sleep. It was really peaceful."

"You said it took you four visits?"

"I didn't have the nightmare until the fourth time. I remember my father being angry, telling my mother we were throwing good money away on a quack doctor. But then on that fourth visit I fell asleep on the bed in his office, and the nightmare came."

"And then you woke up? What did it sound like, when you awoke?"

"What did it sound like?"

"I know it's an odd question, but an important question all the same."

"Well, I'd always thought it was like a book being slammed shut."

"When you woke up, Mrs. Foxworthy, did the doctor have a book on his lap?"

"Yes."

"Leather bound. Plain looking?"

"Yes."

"Are your nightmares completely gone now, Mrs. Foxworthy?"

"Yes, they are. They ended again, on that day when you killed him on the street."

He thanked her for her time and ended the call. With his Sharpie, he wrote Brenda Foxworthy's name on the wall underneath the tagged files. He'd now matched two living nightmares to two specific people—Jepson Heap with the Scarecrow and Brenda Foxworthy with the Bad Cop—both former patients of Dr. Robert Bookman. And the respective hosts for each—Royal Blakely and Kenneth Fontaine, both of whom had seemed to have undergone a sudden and intense personality transformation just before their outbreaks.

Mills had another name for the transformations, and it brought to mind his first case as a rookie. Lucius Oswald. He blew dust off that box and flipped through his files. Lucius was a small, effeminate man. A homosexual, Mills had guessed back then, which later proved right when Oswald's relationship with the attending nurse, Curtis Lumpkin, left him with the AIDS virus and Curtis Lumpkin on the lam. Lucius died two years later inside the asylum, deteriorated like something Mills had never seen before and never wanted to see again.

Mills had been after Lucius Oswald for months before finally arresting him. Lucius, according to his sister, Dorcas Oswald, had begun acting strange over the previous summer.

Easily agitated. Nervous and fidgety. Around the same time he'd started chasing people.

At the time, that was all they had on Lucius. For whatever reason, and without warning, he'd be walking down the street, and then suddenly start walking behind someone. When that someone would grow uncomfortable and start walking faster, he would too, until eventually they'd flee and he'd chase after them, running. For months this went on. Random bursts of following, and then chasing. They'd brought him in numerous times; he'd promise to stop. But then the accident occurred. Lucius Oswald chased an old man named Bernie Buffet down Main Street. The old man panicked, tripped, and fell into oncoming traffic. He was struck by a Chevy truck going forty, and died on impact. Lucius was arrested, charged this time with manslaughter, and after an extensive psychiatric evaluation conducted by Dr. Robert Bookman, who had already broken ground on a new asylum, asked that Mr. Oswald be moved there as soon as it was completed. The judge agreed. Lucius, by that point, had been diagnosed as insane, and was growing crazier by the year.

What struck Mills as odd was how Lucius, even in the tight confines of his cell, and later in his private room at Oswald Asylum, would shuffle his feet like he didn't know where to go. He'd mumble under his breath, and then all of a sudden break off in sprints around the room, across the room, back and forth until just as suddenly he'd stop.

"Chasing Jimmy," Lucius would mumble. "Chasing Jimmy."

Eventually, after so many frustrating visits of getting nothing out of Lucius Oswald other than those uttered words—*Chasing Jimmy*—Mills had gotten him, after a physical threat and literal twisting of the arm, to elaborate. "Who the fuck is Jimmy, Lucius? And why are you chasing him? Why do you chase people? Lucius? You got any marbles left up there?"

"Jimmy Walker," Lucius had then said, stopping Mills cold. "Chasing Jimmy Walker."

"Who is Jimmy Walker?" Mills had asked. "Lucius?" Nothing. "Lucius, who the fuck is Jimmy Walker?" Mills had finally screamed.

Lucius Oswald never brought up the name again, and after seeing the state of nervous anxiety in which the confrontation had left Lucius Oswald, Dr. Robert Bookman took Mills off his visitor list.

Mills paced now, jiggling the Sharpie in his palm like a teacher would a piece of chalk.

Chasing. Being chased.

He knew enough about nightmares now to know definitively that *Being Chased* was one of the more common ones. And now, in hindsight—although he'd spent weeks looking for someone named Jimmy Walker forty years ago—he'd be willing to bet Dr. Robert Bookman once healed a patient by that name. And Lucius had ended up so crazy because he could never find Jimmy Walker. Mills knew for a fact that Robert Bookman treated more than just those living in Crooked Tree. His work was well known enough that parents put their kids in cars and planes and traveled to him, which was exactly what Mills' parents had done with him as a boy.

Mills drew another diagonal line from the central words, *Blackwood; Dr. Robert Bookman*, and at the end of it wrote, *Lucius Oswald, Being Chased*, and then finally, *Jimmy Walker?* His stomach rumbled; it had been a while since he'd eaten. Adrenaline would only take him so far before he crashed. He took his pills and then fixed himself a peanut butter and jelly sandwich, with the notion of getting into Lou Anne Logjam's files from the early nineties as soon as he finished. They'd dubbed her the Witch after she poisoned all those children. Sandwich in hand, he wrote *The Witch* on the wall, and below it, *Lou Anne Logjam*. He stepped back and chewed, eager to dive into her files and see if there was anything that jumped at him.

He wasn't expecting any visitors, so when car tires crunched on gravel outside, he reached for his gun. He saw out the window it was just Father Frank and his vomit-colored Prius, so he put the gun back down on the coffee table and met the old priest at the door. Only a couple of times had Father Frank ever made a house call—one when Linda died, and another when Sam and Linda had staged the intervention that ultimately put an end to his alcohol consumption.

Mills showed him in. "What can I do you for, Father?"

Father Frank held a cane in his left hand and a bottle of merlot in his right. He halted when he saw the living room wall.

Mills said, "I can explain."

Father Frank's rheumy eyes gazed down at him. "No need, Winchester. What I would like though is a bottle opener, a *clean* glass, and a comfortable chair."

"Is this about what we discussed yesterday? About Julia?"

"It is. I'll do my best to explain what I *do* know, as I'm hard-pressed now at my age to find the answers to what I don't."

Before

A MANDA, AFTER SHE'D *calmed down enough to laugh about it, told Ben that Bri would not have done such a thing at home.*

It's Blackwood that brought it out of her. Her mischievous side. The endless bookshelves, the rolling ladders. The nooks and crannies and carved banisters. The turrets and tunnels and hallways and hearths.

Bri had lured her mother to the second floor by tapping a stick against one of the radiators. Eager to seek out the noise, Amanda— who'd been trying to work on a story for the next day's newscast— had searched every room on the first floor before pinpointing the source inside the second-floor study. Bri, wearing a Halloween mask from the horror movie Scream, *jumped out from behind the sofa and shouted. And she'd gotten her good, too, as Amanda had let out the mother of all curse words, loud enough to have drawn both Ben and Grandpa Robert up from the first floor with weapons—Ben, holding the Stephen King book he'd been reading for the fifth time, and Robert, the wrought-iron poker he'd grabbed from beside the parlor's stone hearth, both convinced, by the high-pitched way in which Amanda had screamed, that an intruder had found a way into the house. Amanda was the only one to not think it funny, and she'd told Bri as much on her way out of the room, mumbling under her breath that she hated this damn house and for Ben to handle it.*

With *Grandpa Robert concealing his amusement behind a clenched fist, Ben had pretended to handle it, to reprimand his daughter. But deep down he'd been proud; he'd done the same thing numerous times to his sister Emily at the same age, albeit without the mask, which in truth had unnerved him as well. Not so much the mask itself, but the memory of it.*

"Where did you get that mask, Bri?" Ben had asked her, suddenly serious.

"On the third floor. In the room at the end of the hallway."

He'd taken the mask from her. "We don't go in that room, Bri. We've been over this. Do you hear me?"

She'd nodded, her eyes asking, "Why not?"

"That was Devon's room."

31

Ben tried Amanda's cell for the fourth time since leaving the house; all had gone to voice mail.

"Amanda, call me back. Please. I don't know where you are, but I need you to go to Blackwood. I can't explain over the phone, but I—"

She clicked over. "Ben . . ."

He let out a gush of air. "Where are you? I'll pick you up." Silence. Static; she must still be out in the Hollow, near where they'd found the remains. "Amanda . . . Are you there?"

"I'm here."

"I'm sorry. For everything. I don't know what else to say. Or even how to start fixing it. But at least you know the truth."

"Cocaine, Ben? I thought the drinking was bad. But . . ."

"I . . ."

"I know, you don't remember. And that's why you don't remember writing the book."

"It was the room. It's always been about the atrium."

"It's always been about your weakness, Ben. Temptation."

"Yes." He gritted his teeth. "I'm weak. I've always been weak."

"And you try to cover it by being tough. But that's not you, Ben. That's not the real you. And it's okay."

"Grandpa Robert took me into that room as a boy, Amanda. He—"

"I want to know what's going on, Ben. Not with Robert. With Royal Blakely. With whoever else might be out there. We can talk about the rest later."

"Meet me at Blackwood."

"I'll meet you at Blackwood. But you have to be honest with me."

"I'll tell you everything I know. Just meet me there. I'm on my way now. Promise me you'll come."

"I'll come." She ended the call.

He dialed Emily; she answered on the third ring. "Ben?"

"I'm on my way. Amanda should be there soon." He waited for a cluster of cars to pass, and then turned right toward the woods on the outskirts of town. "Em, we need to talk."

"Yes, we do."

"About Grandpa Robert."

Silence.

"Emily?"

"We'll talk when you get here. Be safe." She hung up.

Both hands on the wheel, Ben took the road more aggressively, and hoped the clunker of a car would hold up. Seated high and fortress-like atop the northeastern edge of Crooked Tree, Blackwood's fifty-seven acres of isolated woodlands was both friend and foe, proudly claimed by some residents as often as it was cursed by others. From the town square, Blackwood's hills loomed large and foreboding, close enough to shade vast portions of Crooked Tree's historic district during the long summer days, yet, by car, still a twenty-minute drive up to the house. The illusion gave credence to the enormity not only of the acreage but of the famous black trees themselves. The illusion, some said, was all part of the allure, part of Blackwood's natural defense against trespassers, as many lost their nerve halfway up.

The house was visible only within the final two hundred yards, and only in the dead of winter when the trees had lost their leaves. Otherwise, Blackwood seemingly appeared out of nowhere. Blocked by trees one minute and before your eyes the next, not so much built amid the trees as it had been built *into* them.

On their fourth date, Ben had taken Amanda to Blackwood to meet Grandpa Robert. Grandma Jane had been dead ten years by then. During the drive, he'd explained to his future wife that no trees had been removed during Blackwood's thirteen-month construction. The edges of the house butted right up to the trees surrounding it. She hadn't believed it until she'd seen it for herself. It was as if the house had been carefully wedged *into* the woodlands. Whatever trees stood in the way were swallowed up into the house's foundation, molded into portions of the stone façade, expertly crafted into the walls and turrets, and through the inner workings of bricks and mortar like wooden veins and arteries the color of coffee grains. The walls, festooned with lichen and climbing vines, soared monstrous and wet, as if the limestone was eternally dripping.

Like many, upon first sight, Amanda had been in awe. She'd promised to bring her camera the next time to video; it was the most unique house she'd ever seen. She never brought her camera. They'd only stayed an hour, long enough for Robert to give her the tour and a glass of wine, but in those sixty minutes her tone had changed from excitement to anxiety. She'd grown pale and dizzy. Robert had escorted her to the nearest reading chair. Later, she'd jokingly asked Ben if his grandfather had slipped something into her wine. She'd apologized to Ben on the way home, hoping it had not been rude of her to ask to leave so abruptly. Following the initial visit, each subsequent return to Blackwood for Amanda had been met with a sense of dread.

Ben coasted onto the gravel driveway, so darkened by the canopy of overhanging trees it was as if he'd entered a tunnel. Twenty yards ahead, with no warning, a deer shot through the cones of light, darting from one side of the gravel road to the other, there and gone in a flash. Ben's heart thumped. He stopped in front of Blackwood's heavily windowed façade. Amanda had already arrived; she'd only been a few miles away, down in the Hollow between Blackwood and Oswald Asylum.

Before Ben could close his car door, Bri was bounding down the porch steps, clearly awaiting his arrival. She jumped. He caught her. The momentum took them into a spin that left him dizzy. He kissed her head, squeezed her tight. She gripped his neck and planted one right on his lips. "Don't ever go away again."

He'd left her many times before, on business trips and book tours, but this was different. Something about their last twenty-four hours apart had been stamped with no guarantee of a reunion, and they'd both known it. He kissed her forehead, hugged her tight, and kissed her again. Aunt Emily waved from the open front door. A second-floor window opened, and then, seconds later, the neighboring window, so that only a thin screen separated in from out. Ben placed Bri on her feet and held her hand. It was Amanda in there, opening one window after the other.

Bri said, "I think Mommy gets claustrophobic."

"Where did you learn that word?" Ben asked.

His daughter shrugged. "From a book."

Ben said to his approaching sister, "Amanda hates the woods."

"Then shouldn't she be afraid of what's out there getting in?" Emily asked with a grin.

Bri was more serious. "I think she's more afraid of what's inside being unable to get out."

32

FATHER FRANKLIN COSTIGLIANO swallowed a deep gulp of merlot, closed his eyes, and seemed to meditate for a few seconds before opening them.

He pointed to the wall, his arthritic finger shook. "There she is." He faced Mills in the armchair on the other side of the coffee table. "Julia."

The priest drank again.

"You might want to slow down there, Father. I need you lucid." Mills stared at the wall, where he'd written *Jennifer, Julia, Ben Bookman,* and *Blackwood,* all with question marks beside their names.

"You need me drunk, Winchester. I need me drunk. You asked me about exorcisms yesterday?"

"Yes. Have you performed one?"

A quick nod.

"How many?"

Another drink. "You won't believe me."

"I will."

"Twenty-seven."

Mills sat so his knees didn't buckle. "You're right. I don't believe you."

"I've performed more in my ninety-two years than any priest should. Of course, most priests never do. Never catch even a hint of it, and even fewer are sanctioned to do it."

"And you are?"

"Ha." Another sip. "No. Of course not. Completely unsanc-tioned, all of them. Getting an exorcism sanctioned by the church is about as difficult as breaking into Fort Knox. The investigations take too long. I tried on five separate occasions in the late sixties and early seventies, all denied. I am not an exorcist, Winchester. So I stopped asking. I did what I could to help relieve the suffering."

"Did they work?"

"Some. Half. But perhaps that's wishful thinking. Not very many, I'm afraid."

"Why do you think we've had so many . . . ?"

Father Frank pointed at the wall. "The same reason you've had so many bizarre crimes."

"And Julia?"

He drank more wine. Her name conjured sadness in him. "Unfortunately, I know her well."

Know, not knew . . .

"She's filth, Winchester. Horror disguised as beauty. Lust."

"A nightmare . . ." He let that linger. Father Frank pursed his lips, as if thinking, but said nothing. "I've seen her in one of my nightmares, Father. Recently. I caught glimpse of one of Ben Book-man's nightmares, and she was in it. I mentioned Jennifer Jackson yesterday and you clammed up."

"I didn't clam up."

"Then what would you call it."

Father Frank swallowed a heavy gulp. "I can't divulge what was sworn to secrecy in a confessional, Winchester. You of all people should know that."

"Even when people are dying? And the town is turning itself upside down?"

"Which is why I'm here." He removed his white clerical col-lar and placed it on the sofa cushion beside him. "About to break promises and shred oaths." Father Frank's rheumy eyes homed in on Mills. "That poor young woman, Jennifer Jackson, believes she is possessed."

Mills didn't even find this shocking. "And you?"

"I know she is." He swallowed more wine. His liver-spotted hands shook.

"When did this start?"

"A year ago," he said, finishing his wine and pouring more. "She felt a . . . presence inhabit her body. A demon of some sort, in the form of a woman named Julia. A seductress of the worst kind.

She tried psychiatrists, doctors, pills, and finally came to me. She'd heard I'd done . . ."

"Exorcisms?"

"It sounds so silly to even say it, but yes."

"We met a half dozen times—consultations, you might say—before actually trying. She'd become a homewrecker. Sleeping with married men all over town, with the sole intent of breaking up marriages. For two days I attempted to rid that girl of her demon. This Julia. But to no avail." Father Frank stared at the wall, as if studying all the lines, markings, and cases. Mills wondered if he would come to the same conclusion as he had. He nodded toward the wall. "Julia. She claims to have come from Blackwood. A room she called the atrium." His eyes shone on Mills now. "Which must be the room you wouldn't speak of?"

Mills nodded.

"That room," Father Frank said, reflecting, finally placing his wine glass, still half full, on the coffee table. "I'd say that's where she originated, but from my encounters with her, I know now she's much older than that house."

"How much older?"

"Like ancient Italy older. Pompeii, older. Claims to have died when Vesuvius erupted. Buried in ash and rock like the rest of them."

"Then how is she here? Now? Crossing oceans, continents, and centuries?"

"I don't know."

"I think you do."

"As do you," said the priest. "But both of us are afraid to say it." He pointed at the wall. "Or perhaps not." He used the arm of the sofa to stand. "She's foul. She's a vixen. A tease. A seductress. Men who've known flesh and covet it smell her as roses, Winchester, but I know her stench differently. She's dirt and dust. She's carnage and mud. When I step into a room tainted by her presence, I smell shit. Human excrement. I smell the devil. Just like all the other ones I've performed over the decades."

Father Frank crossed himself.

"The others?" asked Mills.

"Demons of some form. Both male and female. One as foul as the next."

"At what point do they reach out for your help?"

"When they're at the end of their rope. And they've no one else to turn to." He slow-walked toward the wall for a closer look at all the names Mills had written. "Even nonbelievers turn to God when desperate. They're cautious. They tiptoe around the bush, afraid almost to ask, because the entire notion seems preposterous. First I'll bless houses. I'll bless rooms. Sometimes this has worked, but when it doesn't, I prepare for battle. I've been attacked. I've been bitten by human beings, once normal, who you'd swear had turned rabid animals. I've been cursed at in every language possible, even the languages of the unknown."

"But my question, Father. What prompts those suffering to reach out?"

"Isn't it obvious? Changes in behavior. Some minor, but most, in my case, quite drastic."

Mills stood, walked to the wall, and put a finger on Royal Blakely's name. Next his finger found Lucius Oswald, and then Kenneth Fontaine. Could their changes in behavior all have been triggered by the same dark force?

"What is going through that mind of yours, Winchester?"

"A lot. But also not enough." Mills described in detail the sharp personality changes all three of those men had experienced before either their death, capture, or, in Oswald's case, admittance into the asylum. "They were all patients of Robert Bookman. All part of his life's work. Not only his life's work, but every Bookman psychiatrist before him. Bernard Bookman brought books with him from Vienna." Mills pointed at Blackwood. "Father, I was in that room as a boy. He was unable to help me. He couldn't take my nightmares away. He told my parents he wanted to try something new. Something he'd never done before. They agreed, because what else was to be done? I was a boy stricken with every nightmare imaginable."

"I'm sorry, Winchester. I've told you countless times, you are the most unusual case. Yet here you are still, catching bad guys. Solving crimes. Go on with your story."

"He drove me to Blackwood. He took me into that room. Had me lie down on the sofa. We did the same thing we'd do in his office. He had it set up so that I could easily fall asleep. It was dark. But I was on that couch for no more than a minute before things started to happen. Those books started moving. Subtle at first, but then they began to shake, inching forward like solders marching off a cliff. He hurried me out of the room. He was deathly afraid, Father."

"How do they do it?" Father Frank asked. "How do they get rid of the nightmares?"

"As a boy, every time I was stricken with a nightmare in his office, a loud noise would wake me up. At first I thought it was a clap, but the second time, I saw one of those books on his lap. It was a book being forcefully closed, above my head. He was reciting words . . ."

"What words?"

"I don't remember, Father. But somehow, he traps the nightmares in those books."

"How is that possible?"

"What if nightmares are real, Father?"

"They aren't."

"Julia?"

"A demon."

"What if that's closer to what nightmares really are? When I awake sometimes, I can't move. The mare is still pressing down upon me. What if it's not completely in my mind?"

Father studied the wall. One by one his unsteady finger touched names Mills had written in black ink: *The Witch. The Five O'Clock Shadow. The Bad Cop. The Scarecrow. The Boogeyman. The Screamer.* Father's eyes grew large; he turned on Mills. "Are you saying . . . ?"

"What if sometimes they get out?"

Father crossed himself again. He returned to his wine glass, sipped from it, and listened.

"In folklore," said Mills, "mares ride on the chests of the sleepers. They give them nightmares. They make it seem that they can't breathe. They slide through keyholes of locked doors. They're often seen as . . ." As if on cue, he followed the flight of one as it flew and spun toward the lampshade across the room, black wings clicking on translucent fabric. "Moths."

"And you think Ben Bookman let one out?"

"Yes, and it somehow took over Royal Blakely."

Mills' cell phone vinrated on the end table. He picked it up. It was Sam. "Yes?"

"The Peterson girl has come to," she said, hurried. "She's not talking, but she's aware now that I'm in the room. She follows my finger. My voice. She's having nightmares, Dad. Every time she closes her eyes. I need you to do what you do."

"What do you mean?"

"I know, Dad. I know enough. I'll pick you up in ten minutes. Be ready."

He looked at Father Frank, who was already sliding the white collar back into his shirt, as if not only eavesdropping but ready to roll. "No need. I've got a ride." He hung up.

"Saint Mary's?" asked Father Frank.

"Yes."

Father Frank tossed him the keys. "I'll only allow myself one and get behind the wheel."

"Not two in fifteen minutes?"

"Definitely not two in fifteen minutes." He stood before the wall with his own iPhone. He pressed a button, looked confused. "Damn thing won't take."

"It's on video, Father. You're filming the wall." He switched it over to photo for him.

Father Frank took the picture. "There. For reference." He slid the phone into the pocket of his black pants and followed Mills to the door.

Before

*E*DWARD CREECH WAS *six foot seven and weighed one hundred eighty pounds, fully clothed.*

He wore his dark hair long and uncombed. His eyebrows plumed out like feathers.

He wore his britches baggy, cinched by a belt; it was difficult for his mother to find clothes that fit. He wore sandals for the same reason.

Edward was home schooled, needed no friends, and wanted only to be left alone and play the violin like his dead hero, Paganini.

Paganini had friends, his mother pleaded. He was quite the lothario from what I've read. Don't you want to ever marry, Edward?

I don't want to marry, Mother.

What about playing in front of people? You could tour. You'd have millions of fans.

I don't want fans, Mother.

You do know that some thought Paganini was the devil.

Paganini was not the devil, Mother. He was misunderstood.

Edward was thirty-one and still living in his mother's attic when he felt the breeze crawl under his skin. His attic studio was spacious, with exposed wooden beams and a vaulted ceiling that accentuated the acoustics. He played with the dormer window open so his music carried. He'd been in the middle of Paganini's Caprice No. 24 when the dormer window suddenly slammed shut. He found this odd; the wind had not been blowing. And he'd not yet begun to play so violently—when his sadness turned to rage—as to cause any pictures to fall from the walls.

He put down his violin and bow, felt a tickle on his right index finger, like something unseen had just blown on it. And then it burrowed under the fingernail. He closed his eyes when the tickle turned uncomfortable, and then grimaced when it turned to pain. Up his arm it traveled, through his shoulder and into his chest. Bones tightened and contorted. His head screamed with tightness and pain, and within seconds it had spread throughout his entire body, into his skin, curling him into a fetal position, writhing and moaning on the attic floor.

And then it was gone. No, not gone, but rather, the opposite—arrived.

His mother banged on the attic door. She called his name, panicked.

Tell her you're fine, Edward. Tell her before she calls for help.

Without asking from where the voice had come, he called to the door. "I'm fine, Mother." He said it again, with more force. He waited. She said to be careful. "Okay, Mother."

Her footsteps faded down the stairs. He made it to his feet, whispered, "Michael Bookman." Although he knew no one by that name. He grabbed sheets of paper from his desk and placed them on his music stand. He dipped the quill into the inkwell and drew the outline of a face, and then added eyes and a nose, but no mouth. "Whispers and hushes and screams."

Next he took scissors from a cup on his desk. He sat before his mirror, which was cracked from the day he'd punched his reflection, and began snipping. Next came the razor. Thirty minutes later he was bald. Even his eyebrows were gone.

He liked it.

But what he liked more was that he was no longer Edward Creech.

33

B EN FACED THE atrium's glass wall.
 The glass ceiling was still broken, exposing the room to the elements now for months. The bricked floor glistened with moisture. Puddles sat stagnant. Fuzzy green moss sprouted in the cracks. Sunlight and exposure had faded the spines of some of the books.

"They're not ruined," Emily said behind him. "I don't think they can be." Birds flew beneath the broken ceiling. A squirrel skittered around the tree. Dozens of moths clung to the bark, various species and colors. "Did you see where I marked the trees outside?"

Ben turned toward his sister. "You've been here?"

"Yes. Off and on. But not in several months. And never inside that room."

"What about the trees?" said a young, eavesdropping voice behind them.

They both turned toward Amanda and Bri, who'd just entered the hallway.

"I marked the trees with red paint," Emily said. "Months ago, on one of my visits. The gnarly ones. The black ones."

"The ones like the tree inside that room." Bri pointed from a few steps *behind* her mother, not afraid, Ben surmised, just astute enough to not come closer. "The ones without leaves."

"Yes." Emily approached her niece, squeezed her shoulder. "The ones like that one. Now let's get you back into the kitchen. I bet the muffins we baked are about ready."

"I want to know about the trees," Bri said. "Why did you paint some of the trees?"

Emily looked at Ben. Ben nodded. "She's fine."

Amanda grabbed Bri's arm and gave it a gentle tug. "Come on."

"I'm not moving until I hear about the trees. Why do some of them not have leaves? They look dead, but they're still growing. Aunt Emily, why did you put red paint on some of them?"

Amanda gave up. "Go ahead."

"Because at one time it was only a very small portion of them." Emily looked at her brother. "You remember, Ben? We were kids. We counted. That day, do you remember how many were void of leaves? How many had begun to twist and turn, to darken and grow as if they had minds of their own?"

"Forty-seven," he said, without hesitation.

"Forty-seven," she concurred.

"And how many now have you marked with red paint?" Amanda asked, placing her hands over Bri's ears.

Bri promptly removed them and stepped aside. "How many, Aunt Emily?"

"Over two hundred," she said. "Twelve more since last night."

Ben said, "And you know what's causing it?"

She eyed the tree inside the atrium; even now, in the daylight, the dark bark was covered by moths. "Don't you?"

Bri said, "It happens when a mare touches them. They turn into mare trees. The leaves fall off and then the moths come to drink."

Amanda turned toward her daughter. "Where did you hear this?"

"Grandpa Robert."

"Great, Ben," said Amanda. "My family passes down recipes. Clothes. Memorabilia. Yours passes down nightmares."

Bri said, "Mares sometimes turn into moths."

"And now she thinks nightmares are real." Amanda grabbed Bri's hand again. "Ben, we're leaving. I told you. It was stupid to come here."

Emily's voice stopped them cold. "Amanda, no. If we're afraid of what might be out *there*, trust me, it's safer here."

"Can you at least explain why? Or is that a secret too?"

"Think of it like a prison," Emily said.

Amanda scoffed. "Not hard."

"And a prisoner escapes. Do you think they'd return to that prison?"

"No," Amanda said. "That would be stupid."

"Which is why it's safer here." Emily brushed by her sister-in-law and headed down the hallway toward the kitchen. "Follow me. I'll explain what I know. And also what I've learned since last night."

"Last night?" Ben asked.

"I broke into Grandpa Robert's journals."

"And?"

Emily said to Bri. "Run ahead to the kitchen and check on the muffins."

"But I want to hear about the journals," said Bri.

Emily smiled, ruffled her hair. "Maybe later. Right now I need you to check on the muffins so they don't burn. But don't open the oven without one of us. Just look through the window."

Bri looked dejected, but went anyway.

Emily waited until Bri disappeared into the kitchen. "Grandpa was sick. If not a bit mad. And I'm trying really hard to not think of him as a few other things as well."

CHAPTER

34

AMY PETERSON WAS a pretty little girl with dimples and dark hair.

When Mills entered the hospital room, escorted by Detective Blue and Father Frank, he found the Peterson girl resting on her left side, with a tight clutch on a brown teddy bear.

"You brought me here to watch her sleep?"

"Just wait," said Blue. Amy's eyelids fluttered. "She's been having horrible nightmares. Every time she closes her eyes."

"What do you want me to do?" he asked Blue, testing her.

Blue watched him, possibly testing him too. "Do you remember when I was a little girl?" *Only every day.* "The nightmares I'd have?"

"You were nine." He blinked away the memory of breaking her arm. "Go on."

"You used to sit by my bed at night." Blue watched Amy Peterson instead of him. "I'd get worked up before even closing my eyes. Dreading the nightmare before it happened." She grinned. "You'd put your hand on my forehead. Real soft, like petting a puppy. It was the only time your hands were soft, Daddy." Tears pooled her eyes. "You'd say, pleasant dreams, Sam. Pleasant dreams. Every night I'd believe you."

"But the nightmare would still come." He'd never been able to take his daughter's nightmare away. He wiped his cheeks. "Good goddamn, look at the two of us, Blue. Crying like babies."

She sniffled. "But at least you helped me go to sleep."

"Look," Father Frank said from the doorway.

Amy had drifted off during their exchange, and she'd already begun to whimper. Mills knew what she'd brought him here to do. Although he'd been successful with others in the past, he'd never been able to take his own girl's nightmares away. But it was also apparent that his touch, with Samantha, had done *something* when she was a little girl. He approached the bed to provide that same something to the Peterson girl. He stood over her, waiting. A minute later the little girl's whimpering increased and her body became restless. *Was this when the mare was climbing on top? Bringing about the bad dreams . . .* He delayed another moment; if he was going to have a brush-up with the little girl and take her nightmare, he needed to make sure he was catching the thick of it. He placed his hand on the girl's forehead. Petted the wet hairline. He quietly shushed her, and whispered, "Pleasant dreams, Amy. Pleasant dreams."

Blue had stood from the chair and was watching over his slumped shoulder. Amy calmed immediately. Blue covered her own mouth with a trembling hand.

"Pleasant dreams," Mills whispered again. "Pleasant dreams." Amy calmed even more. After a few more seconds, he lifted his hand from the girl's forehead. Amy slept peacefully. He looked over his shoulder. Blue stared at him; something akin to awe. He said, "And your mother claimed I could never even spell bedside manner."

Blue touched his arm—not the one he'd used to touch Amy Peterson; that one was still humming from the brush-up—and then she moved closer to the bed. She raised the blanket up to the little girl's shoulders and watched her sleep.

Mills wavered.

Blue clutched his elbow and walked him out into the hallway. "Are you okay?" He nodded, stared at her until she asked, "What?"

"How many months along are you?"

She laughed, eyed Mills and Father Frank, who then turned down the hallway to give them privacy. She didn't deny it. "How'd you know?"

"I've made a career off hunches, Samantha."

"Just over three months." She looked down at her waistline. "I'm not showing yet. How'd you know?"

"You got sick at the Petersons' crime scene. You never get sick, Sam. I saw how you looked at Amanda Bookman yesterday. You've been popping breath mints like they were candy. You're quicker to cry. Like you were with the other two. What were their names again?"

"Funny. You can see them again as soon as this is over."

"You don't cry, Blue. You don't always gotta be so tough. You haven't told Danny, have you?"

"No."

"Why not?"

"You know why. He already wants me to quit."

"So do I. Or at least get you out of homicide."

She looked away, checked her phone.

He reached into his pocket and pulled out a medicine bottle. He twisted the lid and palmed four pills into his hand.

She watched him. "What are those?"

"Sleeping pills." He popped them into his mouth, crunched them down to paste, and dry swallowed with a wince of bitterness.

"Dad," she stopped abruptly in the hallway. "You could down an elephant with that many. What are you doing?"

"I need to have that girl's nightmare as soon as possible."

"What? Are you . . . Is that how it works?"

"The next time I close my eyes, yes. Why are you looking at me like that?" He took a step down the hall, wavered again, used the wall as a crutch.

"Do they kick in that fast?"

"No, not typically. When I haven't slept in a couple days, they do."

When the previous ones taken are still coursing through my blood-stream . . .

Father Frank approached, grabbed Mills' other arm. "Do we need to find him a room?"

"He just took four sleeping pills."

"Get out while you can, Sam." Mills allowed them both to escort him to the nurses' station. "Homicide gets in the blood. The adrenaline." He leaned toward her ear. "You know the saying. Our days begin . . ."

"When their days end," she finished. "I got it. Now let's find you a bed before you die."

"How about dinner?" he muttered, starting to slur. "You, Danny, and the boys?"

"Dinner will be fine, Dad."

"Can Father Frank come?"

"Oh, I don't need to impose."

"Father Frank can come." She turned Mills down a hallway, waved for a nurse, who came running toward them with urgency. Blue mentioned an EKG.

"Heart's fine," Mills said. "I've recently started on a nice healthy diet of legumes." He chuckled as Blue handed him off to the nurse. "Do I need to bring anything to dinner, Sam?"

"No."

Just the same soft man I saw back in that room, he thought he heard her say, as the nurse helped him turn a corner. "I'm 'bout to go down for the deep sleep, Nurse . . ."

"Rigsby."

"Nurse Rigsby."

"And what is the deep sleep, Mr. Mills?"

"Little bit more involved than a nap," he said, feeling for the bed she'd just walked him to. "Whatever you do. Don't wake me up until I'm ready."

"And how do I know when you're ready, Mr. Mills?"

"When I start crying. My wife would always wake me up when the tears came."

Before

*B*EN SAT SIDE *by side with Bri, swinging on the porch swing, talking intermittently about her nightmare, but afraid to push her too hard on it.*

"Can I ask you one more question, Bri?"

"Yes."

"Will you promise to tell me if he ever returns?"

"Who?"

"The Nightmare Man."

"Oh. Okay. But he comes all the time, Daddy."

He used his legs to stop the swing. "What do you mean? How long have you been seeing him? Since Grandpa Robert told you the story?"

"Before then. Since I was little. But not anymore."

"And why is that?

"That's more than one question, Daddy. But he won't come back now."

"Why not?"

"Because he finally found my hollow. All kids have a hollow, you know. The place where the seeds grow."

"What seeds, Bri?"

"The nightmare seeds, Daddy. He planted nightmares about Blackwood's trees in Aunt Emily's hollow when she was a little girl. And they grew. Except he calls those Blackwood trees mare trees."

"Good thing the Baku came and gobbled it up then."

She made as if to start swinging again and he released his legs to allow her momentum. "I don't think it was the Baku that killed Aunt Emily's nightmare."

"Oh?"

"She didn't call it. You did."

"Really?"

"And it wasn't the Sandman either, because there wasn't any sand left on the bed."

"How then did her nightmare go away?"

"I think it might have been Mr. Dreams."

35

THE KITCHEN AT Blackwood was spacious.

Robert had always referred to it as big boned—with cabinets that soared, a tall ceiling of exposed wooden beams and trusses, a wooden bar-top table large enough to seat twelve, and a separate breakfast nook with a bay window looking out to the overgrown garden and courtyard where Grandma Jane would take her coffee every morning. It was at the breakfast nook where they'd placed Bri, with two steaming banana muffins with butter, a cold glass of milk, her own notebook for drawing, and freshly charged earbuds to keep her from eavesdropping.

Emily drank Chianti. She offered some to Ben but he declined. "We never lied to you, Ben."

"Concealed the truth then," he said to his sister across the table.

Amanda scoffed. "You would know."

He regrouped. "Em, what happened to Grandpa Robert?"

"He died of a heart attack," Emily said, tongue in cheek.

"That's not what I'm talking about. I know how he died."

"Do you? Do you really?"

"I know someone found and dressed him inside Oswald Asylum, and they did a piss-poor job of it."

"It sure wasn't the twenty-something-year-old nurse that was with him," Emily said with a cold glare down toward her wine glass, which she then tilted for a long swallow. "The one who had him tied up to the bedposts in that room. *She* ran off."

Ben fumed; just one more of those things he'd suspected but never wanted to know.

"One of his many affairs, Ben. One of too many to count, although he sure logged them all in his journals. Like he logged everything he did."

Amanda looked to be growing impatient. "Would it be too crass of me at this point to say who fucking cares about Robert's fetishes? Emily, what did you find in those journals? And what in the hell is in those books inside the atrium?"

Emily hesitated, as if to gather her thoughts for the most well-thought-out explanation, but then settled on the same word now burning on Ben's tongue. "Nightmares."

"Of course." Amanda shook her head.

"It all began with Bernard Bookman," said Emily. "In Vienna, in the eighteen seventies. His work with children, especially in regard to sleep. His birth name was Mundt. Bernard Mundt. And the first time he trapped a nightmare inside a book, it was an accident. Letting that nightmare out was just as much of one, as he didn't fully comprehend the fact that he'd trapped it."

Amanda abruptly stood from the table.

"Amanda, please. As unbelievable as it sounds, it's the truth as I know it." Emily waited for Amanda to sit back down. "Days later there was a murder in Vienna. A murder that strongly resembled the girl's nightmare Bernard Mundt had taken away days before. The next time he was called upon, he tried what he'd done again, with another book. Said the same thing. Performed the same ritual, he called it. Closed the book, hard, at the precise time. And it worked."

"And he let it out again?" Ben asked.

Emily nodded. Robert's journals rested in a small pile next to her on the table. "That night, as a test, he opened the book. The next day, he saw in the newspapers a story of a young man being pushed from the roof of a two-story bakery. It was the same young man who'd visited Dr. Bernard Mundt the day before. His nightmares involved falling from great heights. He broke both legs from the fall, but lived. And told a reporter it was as if his nightmare had come true. The man who pushed him, according to the pusher's wife, had never hurt a soul. The man claimed to have heard voices telling him to lure that man to the roof and push him off. He spent the rest of his life in an asylum. Bernard knew then.

"But others began to talk. Soon he became linked to both crimes. Bernard Mundt fled Vienna and hid in England for three years. There, he continued his work with nightmares, trapping hundreds in books he packed in crates, and eventually took with him when he fled to the United States years later. By then, he'd become known as the Book Man. In the states, he had his name changed to Bookman. He vowed to never again open one of those books once they'd been closed. And he didn't."

Amanda, seemingly unable to look at Ben while she asked the next question, said, "Where does Julia come into play?"

Emily watched them both, treading, as if afraid to reveal too much.

"We know Jennifer met with you within the past year," Ben said. "As her doctor. Therapist. To help deal with whatever that room did to her."

"Which means what we discussed is in secret. Between the two of us."

"Bullshit, Emily," said Ben. "I know what a secret means."

Resigned, Emily said, "As far as I know, from what little I found on her last night in his log books, Julia claims she's from Pompeii."

"Claims?" asked Amanda. "She's somehow inside of Jennifer as we speak. And we don't know where she is." She glanced at Ben. "I'm worried about her too."

"What log books?" asked Ben. "Different from the journals?"

"The journals are exactly that," said Emily. "Daily renderings. Ideas. Thoughts. The log books are more clinical, just lists and lists of . . . nightmares. Medical logs that link every child to his or her nightmare now trapped inside that room. They date back well over a century. This system of logging goes back to Bernard and his first two cases in Vienna. If you went inside that atrium now and opened the books numbered one and two, nothing would happen."

"Because they'd already been let out," Ben said. Amanda stood from the table, removed a wine glass from the cabinet, and returned to the table for a small pour from Emily's bottle. Before Ben could question it, she said, "I'm far enough along. One glass won't hurt."

Emily tapped the pile of journals next to her. "Grandpa Robert showed me the log books when . . . when he decided he wanted *me* to be the next in line," said Emily. "He took me into that room as a girl. Just like he took you, Ben. But I had the discipline. I followed the rules. He showed me how to do it. What to say and when to say it. It's a ritual, like I said, a performance of art. A dark art."

"That he didn't trust me to do," Ben said.

"And for good reason," hissed Emily.

Amanda gripped Ben's hand; the tension eased from his neck and shoulders. Amanda either believed every word Emily had said, or was suspending what she didn't, but either way, the reporter in her took over. "What happened to the two nightmares he let out in Vienna?"

"Like I said, the Pusher, that's what the newspapers called him, he spent the rest of his days in an asylum, hearing voices. That first man wasn't the only one he pushed from a rooftop. There were a half dozen more before he was admitted."

"And the first one? The young woman?"

"Have you ever heard of Hugo Schenk?" Emily asked. "He was a serial killer from Vienna in the eighteen hundreds. Known as the Housemaids Killer. Several of his victims were housemaids. He began as a swindler and thief." She checked over her shoulder to make sure Bri was still occupied with her drawing and music. "He duped women into relationships and marriages only to rape and murder them. He tied boulders to their corpses and dumped them into the Danube. To our knowledge, from Bernard Mundt's notes, Hugo Schenk did not begin murdering them until *after* Bernard unknowingly let out that first nightmare."

"She was a housemaid?" asked Amanda. "That first patient?"

"Yes. And her nightmare was just that. Being raped and murdered by someone she trusted. But even more, she feared drowning. This was why she sought out Dr. Mundt."

"And you're saying that that girl's nightmare somehow became Hugo Schenk?"

"That was Bernard's belief, yes. That the nightmare he let out somehow completed what was already an evil man. Somehow spurred him on to bigger things. For lack of a better word, possessed him. When Hugo Schenk was caught, he was in correspondence with fifty other women he hoped to one day add to his list. Guilt followed Bernard until his death here at Blackwood, inside that room, in the winter of 1922." Emily paused for a drink, a deep breath.

Is that all it was, though? Ben wondered. *Another story? Another legend? Another bit of folklore passed down inside the walls of a house built on it?*

"And Julia?" Amanda asked, refusing to let that thread go.

"You've heard of ancient Pompeii's famous brothels?"

"I've read of what's been excavated," Ben said. "The city was buried by Vesuvius."

"One of the more popular brothels in Pompeii was called the *Lupanare*. Latin for *Wolf's Den*. In life, this was where Julia plied her trade, according to her *imagined* history."

"Why do you say it like that?"

"I've had to piece it together. From what Jennifer knows. From the notes in these journals. Julia was one of the nightmares Bernard Mundt trapped while he was in England, while he was still known as the Book Man."

Ben leaned closer. "Go on."

"At the *Lupanare*, there were rooms used solely for fornication. In history, this was a real place. Famous for the erotic wall paintings . . . showing all sorts of positions of intercourse for sale. Like a sexual menu. Julia claims to *be* the woman in all of the paintings and frescoes and mosaics. When the volcano began erupting, she fled, like all the others, but couldn't outrun the ash and rock. She was buried by it, just on the outskirts of Pompeii, near the Herculaneum Gate."

Ben said, "Pompeii wasn't rediscovered until the seventeenth century, right?"

"Sixteenth," said Emily, opening one of the journals and reading from specific notes that were faint enough and old enough to have been Bernard Bookman's. At that time Bernard Mundt. "That's when the excavations began," Emily continued. "But it wasn't until 1853, when a French archaeologist by the name of Pierre Montague found her body, curled into a fetal position. But perfectly preserved under the rubble. She still had four gold coins in her pocket and the pendant from a necklace in her left hand."

"Jesus," whispered Ben. "In the box delivered to my house, along with Devon's missing shoe, there was a coin. An old, old coin."

"She was mummified, but still *so present*, the archaeologist wrote. He imagined her in life, before the volcano erupted. He imagined beauty and lusted for her. For what his imagination conjured her to be. He named her Julia. This imaginary lover he'd discovered, still mummified. She would be his and his alone."

Bri suddenly approached the table, startled them. "I need to use the bathroom."

"Go ahead," Ben said. "But hurry back."

The hallway bathroom was just around the corner. The bathroom door clicked shut.

Amanda faced Emily. "Go on."

"On the night Montague found that preserved body, he wrote in his journal of a nightmare, the first of many that would ultimately break apart his life. His marriage. Julia, this imagined whore from Pompeii. He began to dream of her nightly, until the dreams became nightmares. Dreams of lust for her, and then nightmares of the consequences. He began to covet the night. He coveted his nightmares as much as he despised them. He was a heartbroken and homeless old man, long past tired of this Julia he'd dreamed up. He heard of the work Dr. Bernard Mundt was doing in England, and traveled to him. Bernard finally rid this man of his burden. He trapped Julia inside one of those books and took it with him overseas with the rest of his nightmares. To the states."

"And Ben let her out?" Amanda asked.

Emily laughed, but the sadness in it left them deathly silent. "Jennifer let her out. She told me she grabbed the book because it was halfway sticking out."

"And something tells me you know why?" Ben asked his sister.

"Because Grandpa Robert knew exactly what was in it," she said. "I used to spy on him down the hallway. He'd be alone in the atrium. More than once he removed that book from the shelf. This book with the Frenchman's trapped nightmare inside it. *Julia* inside. He never slid it back in all the way. The spine of that book was always sticking out, like a tease, like it was the greatest temptation for him *not* to open it. And he never did."

"How do you know?"

"Because she would have been long gone inside someone else when Jennifer opened it. *She* didn't know."

"But maybe I did?" Ben asked. "What are you implying? That I let Jennifer do it?"

Emily's eyes pooled with moisture.

A toilet flushed and water ran in the hallway bathroom; Bri would be back any second. Ben leaned forward, "Emily, what are you afraid to tell me?"

The bathroom door opened in the hallway.

Emily lowered her voice. "When he took me into that room as a girl, I followed the rules. But I knew even then I wanted nothing to do with it. I knew him enough even then to not trust him."

"Not trust him how?" Ben only recognized the rage in his voice after Amanda clutched his hand to calm him.

Emily focused on her wine glass. "On the second night, he handed me that book. The Frenchman's nightmare of this seductress

Julia. The one he wouldn't push back in all the way. I didn't like the way it made me feel when I opened it. It made me feel dirty. I closed it immediately, even before he told me to. The way he looked at me when I handed it back, that sly grin. It still haunts me."

Bri should have been back by now. Amanda and Emily both sensed it too.

Amanda made her way into the hallway, calling out to their daughter. "Bri?"

Ben watched his wife, but spoke to his sister, avoiding any glance at her sleeve-covered arms and the dozens of tiny scars he knew were hidden beneath. "Jennifer said that she listened to you. That in a way, you two counseled each other."

"I don't know why she—"

"Did he ever touch you? Emily? God damn it. Em?"

Amanda's voice sounded from the hallway, panicked. "Ben, Bri's not in the bathroom!"

36

DEEP BREATHS OPENED his lungs, slowly relieved the pressure on his chest.

They'd woken him up, but the mare was not yet gone.

"Keep breathing, Dad. Slow and deep."

Sam? He'd meant to speak the word, but his mouth wouldn't move. *Deep down in the hollow is where he plants his seeds, little girl.* Royal Blakely's voice. Dressed as the Scarecrow, he'd chased her through the cornfield and finally caught her. *I am the corn. I am the fall. I am the harvest, little girl. And you are my Little Baby Jane.*

Mills blinked, moved his jaw, saw Sam's silhouette hovering, her hand on his cheek. The weight of the mare was gone, dispersed like morning mist. "He made her watch." He could make out Sam's face now, feel her hand gripping his own. "Made her watch while he cut them up."

A moth clung to the globe ceiling light.

Mills closed his eyes, saw Royal Blakely's bloody axe, body parts, blood on the walls. The glimpse into Amy Peterson's nightmare had given him a jolt no coffee or pills could provide, and the sudden adrenaline got him sitting up in bed before they could hold him back down.

"I was in the cocoon." Mills slid his legs to the side of the bed, and stopped when the movement made him dizzy. He couldn't have been asleep long before they'd shaken him awake. Father Frank was in the room with Sam, along with the nurse who'd walked him in and a doctor he'd never seen before. "He dragged her across the grass to the barn. Inside the cocoon. He talked to her. Like it was a stroll through the park." Mills gripped his head, fought the headache wanting to form. *The ears were robust. The silks, dark brown and slick to the touch* . . . "Edward Creech."

"Yes. Edward Creech." Blue placed her hands on his shoulders, forcing his eyes to her. "You were screaming that name when we woke you up. Who is Edward Creech?"

"The Screamer. He told the girl that she was next. That the Screamer was gonna get her from the hospital, just like he does at the end of the book."

"We have guards watching her," Blue said. "Nobody is going to take that girl."

Mills glared at Blue. "But he's real, Sam. And he's out there."

Before

D<small>EVON HAD BEEN</small> *missing for two weeks when Ben, newly eighteen, caught their father crying at the living room window, his reading chair pulled up so close to the glass his knees touched the windowsill.*

In his left hand, resting on his left thigh, was a rock glass half full of bourbon. From the glaze over his reddened eyes, it was not his first pour. His right leg shook, the boot heel pulsing up and down like a piston, one of his many ways of dealing with anxiety.

Two months ago, Michael Bookman's childhood nightmare—one his father Robert had gotten rid of when he was a ten-year-old boy— had returned so suddenly that Blackwood had been in turmoil even before Devon's disappearance.

Michael Bookman gazed at the moonlit woods. "Come here, Benjamin."

Ben's heart jumped. He thought he'd been discreet, spying on his father from the hallway. Up close, the fireplace lit half of his father's face. Michael sat stoically, wet trails down his cheeks, as if his bushy beard had been put there for the sole purpose of catching his tears in that moment.

"When I was a boy," his voice cracked. "One night my night-mare got so bad. The screams were so loud, mother and father found me in bed with my ears bleeding." He touched his right ear with his

four-fingered right hand. "I'd dug in so far to get the screams out that I busted my eardrums."

Ben had seen the framed painting in the basement. The replica of Edvard Munch's The Scream. *Robert had explained to him, during one of his many attempts to shed light on his father, Michael, why the painting was eventually taken down and stored. It had hung in the hallway leading to the atrium since Bernard Bookman, a fan of the Norwegian artist, hung it there in 1917. Michael was a little boy when he first saw the painting, and was convinced the bald, misshapen, haunting face in it was looking at him. Watching him. Screaming at him. That night he had a nightmare about the figure in that painting, the way it was holding its ears, portraying pain.* It portrays anxiety, *Robert had explained to his son.* The man in the painting is not actually screaming, Michael. The scream is sounding *around him, through all of Oslo. The nightmare became reoccurring. Michael's version of it became known to him in his nightmare as the Screamer. But in his nightmare, the Screamer had no mouth. It made noises only children could hear, and they followed it into the woods, where the Screamer would then eat them.*

Ben had asked Grandpa Robert, "How does he eat them if he doesn't have a mouth?"

"You'll have to ask your father. It's his nightmare."

Michael's nightmare went on for two months before Robert took his son's nightmare away. Trapping it inside one of those books. And on the shelf it stayed, until one night it was let out. On purpose, Michael felt certain. And he knew who'd done it.

Michael sipped bourbon, kept his eyes on the window, but said to Benjamin. "In German the painting goes by Der Schrei der Natur." The Scream of Nature. *Ben knew this. Robert had explained it all. "In Norway, it is simply Skrik." The Shriek. Michael drank again, this one a deep swallow that left the glass nearly empty inside his grotesque, four-fingered hand. Along with the cleft upper lip, Michael Bookman had been born with six fingers on the left hand, but only four on the right. On that left hand he'd had the extra pinkie that should have been on the right. Ben could never look away from the nubs from the two missing fingers Michael Bookman now had on that left hand. Thick gnarls of scar tissue marred them, like whirls in a chunk of wood. Tired of being bullied, Michael, at age twelve, had come home one day from school, pulled a knife from the butcher block, and severed those two pinky fingers on his left hand. He told his father,* now my hands match. Four on each.

Michael Bookman nodded toward the window. "He's out there."

"Devon?"

"No. The Screamer."

"Grandpa Robert said that nightmares—"

"He lies. Nightmares come true. And mine is out there. Don't trust him, Benjamin."

"You're jealous of him," Ben told his father. "And me. What we share. You always have been." He'd almost called him Dad, but that had never sounded true, had always, when spoken, sounded forced, hurried, coming out like glass shattered on granite. "You've always been jealous." For years it had gone unsaid, until now, and it felt as if a huge burden had been lifted from Ben's heart.

But it drew no reaction from his father, who finished his bourbon with a quick throw-back, never taking his eyes from the dark night beyond that window. "Love him all you want, Benjamin. But never trust him."

Ben stood waiting, wanting to leave the room as awkwardly as he'd entered it moments ago, but he couldn't.

"He screams from the woods," said Michael. "On a level only children can hear. The curious follow the sound." He wiped a tear from his right cheek. "Devon was always curious."

37

Bri's name echoed throughout the house: three panicked voices shouting.

Ben had checked every nook, cranny, and closet on the third floor—even Devon's old room—and was on his way down to the second when he ran into Amanda on the landing.

"Where is she, Ben?" And then louder. "Where is she?"

"I don't know. She's here. Somewhere." He shouted, "Bri!" He stepped into one of the second-floor rooms, flung open a closet door with so much force the hinges cracked the old brittle wood around it. "Bri!"

Amanda shouted from the landing. "I've checked all the rooms. She's not on this floor."

Ben stepped back out to the landing, grabbed Amanda's hand, and led the two of them down the curved staircase to the foyer. Together they shouted, "Bri. Brianna!"

"Please tell me she didn't go outside, Ben. Oh, my God. We shouldn't have come."

"I don't know." Ben's heart was racing, not only from the hunt, but also from what his sister had begun to tell him inside the kitchen about Grandpa Robert.

Emily's voice sounded from the living room, and then the parlor. "Brianna!"

A breeze slithered in from the kitchen hallway. Ben felt it from the atrium's hallway as well. *All the open windows.* He stood silent.

Voices carried through Blackwood when the windows were open. He and Devon used to play tricks on Emily during the summer. Pretending to be ghosts. Amanda shouted their daughter's name beside him. Ben gently touched her arm, put a finger to his lips, urging her to stop. To listen. Emily rounded the corner, distraught and panicked. Ben put a finger to his lips. She calmed, listened to the breeze just as they were.

Immediately, they heard it. "I'm here." A tiny voice. Bri's voice, they could only hope. "Mommy. I'm over here."

"Over where?" Ben tried to decipher from which direction his daughter's voice had come. Amanda must have gotten a better read on it. She disappeared down the main hallway, past the kitchen, where the hallway branched into two more corridors with rooms full of books on both sides. She took the hallway to the left, down a set of stairs that veered to the right and into another hallway. Ben hadn't been down this hallway in ages. It led to the tower—the tower built to house the deranged Henry Bookman in the thirties and forties, so that he could not hurt anyone. The tower, like the atrium, was off limits, locked and chained for as long as Ben could remember.

Bri's voice grew louder, closer.

With Emily on his heels, Ben followed Amanda down another set of stairs, through a gauntlet of angles, until the hallway straightened out to a dead end with a heavy wooden door at the end of it. The door dwarfed Bri, who stood in front of it, waiting; a door that had been too heavy for any of them as children to open without the help of an adult. Ben surged past Amanda toward Bri, wanting to hug her and at the same time reprimand her for wandering off.

Amanda stopped short, panting from panic and out of breath from carrying the extra load of pregnancy. "Bri, we told you to not run off. What were you—"

"Can't you hear her?" Bri said. "I heard her when I came out of the bathroom."

Ben looked up from his daughter to the tower door.

A little girl's voice sounded through the thick wood. "Help me. Somebody help me."

Bri looked up from his side. "See?"

"I'll get the keys." Emily hurried off.

Bri stepped away from Ben. She put her right hand to the wood. "What's your name?"

"Blair," said the frightened voice on the other side of the door. "Blair Atchinson."

Amanda's hand shot to her mouth. "Oh, dear God."

Ben looked up toward his wife, mouthed the words, *She's alive.*

Bri said, "Can you feel my hand?"

"No," said the voice on the other side of the door. "Who are you?"

"I'm Bri. It's short for Brianna. Let's play mirror. My right hand is on the door. Now you put your left on the door." She waited. "Can you see it? The door's a mirror now."

Ben heard Emily approaching with the keys. She fumbled them at first, but was quick to unlatch the bolt. The chains dropped to the floor with a heavy, anchor-like clunk.

Ben spoke into the door. "Blair, we're coming in. You're safe."

"Is he gone?" she asked.

Ben looked over his shoulder toward Amanda, unsure how to answer.

"He's gone, sweetie," said Amanda. "We're coming in now."

Emily tugged on the door, but needed help. The door appeared as medieval as the tower. Ben gripped the handle and together he and his sister pulled.

Dank, fetid air gushed outward as if an ancient seal had been broken.

Blair screamed and cried.

"It's okay, baby," said Amanda, more eager than any of them to get inside to her.

Ben used the heavy chains on the floor to prop the door open. The last thing they needed was the door to close, locking them in. Ben used the flashlight on his phone. The stones underfoot were slick from years of rainwater and moisture. Moss had overgrown the cracks of the pavers. Water dripped. Moths clung to the wet walls. Doves fluttered in and out of the sunlight shining through the dormer windows three stories up near the balcony.

Blair had run to the far wall upon their entrance, and Amanda was doing her best to coax her out from the shadows. Blair wore the pink dress her mother had described to them upon her disappearance weeks ago. The same dress she'd had on in the picture when the alert went out nationwide. The dress was soiled, ripped, the hem at her knees muddy and rain-damp. Her hair was a cluster of nests and tangles. She hugged her arms, shivering. Her eyes were wide open, blinking just often enough to show she was aware of what was happening.

Amanda said, "Blair, you're safe now."

Blair stayed close to the far wall of stones and lichen and cold shadows.

"She'll come to me." Bri approached the girl. They were roughly the same age. Bri wore a jean jacket over her red blouse. She removed it as she got closer, and held it out to the girl. Blair hesitated, and then stepped toward it, shuffling into the jacket and Bri's warm embrace. Bri wrapped her arms around her, patted her hair like a parent would a hysterical child.

"Blair?" Ben said softly. "How long have you been in here?" Nothing. "Have you lived inside this tower since you left home?"

She nodded against Bri's shoulder. "Are you Ben?"

He froze. "Yes. How did you know?"

"The man who took me. He said you'd come."

38

I T TOOK A moment for the name Edward Creech to fully register
with Father Frank, but as soon as the realization struck him, his
knees buckled.

Sam had just entered the hospital lobby, fresh from her phone
call to Chief Givens. She caught his elbow. "You okay, Father?"

"He's at Oswald," said the priest. "Edward Creech is at the
asylum."

Mills readjusted his shoulder holster. "He can't be."

"It checks out," said Sam. "I just phoned Dr. Travis Knowles.
Creech has been a patient there for almost four years."

"And before then?"

"That's what we need to find out." She led the way through the
parking lot to her sedan. "We're not ruling out that he's who you
say he is, but if he is . . ."

"Then who took Blair Atchinson?"

Mills sat tense in the passenger's seat as Blue drove. She periodically glanced in the rearview mirror toward Father Frank in the
back, but kept her focus on the long straightaway toward Oswald
Asylum. "First time I've ever had a father and a dad in the same
car." It was enough to break the tension. Blue watched the rearview
again. "Father, how did you know Edward Creech?"

"We never met. It was his mother I spoke to on two separate
occasions. *About* him. She first approached me at the church, fear-
ing her Edward had gone mad. One morning she found him eating

breakfast at the table. He'd shaved off every bit of his hair. Even his eyebrows. At first she thought he was an intruder. She said his name. He told her Edward's not here."

"It's him." Mills battled the heaviness behind his eyes, the sluggishness of being awake when the meds were still trying to do the opposite. He pulled the amphetamines from his coat pocket, popped them into his mouth, and swallowed.

Blue glanced as she drove. "What was that?"

"My nonya pills."

She shook her head, like it wasn't worth the fight.

Father Frank, from the back seat, asked, "Nonya pills?"

"Nonya damn business." Mills eyed the approaching forest surrounding Blackwood. Oswald Asylum rested at the base of the hill, overlooking the deep ravine known as Blackwood Hollow. "What happened next, Father? With mother Creech and her weirdo son?"

"I advised her to bring him in. But she never did. Years passed before she reached out again, this time by phone, asking me to come to her home."

"How many years in between?" Mills asked, calculating kidnappings in his head.

"Eight, if I remember correctly."

"It's him. God damn, it's him, Sam. Drive faster."

"He's not going anywhere."

"Keep talking, Father. What happened when you got to his house?"

"She walked me up to the attic. That's where he stayed. He played the violin up there. He was a prodigy. But also a recluse. She'd realized he'd been sneaking out at night."

"For how long?"

"She didn't know." He'd loosened his clerical collar. From beneath his shirt he fished out a chain with a cross on it, and kissed it. "Oh, dear Lord. If hindsight only worked in reverse. I had no way of knowing. To my knowledge she knew nothing. Only that he'd gone crazy."

"Why did she call you again? She waited so many years in between. What did he do that made her reach out the second time?"

"He . . . he sewed his mouth closed. With yarn."

Had it taken him that many years to fully evolve into the Screamer?

Blue pulled to a stop inside Oswald's small tree-lined parking lot.

Father said, "By the time I arrived, Creech had locked himself in the attic. I tried to talk him out, but he never answered. Not with words, at least, but with the most bone-chilling violin piece I'd ever heard. On the other side of that door he was stomping and laughing like the devil himself as he played. I never saw him. But I felt him. That violin music. That humming."

"And what then?"

"I left. There was nothing more I could do if her son would not allow me in. I suggested she call the psychiatrist. For weeks he was on my mind, but as memories do, he faded. The next I heard of him, Winchester, was when you screamed his name during your nightmare."

Mills had been inside Oswald Asylum countless times over the years, but had never been in the basement. It was cold and poorly lit.

Space heaters hummed from the center of the room. Light bulbs—one outside each of the four corner cells—hung from a drop ceiling in bad need of repair.

"Our funds have all but dried up since Dr. Bookman's death." Dr. Knowles was middle-aged, but already white-haired. "Which is horrible timing, as the asylum has never been so full."

Mills had caught and arrested at least six of the current patients, Bruce Bagwell and Sally Pratchett being the most recent. *The Boogeyman and the Tooth Fairy.* Two he'd already written on his wall at home.

"We're currently carrying fifty-two patients," Dr. Knowles told them. "Twelve more than we should be. Hence, the basement." The doctor didn't dally; he pointed toward the cell in the far right corner. "There he is. Edward Creech. I can assure you he hasn't been outside these walls since he was admitted four years ago. He prefers the dark. As do the rest of them down here. We call them our night owls." He pointed to the barred cell twenty feet left of the one that held Edward Creech. "There's your Boogeyman, Detective Mills. Bruce Bagwell."

Mills stepped closer. They were never able to get the Boogeyman for more than B&E, breaking and entering. He never stole anything, never hurt anyone. He broke into houses, waited in closets, under beds, and when the time was right, he'd jump out and scream.

"Is he sleeping?"

"Yes. Like I said, more active at night. We do administer daily drugs to keep them calm. They can be excitable." Bagwell looked to be asleep on his bunk. "It was right for him to come here. He sometimes cries himself to sleep. The voices he hears."

"I asked him one day after I caught him," said Mills. "Why do you like to scare children? He looked at me with a serious face, said because that's what Boogeymen do."

"And to think he was once a normal plumber," said Dr. Knowles.

Blue started toward Edward Creech's cell, with Father Frank following behind.

Creech sat on the side of his bed in a light-blue asylum uniform. He slumped with his elbows on his knees, his long hands dangling from wrists that looked rubbery. His hair had grown back. It hung dark and uncombed, like a curtain covering his face as he peered down.

"Edward Creech," said Blue.

"What took you so long?" Edward croaked. His long toes looked like fingers.

Mills excused himself from Dr. Knowles, sidled next to Sam. "Mr. Creech, would you mind looking up from the floor?"

"Creech is gone. Been gone a long time now."

A violin rested against the wall next to his bed, and beside it a music stand and an assortment of bows. "He's not all the way gone, is he?" asked Mills. "He still plays the violin."

Dr. Knowles stood behind them. "He plays every night. Don't you, Edward? The other patients like it. When he gets a little . . . excited, we calm him."

"I play like Paganini." Creech said, eyes on the floor.

"He a hero of yours?" asked Mills.

"Do you believe in reincarnation?"

"I don't."

Dr. Knowles said in a low voice, "They share the disorder of Marfan syndrome. He and Paganini." He raised his voice. "Edward, look up, please. Edward!"

Edward slowly raised his head, used his long, calloused fingers to part his hair. His face was elongated like the rest of him. His cheeks were hollow, his eyes dark, his skin pale. From when he'd sewn his mouth closed years ago, the infection had left him scarred above and below his thin lips, like the stitching of a baseball.

"Some thought Paganini the devil," said Creech. "They called him the devil's violinist."

"Are you the devil?" Mills asked.

Creech smiled; it seemed to cause him pain, so it didn't last long. "I've certainly done devilish things, Detective. But not anymore."

Mills produced a list from his shirt pocket and put it up to the bars. "Can you read?"

"Can you play music?" Creech asked.

Mills gripped the bars. "Can you answer my question?"

Father Frank's hand rested on Mills' shoulder. "Temper yourself, Winchester."

Creech said, "I can read."

Mills reached the list between the bars. Creech scooted down the bed, away from it, as if Mills held a flaming torch instead of a sheet of paper. "Did you murder these children?"

They hadn't told Dr. Knowles exactly why they'd needed to speak to his patient. He watched intently, and when the realization struck him he whispered, "No . . ."

Creech's eyes found Father Frank behind Mills. "Do I know you?"

"We've spoken, yes." Father Frank's voice wavered. "Answer the question, Edward."

"How'd you find them?" Creech asked Mills. "They must all be bones now."

"Did you kill those children?"

"I hid them down deep in the hollow, Detective. Where nightmare seeds grow." Mills rattled the bars. Creech jumped, backed himself against the headboard. "I did what he told me to do."

"He?"

Creech clammed up, ran a hand over his hair.

Mills imagined it shaved, Creech walking through the woods thirteen years ago when Michael and Christine Bookman ran off the road to their deaths. "Did you kidnap Devon Bookman? Thirteen years ago?"

Creech grinned. He had teeth missing, and the ones that remained looked sharp, stained in a way that made Mills imagine blood. "Yes. That's when it all began."

Dr. Knowles crouched down, lowered his head between his knees, realizing the man responsible for the missing Crooked Tree children had been under his care now for nearly four years and no one had known it.

"Who took Blair Atchinson?" Mills hissed, face between the bars.

"I don't know," said Creech.

"Who sent that box with Devon Bookman's missing shoe?" asked Blue.

Creech eyed them both. He seemed genuinely confused.

Mills rattled the bars. "Who took Blair Atchinson?"

Blue touched his shoulder this time, and gently pulled him back. "Edward," she said. "In the books. The Screamer is a myth. A legend kids spoke about at sleepovers. A monster without a mouth. Why did you stitch your mouth closed, Edward? You'd shaved your head thirteen years ago. Why did you wait so many years to stitch your mouth closed? To finish the transformation."

Edward's eyes filled with moisture.

A janitor appeared from the stairwell. His beige shirt had a tag that read *Nathan*. He collected the trash from the cans outside each cell, moving with his hat pulled low and his eyes to himself.

"Not now, Nathaniel." Dr. Knowles stood up straight, noticing now, as they all were, how the janitor's emergence into the room had brought all four patients in the basement to life.

Bruce Bagwell was sitting up in bed now. In the far corner, another patient had moved to the bars, her face pressed in between them, watching as the janitor apologized and started back up the stairwell with his collected bags of trash. Someone in the far corner cell had started laughing, and the longer he laughed the louder he got. Creech was even standing now, his head only a foot from the ceiling. He picked up his violin and started playing. Slowly at first, and then louder, with vigor, gaining steam with each pull and thrust of the bow.

"Hush," Dr. Knowles shouted to the dark corner cell. To Creech he screamed, "Edward, put that down." And then to the greasy-haired woman with her face pressed between the bars, he said. "Sally, back up."

Sally? Sally Pratchett?

And then it dawned on Mills. The tooth inside the box with Devon Bookman's shoe.

The Tooth Fairy. The coin, Julia. The bird claw, what Bruce Bagwell used to scratch the inside of closet doors.

Mills turned from cell to cell. "He built this place *for* them."

"Silence," screamed Dr. Knowles.

Two orderlies hurried down from the first floor with what looked like cans of Mace.

Blue pulled her cell phone from her pocket, looked at the screen, and gave Mills the *I have to take this* look.

Creech's violin playing grew louder, more animated, like the devil himself had now taken control. Bruce Bagwell had begun clapping and jumping up and down inside his cell.

"Detective," Sally Pratchett called out. Mills turned toward her voice. "Ingrid Flint was the youngest of five. The only daughter. Her brothers told her stories of the Tooth Fairy. The thought of someone coming into her bedroom at night and taking her missing tooth from beneath her pillow terrified poor Ingrid."

"Sally," Dr. Knowles shouted. "Enough."

One of the orderlies sprayed something into her eyes. Sally backed away from the bars, wiping at her face with the same fingernails she'd used to pluck out teeth from her neighbor's little boy, and from four more children in the neighborhood before being caught.

"One of the brothers," shouted Sally, as Bruce continued clapping and Creech played on with his violin. "Told her that if you didn't believe in the Tooth Fairy then she'd take a tooth from your mouth instead. Rip it out with her fingernails. Straight from the gums." Sally made as if to rip a tooth from her own mouth, before shouting, "This became *her* nightmare."

She gripped the bars again and continued. "In August of 1937, Ingrid and her parents traveled from Idaho to meet with Bernard Bookman's daughter, Dr. Amelia Bookman. Ingrid left Blackwood cured."

Mills walked toward Sally Pratchett, and the woman backed away from him. She cowered in the corner, laughing.

It was so loud now Father Frank held his ears.

The orderlies had begun to calm Bagwell, and Dr. Knowles was now at Creech's cell, threatening punishment if he didn't put down the violin. But this only spurred him on, louder, more animated.

Blue returned to the basement, stone-faced.

"What is it?" asked Mills.

"Blair Atchinson is alive," she said. "She's at Blackwood. She's been there all along."

Edward Creech paused in his playing to shout at Blue. "I sewed it closed so that I could no longer eat them, Detective. The Nightmare Man always made me eat them."

Before

IT WAS A *warm, sunny morning at Blackwood.*

Devon had just turned eight the day before, and he'd gotten a new fishing pole from Grandpa Robert. Ben had promised to take him fishing, but only after Devon ate breakfast.

Ben had already eaten two slices of buttered toast smothered in homemade strawberry jam made fresh from the Blackwood garden. The apple slices he'd cut for Devon remained untouched on his plate beside the dollop of peanut butter Ben had plopped there with a spoon.

"I'll sit here all day," he told his little brother.

Devon dipped an apple slice in peanut butter and stuck the entire piece in his mouth.

"Chew with your mouth closed, Devon."

He tried, but the piece was too big.

Their mother entered the kitchen without a wish of good morning to either of them, padding in her bare feet across the wood floor toward the sink, in a sheer white nightgown she had no business wearing around the house. The frilled bottom of the nightgown barely reached her long thighs.

"Don't stare," Ben whispered to Devon.

Devon whispered back, "Mom and Dad don't sleep in the same room anymore."

"Eat," he told him, checking his watch, giving his mother a glance at the sink, accidentally catching sight of a nipple through the sunlit fabric as she turned toward them, wiping her wet mouth. Strands of disheveled sandy hair had fallen loose from the bun atop her head. She touched Ben's shoulder in passing. "I'm going back to bed," she told them.

She'd left a bottle of Advil open next to the sink. She'd taken them to nurse a hangover.

Devon had made it through two more slices of apple during their mother's brief appearance. Ben checked the floor to make sure Devon hadn't knocked them there while he wasn't looking. "One more and we'll go."

Devon shoved an entire slice into his mouth and was out of his chair with his fishing pole in hand before he'd finished chewing. He swallowed, said to Ben. "What if we catch a body part?"

"What?"

"In the pond today. What if, instead of a fish, we caught a body part? Like an arm? Or head or something? Or even a dead little boy."

"We won't." Ben watched his little brother. "You got peanut butter on your chin."

On the way to the pond, walking side by side beneath the twisted overhanging limbs with their poles and tackle boxes in tow, Ben looked down at Devon and asked, "What made you say that earlier?"

"Say what?"

"What you said about pulling body parts out of the pond?"

Devon shrugged. "Just curious. And I learned what Daddy's biggest fear is."

"Yeah, and what is that?"

"To be kidnapped."

"He's not a kid anymore. Adults can't be kidnapped."

Devon looked up at him like he was the naïve one. "We never stop being kids," said Devon. "Not completely." And then his mind, as it so often did, changed course—the tree limbs now held Devon captivated as they walked. Black, reaching, mind-of-their-own limbs that resembled live oaks but without the clinging moss. Grandpa Robert referred to them as mare trees. Devon strolled with an attitude Ben found both impressive and disheartening. As Devon swung his arms, sunlight glinted off the Rolex around his thin bicep. The nob of his elbow held it in place, because it was way too big for his wrist.

"What are you doing wearing Grandpa's watch?"

"He gave it to me."

It was the one their grandfather rarely wore, but kept in the desk drawer inside the atrium. "Devon, did you get inside that room again?"

Devon didn't answer. A dark butterfly fluttered around their heads. On second glance, it was a moth. Devon veered off toward it. Ben told him not to touch it, said it was bad luck, but Devon held out his hand anyway. The moth landed on his extended finger, wings pulsing like a heartbeat. Seconds later it was joined by a second moth, and then a third landed on his wrist.

Ben shooed them away.

This angered Devon. "What did you do that for?"

"It's bad luck," he said.

"If you'd left them long enough, they would have filled up my arm. Like they do that tree inside the room." The moths had flown to a nearby tree, and were now clinging to the bark. "Look, they're drinking."

"Moths don't drink," said Ben, although he wasn't sure if they did or didn't. What they did on that tree inside the atrium sure looked like drinking.

"Grandpa calls them night butterflies," said Devon.

"Yeah. So?"

"It's daytime." Devon hitched the fishing pole over his shoulder and headed to the pond.

CHAPTER

39

B LAIR ATCHINSON SAT between Amanda and Bri at the breakfast nook, watching out the window toward the courtyard, garden, and woods, with a blanket over her shoulders and a steaming cup of hot chocolate keeping her hands calm.

Amanda whispered to the girl that the police would be there any minute. Blair didn't respond, but stared transfixed at Amanda's baby bump. Amanda said, "He's moving." To Bri she said, "Do you want to feel?"

Bri immediately moved her hand to the fabric of her mother's blouse, the swell of tight flesh beneath it. Amanda positioned it for her. Bri waited, and then her hand flinched. She smiled. "It's weird."

"It's a he," Amanda said, amused. "Not an it."

This brought a short-lived smile from Blair—since Ben had walked her out of the tower, she'd yet to say a word. Ben had tried to coax answers from her, the number one question being who had taken her. The thing that wracked his brain now was the list, written in white chalk, that they'd found on the inside of the tower wall.

Twenty-one names. A handful had jumped at him. Most notably Father Frank's name, and above him, that of *The Story* reporter, Trevor Golappus, the young man found dead inside Ben's barn. The last two names on the list, respectively, were Dr. Travis Knowles, from Oswald Asylum, and Nathaniel Munt, who they'd so far been unable to identify. But knowing what had happened to the reporter, Ben assumed this was a list no one wanted to be on. The officers had reached out to Father Frank, who was safe with Detective Mills and Detective Blue. Jennifer Jackson wasn't on that chalked list inside the tower, but Ben was still unnerved enough by her behavior in his kitchen earlier that he found himself desperate to bring her in. His calls had gone unanswered. Amanda had tried her three times as well—all had gone to voice mail. Ben's two calls to warn Dr. Travis Knowles had gone unanswered, although someone on staff at Oswald Asylum should have been available to answer the phones.

Ben watched his wife across the kitchen. Blair had set her hot chocolate aside and was standing side by side with Bri, both of them tracking the movement across Amanda's belly. Amanda smiled and gave Ben a look that said *Whatever works.* Ben smiled back, but had just realized things had been so bad between them that he hadn't yet felt his own son kick.

Emily entered the kitchen, wrapped in a blanket lifted from one of the couches. Ben waved her over to the table. She'd been avoiding him. "Start talking," he said to his sister. "The detectives are going to be here any minute. And once they get here, Blair's parents will be notified, and the press won't be far behind."

Emily watched her sister-in-law across the kitchen. "The press is already here."

"She's off duty."

"I didn't think Amanda was ever off duty."

"Quit stalling. What did Grandpa do to you?" Emily made as if to get up. Ben grabbed her arm, eased her back down to the stool. Anguish washed over her face. He went straight to what had pained him now for years. "Does this have something to do with you cutting yourself? As a girl. Jennifer hinted that it did."

"That was told to her in private." Emily closed her eyes. When she opened them, she appeared stronger. She gripped his hand and pulled him to a spot in the kitchen where Amanda and the kids couldn't see them. "Have you never noticed the family resemblance?" she asked. "That none of us—me, you, Devon—none of us look like our father." Ben shook his head, but the rumors, at one time when they were little, had been there. The three Bookman grandchildren looked more like Robert than their father, Michael. "Why do you think Mom liked it here so much? Why do you think she married our ugly father in the first place? Our father with his chopped-off fingers and cleft palate and bad eyes and demons. Huh?"

"No," Ben muttered.

"The great Robert Bookman was her lover," she said. "Our *real* father." Ben shook his head. "Yes, Ben. He was our mother's *doctor* as a child."

Ben felt like the air had been sucked from the room.

Over Emily's shoulder, Amanda stood, listening; she'd come across the room to tell them something and had overheard it all. Wide-eyed, Amanda said, "There's a car coming. The police are here." Ben was too stunned to talk. Amanda gripped Ben's hand and kissed his cheek before leaving the kitchen.

"Look at me," Emily said, turning Ben's face to her. "As a teen. Mother approached Grandpa Robert for help. With her nightmares. Her anxiety. She wanted to be part of this family. She wanted to be in this house. She was sixteen. That's when she met Dad, on one of her visits here. She started a friendship with Michael Bookman then. But it was all fake."

Ben inched out from his position next to the sink so he could watch his sister and the two girls across the kitchen at the breakfast nook. "Did he help her?"

"Yes. In more ways than one, you can say. She dated Michael to stay close to Robert. She was here every day. Michael was on cloud nine. She was stunning and beautiful and he was not. She was fun, funny, the life of the party, everything he wasn't. But she was his. She used him. For their entire relationship, years of dating and marriage. She used him."

Ben gripped his hair as if to pull it out. "So Michael . . . Our *half-brother?*"

"He adored our mother. It crushed him when he found out. Michael walked in on them one night, here, at Blackwood. After they'd married. Mom and Grandpa. That's why he ran off the road, Ben. To kill them both. To end it all."

"One of the many reasons," Ben said, thinking of the Screamer, but also recalling how much Michael hated living at Blackwood. That's why Michael was so quick to move out when he and Christine married, and why Christine had always been so eager to go back and visit.

Often.

"Ben? Talk to me. Say something."

The front door opened. He heard Amanda escorting the detectives into the foyer.

Ben gently grabbed his sister's right arm, tugged up on the sleeve, and turned it so that her forearm was showing—a hatching of tiny old scars, flecks of white cut into the peach tone of her skin. "Did he touch you? Em? Did he ever touch you?"

"Not in the way you're thinking. But with too much affection, for sure, especially with someone who might have been his daughter."

"He knew?"

"Of course he knew. All he needed to do was look." She wiped at tears beginning to form. "But the way he looked at me, especially after I'd started to develop, it turned me cold inside, Ben. So cold it hurt. That's why I was always wrapped up in a blanket. Sat next to a heating vent. A fireplace. I never felt warm here. The anxiety I'd feel around him became physical pain. Real pain." She began crying. Ben wrapped her in his arms, rested his chin atop her head, and urged her to let it out. The guilt in him for terrorizing her with pranks all those years ago brought moisture to *his* eyes too. "I hated this house," Emily said. "I hate this *fucking* house, Ben." He laughed because she never cussed, and then she chuckle-sobbed into his chest. He rubbed her back and whispered to his sister, "It's okay, I've got you now."

She gently pulled away at the sound of approaching footsteps in the hallway. She wiped her eyes, looked up at Ben, spoke quickly. "One night when he was drunk, he ran his fingers through my hair. Told me he's starting to see my mother in me. That I was becoming a younger version of her. That same porcelain skin, so unblemished and perfect. I knew what he wanted. The drugs by then were aging mother. He was growing tired of her."

"So you marred your skin," Ben said to her. "You scarred it."

Emily nodded. "I didn't want to be her." She began unbuttoning her blouse. "I didn't want to look like her." She opened another button, revealing part of her bra underneath.

"Em, what are you doing?"

"She was beautiful, but so ugly, Ben."

Footsteps drew closer in the hallway.

Her fingers plucked quickly down the line of buttons on her blouse, exposing flesh above and below her bra now, where hundreds of tiny healed scars marked her torso, stomach, chest, and the insides of her arms. Ben felt sick to see them all. When she heard talking in the hallway, she quickly buttoned back up. "No more secrets, Ben."

This froze him.

Emily fastened the final button below her neckline, and then wrapped the blanket back around her shoulders. "What?"

"Jennifer, she said the same thing earlier before she left the house."

Emily watched him; she was wrangling with something in her mind, he could tell, and then she said it. "Because even half-sisters think alike."

40

MILLS STOOD INSIDE the tower with Blue, staring at the list of chalked names on the stone wall.

Their crime unit had been in and out of the tower for the past twenty minutes, taking pictures, dusting for fingerprints, looking for hair samples, anything to clue them in to who had locked Blair Atchinson inside the tower. The girl had yet to talk. When Mills had phoned her parents, the mother broke down crying; the father in the background wailed. Blair, though, when asked if she was ready to go see them, had surprised them by clinging to Amanda Bookman's leg, refusing to leave the house.

Mills had knelt down to her level. "Did the man tell you not to go anywhere?" Blair nodded. "You know it's safe to go now. Your parents are expecting you. Would you rather them come here to you?"

Yes, she'd nodded.

Since entering the tower and analyzing the list of twenty-one names on the wall, their team, led by Officer Maxwell, had learned that seven of them—and counting—were dead, all of them brutally slain or missing, all within the past thirteen years. None, though, in Crooked Tree, until *The Story* reporter, Trevor Golappus.

Officer Maxwell entered the tower in a hurry. "Mills."

Mills turned. "No word from Dr. Knowles?"

"No, sir. No one is picking up at Oswald Asylum at all. I sent Fitzpatrick down there to warn the doctor in person."

"It was a madhouse before we left." Mills focused again on the list on the wall. "But the doctor seemed to have them contained."

"We connected another one." Maxwell pulled a small notepad from her pocket. "Number fifteen on that list." She pointed to the wall. "Nick Falcone. He was found murdered on the banks of the Loosahatchie River in Memphis, Tennessee, six years ago. Another unsolved. Tortured, cut up pretty bad. And get this, a baseball-size hole was found in the back of the skull near the top of the neck."

"Christ," muttered Mills.

"Just like number ten." Maxwell said. "And three of the others." She perused her notes. "Numbers five, eight, and eleven. And that's just so far. On the wall there. Peachy Sims, number ten. Lorraine Peachy Sims. Twenty-four-year-old waitress and grad student at the University of Wisconsin. Found in the woods of Forest County, Wisconsin, seven years ago. Again, unsolved. Tortured. Back part of her skull removed."

Blue said, "Call the feds."

"Give it a day," said Mills.

"If there's a pattern of unsolved similars," said Blue, "they'll be in the system. This could be the break *they've* been waiting for."

She was right, but still he balked. *The Nightmare Man always made me eat them.* He couldn't get Creech's crazy grin out of his mind.

"Detectives?" They turned to find Ben Bookman in the tower's entrance.

"Ben, you're not supposed to be in here," said Mills.

"I know. Blair's parents are here. And the media."

"Keep them away from the house," Mills told one of the three techs coming and going from the tower. "All the way around. As far back as you can stretch them. Tape it off." The tech hurried out. Ben stayed in the tower's entrance. Mills said, "Is there something else?"

Ben stepped into the tower. "How was Trevor Golappus found?"

"Murdered," said Blue. "Are you okay? You look like you've seen a ghost."

Ben nodded. "How was Golappus murdered?"

"We can't discuss that with you right now."

Ben pointed to the wall. "The last name. Nathaniel Munt. The spelling just dawned on me. Mundt, n-d-t. That was our family name before it was changed to Bookman. Bernard Bookman built this house. He came from Vienna. His name was Bernard Mundt."

Blue said, "Okay. We're listening."

Ben stepped deeper into the tower. "Has everyone on this list come up dead?"

"So far," said Mills. "We can't get hold of Dr. Knowles, even though we just left the asylum. Father Frank is here with us. And we don't yet know who this Nathaniel Munt is. Do you? Ben? I swear to God—"

"I might," he said. "But you have to tell me how Golappus was killed."

Mills shared a look with Blue. Blue spilled it. "Like at least four others on this wall. He was tortured. Cut up with a scalpel. Or something like it. And . . . a portion of his skull was removed. Back of his head, right above the neck. Expertly done. Perfect hole. Now tell us what you might know."

Ben stared toward the top of the tower. Mills followed his gaze, the soaring expanse of stones, the spiraling stairwell hugging the wall's curvature all the way to the sun-drenched balcony at the top. Ben said, "There was a storm here one night. Devon was five. The next day he'd wandered off, like he was prone to do. I found him in the tower. He'd crawled through a damaged hole in the foundation. From the storm. He was halfway up those stairs, determined to get to the top. I shouted for him to stop. To not move. I'd come up and get him. He told me to stay where I was. He was going to jump from the balcony. And fly back to the floor. Like a moth."

"Did he jump?" asked Blue.

Ben lowered his gaze to them. "No. I made it to the top in time. Told him to never do that again. He didn't talk to me for two days. And then one night in bed, out of the blue, he said, Benjamin. He always used my full name. He said, Benjamin, one day I'll hatch from my cocoon. And the Nightmare Man will know how to fly."

"Ben," said Blue. "What are you telling us?"

"That I think Devon is still alive." Ben pointed toward the list on the tower wall. "And he's been murdering ever since he disappeared."

Silence permeated the tower, as they each took this in.

"In at least five different states, so far," grumbled Mills.

"Six now," said Maxwell, now behind them again. "Number thirteen on the wall. Billy Conklin, eighteen. Found mutilated in Austin, Texas, March, two years ago. Another unsolved."

"The moth in the box," Ben said. "The box sent to me. That was his way of telling me he's fully emerged from his cocoon."

"What . . . ," said Blue. "To become the Nightmare Man."

"And now he's back," Ben said. "An adult, fully formed. One day, not long after I found Devon crawling to the top of this tower, I found him in the cellar. Inside the coal chute. He'd taken an armful of Emily's old dolls with him into the dark. With nothing but a candle and a knife from the butcher block. He'd cut holes in the back of their heads. Every one of those dolls. I asked him why. I was angry. I shook him. He said he was just following Grandpa's story. About Mr. Dreams and the Nightmare Man. He was always telling us stories about nightmares, where they came from. How to take them away. The Nightmare Man planted the seeds. Mr. Dreams was just another story he made up, a legend like the Sandman and the Baku, someone who took nightmares away so kids could sleep."

Mills said, "Ben, the dolls. Why did Devon cut up the dolls?"

"He was looking for their hollows. That's where the Nightmare Man plants his seeds. Deep down in the hollows. Devon was trying to find them."

Mills made his way over to the tower wall, put his finger on the last name on the chalked list. "Nathaniel Munt." He turned back to Blue. "Nathaniel . . . Oswald Asylum."

Blue's eyes widened. "No."

Maxwell stormed back into the tower; Mills hadn't even noticed she'd left. She looked panicked. "Fitzpatrick just called. Dr. Knowles is dead. Along with three nurses and two orderlies. It's a bloodbath at the asylum. Fifteen of the inmates have escaped."

"Creech?" asked Mills.

"Gone."

"Sally Pratchett? Bruce Bagwell?"

"Gone. Both of them. Along with twelve others. It was the janitor. One of the orderlies was left alive, said it was the janitor. Nathaniel Munt."

"Son of a bitch."

Maxwell said, "Before Nathaniel fled with the others, he stripped off his uniform, completely naked. Left the uniform shirt face up on the floor so his name tag was showing."

"Shed his cocoon," Mills muttered. "We should have known, Sam. You saw how those inmates reacted when that janitor entered the basement. It was him. That was Devon."

Maxwell said, "The orderly said he had a tattoo that took up all of his back. She thought it was a butterfly."

"It was a moth," Mills hissed. "He's become the moth."

Ben said, "He's become his own version of the Nightmare Man. He's made him real."

Someone screamed from the hallway, then a wailing sound; they all turned toward the commotion. It was one of the techs, overwhelmed by some news another male tech with glasses then delivered from the doorway.

"Chief Givens is dead," said the tech. "There's been a bust-out at the police station."

"Royal Blakely," said Mills.

The tech confirmed with a nod.

The Screamer, the Boogeyman, and the Tooth Fairy. And now the Scarecrow.

All out.

Before

BEN SAT ON *a courtyard bench, looking out toward the woods. The lurid green foliage and climbing moss. Vines twisted in spaghetti swirls of brown and green. The gnarled trunks and wild limbs Devon once said looked like arms with too many elbows. Tiny pinpricks of sunlight cracked the wooded canopy above the courtyard. It should have warmed him, but Ben felt cold.*

Cold and hollow.

Grandpa had trusted him, and now, with the silent treatment he'd given him the past three days—his failing to close the book when told—it was clear he no longer did.

Could trust be earned back?

Perhaps slowly, over time. But the surge of adrenaline he'd gotten when the words had begun forming on that blank page had been too irresistible. And now here he was, watching the trees without passion, without any hope of one day truly understanding the books inside that room. The tree. The moths.

Ben hurled a rock into the woods, listened for the landing, but the trees buffered the sound. He and Devon couldn't wait to come here, especially for the long stays in the summer. They knew every inch of the house, every step of the woods, the paths and trails, as well as a worn baseball glove. But now he couldn't wait to leave. He looked over his shoulder at the sound of footsteps, and saw Devon coming from the house.

Devon was six years old, but astute enough to know when his older brother was down. He sat beside him on the bench and tilted his head upward toward the overhanging trees. "What's wrong, Benjamin? You've been really quiet."

"Nothing."

"You lie."

Ben recalled the words he'd seen form on that page before Grandpa had screamed at him to close the book. He made up a story so Devon would let it go. "I had a nightmare is all."

This perked Devon's interest. "Oh? What was it about? I love nightmares."

"No, you don't."

"I love them like Emily likes ice cream."

"It was about a scarecrow."

"Really?"

"Yes." Ben hadn't thought of any way to embellish it, so he didn't, and was glad that Devon, at least for the time being, appeared to let it go.

Dark limbs and vines reached overhead like interlocked fingers, forming tunnels and wooden vaults. Devon looked up and said, "Like the arched, ribbed ceiling of a Gothic cathedral."

Ben glanced at his little brother, wondered what made his brain tick. "What do you know of ribbed ceilings and cathedrals?"

"I know plenty. Tell me more of your scarecrow?"

"There's nothing more to tell."

Together they stared at the overhanging limbs. Devon said, "I just thought of another story you can write."

"I can come up with my own stories, Devon."

"But can you really, though?" Devon stared into the sunlight. He often did that until he saw spots. He closed his eyes.

"What's your story?" Ben asked, curious.

"What if there's a story about a scarecrow who comes to life."

"It's been done. Like Frosty the Snowman?"

"No," said Devon. "Not like that at all. When Frosty began to melt, I wanted to scoop him up and drink him like a milkshake. But what if you write a story about a scarecrow that murders people?" Devon rolled his head lazily toward Ben, and grinned. "He murders them, and then chops up their bodies into little pieces. Or maybe they're still alive when he chops them up. I don't know. That can be up to you. You're the writer."

Ben looked to the tree again, hoped his little brother would stop talking. Such thoughts shouldn't run through a six-year-old's mind.

But he wasn't finished. "He sews," Devon said. "This scarecrow. He likes to sew dried corn husks together, with needle and thread." Devon stood from the bench as his excitement grew. "And he makes them into cocoons and hangs them. With all the bloody pieces inside. Cocoons like when caterpillars turn into moths."

41

THE ENTIRE TOWN was in flux.

Police sirens echoed in the distance. Ambulances screamed. Fire trucks wailed. Cycled pulses of panic carried through the woods, up the hillside to Blackwood, where inside the house, all was silent.

Contemplation and anxiety held sway.

The Atchinsons had not quite opened the front door, in a hurry to get Blair home, when the wall of reporters at the tree line gave them pause. And then news of the breakouts at the asylum and police station cautioned them further. Mr. Atchinson made the decision they were staying, which seemed to relieve Blair—she was still afraid to stray too far from the tower. Mr. Atchinson's reasoning was solid. Half the police force was now at Blackwood. There were violent criminals out on the streets. It was safer here, for now, despite Ben's new warnings that he couldn't predict what Devon might do. If it *was* his little brother. Devon had always been unpredictable.

Amanda phoned her parents, insisted they lock their doors, get Dad's gun from the safe, and hide. After seeing what had transpired on the news, they'd agreed. An hour had passed since the breakouts, and as of yet there had been no sightings of the escapees. Something told Ben they were hiding, waiting for dark.

Nightmares liked the dark.

There wasn't a room in the house where Ben could go and not find someone nearby, so for a while, he roamed, pretended to be busy. After what Emily had told him earlier about Jennifer Jackson, he needed to be alone, to gather his thoughts around the fact that their former nanny could also be his half-sister. That Jennifer's mother, Tammy Jackson, had, like way too many in this town, once been a patient of the great Robert Bookman. She'd begun seeing him when she was nineteen, not for nightmares, but for anxiety and restlessness. They'd had a brief affair, one Robert cut off soon after learning that Tammy, a college sophomore at the time, was with child.

Ben had asked Emily how long she'd known. *For all of a few hours*, Emily had promised him, learning of the connection only after reading through his journals the night before. But, Emily had told Ben, she was convinced now that Jennifer had migrated toward their family because of it.

And when Ben had asked if Jennifer knew, Emily had been adamant that she didn't. Or at least if she did, she was the coolest cucumber she'd ever met.

When he thought now about what they'd almost done inside the atrium that weekend, he felt nauseous, but that was quickly quelled now by worry.

Where was she? How much had Julia taken hold of her?

Ben passed Father Frank in the second-floor hallway. They exchanged pleasantries and went on their way. Again. Father Frank had been in and out of most of the rooms since his arrival at Blackwood, and this was the third time in the past hour Ben had run into him. The priest, he told Ben on their third run-in, was blessing every room of the house. Ben had told him to have at it. They needed all the help they could get. The Atchinsons had closed themselves off in one of the second-floor bedrooms. Police patrolled inside and out. Crime scene techs had been in and out of various rooms.

Ben found Detective Mills in the kitchen, looking out the window overlooking the woods, as day was showing the first signs of turning to night. There was a bottle of scotch beside the sink. Mills lifted a coffee mug to his mouth and sipped.

Ben sidled up, asked Detective Mills. "What's in the mug?"

Mills paused, took another sip. "Water."

"Where'd you find the scotch?"

"In the cabinet."

"And you're just looking at it?"

"We all have our peculiarities. I was an alcoholic. Still am. The bad kind."

"Is there a good kind?"

Mills shrugged, turned from the window to face the heart of the kitchen, where across the way, Bri played checkers with Emily. Emily had been determined to take her niece's mind off things. Earlier, Ben had caught his daughter staring at Detective Mills as if she was in awe. Like he was some kind of superhero, Ben told his sister, prompting them both to tell Bri it wasn't polite to stare.

But I've seen him before, Bri had said.

On TV. The news, Ben had explained. *He's around. That's why you've seen him.*

"Sometimes I need to look at a full bottle to remind me," said Mills. "To be strong. Sometimes I even pour it in a glass."

"Why?"

"So that I can pour it out."

"How many years sober?"

"Since Samantha was nine."

Ben eyed the bottle beside the sink. "It's been a few hours for me."

"A lifetime then." Mills downed the rest of his water and placed the mug next to the sink. "Fucking lifetime," he said again, studying Ben now. "Maybe I tagged you wrong."

"How so?"

"Tell me about the sketches. Ones we found in your drawer when Devon went missing."

"It's all bullshit."

"Yeah, maybe. But bullshit's all we got right now."

Ben watched Bri jump two of Aunt Emily's pieces and smile in triumph. "I loved my little brother."

"I don't doubt that. You protected him, didn't you? Tell me about the sketches. I know what they show. The Screamer. The Scarecrow. The all-out carnage from *The Pulse*. Every villain in your future books was detailed in those sketches, years before you wrote them. Pretty sick mind for a teenager, Ben."

"Yeah. Even sicker mind for a six-year-old."

"You didn't draw them, did you?"

"No." Ben focused on his sister and daughter. "Devon was twisted. He was six . . . seven . . . when he drew them. I found him one day, sketching the Scarecrow. The cocoons and blood and hacked body parts. He looked over his shoulder. Said, *Look, Benjamin. You see, I'm bringing it to life.* I was his big brother.

I loved him. I didn't want people to think he was fucked up. So I took them. Put them in *my* drawer, to protect him."

"Are you saying your books . . . ?"

"I wrote them," Ben said. "But the stories, they all came from Devon. His mind. His ideas, sketched out long ago. His world. I was just the vessel."

"Why?"

"Why what?"

"Why did you write them? Why did you feel the need to put it on paper? To go as far as publishing them."

"Because I love books. I've a way with words. I always wanted to be a writer. I . . . It's crazy, but I thought . . . We never found his body, you know. That ate at me. So I never was convinced. Not like Emily was, that Devon was dead."

"You thought writing them might help coax him out?"

Ben shook his head, although in hindsight he wasn't so sure now. "I wrote them thinking it might be cathartic for me. To help get me over the guilt I couldn't shake. And when *Summer Reign* became a bestseller, I couldn't stop there. I kept writing them, thinking that's what Devon would want. The success locked me in."

"And *The Scarecrow*? What made this one different?"

"I don't know, but I think it had something to do with me opening that book as a child. That story consumed me. It's the story I'd always wanted to write, that combination of Devon's idea merged with the feeling I got opening that book as a kid. Leaving it open until Grandpa Robert screamed at me to close it."

"Close it before . . . ?"

"It got out."

"And a year ago?"

"I'd written a third of it. It wasn't writer's block that had me stalled. It was the *should or shouldn't I finish it*. Should I write about something so ingrained? Something that had had me so rattled for years, since I was a clueless boy in that room, that it was like a pressure valve needing release."

"So you went back and opened that same book?"

Ben nodded, eyed the scotch. "I wrote so fast, not so much because I opened it, but because I'd already had it written." Ben tapped his head. "In here, for over a decade. Opening that book just gave me permission."

"And Jepson Heap's nightmare returned."

"In the body of Royal Blakely." Ben nodded again. "I assume that's how it works."

"And their first instinct is to first hunt down the one who created them."

Ben shook his head; it was too much to take in. He wanted to curl up and crawl into a hole. "You questioned my mom and sister when Devon went missing. Emily, she told you I was dark. She worried about me. But it was my mom who told you about my sleepwalking?"

"They both did."

"That's when it started," Ben said. "I'd go out at night, looking for Devon. I'd call his name into the woods."

"It was your mother though who . . ."

"Who what?"

"She told me you used to climb up on her chest," Mills said. "You'd press down on her. Said you truly believed you were a mare?"

"Mom didn't know where she was half the time," Ben said. "We were separated by seven years. Me and Devon. But we looked alike. He looked just like I did when I was his age. She was confused. All the time. It was Devon who'd do that. If Emily had known our mother had told you that, she would have corrected her."

Mills filled his coffee mug with water and sipped from it.

"I know it was Devon who let out Dad's nightmare," Ben said. "What my dad called the Screamer. He went more than twenty years without having it. Robert took it away, you know, like he did. It all started when Michael was a boy. It was that painting, Edvard Munch's *The Scream*. When my dad was a boy, it terrified him. Devon found the painting in the basement one night. Brought it upstairs. Dad saw it and freaked out. He hit him. Beat Devon up pretty good. I tucked Devon in that night. He told me he'd get him back one day."

Mills asked, "He went into that room and let his father's nightmare out?"

"I know that's what happened," Ben said. "Dad started having his childhood nightmare again. Not only that, but he'd begun seeing the Screamer in the woods."

"Edward Creech," said Mills.

"Yeah, so I hear." Ben watched out the window as daylight faded. "My sleepwalking. Me writing my books. I wanted answers, yeah, but it was guilt too. Devon was evil. He'd begun to hurt kids at school. Maybe he was born that way. My family was fucked up, but nobody made him like that. That young. You know, like Bundy. BTK. Gacy. Dahmer. I was afraid of this for Devon. That he would end up like that. Like *this*."

"You said guilt, Ben. What did you do to make you feel guilty?"

Ben said, "Not enough."

42

MILLS HAD ALREADY gone outside twice to scatter the press. Warned them it might not be safe on top of the hill.

One shouted it wasn't safe anywhere. Most ignored his warning, including Richard Bennington, who'd used the *friend of the family* card to try and worm his way inside Blackwood. He was still out there, access denied. When the sun started dipping beneath the trees and shadows started forming, a handful of media vans left, but a representative from each channel and news outlet remained. Two more from neighboring counties had arrived within the past twenty minutes, all eager to question Blair and her parents. Wanting to know if there were any suspects. Anyone arrested? Had the kidnapper finally been caught?

Mills closed the door on them all.

He turned to find Father Frank standing in the foyer. The old priest had both arms full, a cluster of loose papers, journals, and files. Like someone had dropped them all and he'd collected them haphazardly and out of order. "Winchester, we need to talk."

"What is it?"

"Follow me."

He did, into the kitchen, where Ben and Amanda and Emily and Blue sat around the table, waiting on him. "What's going on?" He remembered the intervention to end his drinking so long ago—Father Frank had headlined that too—and the feel of this wasn't too different.

Father Frank pulled out a stool. "Sit." Mills did. Father Frank took his seat at the head of the table, and began to organize the papers he'd been holding.

Mr. Atchinson appeared in the doorway. He held his hand out and Bri walked across the kitchen to take it, but not before she gave Mills another long look. Mr. Atchinson disappeared around the corner with Bri.

Amanda explained that Blair had asked that Bri come upstairs to play.

Mills eyed Father Frank. "What happened to you blessing the rooms?"

"I'm not finished yet."

"Why are we in here?"

"I stumbled upon something in Robert's bedroom. Inside the drawer of his nightstand."

Mills surveyed the table. None of them could look him in the eyes. "Somebody better cut to the chase."

Blue, unable to hide her emotions, looked away. "Hear him out, Dad."

Emily shared a look with Father Frank, and then went right at it. "Robert Bookman, for years, well before he died, was letting them out on purpose."

"The nightmares," said Ben.

"I know about the nightmares," said Mills. "What does this have to do with me?"

Ben said, "I mentioned earlier, in the tower . . . Robert would tell us a story about Mr. Dreams and the Nightmare Man. That the Nightmare Man has been alive since the first sleep."

"The first sleep? What the fuck is the first sleep?"

"Winchester," said Father Frank, his voice wavering. "Listen."

"It was just a story. Folklore," Ben said. "That since the first person ever slept . . ."

"What . . . Adam and fucking Eve? Who we talking about here?"

Father Frank slammed the table with his palm, and after Mills shut up, the priest nodded for Ben to go on.

"Since the first sleep, according to the story, two spirits were born. One planted nightmares. The other took them away. The Nightmare Man and Mr. Dreams. To us Mr. Dreams was no different than the Baku and the Sandman and countless others we were told about. Except Mr. Dreams was a man. A *human* dream catcher."

"For every villain there's a hero." Father Frank showed them a piece of paper, atop which was written the words *Every villain has a hero.* "This was written by Robert Bookman. He started making notes the day you visited here as a kid. Tell them what you told me, Winchester. What happened in that room?"

Mills watched them—the eagerness on their faces gave him cold chills. "The books moved. I had nightmares like no kid he'd ever seen. When he took me into that room all the books started shaking. Like they were trying to walk off the shelves. He hurried me out."

"Those books wanted no part of you," said Blue.

"What?"

"You saw how Royal Blakely reacted when you approached him inside his house. He jumped. And Creech, when you stuck your arm between the bars and asked him to read."

"He didn't jump."

"He wouldn't come any closer either," she said. "And Sally Pratchett, when you got close to her cell, what did she do?"

She scurried to the corner. He swallowed the thought, said nothing.

"He's been charting you from afar," said Father Frank. "Following your progress."

"What progress?"

Father searched through another journal in his pile. "Bernard Bookman. Back when he was still Bernard Mundt. Before he fled Vienna, he came across a new patient. His name was Peter Gruber. A seven-year-old boy who suffered very much like you. Not one reoccurring nightmare, but every nightmare under the sun. Every night they came. He'd been too successful with the books by then to give up on the boy. For two weeks he tried, but to no avail."

"You were born of fear, so fear you shall become," said Emily, dead-eyed, like it had come out as an accident. She absorbed the questions in their eyes. "It's what is said right before slamming the book closed. To trap it in."

Father swallowed so loud it was audible. He sipped from a wine glass. "He could not rid this boy of his nightmares. Sound familiar, Winchester?"

Mills clenched his jaw, closed his eyes. "Go on."

"Peter had what you have. He took people's nightmares. He was admitted to an asylum at the age of seventeen. He was there for seven months, before finding a way to kill himself with an overdose of the medicine they'd been giving to calm him. Peter Gruber shared a room with a man named Dominik Brand, who, that same night, began having nightmares. They sedated him. Secured him to the bed. Different nightmares every night. For a year this went on, until Dominik hung himself from his third-floor window with bedsheets."

"And from there," said Emily. "It jumped to the next person."

"Jumped? What do you mean jumped?"

Father Frank turned another page in the journal. "One of Dominik's nurses, a woman named Hannah Sturm, began having nightmares the day after Dominik Brand killed himself. Hannah was so tormented she fled her work at the asylum. She ended up in Spain months later and ultimately in an asylum there, where she spent the next ten years of her life going crazier by the day. Ten years. They pumped her with so many drugs she eventually died from them, but with a smile on her face because her nightmares were gone. And from there, a doctor from that Spanish asylum was stricken next. It moves like a virus, Winchester." He tapped the journal. "And according to Robert Bookman's theory, Mr. Dreams finally found a host who could handle him. You, Winchester."

Mills shook his head, stood from the table, walked toward the bottle of scotch next to the sink. Blue hurried to him, grabbed his arm. He didn't shake her away.

Father Frank stood from the table with them. "Samantha, your father has been having other people's nightmares since he was a boy. All it takes is a touch. He calls them brush-ups. His parents were desperate. They heard of the work Robert Bookman was doing here. They moved here when he was seven." Mills closed his eyes, nodded confirmation. Father Frank shook the papers in his arthritic, liver-spotted hand. "He followed your progress for decades. He tracked this back all the way to that Spanish asylum. There's been fifty-seven others, from then until now. Tell them when your nightmares started, Winchester. Tell them about your neighbor in Roanoke, Virginia."

"Norman," whispered Mills. And then louder. "Norman Lattimore."

Father said, "The final name on this list before yours."

Mills faced Sam, and then the others. "Norman Lattimore was our neighbor. A teenager everyone thought crazy. I was afraid of him. But also intrigued." He told them how Norman's father would walk him on a leash. He heard voices. One day he'd confronted him in his yard. Norman had whispered something about not being strong enough. "Norman jumped from his bedroom window. Broke his neck. I was the first one to run to him."

"And your nightmares started that night," Father Frank said, the word *night* landing abruptly, a final punctuation. "And he's been taking people's nightmares ever since."

Blue whispered, "But you could never take mine."

"No," Mills said silently, mind churning toward some truth. "I couldn't."

Emily said, "Robert believed early on that you could be Mr. Dreams. No one had ever been able to live with it. Until you, Detective Mills."

"You got it from Norman Lattimore." Father Frank read from the sheet. "And, according to Robert, he got it, as a five-year-old, from a neighbor in Raleigh, North Carolina, a year before they'd moved to Virginia. He tracked your career as a police officer and then a detective, and that's when he became sure. He began letting out some of the nightmares he'd trapped. On purpose. To see if you would migrate toward them. To catch them."

Mills grew weak in the knees, and went down to the right one, light-headed. *Human dream catcher.* Blue held him upright. He felt as if he'd blacked out; his vision had gone dark. When everyone else gasped and began looking around, panicked, he realized what had just happened.

The electricity had gone out. Blackwood was dark.

Someone had cut the power lines.

Before

MILLS COULDN'T BRING *himself to sign the cast.*
Even after Linda demanded he do so. And after Samantha begged him to before all the white space was gone. But he couldn't. The way it fully engulfed Sam's arm up past her elbow made his heart ache, her being forced to keep it at that weird angle. Sticking pencils down in there every twenty minutes to hunt down the itches. Every kid in her third-grade class had signed it, like it was some grand thing to be proud of. Her arm looked like a little broken twig underneath all that hardened gauze and plaster, all because of the way he'd grabbed her.

In anger. In drunken anger. No, he wouldn't sign the cast, but at least the incident had finally led to him getting sober. Her nightmares since then? Those he hadn't expected.

Nightmares were his *realm. Not hers.*

Ever since he'd gotten away from the drink, he'd yet to relearn how to fall asleep without it. He could no longer pass out. Now he spent hours staring at the ceiling, the alarm clock, out the window, and most recently, the hallway, waiting for Samantha to wake up screaming. Linda slept like a rock. He'd be the first by Sam's side, sitting on the bed near her pillow, shushing her back to sleep, petting her head until her eyes grew heavy.

"Pleasant dreams, Sam. Pleasant dreams."

He'd ask her what the nightmare was about. She'd tell him she didn't remember, but he didn't believe her. There were thirty-seven names on her cast now. None larger and more present than Danny Blue, Willard's son, who'd signed it in red marker with a heart in place of the goddamn little a. Danny was her best friend even though he was a boy, and to Samantha all boys were stupid. Mills covered the cast with a bedsheet so he couldn't see it, and then kissed her good night. He waited until she was out, and then retreated to his bed, wondering if it would work this time. He'd taken Linda's nightmares away years ago, when they weren't too much older than Sam was now. Back when he was first realizing about the brush-ups. The strange knack he had for taking on other people's nightmares. His mother always preached it was better to be a giver than a taker, but in his head that always seemed jumbled, backward.

He was a taker. Always the taker, but to him, this kind of taking was giving.

But he couldn't take away Sam's.

And then one day, suddenly, her nightmare went away.

CHAPTER

43

Darkness settled hard over Blackwood.

Outside, dusk had turned the woods to shadows, bleeding purple over the horizon, pushing like an eclipse toward deeper dark. The media remained, but as Detective Mills had reported, casing the perimeter of the house after the power went out, they were anxious, more serious and subdued, secured only by the fact that the police were out there with them.

Inside, candles flickered on countertops, on mantels and coffee tables; flashlights bounced off walls as uniformed cops roamed, searching for what had led to the power outage. Ben sat by the roaring fire in the parlor, staring into the flame as it churned through fresh wood. Three moths spun against the window to his left, tapping to get in. He ignored them; he'd spent too many minutes staring at them already, before Amanda had aggressively closed the window. Now that the night had begun its descent, Amanda had gone in reverse order, closing every window in the house she'd opened upon their arrival.

"We should have left." Amanda paced in front of the hearth. "We should have left when it was light. Ben?"

"It's not safe out there either. *They're* out there, Amanda."

She couldn't stay still. She folded her arms above her baby bump as if cold, despite the heat now permeating the living room. He'd told her about Jennifer. About Robert possibly being her father, as well. Amanda had nodded, soaked it in, but said little, probably too numb to rationally hash anything out. "Do you think Devon is going to come here?"

"I don't know." But he did. *And yes, Devon is coming.* "But he won't get past the police out there. None of them will."

Amanda checked her phone. "I'm on three percent. You have a charger?"

"No." He checked his phone. "I'm on eighteen. I could go all night."

She let out a sarcastic laugh. "Like a sinking ship." Her phone pinged. Her face glowed as the screen lit up. "Great."

"Who is it?" She hesitated, which meant it was Bennington. "What does *he* want?"

"The road's blocked in and out of Blackwood. Somebody from Channel 11 just tried to leave."

"Blocked how?"

She waited for another text. "Tree across the road." More sarcasm. "Must be from the same *storm* that turned off the power."

"Something like that." He was preoccupied by Detective Mills outside the window.

Amanda noticed him too, standing alone out near the tree line. "What's he doing?"

"I don't know." The detective had barely spoken to anyone since the revelation inside the kitchen earlier. Ben watched him now like his daughter had earlier. Like he was some kind of superhero made flesh. Grandpa Robert had told them the story of Mr. Dreams too many times to count. And now somehow it wasn't so impossible. It had gone beyond folklore and myth and suddenly materialized before their eyes as legend. Mills watched the woods out there like he was the first and last line of defense all rolled into one man. Mills paced, then put a phone to his ear.

Who was he talking to?

Amanda stopped in front of the fire. "Ben? Did you hear what I said?"

"What? No, sorry." Detective Mills had just pocketed his phone and run off, out of view. *Where's he going?*

"She's playing with them now," Amanda said. "Blair. Bri's worked wonders with her." From where Amanda stood, the kitchen was visible. Bri was in there at the big table with Aunt Emily; they'd moved on from checkers after the lights went out, to Go Fish by candlelight. Blair had been watching when Ben had last checked on them. And now, apparently, she'd joined in.

"Her parents are with her." Amanda started her nervous pacing again. "Poor girl. Why'd he leave her alive, Ben?"

"He likes to play games. That's what he's doing. He just used her as a pawn."

"Let's hope that's all he did."

"Devon wasn't like that. He's warped. He's sadistic. But he's not like that."

"How do you know? You haven't seen him in thirteen years. He hadn't even hit puberty when he went missing." Ben reached out, placed his open hand on her stomach. She stopped pacing, froze upon his touch. "What are you doing?"

"Is he kicking?"

She gave a snort that said *of all times*, and then gently moved his hand, up and to the right, until he felt the slightest of movements beneath her blouse. He kept it there, over the warmth of her. The life inside her. She stood like that for a minute, him feeling his son for the first time, her rubbing his hand, and in that gesture he felt something resolve between them.

Felt hope.

He looked up from his chair. "Don't cry."

"I'm not."

He stood, wiped her cheeks, kissed her forehead. "Is it killing you not to be out there with the rest of the media?"

"No. I'm where I need to be."

He rubbed her back, felt her laughter against his chest. He pulled away, looked into her eyes. "What could possibly be funny about this?"

"Nothing."

"Tell me."

"Richard. Bennington."

"What about him?"

"You're jealous of him. You always have been. About our friendship."

"Not true."

"He's gay."

Ben stared at her, blinking, confused like he'd be if he'd just learned he had ten legs instead of two. "When?"

"When what?"

"When was he gay?"

"He was born that way, Ben. What are you, a dinosaur?"

"No, I mean, I get that. How long have you known?"

"Since he was thirteen. He told me then. He kissed me out behind the bleachers. And then after, he said, okay."

"Okay what?"

"'Okay, now I know.'"

"What are you talking about?" He found himself smiling, eyes wet like hers.

"He said if he was able to kiss the prettiest girl he knew and not feel anything, then he was sure. And that's when he told me."

"Son of a bitch. Richard Bennington? What about all the women he's been linked to?"

"Façades."

"No shit?"

"No shit."

They looked into each other's eyes. "Why are you telling me this now?"

"I don't know. I promised him I'd never tell anyone."

He put his arms around her and kissed her forehead. He watched out the window—Detective Mills hadn't reappeared. "Amanda." He stroked her hair. "We're not gonna die."

"No?"

"No. Like with all nightmares, we'll wake up to find it was bullshit."

She pulled away, just far enough to look him in the eyes again, which he took as an invitation to kiss her. He kept his lips on hers long enough to taste the salt from her tears, and then he said, "Okay."

"Okay." She grinned. "Okay what?"

"Now I know for sure."

Hurried footsteps from the hallway brought reality back in a flash.

Emily's desperate voice sounded from the opening to the living room. "Ben?"

He stepped away from Amanda, but kept hold of her hand. "Em, what's wrong?"

"Officer Maxwell, she was the one to contact him earlier, so he had her number."

"Who?"

"Father Frank. He was blessing all the rooms. He just sent Officer Maxwell a weird text. Said he was locked in a room upstairs. Third floor, end of the hallway."

Devon's old room.

44

J ENNIFER JACKSON HAD sounded panicked over the phone.

After Mills had gotten over the initial jolt of hearing her voice, he'd urged her to stay calm. To slow down and tell him where she was. They'd been trying to track her down.

"I'm at Blackwood. I'm in the tower."

The Tower? How had she gotten past the guards? The media? Before he could talk her into the main house, to tell her that the door was open, she said, "There's something in here you need to see."

Instinct told him not to trust her. Jennifer, yes—the nightmare she'd become, no. But it wasn't Julia's voice, not the one he remembered from Ben's nightmare. So he discreetly entered the house and listened.

"I think I figured out how to get rid of her," Jennifer said over the phone.

"How?"

"Come to the tower. I can only tell you in person."

Mills turned on the flashlight on his cell phone and navigated Blackwood's dark hallways. And then a background voice sounded through static on the other end of the line.

"Dad, don't. Don't listen to her."

A pained scream.

"Sam?" He increased his pace through the dark. Laughter sounded through the phone. *Julia.* "What did you do? How did you get my number?"

"Oops, I think Detective Blue is injured," said Julia, with another burst of sultry giggles. "Come quick. But don't tell anyone, Detective. Or she just might die."

She ended the call.

Mills turned off the flashlight so no one would see him and follow. He felt the bookshelved walls as he moved from hallway to hallway, remembering in opposite all the turns made earlier when leaving the tower. He followed the breeze, the smell of stale, dank air. His pace quickened. His eyes adjusted to the dark. Within minutes, he entered the final corridor leading into the tower, the door still propped open by the heavy chain that had held it locked for years. He stepped inside with caution, heard only the sound of birds fluttering in the rafters above. A drip from somewhere, plopping in a growing puddle.

"Sam?" He didn't see his daughter anywhere. "Sam?"

Julia-as-Jennifer's voice echoed from above. "Up here."

He peered up toward the balcony, but at that height, and with the shadows, he could make out only one silhouette at the railing. Stone steps hugged the curved wall, spiraling around and upward.

"Sam?"

Laughter filtered down. Or was it crying?

Both.

"Sam!" Gun in one hand, he gripped the curved stairwell railing with the other, and started the climb.

Under the ceiling, birds flew from one beam to another, scattering dust down through moonlight. He called her name again. Twenty steps up, his heart began to thump out of rhythm. Ten more steps. Sweat sprouted across his brow.

"Hurry. I need help." Jennifer's voice again, the false desperation in it reeling him in like the most gullible of catches. "Hurry, please."

"Fuck you," he mumbled under his breath. His only goal: to save Sam. He managed a few dozen more steps before stopping to catch his breath. If he'd had a minor heart attack inside Royal Blakely's house last night, what he felt now was worse. Tightness in his chest. Pain down his arm. Dizziness and nausea. "She's trying to kill me, Blue," he said softly, more to himself than anything. If he was talking, it meant he was still alive.

He climbed a few more steps, leaned against the wall, hand on his chest. He willed himself onward, hugging the curved wall as it spiraled upward. He closed his eyes to the dizziness. Opened them, exhaled. The final curve of the stairwell beckoned him. One stair at a time, he climbed, labored, until finally he reached the landing. Through a patchwork of shadow and moonlight and dust motes stood Julia.

Jennifer as Julia.

But one look into her haunted eyes let Mills know with whom he was dealing. A nightmare as ornery as he'd ever seen. Julia stood ten paces away, in full Roman regalia, a sky-blue silk tunic with a cream-colored stola draped over both shoulders, cinched at the left one by clasps of shiny gold. Her hair was done up in aristocratic curls and flamboyant braids. She twirled, as if to show it all off for him, and then stopped, icy cold blue eyes boring into him, lips painted red.

"Hello, Detective."

Mills leaned against the wall for support. Every movement sent surges of pain through his chest, down his arm. Blue was in the shadows behind Jennifer, sitting on the dusty plank floor of the balcony, her back against the wall. At first glance he feared her dead, but then she began to stir. Her lolling head moved against her shoulder. She groaned. Blood ran down her forehead, around her left eye, and down toward the curve of her jaw next to the ear. From a wound Mills couldn't see. A blow to the head, for sure, but not a bullet.

Mills winced, took a step. "What do you want?"

Jennifer held a book in her hands, a leather-bound book with a number he couldn't make out on the spine, but no doubt one she'd taken from the atrium downstairs. She giggled, "What do I want? Such a silly question."

Mills spotted Blue's gun on the floorboards, and then next to it, the gun she'd always worn around her ankle. She'd clearly been caught by surprise, fooled by Jennifer's innocent voice, knocked on the head and disarmed while down.

Jennifer noticed Mills had spotted the two guns. As if afraid to touch them, she kicked one underneath the railing, off the edge of the balcony, and then the next. Seconds later, two metallic clanks echoed off the hard tower floor four stories below.

Birds scattered at the noise, wings fluttering through dust motes, resettled moments later.

"Jennifer," Mills pleaded. "I know you're in there. I know you want her gone. I can help you."

Jennifer grinned. "No, you can't. She doesn't want to be helped anymore, Detective. She likes what we do now." Jennifer squatted down, her long tunic briefly swallowing her sandaled feet in a silky, flowering bloom. Just as spontaneously, she stood again, her left hand holding the bottom seam of the flimsy garment. She lifted it to her naked thighs, twirled as she lifted it higher, and when she stopped to face him, the tunic had been pulled high enough to expose her naked breasts.

Mills looked away.

"Don't be shy, Detective."

Mills glanced. She'd brought the book in her hands to the opening between her legs. She rubbed the spine of it there, as if stimulating herself, playfully moaning for him—whispering, *Bad Dad*—for show, for him, and then dropped the tunic back down, laughing.

Mocking him.

"You can look now," she said.

Mills did, but with his gun raised, aiming right at her heart.

"You can't shoot," she said. "I've done nothing wrong."

Blue stirred behind her. One of her legs moved.

"You attacked an officer of the law."

"Who, me?" She theatrically placed a hand to her chest. "Oh no, I found her like this."

"Bullshit."

"You're right. I hit her. Hard. But then I kissed her to make it better. On the lips. I licked the wound and swallowed her blood. I whispered in her ear that I was coming for her husband tonight. For good ol' Danny Blue. Loving husband and dedicated father. And that I'd do things to him she never dreamed of doing."

"Stay away from my family."

"Stay away from my family," she mocked. "Is it really your family if they no longer see you? Bad Dad."

Mills inched closer, back pressed to the stone curve of the wall, his gun still on her, but his main focus, now that he knew what those books contained, was on the book in her hand, and what she planned on doing with it. "What's in the book?"

"Oh, this?" She looked at it, faked surprise. "Now how did this get here?"

He took another step, noticed now that the spine's number was *1011*. The number meant nothing to him, other than being just one more from Robert Bookman's list, a list started by the Bookmans over a century ago.

Mills heard footsteps coming up the stairs, approaching through the dark toward the balcony. He aimed his gun toward the steps, waiting for someone to emerge from the darkness. "Who's there?"

Laughter. Male laughter.

"Doesn't this look familiar to you?" Jennifer asked, holding the book out for him to see.

"What's in the book?" he hissed, at the same time glancing toward the curved stairwell again, hearing the slow whisk-whisk of footsteps approaching upward toward the balcony.

Like sweeps from a broom.

"You remember your daughter's nightmare, don't you?"

"Of course I do."

"You tried, but you could never take it away," said Jennifer. "Do you know why you could never take it away?"

"What's in the fucking book?"

She fanned through the pages, opened it, closed it.

The footsteps below him drew closer, louder. *Whisk-whisk.* Mills watched Jennifer, the book in her hands. He turned toward the stairwell to find Bruce Bagwell, the Boogeyman, crouched on the landing, just a few feet away, his face painted in vertical brown and black stripes, eyes and lips rimmed in stark red paint.

"Boo!" he shouted.

Mills lurched, his body slumped against the wall. His heart raged against his ribcage.

Laughter now from both sides.

From Jennifer as Julia, and Bruce Bagwell as the Boogeyman, now disappearing back down the stairs into the darkness of the tower, mission accomplished.

"*You*, Detective Mills," Jennifer said. "*You're* in the book. *You* were your daughter's nightmare."

He shook his head, dizzy, drowned in sweat.

"You snapped her arm like a twig. She could never get past the drunk look in your eyes. The bad look. That's why you couldn't take her nightmare away, because *you* were her nightmare."

Pain. Nausea. He doubled over. Realizing what she planned to do with the book, he willed himself upright, reached out. "Give it to me."

She fanned the pages of the book again. "She told her mother about it. About how scary her nightmares of you were. Bad Dad with the bad look."

"Give me the book."

"Your wife sneaked her off to Dr. Bookman. And he fixed her. Bad Dad went away. But a little birdie told me to let him back out."

He pointed his gun at her. "Don't do it."

And then Blue's voice from the shadows behind Jennifer. "Dad . . ."

Jennifer turned toward Blue. She'd neglected to remove the tiny .380 from the lining of Sam's bra holster.

Clever girl.

Blue fired. Not at Jennifer. At the book. Clipping Jennifer's hand in the process, spinning the nightmare against the wall, blood spraying from the wound, her fingers a mangled mess.

Blue had made it to her feet, gun still poised on Jennifer, who looked up at her, crying, her own eyes now—not Julia's.

Blue must have noticed it too. She lowered her arms, but only briefly, as if to not fall for the same deception twice. She made as if to pull the trigger again, to put the nightmare down for good, when Jennifer stood, slowly, confused and terrified, whispering "I'm sorry," over and over again.

The book Jennifer had threatened to open rested on the balcony floor, in a standing position, pages slightly fanned open. With an outstretched leg, Mills knocked the book on its side, and then brought it in with his foot.

Closed.

Jennifer stood, wobbled, crying. "Tell Ben and Amanda I'm sorry. I loved them. And that I know."

"You know what?" Blue asked, still cautiously holding the gun on her.

"And tell Bri it's okay to be scared. Sometimes."

Before they could stop her, Jennifer hurled herself over the balcony railing. Mills screamed for her, watched helplessly over the rail as Jennifer's body plummeted in a free fall, but looked away just before her body made impact with the stone floor below. He waited a few seconds, hearing nothing, and forced himself to look. Blood pooled around her head. Her neck seemed at an impossible angle. She wasn't moving. No one could have survived that fall.

She was dead.

And hopefully, Mills thought, she'd taken Julia along with her.

Before

BERNARD BOOKMAN WAS *lost.*

Blackwood Forest had swallowed him. For hours he'd been going in circles through a storybook wilderness of brambles and dead-fall, lichen-covered limbs and crooked, moss-covered steps. The over-head branches, so crowded and outreaching they'd blotted out the sun. The air was clean, the gullies deep, the streams lush and running. Bright green moss covered rocks and roots alike, and had begun to trek northward up the lurid black trunks of so many knotted, arthritic trees.

Call it fate or luck, he discovered the clearing, a perfect half-acre oval of windblown prairie grass, in the middle of which stood the tree he'd crossed an ocean to find. Void of leaves, as if fire-scorched and left for dead, yet somehow raging with life. He approached it with caution, saw movement across the dark, wet bark.

Could it be? A real mare tree?

Dozens of moths fluttered, with just as many clinging to the bark as if drinking.

The sunlight should have agitated them, but it didn't.

Bernard stepped to within a few feet of the tree.

The bark looked tarred, like black paint freshly applied to the creases and furrows and grooves. While most of the moths were the drab, ashy-colored ones familiar to most, there were a few clinging to the tree that were not common to the region. Not just the region, but to the states in general. There was a comet moth—touched with shades of purple and yellow—native to Madagascar, one of the world's largest silk moths.

After removing his book of moths from his satchel, he found a picture and confirmed it. He circled the tree in full; the black, twisty limbs cast shadows halfway across the clearing. Next he noticed a twin-spotted sphinx moth. And then a lime hawk-moth higher up on the tree—that species was native to the Near East. Not here. Even higher up, near where the branches had begun to grow outward, he spotted the distinct white and black of a giant leopard moth.

Deer watched from the outskirts of the clearing, a dozen at least, spread out around the circumference, as if afraid to come in.

Afraid of the tree.

Bernard camped in the clearing for three days, painting the moths, charting the new arrivals. He wrote back to his wife and young son in England. He'd found a place to build their home. Named after the forest, he'd call it Blackwood. He sent a picture of the room he'd build around the tree.

It was in that room where he'd keep his books.

45

B EN PUT HIS ear to the door, confirming what Officer Maxwell had just heard on the other side of it.

Like a swarm of bees.

Ben unlocked the door.

"Back up, Mr. Bookman." Maxwell placed a hand on the knob, made it clear she was going in first.

Ben backed away, flashlight in hand, shining the beam at the door as Maxwell turned the knob. She slowly opened the door. As soon as a gap formed, dozens of moths fluttered out.

They both ducked, stayed hunkered as moths flew frantically overhead, all around them. Maxwell opened the door wider, against the resistance of so many moths continuing to spiral out, fluttering in and out of the flashlight beam in strobes and pulses, a dizzying number of moths made insignificant by the number Ben now saw *inside* the room.

On the walls. On the ceiling. All over the bed.

Maxwell swiped at them. They bounced off Ben's chest and arms and face. He clenched his jaw to keep them out of his mouth. He squinted, hunkered lower as he entered Devon's old room. The hundreds hovering over the bed scattered as he swiped at them. Scattered and reformed. He swung at them again, clearing his line of sight long enough to notice what was on the bed. Another body. Unmoving.

Ben turned his face against the tumult and spoke into his chest. "Father Frank."

Moths flickered and danced.

Ben pointed the light at the bed.

Maxwell cleared moths away from Father Frank's face with her hand. He was dead. She closed his eyes. A moth rested on his lip. Another crawled from inside his open mouth. She shooed it away, closed his jaw in disgust.

Blood stained the pillow beneath Father Frank's thin, silvery hair.

Ben rolled the dead priest on his side, gestured for Maxwell to hold him there while he pointed the light at the back of his head. Just as he'd feared, the back part of his skull was missing, a distinct circle carefully removed, like an ice fisherman might bore into the ice before dropping a line.

"He's in the house," Ben said.

Maxwell said, "Mr. Bookman. The wall."

Ben aimed his flashlight to where she was pointing above the bed's headboard. Another list of names. The last name on the list was *Winchester Mills*.

He followed the names upward. *Samantha Blue. Brianna Bookman. Amanda Bookman. Emily Bookman. Benjamin Bookman . . .*

Ben turned back toward the bed. He couldn't leave him in here. He handed Maxwell the flashlight, slid his hands beneath Father Frank's slight frame and lifted. He burrowed his way out of the room.

Maxwell pulled the door closed behind them. So many moths had escaped, the hallway was now inundated by them. Ben lowered his head, carried Father Frank's body through it all. He entered his childhood bedroom down the hall and for now placed the body on the nearest bed.

He closed the door.

Back in the hallway, he found Maxwell waiting, radioing to someone that Devon Bookman was somewhere in the house.

When they hit the third-floor landing, leading downward, they heard violin music.

And then someone screaming.

46

ONE STEP AT *a time.*

Father and daughter descended the tower steps, clutching each other, Mills on the brink of collapse.

He'd told her to leave him up there. She'd told him to shut up.

Violin music resonated from somewhere inside the main house. Julia and the Boogeyman apparently weren't the only mares to return to Blackwood.

Edward Creech had joined them.

"One step at a time," she coached. "We're almost there."

"Sam?"

"Dad, stop talking."

Her radio crackled. Officer Maxwell's voice sounded through static. "They're in the house. Devon is in the house. Moths are everywhere. Father Frank is dead."

"Go," Mills pleaded. "Leave me."

"Where are you?" Blue asked Maxwell, wearily plowing on with her father's dead weight across her shoulders.

"First floor," said Maxwell. "Something's happening outside. Trees are falling. Someone out there has a chainsaw. The press . . . they're trying to leave but they can't."

Screaming sounded over the radio; not Maxwell, but background noise—something happening around her.

And then Maxwell screamed.

Bullets fired.

Static.

Blue increased her pace down the stairs.

Mills pulled away from her, grabbed the rail on his own, and grimaced through pain and dizziness the rest of the way down. She didn't fight him. They were almost to the bottom, the last curvature of stairs.

"You okay?"

"Never been better." He heard breathing that wasn't their own. He cautioned Sam, gripped her elbow. Something moved in the shadows.

She spotted her guns on the tower floor, squatted down to grab them both, while at the same time monitoring the dark surroundings.

Suddenly, the Boogeyman ran toward them from the dark, laughing. "Boo!" He got to within five feet and then hurried away, back into the shadows.

Mills followed the sound of heavy breathing. "Bagwell?"

Footsteps.

The Boogeyman showed himself again, fleetingly, and disappeared into the dark, giggling. Breathing. Mills silenced himself, followed.

Blue turned in a slow circle, ready to fire.

Out of nowhere, the Boogeyman jumped at him them both.

Mills fired.

Sam fired.

Bruce Bagwell screamed in pain, pinwheeling back against the stone wall where those twenty-one names had been written in chalk. They heard moaning and squirming and followed it, their eyes adjusting to the dark.

By the time Sam shined a light on him, the Boogeyman was dead.

Before

"*H*E'S OUT THERE, *Benjamin. Can you hear him?*"

Ben didn't exactly know what he'd heard out there in the trees surrounding Blackwood. Maybe it was the silent screams like Devon was saying. The hushes and whispers.

Maybe it was just the wind.

But the footsteps, the crunched weight over deadfall now sounding out there in the dark, those sounds were undeniable. Someone was out there. Something was out there.

And while Ben, as the older brother, felt so sick he might throw up, Devon took it in stride. Watched the woods like one might a caged animal at the zoo. Curious and interested but not scared one might break out. Ben watched him standing there with his hands in his pockets, unable to shake the memories of what he'd found last month inside the coal chute.

Emily's old dolls with the backs of their heads holed out. Devon had promised he'd not do another one of the dolls like that. Ben made him acknowledge that there wasn't some place inside us called the hollow. Devon had promised. But he'd broken promises before. And he'd been acting funny. Especially since Dad had beaten him for what he'd done with that painting. For bringing back the Screamer.

Yesterday, because of an odd stench coming from the basement, Ben had gone back into the coal chute. The dolls were gone, but in their place were dead carcasses. Squirrels and beavers and raccoons and chipmunks. Each one of them had been cut into. And there were bones, like Devon had been doing it for a long time without Ben knowing. Maybe the bones had been there before, but he'd been so preoccupied by the mutilated dolls that he hadn't noticed.

Ben brought it up again, an hour ago.

Devon said he'd found them. He'd located the hollows in all of those animals and he was proud of what he'd done.

You know, Ben. I'm ready.

For what?

To make that jump.

What jump, Devon?

There's a boy. At school. He picks on me 'cause I'm different.

Devon, what are you talking about?

That grin. He didn't need to say it. He was ready to make that jump.

Devon wore that same grin months ago when Ben found him in the woods with the dead sparrow in his hands, plucking wings off one by one. I'm seeing what it sounds like when they come off. Ben had heard someone coming. He'd told Devon to run back inside. He'd told Emily, when she caught him standing over the bird, that he'd found it dead on the ground. That he'd been sleepwalking.

"Do you hear him out there, Benjamin?" Devon watched the woods, standing casually with his hands in his pockets. "The man without hair. He's Daddy's, you know? He doesn't have a mouth, but he eats children. I should go looking for him."

Ready to make that jump . . .

Ben forced the memory of those words down and found himself saying, "Maybe you should, Devon. Go out there looking for him."

"Like a dare?"

"Yes, like a dare. To see if he's real."

Devon liked dares, and Ben knew that he did.

He took this one and entered the woods, alone.

And Ben never saw him again.

47

MOTHS FLEW EVERYWHERE. Clung to everything. The bookshelves, the ceiling, the floorboards.

An officer was down at the bottom of the main stairwell. Dead. He had to be dead, Ben thought, as he and Officer Maxwell neared the man. Otherwise the dozens of moths resting atop his face, neck, and arms wouldn't be there. He would have shaken them off.

Maxwell knelt down, closed the officer's eyes, and shooed the moths away. She told Ben to wait, but he stepped past her, past the mosaic foyer with the flashlight. He called out for Amanda and Bri, hurried to the kitchen, where he'd last seen them. He shined his light high and low, on the counters and table top, and then into the breakfast nook. He heard crying and sniffling, someone trying to be quiet. He found the Atchinson family huddled together beneath the table.

Before he could get the question out of his mouth, Mr. Atchinson said, "He took them."

"Who?"

"Your wife and sister."

"And Bri?"

"She got away. I don't know where she went."

Blair's thin voice cracked the air like a whip. "She needs to be near him when he dies."

"Near who?"

Blair said, "He took them to the room. The man who took me. He took them into the room with the tree."

Ben grabbed a butcher knife from the block next to the oven, shined his flashlight through the kitchen, and followed the glow into the hallway. Wherever Bri was, he knew she had the good sense to hide, and stay hidden.

Violin music struck up again; his fear for Brianna increased tenfold. The Screamer was in the house. The violin music grew louder. He followed it, and within a few steps pinpointed the location—it was coming from the hallway leading to the atrium. He jumped at what he saw in the foyer. Officer Maxwell was gone, but the body of the slain officer she'd stopped to take care of minutes ago was still there. Another woman hovered over his torso. She wore dirty, light-blue Oswald Asylum fatigues, stained blood red now across the front. She looked up through stringy hair and spotted Ben. Her eyes were dark. In her fingers was a tooth she'd just extracted from the slain officer's mouth. She gave Ben another second's thought and then dug into the man's open mouth for another.

Because that's what Tooth Fairies do.

"Back away," Ben said, shining his light, wishing now he was armed with anything more than a butcher knife. "Back the fuck away right now."

Sally Pratchett laughed, and then resumed her work, even as Ben closed in and moths circled. He shined the light at her, right into her face, and she backed away. Violin music thrummed down the hallway to his right. Outside, a chainsaw ripped and roared and another tree fell. Sirens blared. Gunshots fired, echoed through the woods. He shined the light into her face again and she backed further away, across the mosaic floor and into the front door.

A gunshot fired.

Ben ducked.

Sally Pratchett was flung against the door by the impact. Another gunshot dropped her to the floor, where she cried out and whimpered, the sound of a suffering human, Ben had to restrain himself not to run and help. But deep down he had pity for her. She hadn't chosen this path; the escaped nightmare had chosen her.

It was Robert who was to blame.

Another gunshot stopped Sally Pratchett's breathing completely.

Officer Maxwell entered the foyer, eyes crazed, gun still poised on her target. In her other hand was a blanket she'd grabbed from the living room to cover her dead friend's body. Now, in the light, he saw the officer had died from what had to be an axe blow to the stomach. Ben had been focused on the moths before, and in the dark the wound had gone unnoticed.

Officer Maxwell draped the blanket over her fellow officer.

The axe wound meant that the Scarecrow was somewhere in the house. Ben clutched Officer Maxwell by the arm and pulled her away from the foyer, which was open from too many sides—too much unpredictable dark.

They followed the violin music and entered the hallway leading to the atrium.

48

W ITH EACH CLAP of gunfire, Mills grew more focused as he navigated the dark turns of the house.

He pushed down deep any pains that slowed him, any hints from his body that death was a foregone conclusion. Sam hobbled behind him one minute, ahead of him the next, skittering nervous-like through the hallways, checking every corner and nook and open room with her gun gripped in both hands. It sounded like chaos outside.

Sirens and screams and trees being felled.

Chainsaws.

As they inched through the dark house, Mills realized another name he should have added to his living room wall. Another patient he'd arrested who eventually ended up at Oswald. Ten years ago, he'd brought in Curt Bassey, a male nurse who suddenly quit his job to become a tree cutter. Not by trade or business, but boldly and at random. Bassey purchased a chainsaw and just started cutting people's trees down. When Mills arrested him for more or less being a pain in the ass public nuisance, Curt Bassey mumbled *Fee-fi-fo-fum* under his breath, all the way to the station. Questioned there about his tree cutting, Bassey said because he was the Lumberjack. Not *a* lumberjack, Mills realized now as he followed Sam down another dark hallway flanked by bookshelves, but *the* Lumberjack. Mills had told Bassey that *Fee-fi-fo-fum* was from "Jack and the Beanstalk," and that he was no giant. Bassey was let go and arrested two more times before he ended up at Oswald Asylum, a patient of the late Robert Bookman, until his apparent escape hours ago with the rest of them.

Sam had radioed the officers outside, but no one had answered.

The closer they got to the kitchen, the louder the violin music became.

They followed it.

Mills flinched at the pop of another gunshot, somewhere close. As the hallways drifted back to silence, he heard someone whimpering, but that too faded. He should have seen it coming. Truth was, he had, because that's what dream catchers do.

They sense the nightmares before they strike.

The hairs on his arms stood up.

The stench of Royal Blakely hit him first, before any shuffling of the large man's shoes as he stepped from the darkness of the open closet neither one of them had seen. Mills even saw the axe blade coming, smelled the blood from the Scarecrow's previous victims on it as it came down in a wide-sweeping arc, cleaving through the flesh and bone of his right shoulder before he could pull off a shot of his own. He saw the glint in those dark eyes, popping through the holes of that burlap mask so hastily stitched it was coming loose at the chin in a clot of bloody thread and skin.

Mills didn't drop right away. The blade had been so thoroughly embedded that it held him there, suspended, and it took Blakely's big boot to his chest to dislodge it. Mills didn't know exactly how many gunshots he then heard plug into Royal Blakely's body, but it was enough for him to drop that heavy axe, enough to fell him like one of Curt Bassey's trees outside, enough for Sam to drop one spent gun to the floor and grab for the next one inside her shirt because she *wouldn't* stop firing through her tears. And when that one was spent, she grabbed the pistol she kept around her ankle and emptied that one too.

"Enough, Sam . . ." Mills watched through blurred tears. "He's dead."

Twenty times dead.

Sam was beside him now, clutching his hand and telling him to hold on, but he couldn't hold on when he felt cut in two. "He got me, Sam." She took off her jacket and started ripping. She took his suspenders to use as tourniquets, but it was an exercise in futility.

"Sam, stop . . ."

She worked relentlessly in the dark.

"My thread . . ."

"Shut up about your threads and your three fucking fates, Dad."

He smiled, coughed up blood. "She's beautiful."

"Who's beautiful, Dad? Stay with me. Who's beautiful?"

"Atropos," he said in a gasp. He closed his eyes. "Like you. And your mother."

Sam sniffled, continued working on his shoulder. But she didn't know what she was doing and she was getting more pissed by the second. She was crying and frustrated, and Mills reached up and gripped her arm. "Sam, stop. Let me go."

She stopped. He felt her hand on his head, stroking his thin hair. He choked up more blood. "Dad . . . Tell me about them . . ."

"Clotho," he said in a whisper. "She spins the thread. Of life."

Sam let out a burst of emotion, half-cry and half-laughter. "And oh, what a life she spun."

"Lachesis. She's done measuring, Blue. Baby Blue." He opened his eyes. "Here she comes." He felt someone holding each hand now, one grip much smaller than the other. "There you are . . ."

He let out one last gasp, heaving his chest up off the floor, and settled.

CHAPTER

49

BLUE CLOSED HER father's eyes, looked to her side, saw Brianna Bookman holding her father's other hand.
The little girl smiled.
She'd come out of nowhere.

50

B EN MOVED CAUTIOUSLY with Officer Maxwell down the hallway. When he saw Amanda and Emily on the other side of the atrium's glass wall, and the thousands of moths trapped inside that room with them, his walk turned into a run.

The door was locked.

Edward Creech was in there, prancing and stomping and thrusting that bow across the moth-perched strings of that demonic violin. Moths flew away from him as he played, avoiding his gestures and movements and gyrations.

Ben pounded on the glass, calling out the names of his sister and wife—they sat rope-tied in wooden chairs, placed back to back in front of the far bookshelf. They turned their heads to him simultaneously. Duct tape closed their mouths. Their eyes watched, rapt, confused, and frightened. Moths flew everywhere. On Amanda's head and shoulders. On Emily's neck and arms and lap. On and off shelves, across the stones of the floor, some bouncing off the glass wall, as if trying to get out, but nowhere were they more bundled than on the tree, thousands drinking and crawling and pulsing their wings, all the way up the trunk to the branches and boughs and arches of the shattered ceiling.

Laughter sounded from somewhere inside that room. Ben pounded the glass with his fist until the skin broke and blood ran down his arm.

Officer Maxwell grabbed his arm, tried to pull him away, to warn him of the man now approaching the other side of that glass. Through the flurry of moths.

The source of the laughter.

Ben hadn't seen his brother in thirteen years, but he knew it was him.

Eyes never change—blue eyes like his own, but still empty.

Devon was shorter than Ben, with a thicker build and more closely cropped brown hair, but their faces were so similar it pained him to even look. The glass wall could just as well have been a mirror. But while Ben was enraged and terrified, Devon wore the same casual smile he'd worn before stepping into the woods thirteen years ago on a stupid dare. His blue shirt was unbuttoned nearly down to his naval. His chest was chiseled, and sprawled wide across it were the hints of the moth tattoo. Ink that seemingly ran down both arms and ended at the tops of both hands.

"Hello, big brother."

Ben could barely hear him through the moths and violin music, but he read his lips clearly.

"Hello, Devon."

Devon held up his hand, not to wave, but as a clear sign for Creech to stop playing, which the man did on cue. The Screamer tucked the violin beneath his right arm and stood centurion-like next to the chairs holding Amanda and Emily. Devon gestured toward his sister, and to the sister-in-law he'd never met. "We were well past time for a family reunion, don't you think?"

"Let them go," Ben said through the glass, noticing Officer Maxwell had changed her position in the hallway, trying to find an angle that maximized her chance of hitting Devon while minimizing the threat of hitting Amanda and Emily behind him.

"I'd stop moving," Devon said to Maxwell. "If I were you."

"Let them go," Ben said again. "This is between me and you."

"Do you dare me, Benjamin? Huh? Do you *dare* me to let them go? How about I send Creech into the dark woods, and then dare *you* to go out and find him?"

Creech liked this. A painful grin stretched across that hatching of scars he called lips.

"Don't act like that turned you, Devon."

"Didn't it? Poor little boy lost out in the woods."

"You were born dark."

"Sent out there by his older brother who once loved him. All alone."

Devon took his eyes off Ben. But his attention wasn't drawn to Maxwell, who was behind Ben and to his left, but Ben's right. To the hallway. Toward his niece, Brianna, who, now that she'd fully emerged from the shadows, was holding a gun in both hands.

"Hello, Brianna," said Devon.

Brianna inched closer. The gun was a cannon in her small hands, but her finger touched the trigger all the same, and she looked poised enough to fire. She didn't take her uncle's bait. She didn't say anything back, not with words, at least, but with the biggest *fuck you* he'd ever seen in the eyes of a little girl.

Detective Blue showed herself behind Bri. "Honey, drop the gun." She looked at Ben. "It's my dad's. She grabbed it and ran."

"Where's your dad?" Ben asked, his eyes still locked on the standoff between his daughter and Devon.

"He's dead."

"And there we have it," said Devon. "Mr. Dreams is dead."

Bri stepped closer. "But Ms. Dreams says hello."

"Bri . . . Give me the gun." Ben inched closer. "Honey, give me the—"

Brianna briefly pointed it at him. "No, Daddy." Ben stopped. "I'm not scared." She resumed pointing it at Devon through the glass wall. More moths bounced against the glass, beginning to land on Devon's shoulders and outstretched arms—he was begging her to shoot, making the target easier for her because he didn't think she would fire.

But she did.

The recoil sent her sliding to the floor. The bullet landed high on the wall, shattering glass near the ceiling. A spider web of cracking and splintering etched outward from the bullet hole, and a few seconds later the wall shattered in a waterfall of shards.

Moths flew out by the hundreds.

Devon had dropped to his knees.

Creech had taken the few seconds of panic to come running through the opening, swinging and stabbing his bow like a spear. He connected with Officer Maxwell before she could secure a shot through the fog of moths. Blood spurted from Maxwell's shoulder. The bow had been sharpened—his instrument and weapon. Before he could swing again at Maxwell, a shot screamed from behind Ben, from Detective Blue, and spun Edward Creech into the hallway wall, where he slid down, pulling books out with him as he hit the floor. By then, Maxwell had regained her equilibrium. Creech made a move toward her and Maxwell put him down again with a shot through the chest.

Creech's eyes stayed on Maxwell. Blood pulsed from the wound.

Inside the atrium, Amanda and Emily screamed. Brianna made a move for them, but Detective Blue held her back. Devon had disappeared. Ben grabbed the handgun Bri had involuntarily dropped to the floor. He entered the atrium in pursuit of his brother, and found him in the back, behind the sofa, on the far side of the mare tree, holding his hands out in front like he was begging to be cuffed.

"Ben, don't!" Detective Blue said from the doorway. "Put the gun down."

Ben, with the gun in one hand and the butcher knife in the other, approached his wife and sister. He cut through one of Amanda's ropes while keeping the gun on Devon behind the tree.

Once Amanda's right arm was free, she took the knife and cut through the rest of the restraints, and immediately got to work on Emily's chair, while Detective Blue still fought to hold Brianna back at the doorway.

Ben homed in on his brother.

"You can't shoot me, Benjamin." Devon glanced at Detective Blue at the doorway. "Isn't that right, Detective? There *are* rules to follow."

"Fuck your rules." Ben stepped closer.

Devon didn't budge, didn't move his hands from out in front. "Cuff me. Take me in. I surrender."

"All of this just to surrender?" Ben's finger shook against the trigger. He'd never fired a gun in his life, but didn't think it was possible to miss from this distance, regardless.

"Ben, put the gun down."

Ben glanced over his shoulder. Amanda and Emily had taken the seething Brianna out of the room and into the hallway. Now Detective Blue had a gun on Devon as well, and she was moving in with her handcuffs. "Ben, I got this. Back away. Lower the gun and back away."

"I saw the book," Devon said. "The next one, Benjamin. Your work in progress." He watched Detective Blue's approach now. "Where Mulky's child gets taken by the Screamer . . . What if the detective wasn't patterned after your father, Detective Blue? What if he was patterned after you?"

"Stop talking. Keep your hands where I can see them." Detective Blue closed in with the cuffs.

"What would you do if I said I'd already done it? That I already got into my brother Benjamin's house and saw what he'd written . . . what he'd suggested? Danny and both of your boys?"

Detective Blue's arms started shaking.

"He's lying," Ben said.

"Am I? Try calling them, Detective. I'd be surprised if you got an answer."

"Don't listen to him," Ben said.

Detective Blue swallowed hard, took another step with the cuffs.

Devon turned to Ben. "I know what shampoo your daughter uses, Benjamin. I smell it in her hair at night when I whisper things into her little ears."

Ben had begun to relax his arms, but they quickly stiffened. He took aim again.

He heard a phone ringing and glanced to Detective Blue, who had dialed home while she kept her aim on Devon Bookman. She waited. It kept ringing.

"Cuff me," said Devon. "Let me live out my days in the asylum."

Ben stepped closer. "Why come home only to be caught?"

"So that I can watch. I've been busy, Benjamin. So busy. Now it's time to sit back and watch the harvest come in."

Blue's phone kept ringing. Her face had grown pale. "Don't shoot him, Ben. Please. He's got my husband and kids somewhere . . ."

"What harvest?" Ben hissed. "What have you done?"

Devon surveyed the room, all the books. "It took me days, but eventually I got it done."

Ben shook his head. "You're lying. You're fucking lying."

"All of them, Ben. I opened all of them, and now it's time to watch." Devon held out his arms to Detective Blue. "Cuff me." He turned to Ben. "I've been in your house, Benjamin. I've been in your bed. Sometimes you sleepwalk and I take your place. Amanda is so sweet."

"God damn you, Devon."

"Sam," a voice crackled through Detective Blue's phone.

"Danny!" Tears dripped down Blue's cheeks.

"What's going on?" Danny Blue said, panicked through the phone.

Devon grinned. "Go ahead, Benjamin. I *dare* you." Without taking his eyes off Ben, Devon lowered his stance toward the floor, reached for an open travel crate Ben only now noticed, a crate full of books much like the thousands on the shelves.

"Sam!" Danny shouted over the phone. "Where are you?"

Ben eyed the open crate. "What are those books, Devon?"

Devon grabbed one from the crate, fanned through it, dropped it to the floor, where it rested, spine cracked and pages open.

Ben stepped closer, gun still aimed at his brother, and nudged the dropped book closed with his foot.

Devon teasingly grabbed another book from the crate. "Ever notice there were numbers missing from those shelves?"

"Put it down," Blue said, ignoring her husband's panicked voice over the phone.

Devon opened the next book in his hands, dropped it to the floor. "It's where he kept the worst ones, Ben."

Detective Blue dropped her phone just as Devon kicked the crate over and Ben fired.

The bullet plugged Devon in the middle of the chest. He went reeling back into a wall of leather books. A half dozen books fell from a shelf upon impact. Devon gasped for breath, slumped on the floor with his back and head against the shelves. Blood gurgled from his mouth.

For the first time ever, Ben saw fear in his little brother's eyes.

Devon went pale, his blood on the stones.

Ben held him as he bled.

After

POLICE CHIEF BLUE leaned back in her office chair, rubbed her tired eyes.

Daydreamed of cookouts and sunshine and cold beer. The sound of her children playing. Anything but the prison her office had become. *Slave to the job*, Mills had warned her. And here she was, slaving to a job she both craved and despised in equal measure, the couch across the room still tossed with the blanket and pillow she'd used overnight, despite Danny's begging her to come home and get some sleep. She had a four-year-old missing her mommy.

But with these five bodies found like they were.

It was the most gruesome crime scene she'd witnessed since the Scarecrow murders years ago. Truth was, even after she'd cleaned and scrubbed, she couldn't bring herself to go home and touch her kids, especially the youngest, Winchester, who, unlike the other two, still liked to be held and cuddled.

Not this soon after she'd touched those bodies.

Someone knocked on her door. She closed the file on her desk. "It's open."

A young, redheaded secretary poked her face in the doorway. "Chief, there's someone here to see you."

Blue sighed, checked her watch. "Who is it?"

"It's a girl."

"A girl? She have an age?"

"Somewhere between twelve and fifteen, I'd say. Armed with a notebook and a pen."

"Name?"

"Wouldn't say. Might be a runaway."

"Let her in."

Seconds later, a gangly teenage girl with dark-rimmed glasses, auburn hair pulled back in a studious bun, and a face immediately familiar—just older—stepped into the office and closed the door behind her. She clutched a notebook to her chest, smiled with her daddy's eyes. No doubt about that. Pretty as her mother, and apparently just as bold and determined.

Blue leaned back, folded her arms, and put on a smile. "Bri? Is that really you?"

The teenager nodded. "Brianna now."

"All grown up and . . . How tall are you?"

Brianna took the seat across the desk. "Five eight. Doctor thinks I might grow another inch or two. I'm hitting for the freshman volleyball team."

"Do we have a future Olympian in our midst?"

"No."

After a few beats of awkward silence, Blue asked, "Your mom and dad?"

"They're fine now after the move. Florida heat treats them well and my little brother keeps them busy. They fell in love all over again. Renewed their vows. Kissed at the altar. It was gross." That's all she offered. Blue knew Ben Bookman was writing again. Rumors had him penning something historical. Or maybe it was a western series. Trying to reinvent himself. Again. Amanda was traveling the globe for CNN. Brianna finally added, "Deep down they never got over what happened to Jennifer, though."

"And you did?"

"We deal with things differently. You either get over or get on."

Blue leaned forward with her elbows on the desk. "How old are you now, Brianna?"

"Fourteen."

"Do your parents know you're here?"

"No."

"And you came by?" Brianna didn't answer, so Blue prodded, "Bus? Train? On foot?"

"Train. Then on foot."

"You shouldn't be traveling alone like that, Brianna."

Brianna Bookman shrugged, placed her notebook on the desk. "That tree's still there." She glanced at the door, as if to make sure it was closed and nobody was listening. "The moths are coming back."

Blue tried not to show how the comment had made her stomach curl. "Brianna, this is a treat to see you again. You look well. But can I ask what you're doing here?"

Brianna opened the notebook and rotated it so it was facing Blue. She fanned through at least a couple dozen pages of information and notes and zig-zagging lines and circles—too much like what Blue had seen on her father's living room wall the day before his burial—before stopping on a page marked with the words *Man in the Moon* at the top. And then below it, two more names: *Patricia Kingsley* and *Jonathan Burns*.

Blue eyed the page, and then the two of them watched each other. Brianna looked more tired behind the glasses than her upbeat mood portrayed. Blue was more intrigued than she'd meant to be. She asked of the notebook, "What is this?"

"My work."

"What work? Homework?"

"No, I get that done at school. It's easy." She chewed a fingernail already bitten to the quick. "This is what I've been doing for the past four years. Almost five. Finding them."

"Finding what?" Blue's flesh spread with chill bumps.

"Mares." She pointed to the notebook. "The ones Uncle Devon let out." She tapped the page. "Patricia Kingsley. She was a patient of Amelia Bookman in the late forties. Amelia was Bernard Bookman's daughter. Robert's mother. Patricia Kingsley had a nightmare about the man in the moon. Dr. Amelia Bookman took it away."

"Brianna . . . Are you having nightmares? Like my father did?"

"Yes."

"For how long now?"

"Since he died. I have brush-ups too. Except I call it connecting."

Blue forced herself to look at the open notebook. "What is this?"

Brianna pointed to the page. "You know it was a full moon last night."

"Yes. What does that have to—?"

"It was a full moon last month." Brianna turned back a page to reveal notes and pasted newspaper clippings from the *New York Times*, detailing the accounts of a horrible murder in France, where five bodies were found with their skin removed. "In Paris. You remember the murders there? How those bodies were found?"

"How do you know how the bodies *here* were found? We kept it out of the press."

"I don't," she said. "I just know that there were five found dead. And it happened during a full moon. And I'm good at math and logic and reasoning, and I know how he's done it in the past. But I can tell by the look in your eyes that they're the same. And that he . . ." She turned the notebook page back to where it was. "Jonathan Burns. Is the Man in the Moon. *And* he likes to travel."

Blue allowed her vision to fall on Brianna's notebook.

She picked it up, flipped through some of the pages, and then started at the beginning.

Enjoyed the read?

We'd love to hear your thoughts!

crookedlanebooks.com/feedback

ACKNOWLEDGMENTS

Writing a novel, no doubt, has hurdles throughout the process; it sure takes a village to complete, and *The Nightmare Man* was no exception. The first hurdle for me was the decision to write it in the first place, which would inevitably mean a definitive rebrand for me, as my first six novels were all historical—some of them magical realism, a few dramas, and one historical thriller, in the case of my sixth novel, *The Strange Case of Isaac Crawley*, which holds extra significance for me in terms of the transition to *The Nightmare Man*, my first contemporary horror/thriller/suspense. In *The Strange Case of Isaac Crawley*, the main character experiences a splitting of the mind, and in a sense hosts his own dual nature like that of Dr. Jekyll and Mr. Hyde inside him, and that novel for me just happened to be my own fork in the road, my own splitting of the mind in terms of my career as a novelist. It's much darker than my others, yet still historical, but the darkness of it proved to be the perfect segue into *The Nightmare Man*, my first novel (of hopefully many) under the pen name J. H. Markert. I will continue to write under my own name, James Markert, and have recently finished my latest, tentatively titled *Ransom Burning*, but anything horrifying and contemporary will be under my new pen name. And while the J might be obvious, I won't tell you what the H stands for! But I'm not sure if this novel ever would have been written without the help and encouragement of Kim Lionetti at BookEnds Literary. We plowed through this idea for some time, and saw it through two kinds of endings, and I thank you for planting that seed and pushing me into new territories as a novelist. I'd like to also acknowledge my cousin John Markert by saying that we talked for years about possible pen names for me, and while I didn't use Stephen Kang or John Grasham or Tom Cluncy, I think I settled on the one that works best for what I'm trying to do. But we sure had fun pondering.

I'd like to take a second here to thank Aldan Homrich and my cousin Kaitlyn Tisdale, because I forgot to mention you both in my acknowledgments in *The Strange Case of Isaac Crawley*—Aldan for reading an early version and Kaitlyn for helping me grab all that wonderful research on Jekyll and Hyde and Jack the Ripper. Thank you to Charlie Shircliff, loyal reader and friend, for being the first non-agent to read the finished version of *The Nightmare Man*, back when it was titled *The Hollow*. Your kind words kept me going. To Gill Holland, thank you for reading that 500-page monstrosity of a first draft and finding worth in it. Your support of my work is seemingly endless. Thank you. Much thanks to Matt Martz and Ben LeRoy and Sara J. Henry (Sara, your edits were spot on) at Crooked Lane for catching this fish and reeling it in, and to my amazingly hardworking and diligent literary agent, Alice Speilburg, for not only casting it out into this vast publishing ocean, but first polishing and editing this novel to ultimate readiness when I, at times, had doubts it ever would be ready. Your vision for it was brilliant, so thank you. And this is only the beginning. To Rebecca Nelson, Melissa Rechter, Madeline Rathle, Dulce Botello, Heather VenHuizen, and Kate McManus at Crooked Lane—I believe that covers everyone from publishing to editing and production and marketing to cover design and intern—but thank you! To my brothers and sisters and loyal friends, thank you for the constant support. To my wife, Tracy, breadwinner of over twenty years; maybe soon you'll be able to retire. And finally, to my parents, Bob and Patsy Markert, thank you for always championing the creative mind, buuuuuuut you might not want to read this one. ☺ Of course, if you made it this far, perhaps you already did, so sorry for the gore and scare—I'll blame it on my other personality, J. H.